Catholic Girls

NOVELS

Fort Privilege
Magic Time
The Ballad of T. Rantula
Captain Grownup
Tiger Rag
Cry of the Daughter
Armed Camps
The Better Part
At War as Children
Mother Isn't Dead She's Only Sleeping

SHORT STORY COLLECTIONS

*The Revenge of the Senior Citizens * Plus Other Stories And: The Attack of the Giant Baby*
Mr. Da V. and Other Stories

Catholic

Girls

A NOVEL BY
KIT REED

DIF
DONALD I. FINE, INC.
NEW YORK

Copyright © 1987 by Kit Reed

All rights reserved, including the right of reproduction in whole
or in part in any form. Published in the United States of America
by Donald I. Fine, Inc. and in Canada by General Publishing Company Limited.

Library of Congress Catalogue Card Number: 87-81418
ISBN: 1-55611-063-4
Manufactured in the United States of America
10 9 8 7 6 5 4 3 2 1

This book is printed on acid free paper. The paper in this book
meets the guidelines for permanence and durability of the Committee on
Production Guidelines for Book Longevity of the Council on Library Resources.

This novel is a work of fiction. Names, characters, places and incidents are either
the product of the author's imagination or are used fictitiously. Any resemblance to
actual events, locales, organizations or persons, living or dead, is entirely
coincidental and beyond the intent of either author or publisher.

for Carl Brandt
True squadron leader, Hell's Agents

1

WHAT WAS IT Ralph Schwartz said to her, all those years ago? "What is it with you Catholic girls?"

Unwrapping his and Ag's present, Georgie was not sure. At the time she'd whirled on him, saying, angrily, "We're not girls."

Ralph's knowing smile infuriated her. "You know what I mean."

The trouble was, she did. Now she was not angry but thoughtful, because this same Ralph Schwartz had run away with her old friend Ag and now here was this tacky present—with this note. Here was Georgia Kendall's present from Florida, picked out with loving hands and wry self-knowledge by her college roommate: a light-up Virgin in a conch shell, surrounded by clusters of dyed coral and bearing a decal in Gothic lettering: *Souvenir of Snowy Egret, Florida.* It was a joke, or she thought it was until she found the gift-shop card with Ag's note like a message kited out of prison: PRAY FOR ME.

Something was wrong.

Maybe Ralph had gone to pieces in the tropics. It was an old movie, but it played—the ruined woman, giving up everything for a disintegrating man. She could see the runaways slouched in the watery light of some seedy outpost, miserable and broke.

It would be one of those things: Ag knowing she had made a mistake, too loyal to walk out on it. She pictured her old friend smiling bravely and sipping frosted rum drinks under the sinister, slow arms of a mahogany ceiling fan, while Ralph slow-danced with existential despair. Ag would be murmuring bravely and stirring her Margarita with one finger, watching Ralph slug tequila and talk of Kierkegaard. Georgie saw Ag in crumpled linen, gaunt, romantic-looking Ralph in the classic ice cream suit yellowed by heat and age, and the ruined Panama. With nothing left to live for but each other, with the way back closed off, they would have run out of places to go. Ralph's face would be blue with encroaching stubble, hers pale with remorse.

Not a chance. The truth was that blushing, rawboned, earnest Ag and sought-after Ralph had flown south at Forrest Fulcrum's expense, so Ralph could star at the celebrated Fulcrum Foundation. They had shucked their mates and left families and jobs behind in New Brunswick for an expense-paid idyll at the flossy Fulcrum headquarters. Right now they were basking where the great and the near-great sunned and swam and tortured themselves in exercise classes after which they sat down at the Fulcrum conference tables to solve the problems of the world. When Ag went down the primrose path, she went first class.

Instead of going to pieces in the tropics, Ag had reported in a series of joyful postcards and one awkward phone call, she and Ralph were being picked up and twirled around by the international intellectual mafia. Without credentials Georgie's old college roommate had coasted into a glittering think tank that Georgie herself had applied to more than once, with no luck. If something was wrong now it would be a little thing, some real or imagined slight in the dining room of the triangular Fulcrum tower, or an intellectual confrontation gone awry next to the triangular swimming pool, where Ag and Ralph sizzled daily alongside the world's great thinkers. People in white coats brought drinks to the chaises so they could get sozzled lying down; what could go wrong? Maybe Ag had failed to field a quip by Alistair Cooke, or Ralph had angered one of the oil sheiks or the Minority Whip. Or else some disciple of Germaine Greer or Betty Friedan had asked Ag if she was a person in her own right, or maybe Henry Kissinger had finally told Ralph what he needed to be told sooner or later—that he'd better forget foreign policy, which he knew nothing about, and stick to Swedenborg—but: *prayers?*

What had gone wrong in Florida? She could not imagine, any more than she could imagine what it would be like for Ag if everything had gone right. It had been hard enough for Georgie to grasp the first set of astounding developments: Ag in an affair at all, and with Ralph. Yet gawky Ag, who still wore her old chapel veil when she went to church and always kissed her thumb whenever she crossed herself, Agnes Mary Fitzgerald, who could not keep her head from bobbing every time anybody said "Jesus," Ag the zealous, Ag the exemplary, had run away with glamorous and unreliable Ralph Schwartz, who wasn't even a Catholic. Gawky, loyal Ag had left Brendan and her kids to go to Florida with the disorganized but trendy and Byronic Ralph Schwartz, intellectual *enfant terrible* and academic renegade, who had in turn left the patient Serena one more time—and for Ag!

But: *prayers?*

What had befallen them? She did not know.

She had to talk to Ag.

The surprise, then, was how quickly she got through to Fulcrum. A stranger picked up Ag's phone. There was so much noise and confusion at the other end of the line that she had to shout. "Mrs. Fitzgerald, I said, she's staying there with . . ."

"See if I can (mumble) . . ." There was a clank as the speaker dropped the phone. In the long, expensive interval that followed she could hear men's voices, jostling, static, as if from a police radio, animal noises? Had they forgotten her? Should she hang up and try again? She was afraid to let go.

The animal noises seemed to be getting closer. They separated into words. "He said it wasn't a suicide, it was a cry for help."

"Ag, is that you?"

"Hell yes it's me," Ag cried.

"Shh." Without Ag to pat and say There There to, Georgie patted the receiver. "Shh-shh, it's all right, Ag, really. It is."

"Something terrible has happened," Ag said, between sobs.

Georgie was surprised by how angry this made her. "If Ralph Schwartz has even *looked* at another woman, or lifted his hand to you . . ."

"No no, you've got it all wrong."

". . . I'll murder him." Damn long distance. Damn Ralph Schwartz.

"That isn't it."

But Georgie was launched. "If he's done anything to make you cry . . ."

Ag's tone arrested her. "I think you'd better shut up."

After an unbearable moment in which she became aware that this was not an ordinary crisis, Georgie said, carefully, "Ag, are you still there?"

"It didn't happen to me," Ag said, equally carefully.

"What didn't?"

"It happened to Ralph."

"Ralph!" A secret part of Georgia Kendall twisted.

"Ralph."

"Dear God." Parts of Georgie clenched in a spasm she did not immediately recognize. "Is he all right?"

Right before Ag cracked she thought Ag said, "Not really."

"Are you?"

She thought right before she toppled, Ag said, "No."

It was hard to tell, because all the air Ag had been collecting in short gasps had begun to seep away, along with the careful self-control she had managed for a minute there. Now there was a sound humming over the telephone wires, a strange, unbroken willowing that Georgie knew but could not quite manage to put a name to. It came out of millenial fogs hanging over peat bogs, substance given to an age-old Irish miasma of poverty and tribulation. Her old friend that she thought she knew was carrying on like one of those old ladies in *Riders to the Sea,* just another mourner in the last scene, throwing her apron over her head and wailing. It was . . . Ag was . . . Agnes Mary Fitzgerald was . . . she was *keening.*

"Ag!" It was funny, she thought, you went along the way everybody did thinking you were what, invulnerable, and then something happened to your college roommate, and it was like . . . She recognized the new window of vulnerability Ag had opened: It was like having it happen to you. "Oh, Ag!"

"No," Ag said, weeping, "Ralph."

Ralph. Georgie squirmed: that feeling she would not acknowledge. "Please don't cry."

("I'm sorry," mumbled Ag, who could not seem to stop. "Just give me a minute."

Georgie said, even though Ag could not hear for the renewed keening, "It's OK.")

But she was wild with apprehension, and because she couldn't think of anything else to do she barked. "Stop that. Is Ralph all right?" Ag's reply was immediate, but garbled. Again: Georgie shouted, "I said, *is Ralph all right?*"

"I said, *not really!*" Ag howled.

The rest came at hurricane velocity, a rush of words distorted by a strange, rattling clank—the pearls Ralph had given to Ag, perhaps, or, Georgie thought wildly, the outsized wooden rosary poor Ag had brought to Mount Maria College all those years ago.

Good lord, Georgie thought, she's chewing her beads. She's almost forty years old and she's still chewing her rosary beads. "Ag, are you chewing your beads?"

". . . . . . . !" Ag finished, as if she'd said it all.

She had not answered Georgie's question. She had not, in fact, answered any of Georgie's questions, and the lengthening silence between them was punctuated only by the sound of her breath and the doleful clank of wood or pearl or perhaps it was plastic hitting the telephone mouthpiece all the way down there in Snowy Egret. Georgie had a complete vision of Ag at eighteen: Agnes Mary in a state over something, oblivious to what she looked like to others, sprawled on her bed in a funk, chewing on the wooden rosary. "Oh please! Stop chewing on your beads and talk to me."

". . . edge," Ag mumbled apologetically.

"You say he's on the edge?"

"No, I said on the ledge."
"You mean the whole time we've been talking?"
"Not really," Ag said with a sob.
"Well take it easy and don't do anything to startle him. I read if you ignore these people, they usually come down on their own."
"You don't understand."
"How wide is the ledge, anyway?"
"It doesn't matter how wide it is. Georgie, something snapped!"

Georgie had spent some years as columnist for the other Boston daily; she was giving the premier columnist a run for her money, according to her editor, and she had done some of her best best writing in the area of, what, the personal dimension of public affairs. She'd heard of almost everything at least once and had read about all the rest; in getting at the motives behind the actions of the public figures and ordinary people she wrote about, she'd consulted many specialists. Now she called on everything she knew to help Agnes Mary talk her boyfriend down. "Easy, Ag. Take it easy. This isn't the end of the world. The first thing is pretend you aren't scared he's really going to do it."

"You don't understand."
"Of course I do. The man needs counseling."
"It wasn't Ralph that snapped, it was . . ."
"He would never really hurt himself."
". . . his bathrobe cord."
"Ralph was always kind of a showoff anyway."
"It snapped and now he's gone."
Georgie thudded to a stop. "What?"
"I said, it was the cord to his bathrobe," Ag said clearly. "So he went over."
"Over the edge?"
"Over the ledge," Ag said patiently. "The thing is, Ralph is dead."
"Oh the bastard, bastard!" Georgie said, trying not to cry.
"At least I think he is," Ag said tearfully.
"How could he do this? How could he do this to you?"

"It isn't his fault," Ag said, from the middle of a storm of weeping. "It's mine."

"Like hell it is." Hadn't she written a book about the guilt of the victim? "It's not your fault, Ag, you have to hang onto that."

"You don't know."

"I suppose you went out there and pushed him off." Georgie would have to be cruel in order to be kind. "You pushed Ralph all ten . . ."

"Twenty."

". . . all twenty floors to his death. Now listen. Pay attention. Whatever happened, you didn't do it. You did not do it. Ralph did."

"But it's my fault," Ag cried. She went on in a hushed whisper, wringing out the next words at tremendous cost. "You don't know what he said to me."

"It doesn't matter what he said," Georgie said urgently. "People say a lot of things they don't really mean."

"Not this time. It was terrible."

"Don't do this. Don't do this to yourself."

"He knew what he was saying. He looked me right in the eye." Ag's voice spiked. "What's more, he was right."

"Look, I'm coming down." Georgie was already flipping through the Rolodex, pulling the cards she needed: airline phone number, managing editor's home phone, the new listing for *IN* Magazine. She was supposed to go to New York on Monday for the big interview at *IN* Magazine, but never mind. Her big chance was going to have to wait. Everything was. She and Ag had been friends ever since their first day at Mount Maria College, and Ag was miserable. She had to go down; they'd shared so much past history that Georgie wanted to be with her for this, she could call on the resources of the old days, when Ag had been broken hearted over something and Georgie could still convince her things were going to come out all right. Why did it have to be big old Ag who got stuck with this, Ag, with the terrible life, who had to lose everything? And why did it have to be over Ralph Schwartz, who'd spent his life playing around? She knew without spelling it out that she was going to have to do something to mark Ralph's passing—Ralph, whom she hardly ever saw any more, and wasn't sure she liked. She was going to have to . . . Lord. First things first. "Listen, Ag, I'm going to book the first flight out of Logan. I can probably be there tonight."

There was a long silence, into which Ag's voice dropped like a stone. "Not tonight."

"But you can't go through this all alone. If I come I can take off some of the pressure, help with the . . ."

"Arrangements? No."

"With whatever," Georgie said helplessly.

"Georgie, this is my thing," Ag said, in a voice so low and clear that it stopped her cold.

Hurt, Georgie said, "I thought you needed me."

"I'm fine." Some time between the lines, Ag had come to terms. She had made her adjustments, and out of some knowledge Georgie did not possess, she had made up her mind. "I need you when I need you. I just don't need you yet."

"I'm trying to help!"

"Don't worry, everything is fine. I'll need you later, for the funeral."

"When is it?"

"We don't have a date."

"Monday? Tuesday? What?"

"It depends." Ag went on like a practiced secretary handling an unsolicited phone call. "When we have a time and place, somebody from Fulcrum will be in touch."

"What about the . . ." Georgie's voice broke, not entirely for Ag's sake. ". . . body."

"It's OK," Ag sounded alarmingly calm, "the Foundation is taking care of everything. They want to keep him here. Ralph is, I mean was, kind of important, you know? Look, I don't want to cut you off, but they're waiting for me in the boardroom, and I . . ."

"Oh for Pete's sake let me come and help."

"I told you, I don't want you yet!"

"Well thanks a lot."

"I'm sorry, I didn't mean it that way, it's just that I've got to settle some things, and, you might as well know that in these two short weeks Ralph and I got—well, kind of *central* to things here, and, well, the thing is everybody here is very busy with arrangements and we want everything to go smoothly, and . . ."

"And you don't want me at all."

"That isn't true. It's just. Well this is going to be a very big thing, you know? The people here are very involved with this, they want Ralph to have the biggest sendoff in the history of the Foundation. Mr. Fulcrum himself is flying in from the Yukon where he's been looking after his gold interests, the President may be an honorary pallbearer, and Robert Redford and Nathalie Sarraute are already involved. The thing is, Ralph used to be just mine, but . . ." She took a deep breath. "He belongs to history now. This isn't any ordinary funeral and he wasn't any ordinary . . . I know you and Ralph didn't always see eye to eye . . ."

Georgie stifled a little cry of pain.

Now it was Ag who sounded collected and competent, going on in a there-there tone, "but whether or not you like him you'll have to acknowledge that he really was one of our leading philosophers, and a man like that deserves . . . I mean this isn't just the man with whom I was . . ." Ag's voice broke on the only construction she had for this fact, which demonstrated that she was not brave and new, but only poor Agnes Mary after all, ". . . with whom I was committing adultery."

"God!"

She recovered herself. "When we get it worked out I'll get back to you. I want you and Kath and Mickey to be here." She reached for the right words to wind up the call. "Take care. I'll be in touch."

"Ag!"

"Maybe even tonight." Agnes Mary Fitzgerald, juvenile case worker for the city of New Brunswick, New Jersey, mother of three and estranged wife of Brendan Fitzgerald of that same city, was signing off.

Which Georgie discovered she could not let her do. Without

knowing it poor Ag had raised certain questions, which Georgie would be forced to consider willy-nilly once her friend hung up. "Wait!"

"Can't."

"You have to," said Georgie, because whether intentionally or accidentally, whether as private citizen or figure in intellectual history, Ralph Schwartz had died. What's more, before he had died he'd said something to Ag that had almost overturned her. Had he mentioned Georgie's name? Her voice snagged. "Please don't hang up."

"Have to. They're in the boardroom."

"Oh Ag, please."

"I can't keep them waiting."

"You didn't tell me what Ralph said to you, that was so terrible."

"Oh, that." Ag groaned. "You don't really want to know. It was the weirdest thing. I mean, it was positively terrible, but it was also very strange. What he said to me was: after the first time, he should have known better than to get mixed up with Catholic girls."

"What's so . . ."

"He said they take everything so hard."

". . . strange?" God, Georgie thought. *God.*

"Strange? Oh, the strange part." Ag considered for a long moment in which Georgie squinted with concentration, willing her friend to say something completely other than what she did say. "What was truly strange was the part about the first time. As far as I know, I'm the only one."

"The only woman?" Please God. They both knew this was a lie.

"The only Catholic girl."

"Lord."

"Talk to you later, George."

"Ag!"

Ag was gone.

Georgie would never be certain how long she stood at the kitchen telephone considering the incongruously sweet face of the Madonna in the garish conch shell, or when she drifted back through the empty frame house and upstairs to her office in the turret, or how she ended up standing between her file cabinet and her typewriter table with hands floating up from her sides like something out of *The Night of the Living Dead.* Still she was dazed and wandering, bobbing a little, bumping into furniture; days later she would look at a bruise on her hip and wonder how she had gotten it.

When she got up this morning all she had to worry about was getting ahead on her column so she would be covered for the day she went to New York for the seance at *IN*. There was only that and the matter of, what, winning the interview. Her boss at the paper had given her Monday off so she could audition for the job—monthly columnist for this flossy new magazine. The editor was some Peter Flinc, who said he wasn't going to mess around on this, he was going to be right up front. He wanted a woman, he said, breathing heavily into the receiver. No promises, he went on, sounding a little congested, but he needed the right woman to do this job. She wasn't sure why he reminded her of a trapper clumping in from the Klondike thinking of One Thing Only: any woman would do. Still this could be a big thing for a writer whose reputation had never really extended south of Manhattan or west of Scranton, Pa. in spite of the fact that she had published a book her friends couldn't find in the stores. *IN* was going to be national; they had marketed a test issue and there were already flashy local spots showing on TV. She might hitch her wagon to this one. It would be tough spreading herself in yet another direction, but she wanted the job, hadn't thought about anything else since getting the call, except maybe convincing Bill to let her off the party at the Marlowes' tonight so she could begin an idea book for the interview. Or, she hadn't thought of anything else until now.

Now Ralph Schwartz was dead, and what she had imagined safely buried in the past was stirring, ready to shake the dirt from its face and sit up. She knew why Ralph's death had made her writhe. This was the same uncanny sexual wrench she felt when Bill, Bill, who was not so much her husband as part of her, broke his arm and she saw the bone sticking out—or when something happened to either of her sons—people who were also part of her. She was afraid to consider this. The moment was long past, but it seemed she could not outrun the consequences. The risk had outlasted every real or imagined statute of limitations; it was snatching at her vitals now.

Catholic girls.
He said they take everything so hard.

This was true. In the free and easy early Eighties people she knew boffed everybody all the time, no problem, and yet here she was.

She supposed this was what came of growing up inside the monolith, which is what the Catholic church had seemed like to her at the time—pre-Council, pre a lot of things. The Mass was Latin, the same thing happening everywhere all over the world, which stood for a lot of other things. The church had seemed huge, safe. As kids they had been taught it was immutable: a reassuring and necessary concept at the time; things were more complicated now. When she was little everything inside the monolith was laid out for her in clear blacks and plain whites—who you were, what to do. She and Ag and Kath and Mickey—and Bill, for that matter—had grown up in a world of signs and emblems, good and evils, absolutes. Everything stood for something more than what presented itself to the naked eye. The values were deeper than surface, everything more intense than it seemed to the ordinary civilian without the Catholic sensibility—and the companion package of responsibility. Everything they did had weight on the eternal scales. If she let some jerk from Georgetown deflower her one raw November it was not out of curiosity or daring or even because she had let herself get carried away. It was a direct response to the first major national assassination since Booth shot Lincoln; when she and the guy drove out to Glen Echo to park, her eyes were still red from the long weekend spent mourning in front of the TV, looking over and over at the same dreadful tapes. It was a time for big gestures, time for her to stop crying for President Kennedy and do something major to mark his death. She had wiped that old slate clean in confession the following Saturday, so weighed down by what she had done that she was scrunched in the booth waiting when the college chaplain sighed and put on his stole and came into the confessional. She'd had to tell Bill before they were married. Had to. (He'd said, "You don't have to tell me anything.") When she'd said she did too, and went ahead and told him, she was relieved, but Bill? He dissembled quickly enough but in the seconds before he did, she was afraid of what he might do. Finally he said, "I'm glad you told me," but it was a lie.

Which meant she'd had to carry this other burden for years, and at enormous cost.

What would Bill do if he knew she had made love with this very Ralph Schwartz not before, but after she'd married Bill, while he was finishing up his tour of duty in the waters off Nam? How could she explain that it was a political gesture; she was sick with the war, everybody was sick; how could she get him to see that this, that she had done with Ralph, was only one more cramp in what turned out to be a national spasm of nausea that began with the trouble in Viet Nam?

Absolutists believe in absolute gestures, she thought; when we mess up, we go absolutely wrong.

They quit jobs, occupied buildings, courted arrest because they really thought they were going to stop the war. If Ralph could shelve his dissertation to do this, she could give it her best time. She signed letters in blood and went on marches and even though she was only a city desk clerk she wrote angry editorials the paper never ran. They really thought they could make a difference. On the day she now regretted, she and the rest of Ralph's band of protesters were fresh from an all-night vigil in Harvard Square; they were all young, some were still students, who had marched out from Ralph's loft headquarters, spilling blood and lighting candles because they had to do something to mark the bombings in Cambodia; they'd dug shallow graves in the Harvard Yard, or tried to, places for the four kids murdered at Kent State.

How could she expect Bill to understand it was the war? What was she supposed to do instead, set herself on fire at the state capitol, or open her veins in a swan boat on the Common? Right, it was a very Sixties thing to do; at the time every gesture counted, or they thought it did. Back in the loft that night, kids drifted into corners and lay down in pairs, seeking solace, or distraction; they were like puppies, coupling where they fell, or exhausted refugees who dropped and slept like stones. She staggered into a jumble of pillows behind a pile of cartons and tangled with Ralph, Ralph the brilliant sophist, the fevered activist, who could make any woman believe she was the only one who could save him from despair. He made it seem like their patriotic duty. While Bill was off being a credit to the uniform, keeping the world safe for democracy from the decks of a destroyer somewhere off Saigon; while Bill was fighting the good fight that nobody believed in and she was learning to despise, Ralph and his legions were using everything but force to let Washington know the murder had to stop. Everything.

"Oh Georgie," he had murmured, "you are so beautiful."

Her voice had broken. "Oh Ralph!"

"Oh Georgie," he'd said, and this was the romantic lie, "You're the only one who understands."

"The war." She was crying. "We've got to stop the war."

Feeling his long hands on her face, feeling angry and guilty and moved she had thought: *affair*. It was like something out of a book.

Oh hell, she could have bopped Ralph or rolled away and cracked a joke and left, but like everybody else that early morning she was sick and angry and exhausted and just maybe out of her mind. What she did was not a conscious act of infidelity, exactly, although she could not quite forgive Bill for being caught up in this misbegotten war. It was, rather, a protest against Bill, who had spend his life trying to do right and was doing something so wrong. This had a bizarre logic. She loved Bill so much that she had to betray him with Ralph. Even now she was haunted by the strange, spiteful words she had heard sounding in her head as Ralph pulled her close and she turned toward him; they could have been sounding in her head or somewhere far above them, small but precise: *so there.*

War protest. Right.

By the time she sat up it was too late. At which point Ralph quieted her sobbing and kissed the corners of her eyes so she would quit crying and go back to stuffing envelopes. They spent weeks sending telegrams and telephoning the White House and the Joint Chiefs and lighting candles at public vigils, imagining they could change history just because they wanted to, marching, lobbying, cranking broadsides out of mimeograph machines like bullets out of a Thompson gun. Their *passage* meant nothing to Ralph. He had platoons of women even after he married black-haired Serena Weiner, who was large and calm and coped. He probably didn't even remember. It was Georgie who had spent the rest of her marriage tugging against the one infidelity. Going to confession was the least of it. What would Bill do if he knew? Love and forgive her, she supposed; he had always been one of life's boy scouts, but with an edge. Bill always forgave, but he remembered. He was an absolutist. If he knew she absolutely had, would he absolutely shut her out? Like any good lovers, they squabbled all the time, but about nothing important, and she could not keep from wondering, if she told him, what would their fights be like?

Now Ralph had bailed out without a parachute, and in a more orderly universe this would be the end of it, but unfortunate Georgie's cosmos included a scale of guilt, or responsibility, measuring from mitigated to absolute, and she had never been sure where on this scale the business with Ralph Schwartz was located. At the time, she had needed to construct a rationale. Who else would try to make sense of one quick bash by pretending she was in love with Ralph? Who would have written to him so hotly, just to prove it had been love and not just wickedness. Who else would have kept writing in spite of the fact that he never answered, or written so often or so much? To her chagrin she remembered sending him a love sonnet, although she could not for the life of her imagine what she had found to rhyme with Ralph.

So he was dead in Florida, and her embarrassment was truly over, or else she only thought it was. What had he left behind to threaten her, and where was it now?

My letters. Dear God, I wonder what he did with them?

2

"Georgie, please?"

"Not tonight, I have a headache." It was evening. She had told Bill everything about Ag's phone call except for the implications, which she had managed to bury under a welter of Saturday ceremonies: ice cream at Brigham's, the afternoon ballgame, chores. They had even cleaned out the bird-bath in front of their Victorian heap. Only reverse snobbery would put an architect as successful as Bill into a gingerbread house. Now they were lying in the shuttered bay window at the top of the house and he was importuning her.

"You promised, honey. Please?"

"I just don't feel like it." Georgie threw her forearm across her eyes like an Edwardian beauty fending off the vapors with wet cloths over the forehead: too tired.

"That's what you always say."

"It's really just a bad time."

"You always have some excuse."

"I told you, I'm worried about Ag."

"I'm worried about Ag too, but that doesn't mean I don't want to . . ."

"Oh please."

Bill accused her. "Anything to get out of it."

"I really . . ." They had just finished making love.

"Come on, you know the Marlowes are counting on you."

"I hate parties, and besides . . ." Right now she didn't want to move. Conspiring like bandits, she and Bill had sent the kids out for pizza, bought them off with ice cream and enough quarters to keep them playing Space Invaders until they were so mesmerized by dayglo explosions that they wouldn't notice what the folks were up to and in broad daylight, too. Then she and her partner in crime had sneaked into bed to seize the stolen hour. This meant laying out their clothes so they could dress like firemen if discovered, after which they'd taken the phone off the hook, after which, this. *Not me,* Georgie thought, wrapping her arms and legs around Bill in the shameful, delicious guilt of the survivor, *We're still here.* Surprised by her body, she whipped into the moment like a toy boat into a whirlpool and at some point heard a voice that sounded very like hers unrolling like a ribbon somewhere near the ceiling; she thought she heard it laugh and laugh.

Now she and Bill were lying on the big bed in T formation, he with his chin on her elbow and one large hand tangled in her hair. Huh, Georgie, just this once? Huh? Huh? Crafty bastard, he hadn't even waited for her breathing to return to normal before he started on her with the Marlowes' wretched party: We wouldn't want to disappoint those nice old people, right? Damn Bill, with his promises to keep. Without his infernal boy scout sense of honor, she'd be happy to stay here in bed for the rest of her life. If she didn't address the matter of the party maybe it would go away. She and Bill could lie here for hours, playing in the rumpled covers, woolgathering until they got hungry—or the kids came home.

Who, us? We weren't doing anything. We were just having a little preprandial nap, or: Daddy was showing me the Heimlich maneuver/*pas de deux*/something he learned at Karate class. Sure. Thin excuse. Why not the truth? Anything was better than scandalizing eleven-year-old Tim, who would giggle and fall off his chair choking because it was preposterous, or Matty the righteous, who was already stirred by intimations of his own future but still a prude at going-on-thirteen. You mean you actually . . . eeeew, gross. It was both silly and fun, sneaking around. Stolen times were best and she and Bill managed escalating feats of complicity. She uncovered her eyes and watched the fading spring twilight through the stripes made on the sky by her matchstick blinds.

"Bill?"

He was waiting for her conscience to finish his work.

"You know I hate parties."

"I promised them we'd come."

"You could have said we were busy. You could have said anything."

"It would have been lying."

"Which you never do." She sighed. "Oh Bill, why do you always have to be so square! Scout leader. St. Theresa of all architects. You never even shoplifted in high school." Georgie had discovered this only recently and was surprised first because it was true and second because it made her so angry. He and Georgie would be going along like everybody else and Georgie would come up against this surprising hard core of, what was it, honesty? Moral bedrock that surprised her every time. There were certain things Bill would never do, like sneak in somewhere without paying, or lie. He did not equivocate. Things either were or they weren't. She had rummaged through his memories like a private detective, trying to find something to pin on him so they could be more nearly equals, but he frustrated her. If Bill had ever done anything he was ashamed of they might have a tradeoff: her Ralph for his whatever, but here they were. She accused him. "You never even get in fights."

"I fight with you."

"That's not the same." They fought all the time, wrangling like playmates over little things until one of them started laughing or Bill sulked, clumping around the house like Heathcliff, at which point she knew she had him: shh, I love you, there there. She could not help wondering what would happen if anything big fell between them. Like Ralph. She gave him a little push. "I mean you never punched anybody in the nose."

He rolled and laughed. "What would be the point?"

"Oh stop being so damn *rational*. Everybody who was any-

body shoplifted," she said resentfully. "I bet you never did anything bad."
"Don't be stupid."
Something made her keep after it: his exasperating honesty, her mixture of love and guilt. "You don't know anything about being bad."
"What are you, Medea?"
Georgie said, "You don't know anything about me."
"Lizzie Borden, right?"
"Listen, in third grade I almost killed Tommy Swaggart. I bashed him with the Unabridged. He was out for days."
"So what else is new?"
She had to beg the question. "You probably never even cheated on a quiz."
"Neither did you. Give up. You wouldn't know bad if it came up and bit you on the ass."
"You don't know anything about it!" she cried. How many times had she come this close to telling him? Her breath fluttered. "Oh, Bill."
"Oh George. Georgia," he said, rolling over and sitting on his feet, spreading his hands as if he could take in all her outline all at once, and because she had to stop him from dressing for the party somehow she gathered herself and dived, pulling him back to her. Then they grappled and laughed until her exquisitely tuned mother's ear caught the click of the front door opening and they sprang apart like guilty teenagers, assembling hasty alibis for the kids.

The Marlowes' house crouched on several levels at the top of a long drive, a glittering series of boxes set on the hill by an architect friend of Bill's, whose work he admired but never really liked because, Bill said, his idea of a perfect building was one where no people ever came. Light crashed out onto the swastika of porches, and even from the bottom of the drive they could hear the music, a mezzo disco, half a beat off and spongy at the core. Cappy and Hamish Marlowe had tied wind chimes to the bushes lining the drive, and the terrace was strung with

Japanese lanterns, which meant the Marlowes were having another of their theme parties. Somebody had lofted rolls of toilet paper from the upper porches and the treetops below looked not festive but embarrassed, as if caught naked and forced to grab the first thing that came handy to cover themselves. Bill saw Georgie flagging and took her elbow and pushed firmly, keeping her moving up the graveled drive.

If Georgie's feet dragged and her heart sank it was because the parties in this community were both predictable and terrible.

When they went in they were going to find would-be Nobel-winning chemist Al Hoskins and pallid Sally Watters laminated in a slow dance in defiance of the disco beat, while in a corner Hug Watters, who did something forgettable at Harvard, discussed the law at stultifying length, a prelude to the moment in which he forgot himself and took off his shirt so everybody could admire his pectorals. Always the earnest and inexorable hostess, Cappy would be offering *hors d' oeuvres,* tired-looking tidbits that were already stained by the dye from the colored toothpicks that she had probably put in this afternoon at three. Hamish would be looking for somebody to carve the Virginia ham for the midnight supper (it weighed almost twenty pounds, he always told them, and came in a cloth bag all the way from Tennessee), and by this time Dent Eckersley the lesser poet would have attached himself to another unlucky woman like the great remora, inflicting purple love bites and thwarting all rescue attempts. Although she was chief of service at Mass. General where she worked with birth defects, Patty Sessions would have gone all fragile, concluding that she couldn't walk another step, which meant somebody was going to have to carry her from room to room all evening, in return for certain favors. These were always collectible in the last half-hour, when the music ended and Cappy started emptying ashtrays and Hamish stamped from room to room turning on the lights. He did this in spite of certain occurrences in corners because this was the only way to get everybody out of the house so the Marlowes could go to bed. Jim Sessions, who was in the Communications Center at MIT would be passed out in the howdah chair, and when the last dog was hung Patty would stand on her own two feet like Godzilla rising and lug her husband to the car and drive him home.

It was this complete foreknowledge that slowed Georgie's feet and made her stomach tighten. She knew all the same people would be here and in the end they would all fall into the same attitudes, would do so in spite of the care they had lavished on their costumes tonight and all the hopes they'd brought with them to the Marlowes' event. These things almost always ended badly and yet the guests would continue to waste their best efforts preparing their faces, in hopes, and they would keep coming out to them because there was always the possibility that this time, they might meet the major star who could change their lives, and if they didn't, they would at least say or do the right things, for a change, be witty, or glamorous; this time things were going to be different. They would walk in smiling, on the outside chance that this time they were going to forget or surpass themselves. This time they were going to have fun.

Crossing the terrace, Georgie was surprised once more by that which Bill always seemed to know and she always had to discover: her heart lifted slightly as they reached the door. It was a little like swimming in cold water. All her life she had hated coming to parties, and for good reason. All her life she had dragged her feet right up to the edge. Yet she was always excited, plunging in.

"Hey look," Bill said. "I see a couple of new faces. Wild cards usually help people behave."

"Pray God. Lord, what has Hamish got on?"

"Samurai partygoer," said Bill, who would never forget John Belushi. "Look around. Tonight we're going Japanese."

"Oh God, there's Horace Metcalf." There he was, too, her long-time nemesis, a silver-haired old busybody whose history of the American Midwest had put him on the map. Distinguished as he was, he lurched around in the white suit that he put on every year around Easter and wore to every function up to Columbus Day. Bill said he wasn't a staggering drunk, he had an inner ear problem, but Georgie wasn't so sure. In spite of the surface, he was a meticulous scholar with an extremely orderly mind, one of life's strays whom Bill tolerated endlessly. For Bill's sake Georgie tried to forget the preposterous manner, the potential for messiness, but she seemed to bring out the worst in Horace, who forgot everything he knew and tried to flirt with her. The more she resisted, the more he was ineluctably drawn.

"Watch out for him, he just got back from that clinic in France."

"Clinic?"

"Sex clinic. They put in glands when yours poop out."

"Glands?"

"Goat glands, I think, unless it's carp. He had these things implanted, all around his waist. Hamish says they look kind of like lima beans . . ."

"Bill!"

". . . except they're festering."

"That's terrible."

"Horace doesn't think so.

"He could end up with gangrene, or worse."

"He says if it works they're cheap at any price. He says they've turned him into John the Bear."

"Waste not want not," said Georgie giddily, although this was not precisely to the point. "Watch out, here comes Frederika. Time for your good deed."

"Why me?"

"Because you lead her on."

"The hell I do."

"By which I mean you don't push her in the face. You don't even say no thanks. You just grit your teeth and dance with her and be nice." Georgie slipped her hand under Bill's elbow and turned without missing a beat, saying in the same tone but with a smile, "Why Frederika, how nice you look!"

Frederika Jarvis was a hearty old thing, buxom and straightforward and trying hard to renovate after a bad divorce. She'd done extensive work on the facade, starting with the hair, which had become red, which was alarming, and curly, which it had never been before. She'd shed the rump but she was left with the jugs which she had decided to handle as an asset, which meant her upper portions were not so much swathed as bedded down in chiffon like two outsized Godiva fantasies. "May I cut in?"

Bill managed a strangled, "My pleasure."

"You don't mind if I take your handsome man."

Georgie tried to match her tone, which was a hard trick, since Frederika herself hadn't quite mastered it. She thought it was intended to be alluring so she replied in a throaty voice, "Just as long as you promise to bring him back."

Since the divorce Frederika had done an about face, from frumpy frau with plain clothes and superlative strudels to overdecorated, overblown siren, a wild creation of her own fantasies. She was trying to be something more or less alien to her makeup: sexy. She said, furrily, "We'll just see whether I let you have him back."

"I . . ." Bill began, but before he could finish Frederika had plowed into him with her right shoulder and was pushing him onto the dance floor. ". . . have to help Hamish with the ham," he finished weakly as he backed off in the grips of a force he was powerless to resist. Reduced to silence, he beamed a desperate grin over Frederika's head, which his partner would not see but which Georgie read clearly: HELP. She would, too, after a decent interval.

Except for this, they had arrived late enough to avoid most of the difficult business of the evening. In the corner the local tree surgeon was having at the ham on Hamish's behalf, arranging it on the platter in a modified ivy pattern, and Patty Sessions had selected Hug Watters as bearer. This would definitely prevent him taking off his shirt. He was already pinned and staggering under Patty's weight while she laughed and trailed her chiffon sleeves down the back of his neck. Horace Metcalf was for the moment occupied with a drink in a plastic skull; he had not figured out how to drink it without getting the floating gardenia in his face. Even Dent Eckersley was taken of; he was munching on the neck of a horrified houseguest of the Brills'.

Everybody was buzzing or chattering or dancing and there was the marginal possibility that tonight things might actually be different. Sometimes she thought they were like a clutch of phoenix birds, herself included. Revising their memories of the last gathering, they would rise again from the ashes, and if this one didn't work they would try again. It was so foolish, she thought, or wasteful, that there didn't seem to be much point, and even without Bill here to remind her, she knew that a person had to keep on letting them—a fact that was not really about parties; it was about life.

In addition to billing Heavy Names on their guest lists, the Marlowes insisted on building their parties around themes. They did makeup and wardrobe accordingly, once as Lord and Baby Face Nelson for a Deep Six party and another time as Han Solo and the Princess Leia, a neat trick at their age, which they refused to divulge but was made manifest in ways they had no control over: loose strands of flesh at the throat, rings under the eyes, brown splotches on the hands. Tonight Cappy was splendid in a brocaded kimono with her hair appropriately lacquered and skewered, and Hamish was effective in a simple linen number enhanced by a raw silk obi and a samurai sword. At a honk from Horace Metcalf Georgie veered and headed for her host instead, partly because he was on the far side of the room.

"Well Georgie." Round and shiny Hamish Marlowe was wearing white cotton footlets with the big toes separated, like thumbs, and he stamped his feet in a pattern learned, she supposed, from *The Magnificent Seven*. His personal tragedy was that he had once sold a photograph to the old *Life Magazine*, but he had a family to support and so he'd had to put away his cameras, and now he ran a Boston-based advertising firm. Still, he tried: for example, this costume. The bald head and droopy moustache made the effect not fierce, but touching. "Having fun?"

"Oh Hamish, you look like Toshiro Mifune."

"Do I really?"

"Magnificent. The sword!"

"I know it's silly, but Cappy says when people come here they expect something different."

Her face broke in a first smile. "Of course they do."

"What do you think of the lanterns?"

"Perfect. Everything is perfect."

"Our Nobel prize winner refused," he confided, barely containing his disappointment, "but we're still expecting three Pulitzer winners and . . ." he leaned forward, filled with importance, "they're bringing . . . someone who has a MacArthur."

Georgie tried to smile. "That's wonderful."

"Dance?"

"For you in that kimono, anything."

She was aware as they moved out of the women murmuring in the plant corner: the divorce explosion had left a gaggle of overage singles on the loose. These women were of the generation that had to wait to be asked, and they had been suspicious of Georgie from the beginning: the jeans all those years before Gloria Vanderbilt brought them to the people; the job that took her downtown to the newsroom every day. Although she wrote non-fiction they were secretly convinced that sooner or later she was going to put them in a book. Plus, she could never have lunch. ("I can't *do* like they do," she'd explained to Ag, who was having some of the same problems in New Brunswick. To which Ag had said, "Why should you?" Being well brought-up Catholic girls they had both felt guilty. The fact that it was an amorphous, nonspecific guilt made it more pervasive. This was one of the consequences of being reared in a world of moral absolutes. When that not-quite-right feeling that she identified as conscience nibbled at her, she could not always be sure what prompted it. There was the constant risk of attaching it to the wrong object. In this case neither she nor Ag could figure out whether the guilty feeling came from side-stepping, what was it, Woman's Lot, or avoiding the women themselves.) Woman's lot. No wonder they hated her. Why was she spared their problems? They would never get the truth from her: she wasn't. They assumed she was because she had so many other things to worry about.

Tonight the women clustering in the plant corner had finished vetting her costume and were trashing her character. Maybe it was the small success they could never forgive, or maybe it was only that she was too busy to thump and simmer with them at the health club and would rather eat lunch alone because her food stuck in her throat at their tables, her stomach clenched and she found it hard to smile. Perhaps, in the age-old, unspoken wisdom of the pack, they had divined that she was afraid of them. It was the being judged that scared her; she would never keep her house clean enough; for Georgie the ring around the collar had turned into a vicious circle, proof of her assorted inadequacies. She shouldn't care about these things but she did, which made her feel even more guilty. Although they never alluded to it directly it was clear that they thought even though she wrote for a major daily that would perform exquisite contortions to avoid libel charges, she was going to write something terrible about them and put it in the paper. She could feel their ill will like a dark cloud, settling of its own weight and condensing, viscous and already oozing across the floor. It was only a matter of time before she slipped on it and fell on her ass. She could imagine the joint sigh of gratification, the communal explosion of breath just before they started to laugh. Then Hamish Marlowe twirled, adroitly, considering the flapping scabbard and the white cotton footlets with the toe separators. He bent her backward in a dip that had the patina of an old photograph and whispered, "What are you going to say about us in your new magazine?"

"Whash!" The sword smacked her ankle like a schoolmaster's ruler and she yipped. This was why she hated parties. You started having fun and dropped your guard, which the person sensed: the precise moment at which to gnash off your fingers above the knuckles.

"Upsy daisy," Hamish said, not unkindly. "If you don't want to say anything about the job until it's announced, it can be our secret."

"I don't even know if I've got it." The magazine was called *IN* because they were going to pitch it to All the Right People, just as soon as marketing figured out who they were. If her meeting with the notoriously weird editor Peter Flinc went well she would get a thousand dollars per column per month. She would be read, she knew, south of New York and west of Scranton, Pa. She would once and for all show Trigger Matson, who wasn't even around to see, but that was another story. Who knows, she might be In. It was complicated. *In.*

Hamish said, a little sourly, "I promise not to queer it for you."

"You—what?"

"You don't think they hire people without checking up on them."

"Oh lord."

"I happen to be a good friend of Peter Flinc. It's all right," said Hamish, who seemed to want her to think he had her in his power. "I'll do everything I can."

Georgie said, miserably, "Naturally."

He no longer heard what he was saying. "So if nothing else we'll finally find out."

"Find out?"

He said, smoothly, "Just how far you'll go to get ahead."

"Hamish, they don't want an *exposé*. They don't even want me to sleep with them."

"That's what you think." He just dipped with her and went on in a kindly, even tone of pure dislike. "So after all these years we'll finally have it out in the open."

"What!"

"Just how big your ambition really is."

"Oh look, Hamish, there's Horace Metcalf. Oh Horace!"

"How ugly, and what color."

"Look, he sees us. Oh, Horace . . ." Her strangled call was only a partial measure of her desperation. Horace Metcalf made her teeth clash, but next to Hamish in this particular mood, he looked like a saving grace. "Yoo hoo."

Horace caught Georgie looking and honked joyfully. The sound came straight from the upper beak with the force of a thrown hatchet. It could cut through anything.

"Never mind old Horace," Hamish said. He was doing something intricate with his feet; whether it was from early Arthur Murray or *The Battle at Ichi Jo Temple* Georgie could not say.
"I really have to talk to Horace."
"That old hasbeen?"
At least he had been *somebody,* which would make him no cuter than Hamish, but a lot less unkind. "He was short-listed for the Pulitzer Prize."
"A miss is as good as a mile."
"I know."
Hamish's breath on her cheek was damp; he tried to bend her to his will. "Just when we were getting along so well."
"Mmmmm." She had to get away. In his latter-day posture as aging sex object Horace Metcalf had taken to carrying numerous small objects in his pockets, with the idea that presents made a man irresistible. Tumbling around amid the crumbs and lint were candy bars, penlights, mechanical toys. It was always a mistake to say yes when Horace asked whether you'd like to see what was in his pocket, yet here was Georgie, straining to hail him with an hysterical lilt: "Let's go see what he has in his pocket."
Hamish had her bent backward in a dip. He let go all at once. "Very well."
Flailing, Georgie regained her balance just as the sword fetched her a parting smack on the ankles and Hamish left with a spiteful flip of his skirt. She was relieved to see Horace Metcalf, lascivious carriage and all, because for all his foolishness he was completely without malice. In his prime he must have been something: straight as a lance with a sixth-generation face and a WASPy charm. Now he was bony and bent. His white hair stood up in a Woody Woodpecker tuft and the bridge of his fine nose strained the skin so tight it was only a matter of time before it cut through, exposing itself. The patrician face had given up on Horace and flapped in places, signaling surrender. Still he was dapper if dated in the white suit, and as she approached he reassembled collar and tie and suit jacket, patting himself tenderly in the midsection just above the belt as if to make sure everything was where the doctors had put it.

What was it Bill had said about goat glands? What did he want from her? His welcoming wave would have done credit to the first Douglas Fairbanks, whom he resembled, but not enough.

"Well Georgia, here you are. This is an honor."

"I was tired of dancing."

He seemed so thrilled to see her that he had to give her something. "When you get to my age, little things are important, y'know, like who seeks your company." His voice dropped to a confidential whisper. "Would you believe this is not a wig?"

There was no right answer to this one. She said, cleverly, "Why it looks just like you."

"I want you to be among the first to know," he said in normal tones, "my hair isn't the only thing that's coming back here."

She had to remind herself he was a noted historian. She said, as if to a child, "Aren't the Japanese lanterns pretty, and the banners!"

"Hair, for instance. My head isn't the only place it's coming back, ya know." He said, louder, "Georgia, are you listening?"

"And *look* at the paper umbrellas!"

"All my systems are go, go, go." He nudged her. "Do you want to see what I've got in my pocket?"

"Not really."

"I thought you wanted to see what I've got in my pocket. You might as well know, since the operation, my blood is running high."

If she whispered, she might be able to bring his voice down by example. "Look at the *sake* dishes, and Cappy's kimono!"

"It's running really fast now," Horace said, too loud.

"It has cherry blossoms on the back!" She would do anything to silence him. She tried touching his arm, which was a mistake, because he misconstrued it.

"My blood is in the home stretch," Horace said.

"Shh. That's wonderful."

"For what I paid, it had better be." He was in concert now, an entire flight of Canada geese. "Let me tell you the inside story of my operation."

Cappy was staring; the Brills' houseguest was staring; the Brimmer twins and Hamish, who was sulking, were staring; Patty Sessions was staring from her perch atop Hug Watters, who was also staring; it was too much for Georgie, who yanked the flushed and bugling Horace across the floor and out the front door without a clear idea of which of them she was sparing the embarrassment. "Never mind that now, Horace."

"What?" She was bundling him around the corner and down the bank to the lower terrace so fast that he stumbled and snorted. "What? What? What's the matter?"

"Nothing," she said kindly. "I'm going to let you show me what you have in your pocket."

Trotting along, Horace said, "That's not all I have to show you," but she chose to ignore him.

The first floor of the house would have been the basement in some more conventional arrangement; here the architect had designed a billiard room and a ground-floor kitchen, both giving onto the terrace. Georgie thought eventually some of the guests would filter down and open the sliding glass doors and she and Horace could rejoin the party without any of the usual pains of transition.

As it turned out what he had in his pocket was a windup toy: a tin man on a painted tin motorcycle that went in circles when he set it on the flagstones and touched the lever. After he had it running and Georgie had made as many appropriate responses as she could construct and enact for him, Horace began to talk about his operation with such passion that he forgot how smart he was; it was astonishing.

"It was in a back room, y'know, in the Alphonse clinic in Paris, everything was so hush-hush you might have thought I was going in for an illegal operation, pardon my French, but of course *that* operation isn't illegal any more, even though you mackerel snappers would like to send poor people to jail for it . . ."

Georgie murmured, "Not exactly," but Horace overrode her.

". . . the Alphonse clinic, y'know, named after Dr. Alphonse Alphonse, which may be a pseudonym. His name is a watchword in certain, ah, special medical circles, although of course the Kinseys don't like him, y'know, and Masters and Johnson don't like him and the *Joy of Sex* guy doesn't like him, because, y'know, they are all jealous of him . . ."

"Oh Horace, your toy is running down."

"That's what you think," Horace said in a flash. "Now hush and pay attention. As I was saying . . ." He paused, patting his tender midsection. Were the things really popped under the skin around his waist and what would happen if he strained himself? Would they start flying out like released crickets, or would they drop softly and roll along the cement? Why didn't he go on talking? Oh, right, he wanted to make it clear that he was going to keep her hung on this pause until he had her full attention, and night or day, he was not going to let her go until he had completed his recital. "As I was saying, you might as well know not everybody can get an appointment with Dr. Alphonse because . . ."

Another one of these pauses and they would be here into next Thursday. "Because what, Horace?"

He went on with a vindicated smile. "He's had miraculous results with, among others, the Duke of Windsor."

"But he's dead."

"*Before,* Georgia, before. Now stop being foolish and listen. The man is a count, bar sinister, one of the *finest* French families, but he has to exercise such caution! To tell you the honest truth I was more than a little frightened, y'know, all that backstairs business. I had to meet this sinister man in a black coat at the Deux Magots after which we went through a mass of back streets in a whole series of taxis, it took so much effort to get there that I knew before I even clapped eyes on him that Dr. Alphonse could help me . . ."

Horace's faculties for self-editing had atrophied well before his sex life withered, and Georgie began to fear he had even lost his terminal faculty. She would be stuck here until he tired or died or gave her his full story, which came first would be incidental. Her eyes glazed over but she thought she was still smiling. She would never know what alerted her, whether it was the toy running down or her reporter's sixth sense that the boring speaker had entered a peroration, but she tuned back in to hear him saying, ". . . after which there was a testing period . . ."

He looked so drained that she said, "You mean the operation didn't work?"

"No, it was gangbusters," he cackled, "and ever since then I've been perfectly *exhausted*. The demands alone . . ." He was unbuttoning his shirt. "Want to see what they look like?"

She said, in a naked appeal to his early dancing school persona, "No thanks, let's just sit this one out."

He looked bewildered. "Don't you want to see where they slipped them in?"

And watch them drop out on the terrace? Fat chance. She picked up the toy and wound it frantically. "Let's see how fast we can make your motorcycle go."

Only when she saw his eyes did she realize what he thought she was saying. "Georgia, *you*! Alphonse said this operation turns women into tigers, but I never guessed . . ."

She was calculating whether it might be more useful to throw herself against the sliding glass doors, which were probably locked, or to scramble up the rocks to safety, when thank heavens, the tin man on the mechanical motorcycle made one last spurt and rolled under the rim of the Marlowes' ornamental fountain, a naked stone toddler peeing into an enormous clamshell; the thing was a reflection of Hamish and Cappy's unleashed tastes and completely at odds with everything the architect and the decorator had intended. "Oh look," Georgie cried in relief, "it ran under the fountain."

"Oh dear, we have to get it out."

"My toy!" he cried and fell on his knees in front of the cement monstrosity.

"Georgia, it's one of my favorites!"

"Maybe we can get it out with a stick," she said helpfully.

"Oh yes." His fervor let her know that like the goat glands, this toy had some deep symbolic function. "I do hope we can get it working."

They were both on their hands and knees poking at the large crack in the fountain's base with a stick Georgie had found when she heard Bill's voice. "Lose something?"

Then Georgie fell back on her haunches and beamed in gratitude because he had kept their pact: gorgeous, grinning Bill. "The U.S. Cavalry to the rescue."

"In the nick of time, I see."

Horace forgot his problem in the excitement of having a new audience. He unfolded in stages until he was standing. "Would you believe this isn't a wig?"

"No shit," Bill said politely.

"No shit," Georgie cried in delight and relief. "All his own hair, and so much of it!"

Then, looking past Bill to the large pastel figure approaching, she realized she was not the only one in need of rescue. Here came Bill's corporal act of mercy, the extraordinary Frederika Jarvis, spunky divorcee, giving the lie to the hope that charity was ever something you could check off as completed. Georgie raised her voice in clear warning. "Oh, look, it's Frederika."

"I was wondering where you were," Frederika said, attempting to slip her plump arm through Bill's, which seemed to be welded to his body.

"Oh Frederika, Horace has something to show you," Georgie said with false cheer. "Wait until you see what he has in his pocket."

"You owe me another dance," Frederika said to Bill.

"The problem is," Georgie said, loud, "at the moment it's stuck under this fountain."

"That's the problem," Bill said, stooping resourcefully. This put him *hors de combat,* leaving Georgie to deal with both Frederika and Hamish while Bill used the stick to worry the motorcycle toy out of the soft moss in the crack in the fountain.

"Frederika, you look wonderful." She did, Georgie thought, her face had flushed becomingly.

She patted the Godivas and smiled. "Why thank you."

"And doesn't Horace look wonderful?" He did, too, Georgie thought; with his gangly charm and his white hair shining in the moonlight, he could have been young again.

Frederika rustled silkily. "Oh, hello, Horace, I haven't seen you since you got back from Paris."

"You're a picture," Horace said.

"Why thank you." In spite of her size, Frederika bridled and fluttered.

"And doesn't Horace look wonderful?" Georgie prompted, nudging Frederika forward. "Would you believe this isn't a wig?"

"All my own hair."

Frederika purred, "And so much of it!"

"My dear," Horace said, "come over here in the moonlight and let me tell you the inside story of my operation."

Bill brushed dirt off the mechanical toy and handed it back to its proprietor, smiling. "You'll want to show Frederika how this works."

"Why yes, of course," said Horace, who was off and running. "It would be my pleasure."

Bill turned to Georgie. "Dance?"

They moved together so well that this was a necessity. Holding her, Bill would pull her back into one piece, mending the beginning cracks. She nodded toward Frederika and Horace, who were perched on the lip of the cement clamshell in a parody of some nineteenth-century love scene. "I think we'd better. I think they want to be alone."

Dancing, reinforced and more or less surrounded by Bill in the fortress of her marriage, Georgie surprised Cappy in a naked moment, her face transparent with exhaustion and sagging with disappointment. Their hostess was standing over the shambles at the buffet table with her geisha hairdo askew and her lipstick eaten off except for one smear at the corner of her tremulous smile which was sliding into extinction; the food was gone, except for the stuff nobody would touch; the party was in every respect over although it would be some hours before the last guest had cleared the driveway, and she guessed Cappy saw that it had not been different or even particularly festive; she caught Georgie's sympathetic look and acknowledged every thing with an embarrassed nod that left Georgie equally embarrassed and pensive; perhaps they had both wondered why she and Hamish bothered. Dressing tonight, Cappy must have known that her Pulitzer winners and her MacArthur fellow were never really coming, nor was anybody else that would add luster to the usual crowd. She must have realized these evenings were always all the same, but even knowing, she would have hummed the little refrain they all managed to pick up and buzz somewhere deep in their throats: *not me, not this time*; she would have been certain that this time they were going to find some way to make this one special. So there was the dilemma of these parties: foreknowledge, and the need to keep on trying.

Later, right before she sent Bill to dance with Cappy, who was obviously brooding over the no-shows, Georgie pressed her face into his neck, speaking in such a low tone that he had to bend his head to hear. "Promise we're never going to be like these people." In part she meant all the would-bes and might-have-beens with ambitions that had turned sour, but, more important, she meant the people who seemed so disappointed, not with the way their lives were turning out, but by an insufficiency of love: the squabbling couples, the lonely singles, the unhappily married hostess paddling sadly in the rubble of the buffet.

Bill said, firmly, "It could never happen to us."

Her marriage! "Promise."

"I don't have to promise, it's true." Then her only husband went on in an utter faith that made her want to hide her face in him forever, so he could not look into it and see what she was thinking. Bill said, "We're never going to be like that because we have only ever loved each other."

She strangled. "Kendall!"

"Shut up, Kendall."

It was right before they left the party that Georgie found herself alone in the ground-floor playroom, and discovered that she could not stop trembling. Watching Horace dance with Frederika, she had been struck, almost overturned by the fragility and pathos of the arrangements people made for themselves, found her very life threatened by the precariousness of human love. There was poor Ag, who had run away to Florida with such hopes; there was Ralph. And here was she, in spite of all her attempts to forget or efface or outstrip her moment of betrayal; here was Georgie on the edge.

Sensing her distress, Bill had brought her down to wait in the deserted playroom while he went upstairs to make their manners. Tonight this was particularly important; Cappy expected them to make a fuss because at least one of the new generation of Kennedys had shown up in time to say goodbye. Bill would be back as soon as he gave Cappy a final twirl that left her blushing and giggling, and thanked Hamish and bowed out. They would sneak through the sliding glass doors and cross the terrace and escape through the shrubbery. Never mind Georgie's stockings. She wanted to get out of here the quickest way; she and Bill could crash through the bushes to the driveway once they were clear of the house and head for the car at a dead run and so make good their escape, but meanwhile she had to wait.

Meanwhile she was on the edge. Here was Georgia Kendall on the edge in the Marlowes' unlighted high tech playroom. The night outside was black now, dark as eternity, and through the Thermopane, Georgie could see the edge of the terrace and beyond that trees marching downhill into a darkness so complete that it might have been the waiting void.

For all she knew the void began right here, just outside the playroom, the precipice itself could be just beyond the Thermopane, and as she stared into this blackness she imagined she saw the Marlowes' guests falling into it, dropping past her vantage point at tremendous speeds. The first to fall were Horace and the buxom Frederika, who might have slipped from the roof or from the rail of one of the upstairs porches, Horace with his mouth and eyes wide and his scarecrow arms waving, his white suit dazzling in the night. Frederika went by with her arms flapping in the voluminous pastel sleeves, looking perplexed and even slightly apologetic as she slipped from sight. The predatory Dent Eckersley was the next to drop into her field of vision, waving farewell with a vulpine grin; at midframe he doubled up and knifed past her like a diver, headfirst. Cappy and Hamish followed in full regalia, with their arms and legs arranged in Oriental postures, their white footlets gleaming in the night. They were followed by Patty Sessions and Hug Watters, she in his arms as before; she would be pleased to be carried into eternity, and he would forever have to keep on his shirt. Jim Sessions followed, a mournful solo flier, and he was followed in turn by all the others, everybody plummeting into the unknown in party clothes, still wearing party smiles, the lot all talking and laughing without regard for the catastrophe that had overtaken them, or where they might be going. Some of the guests were gesturing or posturing and some were dancing, but they were all in the attitudes they had assumed for the party and only beginning to be startled by the plunge. As she saw them hurtling past with their clothes whipping in the wind and their hair streaming Georgie wondered whether, if she waited long enough, she was going to see Georgia Kendall herself falling, Bill falling, and what they would look like from the outside. Then from her vantage point she thought, lord, lord! which at the moment was as near as she could come to prayer.

Rushing down the Marlowes' driveway with Bill, she could not outstrip either Ag or Ralph, who were not so much remembered as somehow present, running along beside her, palpable and crowding. Which meant that without reference to anything she or Bill had said since they escaped the Marlowes' house, she found herself asking him, completely accidentally: "What would you have done if it had been me in Florida, instead of Ag?"

To which gentle Bill, *her Bill*, who had never even so much as shoplifted, said immediately, "I would have cut him in half with a machine gun. What's it to you?"

3

A G CALLED BACK in the first hour of the next day, toward the end of *Saturday Night Live.* In the deep rug in the TV room, Tim and Matty lay where they had fallen. Coming in from the Marlowes' party, Georgie found them asleep in a comfortable welter of quilts and pillows and popcorn and family dog. If she had stayed home and wallowed with them she would not be so uncomfortable now. They always begged to stay up on Saturday nights and they always fell asleep somewhere north of the *Love Boat* and south of whatever it was they had waited up to watch. She could be snoozing with them, instead of rubbing the bruise inflicted by Hamish's scabbard and licking teeth that seemed to be scummy with dye from the toothpicks in Cappy's colored *hors d'oeuvres.*

Instead of rousting the kids Georgie shrugged at Bill, who nodded and tiptoed past them to the sofa, where they slouched, beginning to decompress. They would not go to bed until they had run the last tapes from the party through their heads, fast forward, exchanging fragments of gossip to make story. One of the parts of their life together was advancing the novel this community was writing, which, strangely enough, seldom touched on their own lives. It was less a comic novel than a soap opera, but tonight's installment had certain campy overtones, like the budding romance between poor Frederika and fuddled Horace Metcalf in his perennial white suit.

"I don't know what attracted her," Georgie said.

"There's more to Horace than you see," Bill said. "Remember, he was short-listed for the Pulitzer Prize."

"Close, but no cigar," said Georgie, for whom this had implications. At her elbow, the telephone bleated alarmingly; she flinched. Nothing good had ever happened to her on the telephone. "You get it."

"Chicken." When it became clear she was not going to answer, Bill reached across her to pick it up. "It's Ag."

"I can't! Tell her I'm asleep."

"She's right here, Ag. She's dying to talk to you."

"Bill!"

He scooped up Timmy, with his quilts and a stuffed Teddy, preparing to desert. "She's your friend."

Yes. She's my friend. "Oh Ag, I'm so glad you called."

"Sorry if I waked you."

"We weren't asleep."

"That's good. I can't sleep anyway and I guess I forgot what time it was. I just wanted you to know, everything's all set. For the services."

"That's great."

For a bereaved person, Ag sounded pretty much on top of things. "Fulcrum is delaying the funeral so everybody can get down here for the program. They're arranging for complete media coverage, all three networks and the cable news people, which means I won't need you guys until Sunday, Saturday night at the earliest."

"Sunday! By Sunday Ralph is going to be . . ." She didn't have to remind Ag of the state funeral in their freshman year at Mount Maria. When the provincial of the teaching order that ran the college died they had to hold everything until the archbishop could make it back from the Council in Rome so he could celebrate the Requiem. After three days not all the banked gardenias in the world could mask the fact that what remained of Mother Helen was in the grips of something powerful and inexorable.

"Don't worry, he's being cremated. Serena said that way we

could divide him up later if we wanted to, you know, after the funeral?"

"Good lord!"

"A little for her," Ag went on in a voice that was so light as to sound positively careless, as if she were twirling her fingers, "a little for me. Of course I said that wasn't necessary, I mean, when a person is dead the soul is gone, and what would I do with a couple of bones, but you know how Serena is."

Rattle.

"Ag, are you chewing your beads?"

"Of course not. Everything's fine. Why would I be chewing my beads?"

"I was just wondering."

"Everything's fine and Serena is being a prince."

"If you say so."

"You know how she is."

"Yes." Patient Griselda. Or was it Mother Courage? Or did Georgie simply resent her for always being calm? Serena Schwartz was like one of those countries that wins wars by being patient and big enough to absorb all the smaller powers without having to fire a shot. Let other people rage and beg. Serena simply waited, and she always won. Every time Ralph took off she let him go with the same unchanging smile, content to let him chase the speckled butterfly of happiness wherever he wanted, even to the edges of the world, because she already knew that as surely as he went out in search of whatever it was Ralph thought he was seeking, Ralph would come back. Until this time. Now that he was dead and by the coincidence of physical location and timing linked to Ag forever, Serena was, apparently, still winning. When Ralph married Serena, Georgie and Bill went to the wedding; Georgie still remembered looking into that large, handsome face and in spite of or perhaps because of her own folly, feeling strangely betrayed, the way she had when she'd found out that Donny Reickert who suffered unrequited love for her in high school and beyond had actually married someone else when she'd imagined him sitting on some shelf in eternity, pining for her. Did Serena know about Georgie's fleeting encounter? Probably not. When Ralph introduced them her smile was open and generous. "I know how Serena is."

Ag's voice developed a hairline crack. "She's always so damn big about everything."

"Why on earth are they having the funeral on a Sunday?"

"I already told you, they want to make a fuss."

"Who wants to make a fuss?"

"The management here. Nothing like this has ever happened at Fulcrum before. At least I don't think it has. The problem with Ralph is, he is, I mean, he was a public figure. Plus he didn't exactly die in bed." Ag's breath shuddered and her voice dropped to a whisper. "He practically landed on Henry Kissinger." She paused for long enough to recover her breath and went on in a brighter tone. "So they want to give him a big sendoff to counteract the bad press. Mr. Fulcrum himself is coming in as soon as he finishes this deal in Alaska, and we're going to have at least two senators and three college presidents. They're inviting A. Bartlett Giamatti."

"Ralph didn't go to Yale."

"Turns out he always wished he had. Anyway, he liked baseball. Some senators are flying in, along with a Supreme Court justice and a delegation from the American Philosophical Society, and with any luck they get the mayor of Jerusalem out of the Geneva conferences in time to come and give the eulogy. Which means it can't possibly be before Sunday at the very earliest, which means I don't have to face Serena until then . . ." Ag muffled a sob.

"It's not your fault she couldn't hang on to Ralph."

"No, but it's my fault he let go!"

"Ag, put down those beads and talk clearly. Now quit crying, OK? Just cut it out!"

"It's just." Rattle. "Serena. Do you know what she said?"

"It doesn't matter what she said."

"She said . . ." Ag gasped. "She said there is no point in crying over the milk after the cow has stepped in it! Oh George, she's just a prince, and I. I am not worth the paper I'm printed on."

"Ag, are you all right?"

"Of course I'm all right. It's just that Serena is so wonderful and I . . ." Her voice dropped again, so Georgie could hardly hear. "I'm an adulterer."

Before Georgie could stop herself she said, "Not any more."

There was a long, expensive pause in which Ag broke down and cried a little and then sniffled and blew her nose and began again, in a completely different tone. "Which is why I have to have the car."

Georgie started. "What car?"

"My car. The red Datsun. It's in long-term parking in Newark. There's a totem pole on the antenna, so you can find it right away."

"You want me to get your car out of long-term parking in Newark?"

"And pick up Mickey in New York and Kath in Washington and come down in my car."

"If we fly down we can rent a car."

"I have to have *my* car," Ag said.

It was late; Georgie was tired; when they were kids they used to saw back and forth just this way; it took her back. She assumed the old tone. "I'll buy you another one. It was a wreck anyway."

"My car," Ag said. "You don't get it. Listen. My car is all I have left. Sometimes I think it's all I am."

"Don't. You're just upset."

"I'm not upset," Ag said with all the breath she had left. "I'm just trying to hang on." There was a long pause in which she recovered her breath and pulled herself together, a silence marked by one or two mournful clacks of the wooden beads. When she resumed speaking it was in a controlled tone. "George, I have spent the day on this, calling everybody just to work things out. All you have to do is go and get the car, just the way I said. If you do what I tell you then maybe I can make it through in one piece, instead of humiliating all of us. Get me the car, OK?"

"I just think you're not going to want it after the funeral, you're going to want to fly home instead of driving it back."

Ag said, in a low voice, "I don't even want to come back."

"Are you all right?"

"I'm fine. I just have to have the car. What I did . . . What it is, is . . . Everything I have left to care about is in that car. When I ran away with Ralph I left everything behind, I mean everything. My house and my clothes and everybody that mattered except Ralph. I left the kids, who are never going to forgive me, and my boss, whom I don't like, and I left Brendan, who makes me want to cry . . ."

Her *husband,* and he made her want to cry; Georgie said, automatically, "I never liked Brendan."

"And all for a guy that I didn't even know if he slept in his pajamas or his underwear . . ."

"Nothing," Georgie muttered, and quickly covered her mouth.

". . . or what," said Ag, who hadn't heard. "When you go you don't want it to be the end, you know? I mean, you don't want to just—disappear. You want to leave something behind. I mean, look at the pyramids. Everybody wants to leave something. A channel marker, maybe, it's like dropping crumbs in the forest so you can retrace your steps? Do you know what I mean?"

Georgie didn't, really, but she would have agreed to anything because Ag's misery, her desperate courage made her want to weep. "Sure I do."

"Good. I knew you would. So what I did was, I got everything together before I left. I don't know what in God's name I thought was going to happen to us, but when you're that happy for the first time in your whole life, you just know it isn't going to last. I don't know what I thought was going to go wrong, I certainly didn't think I was going to drive him to . . . fall off the goddam balcony." She faltered and quickly resumed. "So what I did was, I got it together, everything I had that would fit in the trunk of my car that is the only thing I ever really owned; I took all my notebooks from college and my letters from you guys and my files from the office and all our picture albums and Grandmother's jet-and-crystal jewelry and my . . . white blazer, I got it all together and put it all into the trunk; I was, all right, I was making something, a time capsule, so maybe next week or a million years from now somebody could dig it up and see Ag Fitzgerald was not such a horrible woman after all. They could see I was just an ordinary mom who loved her kids and did her job until she got . . ." Ag choked ". . . carried away."

In the middle of this recital it had struck Georgie that Ag might not be the only one who couldn't bear to throw anything out. She imagined herself asking, in kindergarten-teacher tones: and Ralph, did Ralph have a time capsule? With Ag in bad shape, struggling for control, she couldn't bring herself to do it.

Ag went on thoughtfully. "Maybe I thought I could be buried with it or in it, you know? You could run us into one of those car mashers and that would be that. Or else I thought we could have a Viking funeral. You could put me in the car and set it on fire and push us out to sea . . ."

"Both of you?"

"I thought so at the time, but it turns out he's gone and I'm the one that got left behind. All he is is rubble now. Ashes and a couple of bones."

"Oh, Ag!"

"Everything that's left is in the car." Ag was trying hard to sound brave and competent. "Books and letters. Baby shoes, Brucie's, I think, my fur coat . . . unless some airport yobbo has already ripped me off. So the thing is, if I'm going to face Serena I have to have my things around me to show who I am, and I want my friends to be here too . . ." In an eyeblink her bravery yielded to despair. "Oh God, George, this is so terrible."

"Damn Ralph for leaving you like this."

"It wasn't Ralph."

Georgie overrode her. "How could he yank you out of your life and not bother to put you back? How could he do this to you?"

"He didn't. Oh Georgie, I moved on him."

Georgie went on as if she hadn't heard. "How could he do this to you, after everything?"

To which Ag responded with a cry. "He did it *because* of everything." And in the next breath she sprang the trap. "So you understand how it is I have to have the car."

Which meant that Georgie had to say at once, and from a full heart. "Oh Ag, I'll get you anything you want."

"Then you'll pick it up at Newark Airport," Ag said in a completely different tone. "Maybe Mickey can come down from Westchester to meet you, and you can head right on down to Washington, you'll have plenty of time between now and next Sunday . . ."

"We can make it in three days."

"Saturday at the earliest." Ag went on in the cleansed, improved tone of a woman who has just enjoyed a good cry. "I'll get Danuta to reserve the room next door for Kath and Mickey, and I'd be . . ." She could not seem to decide whether the right word was: honored, or: grateful, or just: glad, and so she veered slightly, as if they had just finished planning a campout or a field trip, finishing, "and you can bunk with me."

"Ag, where am I going to get the keys?"

"What keys?"

"The keys to your car."

"That's all taken care of. I sent them to Brendan as a parting shot."

"Brendan!" He ought to be booked and convicted and sentenced to life. A year in the stocks might be nice, or a full firing squad. If Brendan hadn't been such a monumental bastard Ag would be home right now, and everything would be fine.

"He doesn't like you either," Ag said.

"I have to ask *Brendan* for the keys?" He was a square-jawed Fordham Irish product who glared at the world like an angry priest, not cruel, exactly, but a psychological wife-beater with deadly accuracy where Ag was concerned. At several dreadful Mount Maria reunions she had seen him demolish Ag without lifting a hand: he would tilt back in his chair with his penny loafers glistening and his striped knit tie barely covering the placket of his Oxford-cloth shirt and with that Irish mug set in an ersatz smile he would simply wipe her out. Erratic as Ralph was, he was a true romantic whose intentions were good. He always imagined he was in love with you at the time, whereas Brendan was a tinhorn philanderer, which Georgie forebore mentioning. "I never liked Brendan."

"Don't worry, you won't have to see him. He's leaving them at the People Express ticket desk, along with the parking stub. I've spoken to them and all you have to do is show ID."

"How did you know I would . . ."

"Because you're my friend."

She was right; Georgie would have done anything for her; in the same position, so would Ag. "I begged you not to marry Brendan, but would you listen? No."

"You also told me not to get my legs waxed." Ag's tone lightened. Georgie could almost see her grin.

"But you did, and peeled like a snake."

"And you also told me nursing women didn't get pregnant . . ."

"Who knew?"

". . . but what did you know anyway?" Ag sounded almost like herself. "So you'll get the car, and Kath, and Mickey? I've already spoken to them and they're dying to come."

Poor Ag! "I wish you'd let us come sooner."

"Take your time," Ag was in no hurry. "Do some sightseeing."

"Sunday seems so far away. Are you sure you're all right?"

"Don't worry, I'm going to be fine. There's this Dominican down here, for a symposium?" He's a Christologist, on a two-month fellowship and he's a really neat guy, so I thought I might get him to . . . I'm going to ask him to hear my . . ."

Georgie's heart twisted. "Oh, Ag!"

"So really. I'm going to be fine. Sunday, OK?"

"OK. Sunday." Georgie secretly resolved to move heaven and earth and their mutual college roommates to get to Florida a little earlier; it was the least they could do for Ag, in addition to which . . . By this time she knew she was going to have to find out whether Ralph had kept her letters, passionate fragments up to and including the sonnet she'd more or less assumed had vanished, along with her *passage* with Ralph. If Ag shored up bits of her past against the moment, had Ralph? He was a terrible packrat in their war-protest days; he used to run off and Xerox everything he got, multiple copies, but those were letters from the White House to put in many hands, and that was war, not love. At the time he had covered her face with the palms of his hands and promised to hold her in his heart forever, but what did that mean? How could she know? It was as if she had buried something embarrassing in the garden and now the neighbor's dog was sniffing at the flowerbed, beginning to dig it up. If they got there early she could help Ag go through Ralph's things. If they existed, she would turn them up and destroy them before Ag even knew. She would be too distracted, piling up bits of Ralph to take with her.

Viking funeral indeed.

4

SHE WAS GRATEFUL to Ag for making the schedule because it left her all of Sunday to write the necessary columns ahead and pack. She could even get to her Monday appointment in New York because Mickey was going to be at her sister's in Upper Montclair ("Don't ask") and they would not rendezvous until suppertime. Peter Flinc had promised her lunch at Lutèce; excited, Georgie skipped breakfast, saving up. Dinner was going to be another problem; Mickey's sister was a lavish cook: three pounds every time you ate at her house.

Tuesday morning they would head out to pick up Kath in Washington. Kath was (she told Georgie) getting her act together, wasn't it thoughtful of Ag to give them time to do wardrobe and everything. Right, Georgie thought. Ag never wanted to put anybody out. In college Mickey was overorganized and Kath was wild and sexy and Georgie was talented, while Ag . . . was just Ag, with hair that was not quite red and a lanky body and all the love in the world to spend, which in the absence of a man, she lavished on her eight younger brothers and sisters.

On the premise that all women ought to be equal Georgie had encouraged her to spin romances. What did they know, stashed in their Catholic College in the pre-Council '60s? The nuns were smart careerists who taught them they could do wonders with their education, but they wanted the one thing the nuns did not have. If they had careers they would have them, but life, they thought, meant romance. Dreaming after lights out, they composed love stories in which they starred opposite this man or that one, writing dialog they might never get to speak, but which they stored up in secret caches, wild fantasies as comforting as diamonds in velvet boxes. Georgie did all right with men but Ag was neither pretty nor graceful, just kind and strong, which meant none of her love stories came true no matter how much hope she put into them—until the others were long married and Brendan Fitzgerald bopped her with his magic wand. Was it for Georgie to point out that he was tight with money, and usually drunk? It would seem mean to suggest that he might not be The One. Instead she and Kath and Mickey cried over their pink bouquets while muscleheaded Brendan did Ag the enormous favor of marrying her, after which he had the absolute nerve to condescend to her and her friends.

It wasn't Ag's fault he turned out to be cruel, nor was it really her fault she was slow to find out not everybody lived in a posture of apology. It was probably her fault that once she did find out, she stewed and then shrugged her shoulders and bent another notch so she could go on carrying her cross without straining her back. Which she did, until apparently Ralph Schwartz . . . Ralph, whom Georgie had . . . Damn Ralph anyway. When Ag shucked Brendan it happened so fast that nobody even had a minute to yell, Look Out. She called Georgie and the others from the airport, told Georgie she was wearing a white going-away suit and it was cold for early May, so Ralph had given her his coat; she was wearing his coat! She marveled that it fit so well and looked perfect with the suit. Ralph, she said, had bought her an orange-blossom lei. It would have been churlish of Georgie even to hint that she might not be the first. Ag was beyond caution, gulping air like a laughing girl, and Georgie . . . was afraid. She respected Ag too much to fob her off with half-truths and she loved Bill so much that she was afraid to let any living person know anything that would point to what she had done with Ralph. No: what she had done to Bill.

* * *

In Newark, she identified herself at the People Express ticket desk and came away with the parking stub and Ag's keys, which had been left by Brendan in an envelope bearing his attorney's letterhead. Right, Brendan. Fast work. The keys were on a metal ring along with one of those keyring replicas of the license tag, the work of the Disabled American Veterans, and to show that Ag wasn't all seriousness, a plastic fried egg. She knew the car because she had driven with Ag to their last reunion, but she could not for the moment bring herself to go to the farthest parking lot and retrieve it. It was nowhere near new, rusted out underneath and fading to pink. Would it start? What if the battery had died? She'd be stranded in west hell while her lunch meeting took off without her: they would all be carousing in Lutèce assuring each other that a woman who couldn't even make a meeting on time was not worth the paper she was printed on. If the car did start, what was she going to do with it? She could spend the rest of her life circling midtown Manhattan in a holding pattern, waiting for one of the garages to disgorge just one car so she could ditch the thing. If she tried to park and walk away from it she would come back to find it had been towed, or worse. She might find the trunk gaping like a dental patient's mouth, all the pieces of Ag's past extracted in one wrench. If somebody burgled the car in the parking lot, that was fate. If she took the car and then it got burgled, then it was her fault.

In the taxi she adjusted her khaki jacket nervously, wondering what in God's name had prompted her to go job hunting in a safari suit. She stretched to check her makeup in the rearview mirror; her eyes and the driver's collided and she recoiled with a little shock. He could have been her mother, letting her know with a grimace that she was wrong again: You're not wearing *that*. She showed her teeth in a disarming smile, at least she hoped it was disarming, but when they reached the Magnum building and he let her out she was certain of his disapproval; his expression said, *country mouse* and as she turned to leave she saw him pick up his radiophone and begin talking: probably sending advance warning to the urbane Peter Flinc.

Broaching the marbled lobby of the Magnum building was like coming into church. It may have been the size of the place or its polished expanses or the vast distance between occupants and vaulted ceiling that intimidated her; people were going back and forth quietly, like monks shuffling along the stone floors of some abbey, dedicated to preserving the hush. At the far end of the lobby the crest of Magnum Enterprises glittered a full two stories high, executed in brushed steel. She resisted the urge to genuflect and cross herself, and addressed the glass-fronted directory, cleverly catching her image in its face. She worked hard on the image and could not make sense out of either her expression or her hair. Maybe she should try not to embarrass the powerful and suave Peter Flinc in some smart restaurant; probably she should ask for a brown bag lunch. Better yet, she ought to put the bag over her head. She got into the elevator moodily, looking hopefully at the Rasta who had slithered in just as the door closed, happily pulling on a joint. His voluminous wine-colored overcoat could be hiding almost anything, and the dreadlocks concealed his intentions, along with the better part of his face. If he bopped her and took her money, she thought, at least she wouldn't have to go through with this. Instead when the doors opened on a plush mahogany-and-leather upstairs lobby, he pulled out a *TIME-LIFE* envelope somebody had given him to deliver and, exiting, brandished it with a savage show of teeth in what she took to be a grin.

Since *IN* was the new baby at Magnum, she expected the offices to be appropriately glossy: the exquisitely appointed nursery in a billionaire father's house. The double glass doors would have the new logo etched in the glass and emblazoned above in pushy neon, and inside everything would be glass and brushed steel and white formica, with the logo repeated in the mossy carpeting. Even the receptionist would be high tech, neo-Barbie perfection slipcovered in *le dernier cri*. Georgie would find the suave if notoriously weird Flinc in the executive offices—two sofas and a VCR, no desk, a ficus in the corner, a

Pollock on the wall and in the aquarium, pirhanas, par for the event. It was already clear that she was not suitably dressed for this encounter, or for Lutèce, but by this time she was hungry enough to go to any lengths; she'd walk in wearing her bathrobe if she had to, anything to get lunch.

The door bearing the number Peter Flinc had given her was marked LOW MAINTENANCE: certainly the wrong place. Nobody answered her knock. Anxious and starving, she went downstairs and phoned.

Somebody shouted, over a background clatter, "*IN* Magazine."

Georgie shouted back, "Look, I'm trying to find your offices . . ."

"Name, please."

"Peter Flinc."

"No, *your* name."

"Georgia Kendall, I have a 12:30 appointment, and . . ."

"Well you'd better hurry. Peter hates to wait."

"That's why I'm calling. He gave me the number of some mop closet."

"Oh, right," the voice said cheerfully. "That's us. You should have knocked."

"I did knock."

"I'm sorry. We're in a state of flux."

It was like walking into a chrysalis inhabited by something that was neither caterpillar nor butterfly. At the moment nobody had decided where the walls were going to go, which meant there were a series of movable units stacked at the far end of a vast space, not far from a lackey on an A-frame, who was holding up swatches for the decorator. There were painters mopping the far walls, which had been pink, with mauve and others streaking the near ones, which had been mauve, with pink, and in the middle distance there were people at work on telephones or typewriters set on everything from lima bean shapes of pink marble to packing crates. Somebody was either hammering or sawing at all times; at all times somebody else begged for quiet. Everything was at odds: the plush chairs with the plaster-spattered workmen sitting in them eating lunch, the mahogany computer stations with the battered file cabinets, the marbled atrium floor with the oversized carton the receptionist was using for a desk.

"I'm Georgia Kendall," Georgie said in the constricted tone she'd used as a teenager, trying to look thin; the receptionist was so skinny and chic that it made her feel fat.

"Right. Mr. Flinc is expecting you . . . As you can see, we're in a state of flux. Color choices. Furniture. He just sent back a whole carload of potted palms."

"I see."

"He said they were the wrong breed." She went on brightly. "*Manhattan, Inc.* called Mr. Flinc brilliant but erratic." Then she whispered as the decorator and her assistant began to argue over a swatch. "That means he has a hard time making up his mind."

"About decor."

The receptionist looked around distractedly. "But he really is expecting you. I just don't see him right now."

"We're supposed to be having lunch."

Was hunger affecting her brain or did the receptionist really say "lots of luck"? With surprising dispatch, she hustled Georgie down an unbroken stretch of mauve carpet and around a bank of chipped and dented file cabinets to the one private cubicle in this morass of improvement. "I'm afraid you're going to have to wait."

"Is this his office?"

The receptionist's voice dropped to a whisper. "He hates to be watched."

"If you could spare some coffee, or a cracker," said Georgie, who was getting faint.

"Wherever he went, I'm sure he's coming right back."

Tacked to Flinc's partition was a Polaroid that unnerved her. It was of somebody in a bear suit with the head tucked under his arm, posing at a costume ball. Even without the mask the heavy brown beard made him look like a bear.

She was reassured by a quick perusal of the desk; she had been around long enough to know how to read upside-down. The mangled copy scored by blue pencil and in some cases hastily reassembled with scissors-and-paste all bore the names of writers she respected, whose work was being eviscerated here. This gave her heart even as she made a quick note to protect herself by contract from this kind of editing. Along with hers, he had books by a number of women she envied or admired or both. Did she have this job or was she one of a whole bevy of ponies turned out to sing a few bars and tap? There were a couple of dummy pages in the clutter and in one corner, revealed by an accidental shove of the pencil she was inadvertently poking with, her own file. She might have flipped it open but she was distracted by the brown satin warmup jacket lettered CAPTAIN BEAR. On the hook behind her hung a transparent garment bag protecting a beaded pink satin strapless evening gown, a fact she noted with a certain giddy prescience, and in an involuntary spasm, carved in stone somewhere inside her head.

"I liked your book."

She leaped away from the dress guiltily, Goldilocks apprehended. He looked like a bear even without the suit. "Where did you find it?"

"Remaindered."

"Already!"

"You're regional, honey, what did you expect?"

"South of New York nobody has ever heard of me."

"Or west of Scranton, Pa. We intend to take care of that."

Georgie started. "How did you . . ."

"If you get the job. Your columns for the daily are good, your reputation is good as far as it goes, but sitting right here I can tell you, if you want to make it, you're going to have to reach. If you want to know the truth your stuff is a little superficial."

She lurched. "Maybe we ought to do this over lunch."

"We're a new magazine," he said, without even seeing that he had wounded her. "We're making a statement here. We're into gut issues. You're going to have to reach inside yourself and pull out everything you've got."

Unless they ate soon that wasn't going to be much.

"You've got to reveal yourself." He was looking at her beadily. "Can you handle it?"

"Tell me what you want."

Flinc pulled out a sandwich and began gnashing at it. "Couldn't be easier. All you have to do is catch where we're coming from . . ."

Brilliant but erratic: right. She forebore saying he was going to spoil his lunch. "Where *are* you coming from?"

"I'll get back to you on that." Georgie expected him to reach for the warmup jacket so they could go but instead he settled back in his desk chair as if the will inside the body had a hard time communicating with it. Then while she waited, he dropped his bushy face into his hands. *A brown study,* she thought. Even his Brown University T-shirt was brown. As he brooded she looked around for other food or signs of food: your jar of peanuts and your coffee urn, perhaps your package of Nabs. *Takeout,* she thought hopefully. *He's ordered and Lutèce is sending it up.* She imagined the cart coming up rattling slightly in the elevator, white cloth with wine bucket and food under silver covers: rack of lamb, anything *en croute* . . . He inspected his belly and looked up. "You have to tell us something from the place inside that hurts."

A bite of his sandwich, perhaps. "You want personal stuff."

"You have to dig deep."

"I see." *Candy, from the machine?*

"Revelations," he growled. "We want deep truths."

She gulped. The only thing she had to reveal was the one thing she had spent her life concealing, and so she said instead, "And you want me to do this on spec?"

"Lady, life is on spec."

If only she could *eat.* "How many people are you auditioning? I mean, if I'm one of a cast of thousands, I'd like to know."

"We're projecting eight million readers. Do you want to do this or not?"

Eight million readers. Hell yes she did. "I need time to think."

The conversation sawed back and forth: the parry and thrust

of two old fencers feeling each other out. He didn't give anything away but as they talked Georgie rummaged for an idea he would like. Still there was the no lunch. It hadn't come and they didn't seem to be going. Was this a plus or a minus? Was he signaling her that she was wasting her time, or was it part of a test? At the midpoint her fuel tank switched to RESERVE and she vibrated with energy. All Peter Flinc's visible pink surfaces seemed to twitch with interest: nose and upper cheeks, startlingly pale lips, the exposed parts of his hands. He began to talk as if she had the job; he made *IN* sound like a combination of *LIFE* and *Vogue* and the Ark of the Covenant with an overlay of *New Republic* for the intelligentsia; *IN* would be devoured by the masses and elite alike (and the pica? Down, Georgie); she would start at a thousand a month. Even though he was talking about deadline schedules and travel money as if they were already in business she knew better than to ask for the warmup jacket yet. What she said instead was, "I think I have an idea."

"Think deep."

"I'll see what I can do." For a thousand a column, anything. Almost. She didn't know whether it was the no lunch or the eight million readers or the chance to show herself to the people south of New York and west of Scranton, Pa. that spurred her, but she was going to go for it. She would give it everything she had: Ag's story, their grief; there was in this a piece of work that she could do. Excited, she couched this to him with a little pang of anticipatory guilt which she stilled by promising herself she would protect her friends, she would disguise their circumstances and change their names so cleverly that even they would never recognize themselves. She said, "An old lover died."

He snapped to attention. "Your lover?"

She said, hastily, "My best friend's. I'm heading to Florida for the funeral. Ah. Immediately after lunch."

"*Whose* lover?"

"Wait until you see the story," she said. "He's a little bit famous. He's dead. Four college roommates, brought together in midlife by somebody's death. I think it has resonance." She invented, extrapolated, spinning details about Kath and Ag and Mickey until they grew larger than life and began to dance on his desk. The pink parts of Peter Flinc flushed, giving him away. She finished with studied diffidence. "What do you think?"

He licked the rim of his mouth. "We'll just have to see."

She had him now and this so dizzied her that she had to twist her tongue between her teeth to keep from telling the whole thing. "Death," she improvised. "Love and survival, and" (lord, Georgie, you are craven, but you do write fast, especially speeches) ". . . the flowers at the funerals inside every one of us."

"I see." He was on his feet and only half listening because the receptionist had popped a Federal Express package like a seed-pod on his desk. On to Lutèce? Georgie sprang up.

When he didn't move for the door she said, "So we may have something."

"Wind it up and let's see if it flies," he said distractedly. "You just dig deep and see what you get and then we'll talk about it, all right? When you're going for a national audience, first impressions count."

"I know."

"If they don't, they're also the last. A first column has to make a tremendous splash."

Like Ralph, falling from the . . . "You mean . . ."

"Blood, tears, everything." He was peering into the end of the package. "Right?"

"And we can talk about it at lunch."

"Lunch?"

"We were going to have lunch at Lutèce?"

"I never said anything about Lutèce."

Brilliant but erratic. Right. She tried for second prize. "But, lunch?"

"I never said anything about lunch. Besides, this is a brand new Updike manuscript." He put it down and began moving her toward the door. "First things first, right?"

"Right." A twinge of nausea distracted her, but whether it was hunger or qualms hatching she could not say. They were stalled at the door; Peter Flinc was shoveling her out and vigorously shaking her hand, which she tried to extract before his grip severed her second and fourth fingers with her sapphire anniversary band. She either had the job or she didn't, wished she could have it on her own terms but needed it in any case, and not only for the money. She was broaching the age at which people begin to guess that they may not be in control of their circumstances. She needed this job not as a hedge against fate exactly, but as something more important: an identity she could retreat to in hard times. If she had to be Georgie Kendall, who tried too hard and sometimes succeeded and was hated for it, and more often fell on her ass but got hated for her small success, who got dizzy at large gatherings and was not always good at life, she also wanted to be this impervious national columnist. Still something else was stirring inside her, some knowledge that she might not want to have to do everything she was going to have to do to get this, and in a crazed and transcendent moment she could not at the time make sense of, she flipped the corner of the plastic garment bag and to what would be her recurring horror, heard herself saying to the woolly Peter Flinc who began scowling even before she finished, said, even though it was clear the thing belonged to the receptionist, who must be going straight from the office to a party, "Oh, is this your *dress?*"

She left without looking back.

Compared to the non-lunch lunch meeting, getting to Newark and getting Ag's car out of long-term parking was going to be a piece of cake. She went via the Waldorf with two things in mind. It was one of the few places in Manhattan where a person could go to the bathroom and fix her face without having to charge a drink to Visa or American Express. Comforted by the hushed privacy and the flossy appointments, she washed her face and wadded her silk shirt into her shoulder bag, replacing it with a red T-shirt that made her feel less like Mrs. Macomber after the gun went off. Then she sailed out past the ruffled attendant and through the lobby like a pedigreed resident fully entitled to the best of service and let the doorman hail her a cab.

In the absence of lunch, she was going to ride to the airport like a human being, instead of taking the bus.

In the absence of lunch, she was visited by a surprisingly full memory of Ralph. Considering the death, puzzling over the reasons, she saw Ralph not as he had been last year in New Brunswick, but as he was in their peacenik days, the rangy visionary, persuasive, angry and intense. Yes she had been angry too: at the war, at Bill for being hers and still going so far away; with Bill gone for six months she had seen what was coming and run headlong into the collision, meeting Ralph midway. The first shock was that Ralph had *smelled* so different; of pipe tobacco, yes, and the grass they had been doing, and sweet wine, but beyond that there was the fundamental smell of Ralph, who was not Bill. A woman who had taken many lovers might have had a different scale of comparison but for Georgie there was the astonishing difference in touch; it was like—lord, the strangeness of the first new dentist she went to after Dr. Garry died; doing this, that she had never imagined doing, she was struck by the extraordinary difference in touch. She could still remember how strange Ralph's hands had seemed, feverish, hungry and (Ralph! what drew women like a magnet) ineluctably sad, unlike the joyful Bill. That night he was trembling slightly, also a surprise after Bill, who was well-muscled and not so much composed as compressed in his excitement, and who knew her to the heart; she supposed it was the significance—*affair*—as much as anything that had carried her, that and the fact that in everything he did Ralph lagged behind her desire so that instead of running in tandem she was racing, thinking: Hurry.

Hurry. God she was ashamed.

What had she been thinking of? What was Ralph thinking of, standing out there on the rail last Saturday, envied intellectual in the prime of life, adored by the woman he said he loved? *It snapped,* Ag said. What snapped? Was it the bathrobe cord or was it Ralph? Had guilt roared down on him like an express train then—his own, Ag's, hers—and rushed him off?

It seemed to her then, riding along in the gritty back seat of a Yellow Cab that this piece she was going to write might turn out to make sense of all of this: Ralph's death, what she had done. It might be her way of atoning not for the moment but for the betrayal—doing this to Bill and being afraid to let him know.

The problem was how to do this while protecting all of them—her secret, her old friends. If she cast the piece in the terms of her book—not guilt and expiation but the guilt of the victim, she could push it to some universal—what? She wasn't sure. She knew right off she was going to have to change the names. Trying to get down something that would make sense of it, she was still making notes when the cab jerked to a halt in front of the terminal and the driver let her out.

She did three prepackaged brownies with the fervor of an addict before she felt strong enough to pick up the luggage she had checked when she flew in this morning and go to Ag's car.

The car was not hard to find. Ag had hoisted a plastic totem pole on her car antenna: she got a new one every year from some Indian mission she had sent money to back in 1969, but Georgie unlocked the trunk just to be doubly certain she was in the right place. This was a mistake because the bits of Ag's jumbled past were all in there all right, ready to cascade out and overwhelm her. All those boxes and books and undigested lumps of memory had been tied and stashed and covered with, lord, they were covered with the once-coveted white blazer with the college seal, the cherished symbol of general excellence which was yellowed now, and stained with grease from the lid of the trunk. It had been given to Ag for achievement in athletics, in the raw, vernal and confused days when such things had seemed important. In the orderly, contained world of their tiny girls' college she and Ag and Kath and Mickey had flourished, fixed in such perfect faith on the fact of God's plan and their place in it that they didn't always notice or protest when somebody tried to make them believe the little details, like who won what and who stood where in the May procession, carried reflected significance. Georgie knew you could still love God and not even want the blazer; Ag had cried when Sister Mary Thomas shook her hand and put the blazer around her shoulders. Oh, Ag. Ag's car gave off the scent of a long-deserted room, all dust and compressed silence and what smelled like Oil of Olay. In spite of encroaching wrinkles Georgie had resisted the company's promises because she'd rather shrivel like a white raisin than smell like other people's mothers. Or maybe, she thought, turning the key, she didn't want to smell like Ag, exuding, was it grief or loss or simply defeat?

The motor started easily and she gunned it, trying to get away from her misgivings, which she managed to outrun until she had paid the parking attendant and filled the tank and started off.

The trouble began with the plastic totem, which she had forgotten to remove. It blew off the antenna and bobbled under the wheels of the driver behind her, the efforts of many grateful Indian children mashed to extinction on the Pike. She remembered Ag explaining her visit to the mission with the same sweetly girlish shrug she had used to explain away all her idealistic gestures: the year in the settlement house soup kitchen before she met Brendan, the time she tried to get Mother Teresa to let her take the veil in Calcutta, which she did years before anybody knew who Mother Teresa was; her futile attempt to adopt the fifteen-year-old junkie recidivist. Ag would forestall questions by saying: *We are so lucky. It's time for us to give something back.*

But when they were that young such gestures had seemed possible; she and Kath and Mickey could even imagine, with Ag, that her efforts would work out. Then she found a more manageable cause: the choleric Brendan, whom she intended to give eight lovely babies, whom she would change into a happy man as soon as they got settled down, whom she would soothe with a big smile and a frosted shaker of Martinis every night. Fortunately Ag married late and had a fertility problem so they only ended up with three; otherwise—that old idealism extended to the limit—she would still be popping babies like fresh toast for an ungrateful Brendan, as many as her body allowed. She would be feeding and hugging and shushing them so that big bastard could watch his Monday Night Football in peace. She would still be safe in New Brunswick, and so would Ralph.

Unfortunately, when he came home at night that big bastard Brendan brushed past the big smile without even seeing, seized the frosted shaker and upended it into the open gullet he had expanded at all those college picnics in the dear dead days before he met Ag. Ag went on to a next cause: Ralph Schwartz. Say his wife didn't understand him, say he couldn't get his book written with his unhappy homelife under the vigilant eye of Serena who didn't understand him, say he was ready to tell his quarry anything so he could have his way with her.

What was Ag's mood when she locked the trunk of her car on all this stuff two weeks ago? How many were her hopes and how few her fears and what was she thinking when she posted the keys to Brendan, was she glad or anxious or valedictory or what?

Something about the speed at which the utility poles were passing alerted Georgie to the fact that everybody else on the road seemed to be standing still. She was racing. Why? Decelerating, she realized that she was even more anxious to talk to Mickey and Kath than she had thought. She needed to see herself as she had been, unsullied George reflected in their faces, to be sure after everything that unlike poor Agnes Mary the three were still all right.

Give back some of what has been given. Oh yes. Oh, Ag. Thus Georgie, already feeling guilty because Ag was essentially so good while she was fixed on how to get this job without betraying anybody she loved.

5

The most puzzling thing about Mickey's sister Jane's house was the string tied to stakes in a line that exactly bisected the front lawn. The line ran all the way from the bushes in front of the house across the flagstone walk and the grassy parkway to the curb. When she recovered her balance and tried to trace it, Georgie saw that it was fixed at the far end by a permanent-looking metal stake. On the driveway side of the string the bushes were trimmed and the grass was neatly cut; on the far side, where the front walk led to the porch steps and the front door, bushes competed for space and weeds wrestled the grass to the mat.

Hurrying for the house, Georgie had been too preoccupied to notice any of this until she felt something whip across her ankle, sawing at her bare flesh with an ugly bite that threw her off balance and almost yanked her off her feet. A child sing-songed, "Watch out for the string."

"Ow!" Georgie tried to kick free. The string was making sawmarks on her leg; it clung like a piece of powerful web from which hung a jagged shard of orange crate.

"And you'd better put Daddy's stick back where it was."

Furious, Georgie said, sweetly, "Is this your string?"

The eight-year-old regarded her from the front steps. She looked like a figure in a Rousseau painting with a round face and glazed expression, apparently unaware that she was about

71

to be swallowed by the creeping undergrowth. "Do you think I'm a baby?"

Georgie held up the shard of orange crate with a smile that oozed. "Is this your stick?"

"What would I want with that stupid old stick?"

"Then what . . ."

The child said patiently, "Are you here to see Mommy or Daddy?"

She might be here to do murder. "I'm here to meet your Aunt Michele. Now what idiot put this . . ."

"Then you'd better get off Daddy's side of the grass."

Georgie disentangled her foot. "Daddy's side!"

"You have to come over to this side anyway, if you're a friend of my Mom."

"Well I'm a friend of your father's, too, or I was." The child's walleyed look of distress prompted Georgie to change the subject. "What's your name?"

"Bethy. You can come over, but you'd better fix the stick."

"The hell with the stick."

"It's important." The child was just about to cry.

"OK, honey, I'm putting back the stick, OK?" Bethy's expression made her add, carefully, "Is the car all right where it is? I mean, the driveway is on his side."

"You've got to park somewhere," she said wearily. "They both know that."

"What about you? Are you on a side?"

Clearly prepared in advance, the child said, *"Amicus curiae."*

"Right." Georgie winced. Friend of the court. Jane had married a law student while she and Mickey and the others were still running around in gym suits with their bare legs lashed red by the elements, chasing hockey balls. At the reception they had touched handsome Beck's sleeve with lust and envy and competed for dances with him, all of them choking on unspoken questions that would overflow as Jane ran past, ablaze with expectation in her peach silk going-away suit. Their speculations followed her down the club steps and away on her honeymoon, off the airplane and into the wedding suite, into bed . . . Georgie remembered sitting on the country club steps until the last guest to leave tripped over them, Mickey fuddled with champagne and incongruous in her aqua bridesmaid's dress and the others sprawling in their incongruously ruffled flowered cotton dresses, four college freshmen with their knees spread like benched ballplayers, smoking in a tipsy reverie. They surmised and embroidered until the imagined wedding night ran purple with the blood of passion and crushed roses, until the air reeked of bodies in collision, the four of them elaborating until prudish Mickey had to stuff her aqua lace mitts in her mouth to stifle her shrieks. Were they ever that young? Georgie thought so. In 1961 the Sixties had not even been imagined; they would not be realized until 1967 except in a few places more advanced than Mount Maria College, or less safe; these Catholic girls had been born in the first half of the twentieth century and their sensibilities were formed in a time that, mysteriously, still existed in 1961; there would be cataclysmic accidents and surprises in the next decade: nothing and nobody left unchanged. Still they had managed, Georgie thought; they had tumbled into the Eighties more or less adapting; she, at least, enjoyed it; whatever happened, she was ready to go with the flow. But there was one leftover, or price tag attached to growing up with that measure of security: not shock or even regret at the way the world seemed to be going but, what, susceptibility to wonder. A lot of the time she was surprised.

"Are you coming in or what?"

"In a minute." Jane's front porch ran across the front of the house in the old style, spacious and hospitable. As Georgie came up the steps she could see all the wicker had been clumped at the near end, while at the far end a wooden swing dangled forlornly from rusted chains.

"I haven't got all day."

"Bethy," Georgie mused. "You must be the baby." In this circle you sent presents for the first child, a card for the second, after which you simply shrugged and smiled at each addition. Jane's boys were almost grown. Georgie had heard about her postscript from Mickey, who'd had to adopt her own two. ("You'd think if you could have your own, you'd want as many babies as you could manage." "Oh, Mickey, maybe not.")

"I'm not a baby."

"The youngest."

"The last rites," Bethy said. "Born ten years after their last child. Boy were they surprised."

Abashed, Georgie offered, "I bet your brothers were thrilled."

"They wanted a dog."

"That's a very pretty dress."

"Anyway, they're in the kitchen."

"Your folks?"

The little girl looked at her with Jane's eyes, saying, wisely, "Don't you know *anything?*"

"I just thought . . ."

"Mom and Aunt Mickey, all right? They have to make hay while the cat's at work." She turned with a flip of her skirt. "Daddy asked if they could be out early because he has a big date tonight, I don't like her, but at least she's not as bad as Albert."

"Albert!"

"Forget I said that. If Aunt Mickey knew Mom was going out she'd croak."

"I promise."

"Mom would murder me."

The child looked so worried that it made Georgie want to hug her and beg her to stop. "Really, I won't say a thing."

Going into Jane and Beck Courtney's house, Georgie was struck once more by surprise at the fragility of other people's arrangements. The last time she was in this house everything was new. She remembered being impressed by the rich grassy color of the wall-to-wall carpeting and the white shutters Jane had selected instead of draperies. She'd been the first person Georgie knew to have not one Eames chair, but two, a gutsy choice given the conventional lines of the white upholstered sofa and matching chairs. Jane's boys must have been one and three then, adorable in fuzzy blanket suits that made them look like cuddly bunny rabbits, and looking at them, Georgie had thought that for Jane, at least, everything had come true. Later, struggling with her erstwhile career and her unwieldy little boys in their smelly nighties, she had wondered once more why some people were much better than others at certain things:

Jane, for instance, who had kept her life in perfect order; she had even managed to do this and keep a part-time teaching job. In a way, she had counted on Jane for certain things because she was everybody's big sister; in a way Jane was trying out everybody's future; they could look at her and imagine where they would be in a few more years; it seemed right for somebody to go ahead of them to show the way.

Forgetting her purposeful little escort, Georgie strayed into the living room and was sorry she had. The first thing was that all Jane's plants had died; the green carpeting must have been worn through in spots because somebody had thrown bathroom shag rugs down in certain places, without noticing how ugly they were, or how badly rucked up. The sofa and matching chairs had long since been slipcovered, and looking at the rest of the furniture, Georgie realized that most of it had quite simply been used up, as apparently the marriage was used up. Somebody some time ago had quit gluing and mending things and replacing light bulbs, and this same person or people had apparently given up everything except the most perfunctory cleaning because there was nothing to hold them here. The broken Eames chairs and the cracked glass coffee table and the dingy shag rugs all spoke of some larger, psychic neglect.

Until recently, Georgie had operated on the assumption that people she liked cared about the same things she cared about. Married to Bill, she had managed to believe that most people lived together more or less smoothly and loved each other in spite of what you read. Bad things happened to people, but not people you knew. After all these years of womanhood she was at heart a Catholic girl, who believed you got married because you loved the person, and you lived together and made love and had fights and made up and made love again because you were certain you would always love the person; you had decided to be together and have fun and take care of each other until you got old and a truck hit you both at the same time and you died. She and Bill had danced at the Courtneys' twentieth anniversary; they had once almost rented a summer place with the Courtneys and Mickey and Howard, and now

Beck Courtney was coming home to change for a date and here she was in Jane Courtney's house, which looked not dirty, exactly, but forlorn, worn out and used up, as if the people who still ate and slept here had long since given up on it, along with the enterprise. The house answered any questions she might have.

From the kitchen she could hear Jane's voice. "After all, I have to have my life."

She could not hear what Mickey said.

She called, "Jane?"

But Bethy was standing in the doorway like a little sentry waiting for the countersign. "Mom, it's a friend of Aunt Mickey's. Is it all right if she comes in?"

"George!" Jane burst into the hall and embraced her, thrusting aside the protective child as carelessly as if all her efforts meant nothing and rules were only for little kids. Mickey's sister was a little thicker in the waist and her light brown hair had the new yellow sheen that comes with a rinse designed to cover encroaching streaks of grey. She looked tired and at the same time excited, like somebody about to begin a race.

"I'm so sorry," Georgie said.

"Don't be, it was a long time coming. But here you are. Mickey, it's George." Jane pulled Georgie into the kitchen a little too fast for Mickey, who seemed to be assembling herself hastily because, close as they were, the college friends had always measured themselves against each other and Mickey knew this and had gone to lengths to win the tossup at least this once.

"You look wonderful." It was true, Mickey did. Gold disc earrings just brushed her neat bob, and although she was plump her powder blue silk shirt was neatly tucked into a belted linen skirt, reminding Georgie that in college Mickey had always pinned her shirttails to her underpants because she would rather die than have them come loose. Mickey had always been the tightly collected one, organized to the point of hysteria. She was so carefully brushed and dressed that Georgie and the others sometimes found it necessary to spring out at her and tickle her until her hair was wild and her shirttail ripped free of the pins and flew. This was the woman who kept three different kinds of stationery from the time she was in high school, because you never knew who you might be writing to. Neatly put-together as she was, careful, combed, well-kept, she insisted on everything in its place in the secret conviction that if anything slipped, if her shoes came untied, she would come unglued.

Mickey was saying, "Thanks. So do you."

"No." It was both true and not true. Georgie maintained a good, taut body and an excellent haircut but her khaki shirt was rumpled and thanks to the string, her ankles were a mess. "Not really. I'm a wreck."

There stood between them the old conversation, so well-rehearsed that they no longer had to say their lines. *"If you let go on one little thing, pretty soon the big ones are going to follow."* Georgie: *"It wouldn't hurt you to let down a little bit just this once."* She always ended being angry because she knew what she meant by this and could not express it or make Mickey see. Mickey knew too, and would not acknowledge it even grudgingly; yes she would rather die than relax even half an inch. Mickey had always had a step-on-a-crack morality and it came to Georgie that the drive to Florida was going to be harder than she had thought. She did not really want to hear Mickey on Ag's poor love affair and knew that Mickey was too compulsive, which Mickey thought of as honest, to let the matter rest. She would worry the subject like a rat-terrier until she had brought Ag up on charges and tried her and disposed of her case; she might even hand down a merciful sentence but the verdict would still be *guilty* and she would expect Georgie to assent, keeping at her until finally Georgie would be forced to bind and gag her and lock her in the trunk. Georgie remembered herself in one of those pre-Council theological arguments, grabbing her impassioned and unyielding roommate by the shoulders and shouting into her reddening face: "Dammit to hell, God's umbrella is bigger than you think!"

But now Mickey was clearing her throat nervously. "How's Bill?"

"Fine. How's Howard?"

"Oh, Howard is just fine. How's your job?"

"Fine." Mickey believed a good mother should stay home all day every day, in case. Maybe Georgie would get a column out of this. She would call it "At War With Absolutes" and they could run it in the month after they carried her introductory column, if she got the job. The job. She and Mickey were both judging, fearful of the other's judgment; Georgie was blushing for no reason ("Is that your *dress?*" Oh God).

"I bet you're thirsty," Jane said.

Georgie seized on the new topic with relief. "Parched."

"My Cokes are in the fridge. The beer's OK, but I'm afraid everything in the bar is Beck's."

"I don't understand."

Bethy said, helpfully, "Separation agreement."

"I see."

"Bethy, honey, isn't it time for *The Brady Bunch?*"

"It hasn't been on for years."

Jane said, pointedly, "I'm sure Daddy won't mind if you watch his television set. Upstairs." When the child hesitated, she said in a tone that brooked no argument, "Upstairs."

Like the front lawn, the contents of the refrigerator were divided, but here the shelves were labeled, just in case. About Jane's famous gourmet dinners: she could forget about a gourmet dinner. It was going to be short rations here. There were identical packages of marge and cheese and milk and produce and even duplicate loaves of bread: the top of the fridge was hers, the bottom was his, but somebody had initialed Beck's half-gallon of milk, which sat uncomfortably next to Jane's quart of Ultrathin because it was too tall to stand on the bottom shelf. This made Georgie wonder if she was going to blunder into the bathroom and find the paper labeled, square for square: his and hers. She would not say afterward what perverse impulse drove her but she took a bottle of Perrier off a shelf that was clearly marked as Beck's and opened it with a grin at Jane's look of disapproval and Mickey's little gasp. "That's Beck's!"

"I'm his friend too."

Jane said, grimly, "When you can't afford separate houses, you have to find a way to draw the line."

"I'm sure Beck won't mind."

"While you're at it, why don't you fry up that filet he's got stashed?"

Stung, Georgie said, "It must have been some fight."

Jane was cold. "I don't think you know what's going on here."

"Apparently not."

Mickey said, "If you'd just put back the Perrier . . ."

"I don't think he'd mind. After all, we're still friends."

Mickey was incredulous. *"Friends,* after what he's done?"

Georgie had always liked Beck. "Whatever it is, I'm sure he's sorry now. Maybe if you sat down and talked it out . . ."

Jane was getting angry. "It's too late for talk, all right? It's all over, all right?"

"It's all over and his stuff is still in your fridge?"

Jane flushed. "He has to keep it somewhere."

"But if things are that bad . . ."

"Not everybody can afford to break up in style." Jane's face began to crumple. "You don't know what we're up against here. The legal fees alone, the boarding school and college fees, his shrink, my shrink, it has to come from somewhere . . ."

"Oh, Jane, this is so *sad.* But all his stuff is . . . If he . . . If you . . . Ah. Where is he living?" It dawned. "Oh, *no.*"

Jane would not look at her. "He can't afford to move." Then she started at a new sound: Beck's car in the driveway. "Come on, let's get our stuff. I really don't want to have to see him right now."

"But this is Beck," Georgie said. "Beck, that you used to love."

Jane said, bitterly, "I don't think you have any idea what it's been like."

Georgie finished weakly, ". . . that used to love you."

Jane wheeled on her. "In this kind of war you take no prisoners. Now let's get out of here before I have to talk to him." Jane was collecting things like an angry householder determined to leave nothing for the enemy but a little scorched earth. She had everything on trays: beef mixture, bread. "Mickey, get the salad, and George can bring the drinks."

"Hurry," Mickey said through gritted teeth.

"Oh, wait."

"Now." Jane headed down the hall in the determined shuffle of an egg-and-spoon racer anxious to hit optimum speed without spilling a thing. "He always comes in the back."

"Wait a minute." Georgie was overwhelmed by wonder and sadness and conflicting loyalties.

Mickey hissed, "Georgia Mahan Kendall, hurry up!"

"I want to say hello to Beck."

"Well I don't. Beck Courtney is a rat." Backing into the doorway with her tray, Mickey gave Georgie a last grim look and kicked it shut.

Alone, Georgie began to wonder what foul monster was coming up the back steps, whether the handsome Beck had turned into something else since she last saw him, some coarse brute that she wouldn't even recognize. When the back door opened she grinned with pleasure and relief, as she saw Beck's same old good-looking face split open and shine at the sight of her. They hugged without speaking, after which Georgie said, "Well."

Beck said, tentatively, "Well."

"Look what's happened to you."

At second glance Beck had a gaunt, untended look; he had dropped a few pounds; the gaudy shirt was new and his hair was unkempt. "It is kind of awful, isn't it? At least you're speaking to me."

"I'm never not speaking to you." She tried to begin. "I'm so—"

But Jane whipped open the hall door, saying, angrily, "I thought we were going to have the house to ourselves tonight. I thought you had a date."

Upon which Beck made a lighting change before her eyes, dropping into a feral slouch that would have done justice to the later Mr. Hyde, who in his last days underwent the change without regard for who might be watching. The face he turned to Jane belonged to someone else. "I thought I did too, but I don't, OK?" His angry shout surprised both of them. "But it's my hour in the kitchen, so you can stay the fuck out of here."

"I suppose you think this happened overnight," Beck said mournfully. He joined Georgie who in a fit of depression had fled to the porch swing, where she dangled her feet pensively, wondering if she could survive a night in this bristling fortress.

She and Mickey and Beck's soon to be ex-wife and daughter had crouched on the front porch wolfing their Sloppy Joes while Beck rattled dishes and crashed pots in the kitchen, after which they waited for him to retreat to his study with a tray. Then they cleaned up their part of the kitchen and sponged the counter they had used. Jane pointedly ignored the dirty saucepan Beck had left, along with the crumpled foil from his Sara Lee nut bread. The women repaired to the living room, where Bethy picked up and relayed messages and brought back replies: about his plans for the weekend and when they would meet over the household bills. After the third long-distance exchange Jane explained, wearily. "Believe me, it's better this way. It's better for us and particularly for Bethy. When the two of us are in the same room it gets really ugly. He hates me and all I want to do is murder him."

It was dark now, and Georgie had fled the women's armed camp in front of the color television. Beck was saying, "I suppose they told you how it happened, Jane's version, naturally."

They hadn't, really. They had sat around saying ugly things about Beck. "I don't know how these things happen," Georgie said.

"I don't think anybody wanted it. They never do." Beck sighed. "I suppose it's at least partly my fault. The thing is, a man does get to a point in his life where he's got his wife and he's had his kids and his house is almost paid for but he doesn't know how in God's name he's going to pay for all those colleges; he's never going to be out of debt or, all right, any younger; he reads in the papers that his sexual powers are diminishing, and then. He just looks out the window and sees the whole rest of his life, which is going to be more of the same and longer than he would like . . ."

"Don't think that."

"It's true. It's going to be long and every mile up to the last one is quite clearly leading downhill. What happens is, you look out and you think, My God, is that all there *is*?"

"I know." To her surprise, she did: one more reason she had to have the job. ("Is this your *dress*?" The stupidity!) "But you don't let that get in your way. I mean, you don't let everything go." She faltered. "Do you? I mean, if it looks that way then you have to try and change it."

"That's exactly what I did." His voice was ragged. "All right, I got thinking I was like the phoenix bird, I met this girl, and when I was with her I thought I could do anything, I thought, Hey, it doesn't have to be this way, you know? Trouble was, Jane found out. And you want to know what made her maddest? That it was this kid."

"Did you want her to find out?"

"That's possible," Beck said. "It didn't help that this girl used to go out with Billy, you know?"

"Billy?"

"All right, this girl used to go out with my oldest kid. She used to come around when he wasn't here, and we got to talking . . ."

"This was all about a high school girl?"

"College. Her name is Nelda." With one small gesture his hands described their whole affair—the novelty, the renewed passion, the discovery.

"All this . . . your house, your kids, your *life*, over a high school girl?"

"College. It had to be somebody. How am I supposed to explain, she made me feel like we were the same age." Beck shrugged. "Nelda's a sophomore at Berkeley now."

"And Jane won't . . ."

"She won't and I can't." Beck said. "It's crazy, right?"

"A sophomore. I thought when these things happened it was supposed to be a grand passion, you know, bands playing, white horses, the works."

"At the time I had to tell myself it was." His hair had begun to grow over his ears; he touched the fringe thoughtfully. "It wasn't, of course. She wasn't even very smart."

"It seems so sad."

"It didn't at the time." Beck's expression was hard to make out. "You know, it's really funny, here we are in the Eighties and everything, and nine tenths of the world goes out and does this kind of thing all the time and nobody even notices, and everybody says, Yay yay, it's about time. They're all at it breakfast, lunch and Christmas with no guilt and no hard feelings and I get into this one affair and not only do I feel too guilty to enjoy it . . ."

"Oh, Beck!"

". . . terrible, but my wife will never get over it."

"Maybe if you give her time."

"Some things you can't ever put back together," Beck said. "And she'll never forgive me, either. It doesn't make much sense."

"I know." Georgie was troubled once more by the matter of absolutes. "We believe this, so we do that, and hell yes we take things hard, but God . . ." Her voice was unsteady. "We are supposed to forgive each other."

"I just went too far," Beck said, "But you know, too far is closer than you think. Jane hides it better than Mickey, but she's a lot like Mickey in a lot of ways, which I guess I knew from the beginning. In a funny way it was why I married her. You always knew exactly where you were with her, and that things might change, but she would never change, but now . . . When I went off with Nelda I could see how it was going to end but she was young and pretty and she made me feel, OK, how many times have you heard this one? I thought my life was almost over and she convinced me it was all still ahead. I knew how it would end but I had to try it anyway. Which is what's so confusing—how you can see it all, and go right ahead."

"Eve and the apple." My story exactly, Georgie thought in spite of her efforts to deny it, and quailed.

From inside came the sound of the phone, Jane calling to Mickey in a stagey shout. "Sis, it's for you. Better take it upstairs."

"So I guess it's that you're absolutely married or you've absolutely not, and Jane is never going to let me forget it and I can't."

Under cover of darkness Georgie nodded: *absolutely married,* in which she and Bill lived and believed. But all this misery, over one bad moment. "One slip."

"God will forgive me before Jane does."

"One little slip . . ."

"Georgie, it's Ag." Mickey poked her head out, pointedly ignoring Beck. "She says she has to talk to you."

"The other thing," Beck said, "the other thing is, once you've breached the fabric I don't know if you can ever mend it right. There is always going to be this weak place in between you, no matter what you sew it up with or throw over it or try to pull it back together with. I don't know if I want Jane back now even if she wants me back, which is possible. After what she said to me. After what I said. After what we've said and done to each other it's probably too late. I'm not making any sense because it doesn't.—Does it?"

"Georgie, telephone."

"I don't know," Georgie said. "I don't."

"George!"

"Oh Beck I am so sorry." She squeezed Beck's hand and when he returned the clasp and let go reluctantly, she got up and went inside. Mickey led her to the upstairs extension, which had Jane's initials on it in peach nail polish.

"Ag," she said in a low voice, "everybody here is crazy. How are you?"

But Ag didn't hear. "George? Listen, I was so upset I forgot to tell you, about Ralph? He never came out with it exactly, but he seemed to have this unrequited *thing* about you, he was probably drunk but he said he had brought *along* something of yours?"

Georgie said, hollowly, "He *what?*"

"Heaven only knows what he was talking about, a signed copy of your book, maybe, or something from the papers that he cut out. Listen, how well did you *know* Ralph anyway?" Ag did not wait for an answer, but hurried on. "Never mind, it's none of my business, it doesn't matter, at least I don't think it does, but I just thought, in case it did? If I can find it . . ."

"Don't bother."

"It's no bother, really." Bereavement made Ag generous. "If he had something of yours . . ."

"I said, don't *bother.* Please."

"You ought to have it to remember him by."

6

ALTHOUGH IT WAS CLEAR that Jane and Beck had devoted considerable energy to the rituals of separation, even a lawyer could not plan for every territorial contingency. There was a certain stickiness over where Bethy was at a given time, which parent she was doing errands for, and even worse problems arose over traffic patterns, giving Georgie and idea that if these two ex-lovers and sworn enemies met they would tangle with a clatter of armored scales and sinewy tails flapping, like the Dynavision lizards in one of those movies about the dawn of the world. The worst confusion was attached to bathroom privileges, which Georgie discovered too late to help Mickey. The house had been divided so that Jane used the master bathroom and Beck, who was sleeping in the back bedroom, took the one at the far end of the hall. This presented no problems to Georgie, who assumed Beck wasn't going to mind; they would pass like ships in the night, no problem. The trouble was that Mickey was a partisan who writhed in distress when she discovered that Jane had locked herself in the master suite with the one bathroom Mickey would consent to use. She looked like a schoolgirl in the smocked Celanese nightgown with the sprigs of violets, clasping her hands with a look Georgie recognized. "Where am I going to wash my face?"

Georgie had spent her life trying to get Mickey to call a spade a spade. "You can brush your teeth in the kitchen sink."

Mickey reddened. "You know what I mean."

"Back bathroom. No problem."

Mickey said, stiffly, "It's Beck's."

Georgie said, with malice, "Beck won't give a shit."

"I would feel compromised. Besides, I don't want Jane to think I'm on his side."

"Well, are you?"

Mickey shook her head. "It's much too late for sides."

"Better ask Jane to let you use her bathroom."

"Genghis Khan couldn't get in there without a key. Her lawyer told her to keep that door locked. Besides, she's asleep."

"Wake her up."

"Not on your life."

Georgie knew better than to argue; Mickey could never be budged. She, however, was permanently scarred from the time in freshman year when Mickey, *in extremis,* had refused to use the only available toilet because it was in a men's room. "I remember a person that wouldn't go when they had to and they ended up in the emergency room, being catheterized? And Delia's great-aunt was such a prude that she popped and died because she couldn't bring herself to do it in the bushes when her car ran out of gas."

"George!"

"So you'd better do something," Georgie said cold-heartedly. She rolled over on one of the maple twin beds and pulled up the plaid bedspread, doing her impression of a person sleeping. It was tough work because the overhead light was still on and she could feel Mickey's eyes on her. Through cracks in her lids she could make out the Courtney boys' neo-punk decor, which was strangely diffused by team pictures and maroon-and-gray banners that read ST. CANISIUS, to say nothing of the bedding trimmed with nautical borders and the badly worn stuffed bunnyrabbit propped on Billy Courtney's desk. If she made a half-turn she would see the model rockets suspended from the light fixture and, standing underneath, Mickey still dithering. After a long while she heard Mickey go out with a sigh, and then, surprise, she heard Mickey tiptoeing downstairs. After an even longer while she heard sounds in the night: Mickey relieving herself in the garden, crunching bushes and muttering in

the dark. She had made a gratuitous trip to Beck's bathroom and was back in bed by the time Mickey crept in.
"George?"
"Goodnight, Mickey."
In the darkness Mickey persisted, saying, dolefully, "I couldn't remember if it was cats or dogs that are supposed to bury it."
"Raccoons," Georgie said laughing. "Or else it's their food."
"I kept expecting Jane to come after me with a rolled-up newspaper." Mickey giggled.
"Or Beck."
"They'd probably fight about whose fault it was."
"Beck's, because you wouldn't use his bathroom."
"Except that I'm Jane's sister, so it would be hers. Oh George, things are just awful here, aren't they?"
Georgie discovered that she was in some pain. "It's like being in a wreck."
"When they broke up I got this funny feeling, like it was *me* they had betrayed, Beck by having the nerve to step out on *my sister* and her by trying to cover up." Mickey rolled over in a sad rustle of nightie and bedding and Oil of Olay, perhaps wiping her eyes on the sheets with the nautical border. "This just never used to happen, did it?"
"Not to people we knew."
"What *happened?*"
"Things, I guess. Things happen. Times change." This so depressed Georgie that she said, "Maybe we should both shut up and go to sleep."
"I mean, people didn't used to be this way. George? Did they?" Mickey's tone called up the ending to *Of Mice and Men*, Lenny and George stalled just outside the Promised Land; the number she and Mickey used to do: *Will there be daiquiris and cute boys when we get to heaven, George? Will they all come down to meet us and will we be thin and beautiful?* To which Georgie would reply: *the fountains will run with cocktails, Lenny, they will carry us on their shoulders and they'll stand in line to dance with us because we are so beautiful. George, do you promise?* "George?"

"Maybe they did and we just didn't know it. Catholics were supposed to keep it together, no matter what."

"Well, I still think they should. If you pay attention to the little things . . ."

"I know, I know. The big ones will follow," Georgie parroted. "Sister Clarice didn't know everything."

"I liked it better when she did. I mean, we used to have it all laid out for us. What to do to get to heaven. What not to do. Where to begin."

Georgie was surprised by a rush of nostalgia. "That was in the seventh grade, Mickey."

"You know that's not what I mean."

Right, she did know. "Right."

"I mean we used to have something clear-cut, that we could go by."

"Maybe it was never that simple."

Mickey persisted. "I think it was."

"Well that's all changed." This was true. When they were little, change was already stirring; by the time they were in college change had thrown open the doors to the monolith to let the fresh air in. A lot of small objects got blown around; the outlines to some of the larger ones looked different. What was interesting was that they had gotten rid of some of the smaller things: meatless Fridays, fasting during Lent—little rules that were easy to keep, which left the rest of what you were supposed to do in sharp relief: what might be hard. Certain parts were still immutable but it was getting harder to figure out exactly how many, or where or how to draw the line. "You have to find your own way now."

"We used to travel first class with a guide and a map," Mickey said wistfully. "It used to be easy to be good."

"Maybe we just used to think so," Georgie said. She did not have the heart to break the news to her friend that in this decade not everybody was worried about being good.

Mickey's voice quavered. "I used to think it would be a wonderful thing to convert people, but now . . ."

"Shh. Shh." She tried to divert Mickey, saying, "I bet they

buy the two-color toothpaste, so they can divide it? When it comes out the red stripe is his . . ."

". . . and she takes the white. Probably the sugar bowl has a line across it," Mickey said in a lighter tone. "And the toaster."

"Maybe Jane does too."

Mickey was beginning to laugh. "They put it on with Magic Marker."

"Right. He gets the left side . . ."

"And she takes the right," Mickey finished with a muffled shriek.

"They even got their pubic hair dyed, his are dyed red . . ."

Mickey's giggle was delightful. ". . . and hers are dyed white."

Hearing her like this, Georgie remembered how they had gotten to be friends in the first place, and for which reasons and why, in spite of the prudery, the rigid lines Mickey drew for herself and could not be induced to cross, they were still friends.

Then Mickey's voice came out of the darkness on an altogether different note. "Oh George, why can't people be good and be happy?"

And Georgie heard her own voice coming straight out of the end of that stupid movie, George to Lenny, soothing and unconvincing: "When we get there, Mickey, they will."

But the question recurred in the darkness of early morning like a beer commercial jingle that would not quit. Georgie woke standing in the middle of the kids' shag rug, stamping to shake off the locusts that swarmed, devouring her from the toes up. It took her a minute to figure out what she was doing in the dark in the middle of a strange room with her breath skidding and her heart shuddering, and another minute to take herself in hand.

Beck had left the light on in the bathroom, thoughtful man. She noticed as she passed the door on her way back to bed that his bedroom light was on, making a bleak line around the door. Had he been up all night numbering his miseries or had he waked with night frights or morning anxieties? She imagined

him grappling with the dry swallows—Beck, whom she and Mickey and the others had adored and counted on to be happy, and be good. She raised one hand in salute: *Yes, Beck. I am sorry. We all are.*
Why can't people just be good and be happy?
I *said,* Why can't people just be good and be happy?
I don't know, Mick. It beats the hell out of me.

If the world was resting on the back of a turtle, she thought, when it became clear that she was awake for good and it was too early to do anything about it, what was the turtle standing on? If it was absolutely logical for an absolute deity to set down absolute standards, how far down did the absolutes reach? Sister Clarice notwithstanding, she had picked her way through this thicket every day of her life. Back then, they were taught if you paid attention to the little things, the big ones would follow. After which Pope John called the Council, which did away with a lot of the little things. At the time she and her friends called it VAT II; a friend at Georgetown made fake whiskey labels and put them on everything; at the time they were excited and dazzled and confused, hopeful in spite of the older people who were, rather, confused and resentful. She remembered Mickey digging in her heels at the liturgical changes: Look what they've done to our Mass! Right, they had been pulled into some aesthetic sacrifices, she'd told Mickey, adding: Look at it this way; it's the price we have to pay. For what, exactly? Freedom, Georgie thought, with which had come (she groaned) increased responsibility.

Why can't people just be good and be . . .
Shut up, Mickey. Will you just shut up?
"Did you say something?"
Oh shit. "I thought you were asleep."
"In this madhouse? Are you kidding? Besides, I think there's a dog under my bed."
"Sure, and there are really locusts crawling up my legs."
"No, really," Mickey said with barely stifled hysteria. "Something's moving. Don't you hear it? Shh. There is definitely something under there."
"There is not," somebody said from under the bed.
"Bethy, you little sneak!" Mickey rolled off in a welter of

covers, making a lunge under the dust ruffle. "What are you doing under there?"

"Leave me alone. Can't a person get a little sleep?"

"Sleep!"

In the dawn light Georgie began to sort them out: Mickey militant in the flowered nightie, Bethy struggling.

"Bethy, were you spying?"

"I wasn't doing anything." Bethy began to cry.

"Shh, for Pete's sake," Mickey said urgently.

But it was too late; the door opened. "I think you'd better let go of her."

"Daddy!"

"Beck!" Mickey tried to cover herself all over all at once: face, breasts, belly, pubic triangle, thighs, in spite of the fact that everything but the face was fully obscured by masses of sprigged cotton smocking; she clutched herself in distress because she would never have enough hands to go around, and Georgie was unhappily certain that not even Howard saw Mickey without anything on. Finally she seized the bedspread and managed something halfway between late toga and early mantle. She was looking outraged. "What are you doing in here?"

"What are you doing to Bethy?"

"Look what you've done to her," Mickey said angrily, "Is this a happy child?"

"There's nothing the matter with Bethy," Beck said defensively. "She's cool. She can live with this."

Apparently wakened by the sounds of confrontation, Jane had arrived close on Beck's heels and now she plunged in. "Knowing her father is a philanderer? You've turned her into a basket case."

Beck had an arm around his little girl. "That isn't true. Bethy, tell Mommy you're fine."

"She's been a wreck ever since you started deceiving us. Bethy, come here."

"Mommy, I have a stomach ache."

"She's a perfectly normal, healthy . . . Bethy, where are you going?"

Bethy escaped as her mother said, to the room at large, "See that? She's practically psychotic. Look at her, sneaking around and sleeping on floors. She doesn't know who she can trust any more." In a Q.E.D. tone Jane said to Georgie and Mickey, "She's been that way ever since Beck started the divorce."

Beck slipped into a dignified courtroom stance so easily that even Georgie forgot he was standing there in his black Calvin T-shirt and underpants. "I think you're confusing the witnesses here. Who first raised the issue of divorce?"

"Well, whose fault was that?"

"If you want to start assigning liability . . ."

Georgie and Mickey exchanged looks and withdrew with whatever clothing they could grab in one pass. Georgie dressed in Beck's bathroom; with a look intended to convey loyalty, Mickey went into Jane's. In the kitchen they dawdled over an extended breakfast, waiting for Jane and Beck to conclude hostilities or move on so they could sneak back and retrieve their bags. When the argument rolled downstairs, Beck and Jane tangling on the landing in all the lather and commotion of a major dogfight, Georgie jerked her head in the direction of the kids' room. They had to wait until the door closed on the study, where Jane and Beck were hissing over codicils and provisos and supplementary lists. When it seemed safe to pass, they went upstairs to pack.

They had finished and were checking for forgotten items when Georgie said, thoughtfully, "Mickey, are you ashamed of your body?"

"Who, me? Why no." Even though she had her head stuck in the closet for no reason, Mickey's tone made it clear that she was red to the eyes and beyond, into the first wave of that neatly cut hair. "No, of course not, don't be silly.—Why should I be?" Turning from the safety of the closet she ducked her head and began rooting in her pocketbook with angry concentration until she fished out a breath freshener, which she sprayed in furious bursts, like a householder going after cockroaches. Then, without missing a squirt or even changing her tone, she finished: "Bodies are a pain in the ass."

7

SNEAKING AWAY under cover of the Courtneys' morning fight, Georgie had trouble getting past the closed study door. Mickey, who had put on white shortie gloves and a suitable headband for the trip, dug in her heels and with a guestly smile, made as if to knock.

"What are you *doing?*"

"We have to thank them."

"Mickey, they're fighting."

"I don't care, they're still our hosts, and it's polite."

Georgie grabbed her by the cotton-covered knuckles. "Forget it. We'll send them a nice note from Florida."

Behind the door the Courtneys had moved from the explosive opening volley of beginning battle into the measured muttering of the middle stage, which would devolve into whining and then crying. Practiced long-distance wranglers, they knew how to conserve energy, so if called upon to rise to the occasion, they could fight for eight nights and eight days, exhausting all spectators and outlasting any attempts at mediation, and still emerge as fresh as daisies with no ground lost and not one inch gained. Georgie expected to escape unnoticed; she could shovel Mickey in the car and bomb down the New Jersey Turnpike in the pre-rush-hour lull; they could be halfway to Washington before the happy couple broke for the first intermission. To her surprise, just as she got Mickey stowed and turned on the motor, they popped out of the front door.

Beck and Jane seemed to be, if not dependent on audience, at least aware of it. They must have come up for air as the screen slammed shut. Now they spilled across Jane's uncut grass and Beck's manicured portion willy-nilly, springing along in their bare feet without regard for stakes or strings. They were glowing like honeymooners; they probably got off on this, Georgie realized. Remembering Beck's lament, her quick sympathy, she felt somewhat bilked, because it was clear that in their complicated union they had withheld or distorted information and now for whatever reasons it was she and Mickey who seemed diminished, while the Courtneys bloomed. They hadn't stopped to dress. Jane was still in the forbidding cotton shift of the wee hours, a distressed-looking brown number that would have depressed Mother Hubbard, while Beck looked sexy and lithe as a runner in his color-keyed underwear, as easy and composed as if he'd turned out in his lawyer costume, all four layers.

"Oh lord, he's in his underwear!"

"Smile, Mickey. Wave goodbye. We're getting out of here."

Naturally Ag's motor strangled and Georgie grabbed at assorted knobs and levers like an escapee in a bad dream. She was anxious and rushed and at the same time distracted by the disparity: sleek Beck, lumpy Jane. If, as she believed people did send messages with their bodies, there was more than one reason for the Courtney breakup. Which came first? Beck's pecadillo or Jane's don't-touch body slipcovers in mud tones? What were they trying to tell each other? The world? She had a wild vision of a solar explosion or a Martian death ray ripping into the atmosphere while an innocent populace slept, tangling airwaves and synapses and garbling everybody's messages. What bizarre signals had these two started exchanging, and at what point had they stopped caring enough to want to keep trying to decode them?

She did not want to talk to the Courtneys because she could not for the life of her figure out what she was going to say, and so she blew kisses and scratched off while they mouthed farewells and Mickey tried and failed to deliver separate but equal valedictory addresses without actually looking at Beck's underwear. Georgie shot backward into the street, transformed in a flash into a demolition derby driver backing into position for the Slide for Life. Jane sprinted across the sidewalk and vaulted the border to catch her on the turn.

"Message," she gasped, thrusting a piece of paper in Mickey's window. "Yesterday. Bethy forgot."

"Jane," Mickey began painfully, "If you would just *see* somebody about your problems, tell Father O'Shane..."

Fortunately this was lost on Jane because Georgie was halfway to the corner, where she made a turn Paul Newman would have admired and bombed into the straightaway. She felt better already. By the time they reached the turnpike, she was going to be fine.

Mickey was puzzling over the paper Jane had thrust on her. She crumpled it up and threw it out the window. "I don't know any Peter Flinc."

Which was how Georgie ended up flogging Mickey back along the verge in search of the lost message, and how she ended up in a pay phone talking to Peter Flinc. She could not fix on what the editor of *IN* was saying because there was an echo pinging around inside her head. ("... they're the money behind the magazine, and I thought if you and they talked..." "I don't have much time in Washington." *Oh Mr. Flinc is that your dress?* "It may be a good idea for you to pitch your idea directly to them." "I thought you were in charge." "I told you, we're in a..." She finished for him: "State of flux." *Is that your dress?* "You take my point. If the Lawtons get behind you, you're in good shape." "You mean I get the..." What did I say to this man yesterday? *Is that your...* "No guarantees, but I'll see what I can do.") She would promise him anything precisely because he hadn't brought up the terrible gaffe about the dress.

This, then, also explained how she found herself doubleparked in downtown Washington, trying to euchre Mickey into taking a taxi to Kath's. If she dropped Mickey here, she could head straight to the Windhover, where the Lawtons lived. Unless she dropped Mickey and went direct, she was going to be late for her meeting with the couple who were bankrolling

IN. It had occurred to her to ask Flinc how come he had to deal with backers when Magnum was supposed to be the parent company, but she had been so embarrassed by the dress fiasco that she was afraid to try her luck. Instead she had fixed on this appointment in the conviction that if she, what, passed, or won the meeting, she would have the job. It would be nice to get to Florida already knowing; she'd be more relaxed and better able to help Ag; she didn't know whether it was the being on the hook over this or the business of Ralph or both that had undermined her, but she had the idea she'd be in better shape if she could settle at least one of her difficulties. This left her sitting tight in downtown traffic on F Street, on the verge of the first of a series of tactical mistakes. She gunned the motor impatiently and waited for Mickey to get out.

"Mickey, if it's money you're worried about, I'll pay for the cab."

Mickey said, grimly, "I'm worried about our stuff. It's going to be stolen out of the car."

"If it does, I promise I'll make good."

"If we lose it, what are we going to wear in Florida?"

"I'll buy you a whole new wardrobe."

Mickey looked worried. "What about Ag's stuff?"

"I told you," Georgie said urgently, "I promise, I'll take care of it. Now will you just get out?"

Mickey's eyes took on a crafty glitter. "I can drive around the whole time you're inside," she said with a please-don't-leave-me look. "That way I can watch the stuff."

"Oh please, Mickey, I can't . . ." There was no way for her to say it: that where she was going she had to act like a grownup, an impossibility with her old college roommate circling the block in another college roommate's car. "Listen, Kath is expecting us. If you don't show up she'll be worried."

"That's another thing. Washington is dangerous."

"It's a hell of a lot less dangerous than the New Jersey Turnpike. Look, there's a taxi, will you hurry?"

"You don't even know these people."

"Look. The taxi's waiting. He's turning around."

"They aren't even friends."

"Come on, Mickey, give me a break."

"You don't even know them and you're treating them better than me." Mickey was regarding her with a strange expression that Georgie would have reason to reflect on later, and regret. Looking back on the mutiny, she would have to remember that by the time they headed south from Washington, Mickey was beginning to get weird; she would have to date the beginning of Mickey's decline from the next moment, in which she reached over and opened the door and shoved her protesting friend into the street. "Georgie, for God's *sake!*"

"Sorry, Mickey, but I have to get this job."

From the curb Mickey said, resentfully, "I don't see why."

There was no way for her to explain to Mickey what kept her twitching in the eternal tapdance. She was not altogether sure she knew. As she scratched off, Georgie found it necessary to try to explain, more for herself than for her testy friend, who would never understand it even if she could hear above the little car's roar of departure. Georgie herself was somewhat surprised by the answer, which both made sense in context and didn't, since she still assumed she could stop any time she wanted to: "Because I am tired of hustling."

She would not hear what Mickey said.

Once she had gotten shut of Mickey, Georgie abandoned Ag's car to a parking attendant in the Valet Parking uniform without even a twinge of conscience, and went into the Windhover without a backward look. If the coked-up adolescent in the uniform totaled Ag's car in a chicken race in the bowels of the Windhover, so be it. If vandals crept from behind every stanchion and stripped it to the axles, fine. Let the winds take her canvas bag and Mickey's satchels and Ag's accumulated treasures; this time she was going to have a lunch meeting where she actually got lunch.

What had she and Mickey eaten at their pre-dawn breakfast? Bagel, she thought, the best thing they could find in Jane's part of the divided refrigerator: half each. Going up in the elevator, she realized she was out of fuel and running on vapors. Never mind. If the Lawtons were the magazine's major backers, they would certainly be rich and they might even be kind. She pictured them as graying and settled, older, maybe even parental; they would be gracious hosts with frosted drinks and *hors d' oeuvres* waiting for her in their brocaded living room; they would coat her jangling nerve-ends with creamed crabmeat, or perhaps a little quiche. She wanted to bury her face in white food: creamed chicken, vichyssoise, soft rolls; she would rub rice in her hair and pat cream sauce on her wrists and neck and armpits, after which she would feel much, much better. Sated. Calm. Waiting in the plush hallway outside the Lawtons' door, taking in the gold flocked wallpaper and the directoire tables with matching vases of spring flowers, Georgie knew that she was going to like it here. These nice old rich folks would be delighted to meet her and they were going to like her idea so much that they'd want to settle her fate right now. They were the money behind *IN*, which meant they had the power to give her the job. She was so comforted by this vision that she did not stop to figure out precisely what her idea was. She'd have plenty of time to work it out while pretending to cut up her chicken Kiev, she thought. She had put in enough time at meetings to know her best tactic was to let them lead. She could cook to their order, she thought giddily.

The youthful maid came to the door in jeans; in pierced ears, she wore rhinestone studs. She made trim Georgie feel like the circus fat lady. She did not immediately let Georgie in. "All right," she said, several uncomfortable seconds after Georgie had finished explaining. She took off the chain latch. "Come on in."

She led Georgie down a barren corridor into a bleak living room which had been whitewashed and rubbed and then furnished in brown wrapping paper and early painters' ladders, with the occasional side-chair wrapped in cheesecloth tied with brown string. Except for the string and the wrapping paper there was no color; there was nothing except white on white on white. It was like being in a Magritte. She knew better than to look for green apples, starved though she was. There was no food here and no sign that people actually sat down.

Only the Bentley of all coffee tables and the white-on-white minimalist painting above the swaddled sofa made it clear that this was a design statement and not the midpoint in an intercontinental move. Waiting for Robin Lawton to come in, Georgie took in the minimalist sculpture in the corner nearest the sofa—string depending from a tenpenny nail to an artful coil on the parquet—and wondered where the Lawtons would take her for lunch. She had no idea how big this place was, but there were no traces of bacon cooking here, no clinging odors of onion, no signs of cooking anywhere. Maybe the Windhover had room service; at the touch of a buzzer uniformed striplings would come in with laden trays. Maybe she did the Lawtons an injustice and there was an elegant cold lunch waiting in the fridge. She wondered whether they would eat off their laps or out on the terrace, where the decorator had upended three medium-sized cable spools around a cast bronze number that must have been aged in the Mindanao Deep and brought into the apartment by block and tackle, at enormous cost. The money tied up in the items in this room alone would have supported the citizens of an undeveloped country for months.

Maybe they're so rich they don't have to eat. There would be Perrier in the refrigerator, limes, a shriveled olive and nothing else. But there was a little mirror on the coffee table; she groaned. Maybe all they cared about was coke. She knew she should be figuring out how to pitch her idea to these people, or at least practicing her smile, but all she could think about was how hungry she was.

Then Robin Lawton came in and her hopes for lunch grew wings and flew out over the terrace rail. Clearly, food was not one of his things. Even in jeans and a bulky sweater tucked into the institutional-size concha belt, he was as lithe and trim as the maid, who was not the maid, of course, any more than the studs in her ears were rhinestone; they were diamonds. Apparently these people really were so rich they didn't have to eat. Oh lord.

"Sorry I haven't read your book. Thanks for coming anyway."

She heard Mickey speaking in her voice. "Thank you for having me."

"Sit." He waved her to a wrapped side-chair and sprawled on the sofa, regarding her with a face that she realized with a shock was younger than hers by at least five years in spite of the fretwork of wrinkles from too many seasons in the sun. "Now . . ." The cornflower eyes were intense. "Tell me why you're here."

She was slipping fast. "You didn't send for me?"

"Hold it a minute. Hang on for Anthea. We only want to do this once." He said, confidentially, "She's in the kitchen."

Something in a hollow place north of Georgie's sternum turned over like a silver fish.

At the sight of Anthea in the doorway behind Georgie he produced a smile so brilliant and accomplished that it must have been rehearsed. "Here she is, with tea."

Food.

Sort of. Anthea Lawton produced a pot of tea and a plate of nasty-looking cookies, which she had arranged in a tight swastika to keep them from interfering with the painted design. She slapped the painted plate onto the Bentley of all coffee tables just out of Georgie's reach. In meetings you waited for the others to go first, which meant she had better wait. Feigning indifference to food, she cribbed a smile from early Liza Minnelli and waited for Robin to begin, which he did not. After three more trips to the kitchen for cups, sugar, spoons, Anthea perched at the far end of the sofa with her hands folded and her knees clamped tight. She regarded Georgie with a look so guarded that she could have been preparing to lunge away from anybody who was stupid enough to try to make her eat. Robin said, "Now."

"Now?"

Anthea said, "What Robin means is, tell us why you're here."

"Peter said it would be good if we met."

"Oh, Peter," Robin said carelessly. "You know Peter."

"Not really."

"He doesn't care what comes out of his mouth."

"What Robin means is, publishing breeds strange bedfellows," Anthea said.

Robin said, "Peter will say anything."

"I see."

Anthea bore down. "To be frank, we don't know your work."

"I'm not very well known . . ." south of New York or west of Scranton, Pa.

"Still, Peter is high on you. He said something about . . ." Anthea prodded her husband, who finished:

"Some winning idea of yours."

"Gangbusters," Anthea said without enthusiasm.

"Gangbusters?"

"That's what Peter said. He wanted us to meet so you could lay it out for us."

My God, what had she told the man? She could not remember. What was she doing here anyway? She was reminded of her nightmare titled The French Exam, in which there were a hundred questions on the paper and her mind was blank. She stalled. "My idea." *The main idea.* Her kids' teachers told them this was what you put in a book report. *The kids.* She had two, thank you, they were eleven and going on thirteen, she was married to a man who loved her and unlike this heartlessly modish rich couple she had worked for her living all her life. Looking at them, she thought this was not such a bad thing. Outside this room she was a lot more than a starving, importunate nobody; she was somebody with a place to go home to and a family that cared; no matter what they said or did to her here, she could hold her own. She wondered idly what would happen if she started shouting, "I WANT YOUR MONEY," or only, "GIVE ME FOOD." Hunger and fatigue had so fuddled her that she wasn't sure she had an idea to pitch to them, or if she did, what it was going to be, and so she waited, trying to figure out what she was going to say. When it became clear that she was not going to go on, Anthea nudged Robin, who prompted her.

"Yes, your blue ribbon idea."

Georgie leaned forward. Hunger and exhaustion had left her in an altered state in which she could not be sure what she was supposed to do or what they expected. If she kept quiet for long enough, they would feed her her next line.

Anthea lifted one eyebrow and inclined her head.

The silence got worse.

Robin said, "Unless you've been wasting our time."

At which point Georgie was stripped forcibly of the illusion that the worst thing she had said to Peter Flinc was, *oh, is this your dress?* because Anthea went on. "He said you were going to rip the lid off some old love affair."

"I never said he was my lover."

"He said you were working on a confession," Robin said.

Anthea licked her thin lips. "Confession is very *IN.*"

"We'll want to know what your husband thinks."

"By the way, does your husband know?"

"Wait!"

"About the lover," Robin said.

Lover? Ralph! "I never had a lover," Georgie snapped. *My husband, my life!* "It was my best friend's lover."

"That's not what Peter said."

She grinned carelessly. "You know Peter, he'll say anything."

Robin said, "If there isn't any lover, there isn't any point."

"I'm working on something a little bigger," Georgie said. In her altered state she was not altogether certain what else she said, but she was galvanized, pacing briskly from stepladder to minimalist sculpture to second stepladder to terrace doors and back. She would pitch her story while stalking the perimeter, on the premise that a moving target is always harder to hit. She shucked her khaki jacket with a grin, so her red shirt blazed in the colorless sitting room. She went to the terrace doors and back to the first stepladder with increasing confidence because she thought she could keep their attention as long as she stayed on her feet. Talking fast, she picked up the end of the minimalist string sculpture, looping it over her hands with such concentration that they both snapped forward to watch. "Three college roommates at midlife, drawn to the side of the fourth roommate by a tragic death." *Have to protect them,* she thought. "I intend to use composite characters, to get to a universal truth." She had made a cat's cradle. "Women in transition," she said hastily, watching Anthea's eyes because by this time she thought she knew which of them was in control, and without thinking she held out the cat's cradle, which Anthea took on her own hands. "Death. Tragedy. Self-discovery. Rebirth. Then, she accidentally said, "It has repercussions because the dead lover is Ralph Schwartz."

Robin jerked to attention. "The great Ralph Schwartz! The noted philosopher. This is better than I thought."

("I never heard of him."

"Believe me, our audience has."

"A philosopher. I was hoping for something a little more central," Anthea grumbled.

"Listen, the man is a very big deal.")

"Poet-philosopher of death," Georgie said to Robin, redirecting her efforts. "You remember his groundbreaking book."

("National Book Award. MacArthur. The works," Robin explained to Anthea, who was still skeptical. "You know."

"Intellectuals are bad box office."

Robin said, "Womanizers aren't.")

"He's your sexy intellectual," said Georgie, feeling a little cheap. The balance of power seemed to be shifting. She played to Robin. "We're talking existential love and death." At Robin's flicker of dissatisfaction she began to spin a little faster. "Of course it isn't all going to be existential. We're also talking about four women, together again after twenty-some years. We. Ah." She heard herself gulping air. "We may end up at some kind of moment of truth."

"It wouldn't hurt," Robin said. "Anthea, what do you think?"

"I don't see what all this says to a national audience."

Georgie thought fast. "Well, there are the celebrities. *IN* people. Picture possibilities."

"Where did you say this was?"

"Beyond Palatka, outside the town of Snowy Egret. This is a major think tank." She had left something out. "The Fulcrum Foundation."

"Fulcrum!" The missing ingredient.

Now Anthea's eyes quickened. "We may be able to work with this."

Bingo. "Fulcrum. Midlife crisis, love and death in the intellectual powerhouse." Inspired, she went too far, promising that which she could not necessarily deliver. "Maybe some inside dirt on Forrest Fulcrum himself."

Anthea pounced. "An exposé."

It made her uneasy, but she did have her audience: for now. "Perhaps."

Robin bit hard. "How soon can we have a draft?"

"How soon do you want it?"

"We'd like to get moving on this at once."

"Wait a minute," Anthea said crossly, "Let's not move too fast."

"I think we can get something going with this."

"It's not what Peter promised us. What Peter promised, as you may or may not remember, was a woman's marriage threatened by the death of an old lover. Self-exposure. The kind of thing we want."

Georgie gave them a brash grin. "Peter promised you junk."

"I don't think . . ."

"Anthea, remember whose store this is."

She gave him a look that would have felled a charging crocodile, but, surprisingly, fell silent.

The Lawtons' lives appeared to be more complicated than most and she still was not certain who ran the show here, but in a phrase Robin had made it clear where the money was. She turned to him. "I can get a draft out tonight."

"Right. In the morning we'll talk."

Anthea said, "I don't think Peter is going to like you committing without a phone conference."

"I don't care what Peter likes. Now Mrs. Crandall . . ."

"Kendall."

"Kimble."

"Kendall."

"Whatever," Robin said. "Let me tell you what I want . . ."

So it was that Robin outlined his ideas while Anthea frowned and Georgie made hasty notes. At this point she was ready to promise almost anything to secure this job, partly because she was a born Type A which meant she had never been very good at losing, and was even less good at suspense, but more important, because she had to do something to cry off the threatening wolves which at the moment were running dangerously close to the runners of the sledge.

This was how Georgia Kendall, who might possibly be found dead of starvation before she ever escaped the Windhover, reduced to a yearning skeleton just inches from the safety of the street, heard herself offering to deliver a draft of her lead and an outline of the first installment of what now sounded like a major series not in the morning, but by five o'clock tonight. It was past one and she couldn't remember whether Kath had a typewriter, but she agreed without a second thought. She didn't know why but it reminded her of being in the hospital having certain babies; you went in with a normal modesty but by the time you were finished with the medical exigencies, you were so anxious to get it over with so you could get out and go home that you didn't care who looked. She had walked in here cold and fished a commitment out of these people with only slightly less effort than it took Byron to retrieve Shelley's still-quivering heart from his burning chest. She offered to finish the job and get her offering duplicated and into Express Mail by five o'clock so these barracudas and the rotund Peter Flinc could eviscerate it first thing in the morning by conference telephone. She would kill herself doing this and she would, further, hand-carry two copies to the doorman at the Windhover for the Lawtons before dinner tonight, yes indeed. Robin smiled. Anthea almost smiled. Yes. At which point Robin, who had been brought to his feet by her amazing free offer to throw in an interview with the eminent and elusive Forrest Fulcrum, seized the cookie plate and thrust it at her in a spasm of largesse. So that Georgie, who was so spent that she would have agreed to deliver her piece *viva voce* if called upon to do so, found herself close to food at last, blinking into the tightly organized cookie plate. Robin held out the desiccated goodies as if it were the job he was proffering, saying, "Help yourself."

Why did this victory make her feel soiled? Why did even these mean-looking tea biscuits look good to her? "I can't," she said because she felt so compromised. "I ate before I came."

8

"B<small>ILL</small>?"

It was evening in Kath Hartley's house, and Georgie was calling home because she needed to touch base. She sat at the triangular phone table on the landing at the top of Kath's Georgetown Federal. Kath and Barry had redone it in the first years after their marriage, which had ended some time between the last college reunion, when Georgie last saw them together, and tonight. She knew she should have seen the signs; the strange combination of pride and fear of scrutiny at those things brought out the worst in people and put it right up front. At that last party at Mount Maria, Georgie looked up from the phone number she had just taken from an old classmate whom she would never telephone; distracted by a flash of movement, a slight disturbance in the air, she looked up to see Kath running out of the dancing party and into the late spring night, a frantic white blur in a Mexican wedding dress coursing past the plate glass window of the college lounge, while handsome, beautifully groomed Barry, the careful mathematician, sat stoically at the tiny corner table where they had been locked in unreadable attitudes—hers passionate, his unnervingly still, for more than an hour. Georgie had a flashing impression of Kath's eyes black in her white face, her black hair streaming as she streaked past the window, saw that Kath was barefooted and knew as surely as she wanted to go after her that she'd better not. Within seconds the impassive Barry had gotten up unhurriedly and started out after his wife. Something about this struck Georgie cold; when she reached for Bill's hand she could barely feel his fingertips because hers were numb.

When she got here this afternoon after her seance with the Lawtons, Kath took her aside and said, hurriedly, "I guess you already know I've shucked Barry."

Surprisingly enough, she did.

"I have, I mean, I did, but I kept hoping," Georgie said, with some of the same disappointment she'd felt at Jane's. It was as if little bits of her past kept dying. "I kept hoping you'd get it back together, you know?"

Kath's violet eyes sat in black shadows; her hair was black and her expression was black. "There are some things you can't put back together," she said.

Georgie could not keep from saying, "I just wish."

"Well don't." After a moment Kath said in a strange, dry voice, "There's another thing."

"What?"

There was a little silence in which Kath might have been doing one of Barry's bizarrely abstract problems in her head. "I guess I'm not ready to tell you."

Georgie was impatient by this time; she had a piece to write, she had to go to the bathroom, she had to ... "Kath, for Pete's sake."

Then her beautiful friend, who had gone extremely pale, considered for another moment, apparently choosing and discarding ways to present what she wanted to present; finally she gave up on all of them, saying in a funny, flat voice, "Just let me be what I want to be," and Georgie, in a compact she did not understand but agreed to because they were friends and had been friends for so long now, sealed it, saying:

"Anything you say."

"Look, I've got to go down to the kitchen and see to supper." She left Georgie with a charge, carelessly tossed over her shoulder. "Explain it to Mickey, will you?"

"OK," Georgie said.

Of course she'd reckoned without her deadline for the Lawtons, which drove everything out of her head before she reached the top of the stairs, so that she went straight to the typewriter without a thought for Mickey, or a word of explanation or anything else that might get between her and finishing the job. As a result Mickey was fuming in the ruffled guest bedroom with no news broken or mitigated; she sat neglected, while faithless Georgie clung to the telephone, driven by an urgency fueled by certain visions of Kath.

Kath had always been the visionary, the natural beauty with an intuition that transcended logic; before anybody explained, Kath knew; when they were in college Kath talked about sex and religion with equal passion to impressionable young men who confused one for the other; Georgie remembered Kath arriving back at Mount Maria in a car stolen from her escort, weeping and furious; she had thought he was a better person, she'd said angrily, reassembling her evening gown. The bastard could whistle for his car. If he had to walk home from the Shoreham, where she'd decked him on a balcony, it would serve him right. She could still see Kath's angry face: *I was trying to explain the TRINITY!*

Kath was another of life's absolutists; Georgie remembered Kath looking goofy in sweat clothes with her pink-framed glasses at the end of her nose and her freshly washed hair rolled up on socks as if that would discipline the curl, explaining that death was better than dishonor in any circumstance; she would not have said she was saving herself for the right man because she flirted with disaster of every possible kind at every possible opportunity, but, strangely, she kept herself apart from any really close encounter with an energy that made Georgie think of St. Joan leading platoons of impassioned virgins. Kath wouldn't settle for ordinary guys; she wanted archangels. What she got, finally, was Barry—blackly handsome, rich, imperious in a way that made Georgie want to push him to see if he would lean. At the time Kath fell for the manner; she loved him because he ordered her around. So all right, from the beginning it was doomed. This did not explain why Georgie was disturbed now or why, clinging to the telephone, she kept misdialing in her anxiety to be in touch with Bill.

The trouble, she supposed, was that of the roommates, Kath was the most like her, or Georgie thought she was, because in some ways Kath was Georgie idealized; she was fierce and headlong where Georgie combined fire with caution; Georgie was quick but Kath was quicker—intuitive, people said, the way the best artists are, or was it brilliant. Georgie had the small success, the reputation, but Kath—it didn't matter that what she put down was not always consecutive and didn't always make sense because it was so clearly gifted—Kath was a born poet. When the two friends checked themselves out in the hall mirror at Mount Maria before going down to the heavily draped and cushioned parlor to meet the guys, whoever they were, it was clear that Georgie looked pretty, if a little haphazardly put together—wrong belt, maybe, or wrong shoes for the dress—but it didn't matter what Kath put on because she was a natural beauty. Kath could forget birthdays or promises she had made; she could be sloppy about her assignments or late for dates or careless with people who loved her because she was wild and gifted and in the funny, limited way of small communities, she was famous.

If it was the headlong, undisciplined quality that set them apart, it was also what Georgie most envied. All her life she would worry about other people's feelings and being late for things and failing to keep her promises. What would it be like to wake up some morning and not give a damn about any of these things? She thought it would be wonderful. At the same time she understood it was this recklessness, this profligacy with talents and self and word given or broken that had spilled Kath out in midlife with no *more* than she'd had at the beginning. Fleeing her talents, Kath had taken brief twirls with graduate courses in this and that, had a fleeting romance with public relations and another fling with art history; she'd had two miscarriages that Georgie knew of and when she opened negotiations with the agency that placed Vietnamese children, Barry had refused to adopt; she'd started work in a library once, in a travel bureau another time; once she'd even stifled the laughter that rose at the very idea and trained to be a stewardess—*not* flight attendant, not anything Barry would approve. That time she had backed off at the last minute because of Barry; her marriage? "It seemed like a good idea at the time," she'd told Georgie, earlier today. So had her affair, the one that had ended it.

So there was this, too, that worried Georgie. If Kath possessed certain qualities of Georgie's, extrapolated, or pushed to the limit, she might also be some kind of forerunner, staking out their shared areas of vulnerability. Hence Georgie, on the phone. She wanted to crawl through the wire and into her own kitchen at this hour, to touch base and stay there, where it was safe. She needed to hear Bill's voice leap at the sound of hers, to be reminded that things were still the same with them. He did not answer on the second ring, or even the sixth one. When he did pick up the phone she started talking uncontrollably.

"Oh Bill, either this is the best day, or it's the worst."

But an alien voice cut her off; it sounded like a flight of Canada geese being stuffed into the receiver headfirst. "Honk-awho is it?"

In the background she heard pots crashing, heralding some kitchen disaster. "Wait a minute. Who is this?" She already knew.

"Who is this?" Horace said.

"Oh my God, Horace, what are you doing at my house?"

"Collecting notes on the makeup of the American Catholic consciousness," he said with some dignity. "It's for my book on American thought. And who are you?"

"Horace, it's me. I have to talk to Bill."

"Georgia, is that you?"

"Please, Horace, I'm—"

"Why are you always so impatient with me?"

"I'm sorry, I have to talk to Bill, about this problem?"

He said, morosely, "It might interest you to know that I have problems too."

"I'm sorry. Really. Is Bill there?"

"But they don't mean anything to you."

Inspiration struck her. "I'd love to hear about it, but I'm calling long distance."

"Long distance!" Horace had grown up in the era of crackling connections made at great cost over faulty wires. Long distance was expensive magic; it took precedence. "Bill, it's long distance." He dropped the receiver with a crash. He was gone an unconscionably long time.

During which Georgie hung on while in the little bedroom Mickey huddled grimly in front of the guest TV. *Bandstand* couldn't be that great, Georgie thought, after she'd tried and failed to catch her old friend's eye. *Oh, I get it. Mickey isn't speaking to me.* She had not forgiven Georgie for stuffing her into the cab and sending her on ahead, much less pushing past her to get to the typewriter when she finally did arrive. What had Mickey said to her?

"I don't see why this article is so important."

"If you have to ask, you'll never understand."

This was true. It was also one more reason she was at the moment unfit for conversation with anybody but Bill. They had been together for so long that they were essentially the same person; what she needed, he supplied. She could hide her head in his chest in the worst of times and think things were going to be all right, and when she was up, happy, high on something she had just accomplished, she needed to touch, be with, tell Bill because he was the only person who really cared.

Getting a head start with yesterday's notes, she had emerged from a concentrated effort and her orgy of Xeroxing and delivery with some of the same feelings Diana Nyad must have had swarming out of the English Channel, a little dizzy and still rocked by remembered waves. She had to talk to Bill, who felt most of the same things. Mickey was withdrawn and huffy, and in the tiled kitchen four floors below, Kath and her nephew were rattling and crashing pots. If she tried to explain, Kath would narrow her eyes in a kind of puzzled resentment because this was where the difference between them fell; Kath was brilliant but Georgie followed through. Committed to finishing everything she started, Georgie could be a Martian describing some vital alien ritual in a language nobody knew. Who else cared about the fulfillment of arbitrary tasks according to a self-imposed deadline? She was like a long-distance swimmer trying to improve her form or shave seconds off the next mile; it wouldn't show. They could have the block party and the torchlight parade for the flashy high divers; for her, finishing would have to be the prize.

Mickey was trying to get her attention.

"In a minute, I'm on the phone."

Mickey's voice was congested. "We have to talk."

There was life on the line at last. "Georgia?"

"Bill!"

Mickey beetled at her from the slipper chair. "I'm not kidding, it's important."

Honk.

Stretched too far, she snapped. "Oh Horace, go away!"

Bill cut through. "Honey, it's me. Horace, if you would just . . ." The old man's voice receded. "Sorry about that. Fork in the Dispos-al, Horace's fault."

"How the hell did he get in our house?"

"Drawn like a leper to the feast, I guess. That's it, Horace, put it out back, along with the rest of the garbage, all right?" Bill went on in a lower tone. "He knows I'm a soft touch. He heard you were gone and he figured I might not mind. He said he wanted to go over his notes for the new book, but if you want to know the truth, he and Frederika have broken up."

"They only got together Saturday."

"He said it was too hot not to cool down. He sublet his apartment on the spur of the moment and as soon as Frederika found out he was taking it for granted, she kicked him out. So I had to . . ."

"You mean he's *staying* with us?"

"He says it's for research interviews. I'm supposed to give him insight on people like Spellman and Joseph Kennedy."

"But you're not even Irish."

"But I'm a Catholic. He thinks I know something he doesn't about how other Catholics think."

"And he's staying in our house?"

"Honey, he didn't have anywhere to go. Corporal act of mercy, all right?" When she didn't say it was all right, Bill said, "I promise to get him into an apartment before you come home. He's really trying to be helpful, he begged me to let him make his special antipasto, which is how the fork . . ."

She didn't mean to sound angry, but she did. "In my house!" She backtracked at once. "I'm sorry. Tell him I'm sorry I yelled."

"Are you OK?"

"Barry and Kath are split."

"Right," Bill said. "I guess we knew. Tell her I'm sorry."

"And the Courtneys. They've cut up the house like Solomon's baby. It's the worst."

"I'm sorry."

"Lord, Bill." She drew in her breath. "What if it's going around?"

He did what she counted on him to do—pulled her down with a don't-be-silly-tone. "It's not. Relax."

But he didn't know about the letters. Her voice snagged on it and wavered. "What if it's something you can catch?"

"Stop that."

"Right," she said, in some pain. "It's just . . . Ow!" She gasped at a hand on her shoulder and spun around. "Mickey, good grief!"

In Boston, Bill said delicately, "Same old Mickey?"

"Right."

For relaxing, Mickey had chosen an old Mount Maria sweatshirt, mysteriously clean and bright after all these years, unless of course she'd ordered it fresh from this year's catalogue. Her skirt was pleated like a schoolgirl's, her idea of what women, or was it ladies, wore in their leisure time. Maybe, Georgie had thought more than once, Mickey's problem was that she had been born thirty years too late. She had, for instance, always felt compromised in pants. Her favorite piece of jewelry was her grandmother's lavalier; it was old-fashioned, like Mickey, sweet and out of date. Right now she was huffing at Georgie's elbow, looking proper and, what, importunate.

"Georgie, this can't wait."

"Bill, Mickey is . . ."

"Call me back. I love you."

"Me too."

". . . have to reach a position," Mickey was saying. "Before we go down to dinner."

"What?"

"We have to settle this before we eat."

"Eat," Georgie said wistfully. Deprived of lunch, she had snorted some Nabs and a Snickers bar on the run, which she had been forced to chase with half a package of the world's greatest living antacid. "Is dinner ready?"

"How am I supposed to know whether dinner's ready? Nobody ever tells me anything. I got here all by myself and Kath didn't tell me anything and you got here entirely too late and I thought, she's late, but at least she'll stop and talk to me but you were so tied up with your stupid article that you wouldn't tell me anything but I found out a few things anyway. . . ." She paused and caught her breath. "Things you had better know. Now come on in here and let's get this settled. If nothing else we have to make a solid front." Mickey tugged her into the TV room with the look which in college she had reserved for heavy business like honors violations or people who lied about where they were going to spend the night.

"What is your problem!" Georgie did not mean to sound angry; it just slipped out.

"Me?" Mickey was huffy and clearly hurt. "Why nothing. I don't have any problems. Everything's just fine."

"I'm sorry, Mickey, probably I'm tired. Now what's the matter here?"

"Funny you should ask." As of yore, Mickey had bruised like an enormous tea rose; even at her most delightful Mickey had always been too easily wounded; it would take a CAT scan to locate all her vulnerable spots, more psychic power than Georgie possessed to stay clear of them. "If you have to ask, maybe the problem is with you." Mickey went to the door and listened for a moment, after which she closed it and turned up the volume on the TV like a practiced spy. In another minute she would be lifting picture frames and feeling under tables and lamp bases looking for hidden microphones. She pulled Georgie down so that they sat facing, so close their knees bumped and when she had Georgie's full attention she said, hoarsely, "There's something going on."

"Oh look, I'm sorry, I was supposed to explain for Kath, she didn't have the heart to tell you herself, she and Barry are . . ."

"Any fool can see that," Mickey said impatiently. "Listen, we have a lot more pressing problem." Her voice dropped to a portentous rasp. "You know Kath's nephew?"

"Not really." She'd barely seen the rangy kid in the background; he'd headed down to the basement kitchen as Kath let her in.

"I don't think he's really her nephew," Mickey said.

"So?"

"Don't make me spell it out."

"Oh Mickey, he's only a kid."

"That's what you think."

"He can't be more than seventeen."

"That's the point. I think we ought to get out of here."

"Before dinner?"

"Before we get tarred with the same brush!"

"How could we possibly . . ."

"You know what happens to divorced women. It's just so *sordid*."

"Oh good grief."

"As long as we stay on here, we're part of it."

"Part of what?"

"Whatever's happening."

"Mickey, how could we possibly . . ."

"Susannah and the elders," Mickey said significantly. "Guilt of the beholder."

God, Georgie thought, she read my book. "You don't think we're . . ."

"It looks like we're *approving*." Mickey finished after a heavy pause. "With knowledge comes responsibility."

"Invincible ignorance," Georgie parried, like lightning, a bolt straight from Theology Three. At Mount Maria the visiting Dominican had introduced the concept; you could not help what you could not know.

Mickey brightened. "Do you really think so?"

"If he isn't her nephew he's probably a student of Barry's, or a family friend. Besides," she lied boldly, "I heard him call her Aunt Kath. Now if you'll excuse me I'm going down." She became aware that Mickey's shiny Bass Weejuns were planted on her sneakered toes. "I wonder, would you mind getting off my shoes?"

"I think I'll wear the blue, with my lavalier."

"You don't have to dress for dinner."

"It's navy," Mickey said inexorably. "What do you think?"

Georgie sighed. "I think that will be fine."

"I just wish Kath wouldn't *do* this."

"For all you know, she isn't doing anything."

"What if he isn't her nephew?"

Georgie turned impatiently. "Are you coming, or what?"

From the landing she heard Mickey calling mournfully, "Would you tell them I'll be down as soon as I get dressed?"

She couldn't be certain whether it was sympathy or malice that prompted her to call up to the anxious Mickey, right before she plunged for the basement kitchen and light and music, conversation, food, "I think I would forget the lavalier."

9

It seemed appropriate for Kath to have custody of the Georgetown house because in the absence of anything more consuming, she had thrown herself into revamping it for Barry with the same passionate concentration with which she'd used to begin a poem. Kath never did anything halfway. She never did anything for very long, either. It might just be a matter of heat and velocity: anybody who started that fast was bound to burn out, but there was always the possibility that for better or worse Kath was in fact casting for something she would not necessarily know on sight. Whatever it was, it had left her restless and impatient; nothing else would do, and she had a way of giving things up before they were fully undertaken because she seemed to know, sooner than anyone, that a given enterprise was not The One. *Why waste time?* Georgie could almost see this, but even at this distance she could not be certain whether Kath was running out of control because she was spoiled and scatty or whether, rather, somewhere—ahead or behind?—she heard the snuffling of the hound of heaven.

Being in Kath's house was a little bit like being inside her head, except that everything was finished here. Coming down the last flight of stairs of a house that had been gutted and refinished in Kath's image, Georgie stopped on the last landing to look over the railing before Kath saw her and they spoke. She had the idea that if she could just read the surroundings, she might be able to understand.

Everything in the place reflected Kath: the bright colors and strong lines, the sense of fun, the imagination. For all his forcefulness, his strong good looks and physical magnetism, Barry was still a mathematician, blind to everything but certain patterns inside his head. He wouldn't notice whether his wife wore white or black, only whether she fit within the logical construction he had made to stand for their marriage; he wouldn't notice if the walls were painted dayglo pink or papered in polka dots, nor would he much care. Kath had done all this, tiling the ground-floor kitchen and whitewashing the foundation walls, choosing the multi-colored Danish rug for the sitting area at the far end. She had studded the walls with Mexican grotesques out of papier-mâché; on the mantel sat a row of candy skulls. She had right-angled two narrow water beds in the corner nearest the door to the garden, mounding them with brilliant cotton quilts and pillows from a dozen cultures.

The young man or was he a boy working in the kitchen area fit perfectly, in his trendy shirt and tight jeans and moon shoes that would have excited the envy of an astronaut. He and Kath were jabbering over a recipe like children, while on the stove something bubbled and in the oven something else roasted and spat.

Georgie wondered whether there might be some way to send this kid on an errand so she and Kath could talk; she wanted a minute to take her hands and ask her what was happening. She didn't know whether it was her own obtuseness or psychic naivete that left her baffled every time a marriage came apart. Was she so dumb she still believed all the good old things people used to believe in the good old days? Probably. Longtime student of Kath as she was, even knowing Barry as she did, she couldn't quite make it out, any more than she could make out who the kid was—in spite of Mickey's dark suspicions—or what he was doing here. But here he was and here they were, he and Kath bumping dark heads over the recipe book, Georgie lingering on the stairs.

From her vantage point Georgie skimmed counters like a speed reader, looking for *hors d' oeuvres*. When Lance, if that was his name, emptied a sack of raw peanuts into a chopping bowl, she leaned out too far, missed a step and fell.

"Oh, George, I thought you were dead. You took forever."

"I had to do this thing."

"You always were compulsive." That look: what I wanted, you have accomplished.

Not really, Kath. Not yet. "Yeah."

"Where's Mick?"

"She has her own compulsions. You know."

"Whether to wear the lavalier," Kath said. "Doesn't she know it's only us?"

"That's the whole thing," Georgie said. "When she dresses for dinner she doesn't mess around. . . ." She tried hard to keep from swallowing her tongue. "About dinner. When's dinner?"

"That's up to Lance." Kath put him forward with a tentative grin. "You haven't met Lance."

He was older than he looked at first blush. How old? Even listening carefully, Georgie could not pick up a job description or familial reference or anything else that fully explained his presence. So his name really was Lance. She said, "Hello, Lance."

Someone at Sassoon had clipped and raked Kath's hair in a cut that accentuated the elegance of her features. Something, emotional hardship, perhaps, had given her a new leanness that Georgie would murder to attain. She had thrown out her old wardrobe along with Barry and she looked tough and glamorous in a black shirt and pants and suede boots that crumpled like a pirate's. If in context the butcher's apron was surprising, it was also chic. Kath could have been any age—Georgie's, his. Lance was too young to have to worry about how he looked. He was graceful and well put together in a shirt that was a sight gag. It had suffered an attack of zippers; they crossed the neck and ringed the biceps and made random slashes across the front. He was not that much older than her Matty, Georgie thought with a wrench. Matty had just this year stopped being a child. One night at supper she caught him in the middle of the change; as she watched his outlines blurred and shimmered, forecasting the man he would become. Sweet kid, she thought, without knowing whether she meant Lance here, or her son.

"Say hello to George."

"Hello, George." At a look from Kath he corrected himself. "Mrs. Kendall, I mean."

"Georgie," Georgie said, drained of everything: strength, energy, will. She said, not so much to Lance as to her old college roommate, "Don't make me feel old."

Lance was saying, affably, "OK, George."

"Is your name really Lance?"

He colored. "It was really Benedict, but ah, you know."

"He's staying here for the summer. His folks are in Rangoon."

These small crumbs made Georgie grateful. At least he had parents. "I see."

As she reached for the peanuts Kath fended her off. "Those go into the dish. What do you want to drink?" Something, probably the presence of the kid, kept Georgie from offering to help or throwing herself on Kath as she would have even a week ago, groaning, *I'm starved.* "I'd better not have a drink."

"It'll be good for you," Kath said, aiming her at the corner couches like the spinner in Blind Man's Buff. "This is going to take a while, but it's worth waiting for. Lance is cooking African."

Without wanting to she ended up juggling an unwanted beer and a bowl of dried soybeans on one of Kath's water beds, *hors de combat,* while Kath and Lance moved like accustomed partners at the stove. Barry couldn't even boil an egg, thought Georgie, who had a secret theory about people who were not good at food. She was, however, starved and uncomfortable but afraid to move to Kath's beautifully set table for fear of fainting into one of her Picasso plates. She had always hated water beds because no matter how careful she tried to be, or how still she sat, they lurched and sloshed. There was nothing to hold on to; the covers on this particular inflated instrument of torture had begun to slide and all her attempts to remain upright were foiled. She hurled herself at the pillows in a last-ditch attempt at stability and ended up reclining, so close to the moving surface that she could hear the water gurgling; agitating the spilled soybeans, it jiggled with every breath she took. Becalmed, Georgie fought off seasickness in the presence of incessant lapping of waves. Kath and Lance seemed in no hurry, clearly taking pleasure in the business of creation here, and she had the sudden fear that they would extend this, chopping nuts and dicing yams into tomorrow because it was so much fun. Growing sicker by the minute, Georgie cursed water beds and travel and particularly Horace Metcalf, who would have eaten most of the casserole she'd fixed especially for Bill, gorging on her food, while its maker floated helplessly, waiting for the yams to blend, or cook to mush, if that's what Lance wanted, so she could eat. Even more than she resented Horace she resented the kid for being so young and self-assured and physically attractive and for cooking African when all she wanted was to eat beans out of a can if necessary, anything so she could go to bed. She would be dead by dinnertime, if there ever was a dinnertime.

There was a stir at the top of the stairs.

"I hope I'm not too late."

She heard Kath swallowing laughter. "Oh Mickey, how lovely. Your lavalier."

Later Georgie wished that she had died. It would have short-cut hours of suffering. Lance was a foreign service officer's brat, which explained his ease with the three of them; he was also intelligent and handsome in an irregular way, but there was something else about him that Georgie could not quite pin down that disturbed her then and nagged at her now, in the middle of the night, a hunger or maybe it was a feral quality— it was a little like making friends with an animal; it was so attractive that it was hard to keep from touching it, but there was no way to tell how long it was going to be there or whether it would bite. Mickey was riveted; she might have been at a movie that she could not foresee the end of, afraid to look, afraid to look away.

His cooking was glorious. It was almost worth waiting for, if waiting was ever worth it. For the first time since home she'd had enough to eat but now, at the pitch of three A.M., she was paying the price. She was in the tiny guest bathroom at the top of the stairs, twisted by cramps. Raw peanuts, she guessed, unless it was the pilaf or the rich sidedish made from a root vegetable Lance declined to name. Either that or it was the

Lawtons' cookies, fixed in her memory like a polyester resin food sculpture; they were still glistening on their plate in that darkened apartment, reproaching her from beyond the grave. Maybe it was the acidic properties of Peter Flinc. She couldn't blame Kath, or Lance, whose behavior at dinner was unexceptionable, nor could she blame Mickey, who had sat there in her navy silk dress fingering her lavalier and trying to find the right way to behave in a situation she did not approve of and could never understand. Georgie was going to have to conclude that her misery was the natural result of her own folly, whether tonight at table or all those years ago she could not say.

Whatever the reason she was suffering the tortures of the darned here on the plush bathroom rug where she had come to rest curved around the cold porcelain which, in proximity, she found strangely comforting. She was stranded far from her loved ones, beyond the reach even of the world's greatest living antacid; her miles of spasming intestine must look like the knotted fancy-work sailors did on long sea voyages and, worse yet, she had started hearing noises over the rumble and swash of her inner turmoil. She saw a white strip of light flash into the space under the door. Somebody was at the door at the bottom of the stairs, outside the room where Kath had slept with Barry for so many years and where she, Georgie, had assured Mickey (only tonight) that Kath still slept in solitary rectitude. When the door opened, out of Kath's bedroom like a gust from the past blew the original Beatles recording of "Lucy in the Sky with Diamonds," straight from the year they were all married. Rotten luck, that all their lives should erupt in the year of a Beatles revival. Wait a minute, she thought, My life is not erupting, it's only my large intestine. It's Kath's life, she told herself, as a volley of thumps and giggles drifted up like a seismic intimation. She tried to pretend this came from next door or outside or the TV in front of which Mickey was snoring, but she knew better. Lithe Kath and rangy Lance were together in the bedroom at the bottom of these very stairs; if she tried to escape the bathroom now they'd almost certainly hear. What had she told Mickey? Kath would never, good lord, her room is too close to ours and this is *Kath.*

It was not Kath's having a kid lover that bothered her; it

wasn't even that she was trapped in the bathroom, a helpless and unwilling witness; it was, rather, being forcibly reminded that no matter what you did to forestall or prevent such moments, no matter what you shored up against them, nothing in life stayed where you put it. In spite of what they'd been taught at Mount Maria, and everything they had taken for granted at the time, nothing was certain. In a way, Georgie thought, she was as rigid as Mickey was. In spite of her acuteness, her willingness to adapt to the times, in her heart she expected certain things to remain constant; like the rest of them, Kath had married Barry before God and forever. Yet here Kath was. There was Ag, in Florida. Here was George.

Here was Georgie, drained and lying prone with her face mashed into the immaculate beige fluff while Kath and that clever, sexy boy . . . It was Kath's business, she reminded herself; it was Kath's life, she told herself firmly, but could not efface the image of Lance stripped to the essentials. Damn the Beatles. Damn Ralph Schwartz anyway.

She was afraid to get up and totter back to bed; they might blunder out and discover her. Instead she pressed her rapidly chilling body into the fluff and pulled down the bathmat to cover her rear. If God loved her, time would pass with merciful speed. She would wake up and it would be morning.

Not a chance. After an indeterminate amount of time in which she may have dreamed bad dreams she heard something thumping down the hallway like an approaching mole; maybe, she thought, beginning to be frightened, maybe she had waked into an outtake from *The Mummy*. It dragged itself along and bumped and slithered, trailing cerements. Mickey. She tried the bathroom door, muttering angrily when it would not yield. She rattled the handle and after she had tried the door with the entire weight of her swaddled body she said, too shrilly, "Georgia, are you in there?"

Who the hell do you think is in here? Georgie thought, too mortified to answer. At this volume Mickey was going to bring out the police.

"Georgie?"

"Shhh."

"I knew you were in there."

"Mickey, shut up."

"Why didn't you answer me?"

"In the name of heaven, shhh." Georgie got up and pressed her mouth to the crack. "Shut up or they'll hear."

"Who will? What are you *doing* in there?"

"What do you think I'm doing?" she lied through the crack. "I'm going to the bathroom, now will you go back to bed?"

Mickey was gruff and urgent. "You're not the only one who has to go."

Georgie heard sounds Mickey was too pressed to notice. "They're coming."

"Who's coming?"

"Shh!"

It was too late. Kath said, from the foot of the stairs, "Mickey, for Pete's sake!"

"Eeeeek!" Georgie didn't have to see modest Mickey clutching the raincoat she wore over her fuzzy bathrobe and the spriggled Celanese nightie. "I was trying to get into the . . . Kath!"

(Kath, *sotto voce*: "Lance, I'd better handle this.")

"Oh my God, Kath, there's a man in your bedroom."

There was a fusillade of stamping, thumping and murmurs and doors slamming: Mickey retreating in disarray, Georgie supposed, while Lance drew Kath back to bed. This was followed by what seemed like hours marching toward dawn, which was actually breaking outside the bathroom window when Georgie concluded everybody must be asleep and it was safe to go back to bed. She stretched, stiff from all the time she had done on the rug. With excruciating stealth, she escaped.

Naturally she ventured out just as Lance emerged from Kath's room, turning in the doorway for a last embrace and at a murmur from Kath, who saw her first, Georgie fixed in the glow from the tiny skylight. Kath slipped back into her room with a foxy grin but Lance stayed put, perfectly at ease in gray cotton bikini underpants. In the second before she broke his gaze and plunged for her room he acknowledged his position here, hers, everything in one gesture, leaving her scorched and so embarrassed that it was late the next day before she even noticed her stomach's revenge had ceased sometime in the night.

She wouldn't have minded dying right there or going to bed for the rest of her life but Kath was at the door in seconds, drawing her downstairs to the kitchen so they could talk.

"I suppose you're wondering what Lance and I were doing."

"Not really."

"You might as well know I'm in love with him," Kath went on with brash confidence. "And he's in love with me."

In spite of the hour and the tousled hair and the outsized T-shirt, Kath looked so pretty and hopeful that Georgie choked out an equally hopeful, "That's wonderful."

"I just thought you ought to know." Her voice trailed off.

"You really don't have to explain to me."

"I kind of do." Kath's eyes kindled with the look they got when she was about to start something. "I've left the church." She squinted, apparently waiting for Georgie to express the wrath of God.

Georgie did not fall off her stool. "Oh, really? Oh. OK."

"Aren't you shocked?"

"I don't think so."

Kath seemed disappointed. "I thought you would be. After all these years. I mean, you're still in it, right?"

"Yeah."

"I thought so. After everything."

Georgie shrugged. "In spite of everything."

"Isn't it weird?"

"Yeah, it's weird. Don't ask me to explain." She did not add: and please, don't you explain.

"Let me tell you what it's like."

"You don't have to," Georgie said.

"Yes I do, OK?"

It was not OK, but she had no choice. "If you say so. OK."

"It's really funny how it started."

"What, Lance?"

Kath shook her head. "Everything. You don't start with Lance, Lance is something you arrive at. He's cute and he thinks I'm wonderful and he needs me and it's amazing. We're in love. But whatever is happening with me right now ... what I think I'm doing ... would you believe it started with birth control?"

Georgie winced. "I'm afraid I would."

"Barry never wanted kids." Kath grimaced. "Imagine our surprise when after all those years of me feeling guilty over preventing it we found out he couldn't have them anyway. He decided it was that year's project and when it didn't work in the first ten minutes he said we had to Take Steps. You know how Barry is."

"I know how Barry is."

"He wants everything done yesterday. Well surprise. We took steps, which is how we found out his sperm count is zilch. Ego up the tubes, and all those years I'd been using—you name it, I used it, and feeling terrible, you know. Guilt. In spite of the flap, and all the people that said it was OK. Not feeling wrong, exactly, just never quite feeling right. Do you hear me?"

"I'm afraid so."

"And as it turns out, for no reason. Birth control. Isn't it a riot?"

"If you want to call it that." They had galloped through the Sixties under the illusion that things in the church were changing faster than they really were, and conducted their lives accordingly. If you could cancel a lifetime of Latin masses and Lenten fasting almost overnight, clearly other things were changing too. Then that one blew up: letter from Rome on human life. Was there any other body in the world that went into convulsions at the drop of one word from the top? There was everybody on the barricades, clergy, civilians, even bishops and cardinals all sawing back and forth over the intimate question, which was not really over what people did together in bed; it was about conscience and authority, or was it conscience versus authority. Even that was not clear. Protest rattled every window in the monolith; untidy doubt blundered in and set up housekeeping in the lobby, where it had been making itself at home ever since. People either tried to pretend it wasn't crouching there or else they acknowledged the mess and learned to live with it, or they chucked everything and left. Georgie fell into the second category, nudging doubt to one side to make room for her because she intended to stay, which meant she had spent her life considering, because no matter how she tried to arrange herself she could not get altogether comfortable. Ralph Schwartz was right. Catholics did take everything too hard. Which was, of course, the whole thing.

Kath was saying, "All that transgression, and for what turned out to be no reason. I figured I might as well be hung for a sheep as a goat."

"Who said you had to hang at all?"

"It's an absolute system. If what I was doing was absolutely wrong . . ."

"What if it wasn't?"

"It was still disobedience."

"You always did push everything to the limit."

"Yeah. Well, anyway, if what I was doing was absolutely wrong, I figured I must be absolutely out of it."

Georgie said angrily, "Nobody is ever absolutely out of it."

Kath was serene. "So if I'm absolutely out of it I can do absolutely anything I want. So that's just awful, right?"

"Not as awful as you want it to be." Georgie went on, with an effort, because these things were complicated and abstract and in a funny way, so personal that they were hard to talk about. "He's never going to give up on you."

"Then I'm the one who gave up on Him."

"That's not as easy as you think."

Looking tired in the early light, Kath ran her fingers through her thick dark hair. "In a funny way, it's kind of liberating. I figured if there were people ready to write me off because I'd let down on the one little thing, I might as well shoot the works." She grinned. "You could call it the domino theory of departure. So I'm out of the church all the way. You understand it's the logical extension of an ideological position."

Georgie flared. "But you don't *have* to—"

"You may not have to, but I do."

"Well you don't have to explain it to me."

Kath went on explaining anyway. "It's something I had to do."

"Then don't apologize."

She persisted. "I mean, I know what I'm doing."

Georgie sighed. "I wish I did."

"The thing is, if it used to be a sin to eat meat on Friday and now it isn't, what did they do with all those poor people, and for what, and why should somebody like me have to feel guilty about something that people can't even agree whether it's wrong?" Kath's hands were all knuckles, which she began to gnaw.

"For God's sake, Kath, if you're comfortable with it . . ."

"Oh, that," she said. "That's over. What's more I am very damn comfortable with this. All right?"

If she was she didn't look it. "How did you happen to meet Lance?"

Kath brightened. "Funny you should ask. Barry turned out to be selfish beyond belief, you know? When the baby machine didn't work according to expectations he just switched me off and stuck me in the mop closet, No time for that now, Down girl. So I started stepping out on him. Around the time he figured he would rather move out than bump into my boyfriends on the stoop, he was renting rooms to students, of which the last one was Lance."

"He doesn't look like a math student."

"Lance is going to be an expert in international law. I'm helping him through school."

"I see."

"He's a kind of a diplomatic orphan, you know? His folks are in Rangoon, he wouldn't go along and so they cut him off without a cent. He may be young but he's eight times the man Barry was, and stronger and more loving, and the last time Barry gave me a hard time Lance punched him in the nose and kicked him out." For whatever reason, the hour or the circumstance or an excess of emotion, Kath was so close to tears that Georgie had to say some mitigating thing.

"He seems very smart."

"Smarter than Barry, you can bet." Kath smiled gratefully. "I'm trying to help him finish his education. I suppose you think what we're doing is terrible."

Georgie shook her head because at the moment she could not speak.

"I know it looks bad, me taking advantage of a kid, but it isn't that way."

"What if he's taking advantage of you?"

Kath bared her teeth. "Don't!"

"I'm sorry."

"He's young but he loves me and he's more of a man than Barry ever was. I know it sounds dumb but he's the only person who ever really understood me, and God knows he's the only man who's ever been truly nice to me." They both knew not all of this was true but Kath was constructing a narrative that would make sense of this passion or infatuation or temporary insanity; she needed to do this more than Georgie needed to warn her about Lance. "Isn't it funny that when I cut loose and try to be bad this is the worst I can come up with? It's like those nights when you're little and your parents leave you all by yourself, you know, after you've drunk all the ginger ale and read all their sex books, what else is there left to do?" She finished softly. "Lance *is* special, isn't he?"

"Please don't get hurt.—Look, if we're going at ten, I really have to get some sleep. It's been a bad night." She said this over her friend's shoulder because she had found it necessary to grab Kath and hug her quickly to keep her from seeing, what, the future written in Georgie's face. "Take care," she said quickly and let go.

Dear Kath. *Please don't let anything happen to her.* On the first-floor landing she put both hands to her face for a moment because she was determined not to cry. She was troubled, feeling exhausted and tender and anxious to warn Kath without knowing how, knowing only that it was important. It was important because in the last moment before dawn, before Lance headed downstairs and she plunged into her bedroom, he had fixed her with a long, insolent stare, after which he'd cupped his hands under his crotch and jerked himself forward in a quick, contemptuous bump.

Maybe she could prepare Kath in stages, she thought, and brightened. *Thank heaven he isn't coming on the trip.*

10

As it turned out Lance was going on the trip.

When Georgie and Mickey came down with their suitcases, Lance was in the front hall with his backpack, waiting for Kath to put on her amber so he could do the clasp. Amber, with khakis and a string sweater; a kid boyfriend; it was all so chic and relaxed that it almost made sense—would have, Georgie thought, if she trusted Lance, which she did not. Watching Kath duck her head in front of the mirror, seeing Lance's clever hands working at the nape of her neck, Georgie understood how this had come about. He was still in the act of *becoming*; YES that was sexy; so was he. Lance was too young for early signs of his true self to mar or brighten his face, too new for his body to record dissipation or illness or unhappiness or even misgivings or regrets. Lounging with his knuckles brushing the back of Kath's neck, he shimmered with potential in some of the same ways Matty Kendall did. He could be anything. Might already be. It was clear why Kath might think he was the answer now.

Poor selfish Barry with his impossible standards and his faulty apparatus; he could have been a living demonstration of his all-time favorite, Goedel's Theorem of Incompleteness, the hand perpetually reaching for the perpetually receding cup; poor sterile Barry with his imperious manner and his unfortunate sense of order. He didn't stand a chance. There was the marginal possibility that Georgie had been wrong about Lance in spite of the bump in the night. Maybe in the bad light she had misapprehended him and he was only scratching himself. Maybe it was a little kid trick and not what she thought. She wanted to believe this was the case.

Next to her, Mickey was inflating like a Macy's Thanksgiving Day balloon, hands first, her face red with distress. She kept nudging Georgie and mumbling, trying to push her forward. *Do something,* she said with every line of her body; *aren't you going to do something?* Gentle, staid Mickey had been born into a world she had not made and now her friends, whom she had trusted, seemed more in tune with it than she did.

No. They were more in tune with it than they were with her. When Georgie did not respond to her prodding she gathered herself, brave, for Mickey, and spoke right up. "You're not *bringing* him!"

"What if I am?"

Mickey had swallowed so much air that Georgie could barely make out what she was saying. "Not the whole way."

"Why not? I need him to help with the bags." Kath had the funny, arrogant look she got when she was afraid she was about to be hurt. It was not so much sad as gripping to see the two of them in a standoff: Kath, who had always said she didn't care what people thought and who because she too was all potential cared desperately, and Mickey the rigid, who was not so much protected as trapped by a wall of propriety. Sometimes Georgie thought she was trapped in there with the cask of Amontillado, and unless something or somebody prevented it she would be walled away from them forever; it was only a matter of time before the last brick slid into place.

"You're bringing him now?" Mickey was inflated to the point of misery. "Now, when there's been a death?"

"Now most of all. Besides," Kath said, trying to sound efficient and matter-of-fact about it, "there are some people at Fulcrum that Lance needs to meet."

"At the *funeral?*"

"At Fulcrum. There are people there he needs to meet if he's going into international law."

"What's everybody going to think?"

"One thing Barry did teach me is connections are important. If I can help somebody's career, even a little bit . . ."

"What's Mr. Fulcrum going to think?"

"You never heard of Mr. Fulcrum until yesterday."

"I keep up. I know who Mr. Fulcrum is."

"What do you care what Mr. Fulcrum thinks?"

"I just don't want to give scandal in front of Ag."

"Mickey, for God's sake, this kind of thing happens all the time now. People take it for granted."

"That doesn't make it all right."

"You're the scandal," Kath said. "If anybody's out of place these days, it's you."

Georgie was spared the rest of this exchange by a call from Anthea Lawton.

"Mrs. Kendall, I wanted you to know that Robin and I have finished your piece."

And? "That's wonderful." She had worked faster and better than she ever had before; she knew the piece was good but she was waiting to be told. She was like a cat with its back arched, waiting to be stroked.

Anthea said. "We think it's going to be very exciting, but."

Georgie sagged. "But."

"And we've talked to Peter about it. At length."

"And he says it's right on target," another voice said so unexpectedly that Georgie jumped: Robin Lawton, on the Totalphone. She couldn't read anything in his tone either.

"What Robin means is, Peter agrees with us."

Georgie thought, *oh shit*. "Agrees. With. You."

"About what's needed," Anthea said cosily, slipping in the knife.

"Needed!"

"In your piece."

She said, defensively, "I thought you said it was right on target."

"No, that was Peter," Anthea said. "There are some good things in it, but we see real problems with it as it stands."

"It's a problem with the love affair," Robin said. He left it to Anthea to stick it to her, which she did.

"At the moment, it just isn't there."
Georgie bit the inside of her mouth. "You mean the roommate's love affair."
"Whatever. You need to face facts."
Robin said, almost at the same time, ". . . but keep it low key."
"Robin, don't confuse her."
"I was just—"
"Do you want me to play it up or play it down?"
"We want you to rethink it," Anthea said. "The part in outline looks more or less OK, but I'd pay particular attention to the lead."
"What's the matter with the lead?"
"We're agreed on that." Robin said, "Just look at it, and you'll see it too."
Anthea said, "Can you wait a minute? There's another call coming in."
"What do you want me to . . ." But it was too late. She was on HOLD, where she spent so much time that she expected somebody to turn on Muzak or tell her a company operator would be with her shortly and she should use this interval to get out her credit card.
When Robin got back on the line he sounded tightly controlled, like somebody emerging from a major fight. "Are you still there?"
"Of course I'm still here."
"Oh good. Thank you for bearing with us. Anthea has . . . Peter has . . . We've agreed that if you do this right, we want to give it a lot of space."
"You haven't told me what you want."
"We may want to make it the cover," Robin said.
"The cover!"
"If you can do what we want."
"In the matter of . . ." She was waiting for him to finish her sentence, which he did not.
"Which means we need it soonest," he said, and hung up.
Which either was or wasn't just as well, because the minute she put down the receiver her second call came in. It was from

Peter Flinc. When he growled a furry hello she said, "About my piece."

"The Lawtons will have told you what we want."

"Not really."

"There are some real problems."

"Robin said you said it was right on target."

"If you want to know the truth I think it's low and a little to the left." Flinc muffled the mouthpiece while he talked to somebody in the office, leaving Georgie to dangle until he finally uncovered the receiver and let her hear him telling somebody, "By all means it's worth ten thousand dollars, I love every word the woman writes . . . Sorry," he said to Georgie in the next breath, "We're concluding a one-shot deal with Joyce Carol Oates, her agent is in the outer office and . . ."

Outclassed again. "That's wonderful."

"But I think you're going to give her a run for the money once you get this thing in shape. I just called to tell you to take your time, we don't want you to rush a good thing or you'll run it out of shape." Flinc let his voice drop to an intimate husk; in another life he might have been a high school hotrod trying to put the make on her.

"Rush it! I wasn't rushing it. You wanted—"

"By tonight."

"Tonight!"

"That is, if you still want the column."

"Of course I want the column."

"And we'll up the ante for a cover piece." Without changing his tone or bothering to put his hand over the mouthpiece he said, "Margaret Drabble? Fine . . . Now, are we clear?"

"Not really."

"Good. Which is why we need it by wire, and tonight. Think cover. Think big."

"I'll see what I can do." A cover. It might not make her name, but it would help.

She had been aware, as she hung on the phone, that there was a shadow in the doorway to Kath's pretty sitting room, but she had been too embroiled to turn around and look. From the hall came the last strains of Kath's and Mickey's argument, which was segueing into an uneasy truce, but Lance was watching her from the doorway and as she turned and recognized his presence, he slipped into the room like a hunting dog on the track of something succulent.

His smile was designed to let her know he was still only a puppy. "You're working for a magazine?"

She shrugged. "Or not."

"I read your column the whole time I was at Harvard."

"Harvard!"

"Well, sort of." He struck where she was most vulnerable. "I liked your book."

"You read it?" She didn't even know whether Kath had.

"You really know how to get to people, reach them where they hurt." Crafty Lance.

"You're, ah, hurting?"

"It's not important. Look. I thought maybe if I could get some of it down . . ."

"You want to be a writer."

He lifted his shoulders with a self-deprecating grin.

"I thought it was international law."

"Sometimes a person is more than one person."

"Not necessarily."

"Let's face it, Fulcrum . . . Well there's a Supreme Court justice I need to talk to, along with . . ." He seemed to have left his face open. For whatever reasons he appeared to be asking for her help.

"Burke Marshall and Eugene V. Rostow," she supplied. There was the *marginal* possibility that Lance was on the level.

"If a person could talk to one of them, or all of them, I mean, get an interview . . ."

"I don't do interviews."

There was that ingenuous, hopeful grin. "I mean me. I want to do it. Do you think there's a chance they'd let me talk to them?"

Even though she still didn't trust Lance she could not keep herself from softening. "They might. You're cute. You might be able to get to them where an old reporter can't." It had always been her weakness that she got off on doing favors. "If I can help . . ."

"Anything you can do . . ." He was standing directly in front of her by this time, taut and attentive in a black Shetland sweater and no shirt. If she wanted to she could touch the pulse beating in the tanned hollow at the base of his neck. Under the dark, thick eyelashes, his eyes were a clear gray. "I'm bringing my portable that you've been using."

"Oh, was that your typewriter?"

"I thought if you wanted to, you could use it on the trip."

"How do you know I'm going to need a typewriter?"

Under the tan the blood rushed to his face. Of course he'd heard her on the phone. "It's yours. If you need anybody to do legwork on the trip . . ."

"That's very nice. I'll let you know."

The dark, straight eyebrows seemed to tilt up at the ends; they looked smooth enough to touch. "And if I can reach these guys, and I write about it and it's any good, could you help me figure out how to publish it?"

"I'll put you in touch with my editor in Boston." She added, in a spasm of generosity, "You can use my name."

The ease with which he had brought her to the point where he had been leading her made him careless and he sprang too fast. "I'd rather do it for your new magazine."

Fatal error. Right. OK. "Ooops," Georgie said, recovering herself so quickly that he missed the transition. Inexperienced hustler, he didn't even see it happening. "Time to go."

Lance failed to catch the alteration in her tone. He went on eagerly. "We make a good team."

"Give me a break!" He was following so closely that she could feel her back getting warm; his breath stirred her hair and unless she did something fast he was going to put his arms around her from behind and assume they'd made a pact. In her hunger for Bill, in the moment before she freed herself she might feel her body sag against him, inadvertently sealing it. She had to do something fast. She needed to nail him, which she did just before they broached the hallway, where Mickey and Kath stood with their heads bent over a road map, formalizing their treaty.

She bristled, growling through clenched teeth, "You do one thing to hurt Kath and I'll murder you."

11

WHEN SHE WASN'T DRIVING, Georgie slouched in the back, working on her piece. She had taken her Xerox apart from the top without any clear idea of what the people at *IN* expected from her, except for her to make it different, which she had to do without hurting anybody she cared about. She had the idea that doing this was like completing a puzzle; she would keep on rearranging the pieces until the last one snicked into place and locked. Then she would get the prize.

Hiding behind her clipboard, she could pretend not to hear Mickey's labored attempts at polite conversation, the lumpy silences that followed while Lance slouched deeper and Kath scrambled for some tactful thing to say. Flushed and desperate, Mickey seemed incapable of being quiet. She had to tell them all about Howard and their life in Bronxville and the twins; they were the stars of the third grade in every respect and even though they were adopted everybody said they took after her. She even told them about the study group she belonged to in Bronxville, a circle of women who had put aside their careers so they could attend to their families, she said with a significant look at Georgie. But, she said, these were not just *housewives*. They were intelligent people who read all the great books and wrote papers about them, although not everybody thought the same books were great. Next she retreated to the relative safety of her flower garden, naming every rose Howard grew, following this with a catalogue of vegetables and insect pests, after which she unfolded her routine of seasonal plantings and mulchings in a protective litany. She went on beyond the point of polite conversation to stultification, numbering the parts of her life so compulsively that Georgie saw she was summoning them as if they could make her proof against whatever outrage was to come.

"If you can't do important work," she said with tears standing in her eyes because nobody was listening, "at least you can try to have a beautiful life."

"Right on, Mick," Georgie murmured, and bent to her task.

If Mickey had always been the most tightly organized of them it was because she lived on the narrowest margin of confidence. Mickey had always been one of life's C-plusses, average in intelligence, unlike Georgie and Kath, ordinary-looking, unlike Kath, not good at sports like Ag, and with no distinguishing talents, and because she lacked the spark or whatever it was that made Georgie what their teachers used to call creative and Kath gifted if erratic, she made an art of being ordinary, establishing a tight set of norms with the idea that it was fitting in that mattered, and any attempt to stand apart was, rather, an aberration. She could manage this in Bronxville, but it was hard for her here, in the presence of her two old roommates. Mickey was always too polite when she was anxious and right now she was miserable; Georgie watched her knot her hands in her navy blue lap and envied the placid simplicity of the life she had created in an old-fashioned household where Mom stayed home so everything could run smoothly, where systems were an end in themselves and the stakes were low.

It was cruel, she thought, to lift Mickey out of her neutral living room with the rose brocade side-chairs, to tear her away from her peach bedroom and her pink eight-year-olds and the genteel discussion group and her orderly kitchen with its every surface burnished to extinction. She should be among her glistening appliances, cutting out cookies with a sugared wine glass, not here. Poor Mickey ought to be safe at home instead of barreling down the highway with two maverick roommates and a psychotic college dropout, heading for a microwaved fried platter in some unspecified motel at an hour they hadn't even fixed. She wanted to be nicer to Mickey, to make up for it, but when Mickey's conversation suffered a terminal convulsion, she leaned heavily over Georgie's shoulder, trying to read her notes. Georgie turned her clipboard protectively.

"George?"

She had been unfurling a sentence straight from these reflections; she tried to hang on to the end of it. "Mmm."

"What are you writing?"

"Nothing."

"What do you mean nothing? Everybody can see you're writing *something*."

"It's for *IN*," Georgie muttered grimly.

"I thought you already did that."

She was trying hard to hang on to her thought. "Mmm."

"On your way to a *funeral?*" When Georgie did not answer she went on, "I suppose even if it was *my* funeral . . ."

"Shit!" The end of the sentence whipped out of control and flapped in the wind, about to be torn from her grasp. "Will you shut up?" Mickey began to sniffle. "I'm sorry. Please. I have to do this."

Unfortunately, she did. She had led her life in the belief that if she could just manage to take the right steps in the right order, she could be a winner. It was embarrassing, but she had been born wanting a major success. She wanted to be known, OK, south of New York and west of Scranton, Pa., God help her, she had hit the ground running in a time when it was chic to pretend she didn't care. It was a little shameful, like admitting she wanted to be a beauty; if she managed even the semblance, she was supposed to act surprised. This old thing? It's nothing, really. Secret of my success? Garsh, I dunno. I didn't do anything to deserve this. I guess I just happened to be in the right place at the right time.

It was funny, having to dissemble, when she knew as well that the rest of the flock was ready to shun her or peck her to death if she failed. Yes she wanted to win at life. Yes it was crazy, but so was trying to get to heaven; if a person was born wanting it a person kept on running hard no matter what the outside indicators, would do this without even knowing the outcome but in the joyful expectation.

She had been this way pre-assassination, when aspirations were supposed to be unbecoming to a woman, on into the years when somebody decided women feared success—a story made up after the fact, she thought, by people explaining why they hadn't made it. She ran on, jumping higher as obstacles fell in her way, carrying her accumulating life on her shoulders because winners didn't shuck the people they loved just so they could run faster; they simply bunched their shoulders to take on the extra load and put on the gas. She did this in the conviction that there was a logic to her progress. She was either going to arrive or die trying; if she stopped running she was dead anyway. Sometimes, as today, she dreamed of retiring from competition, slipping into a peach peignoir and disappearing into a five-pound box of chocolates; she thought of getting fat; she wished for the dreams of an everyday housewife, she wished she could be like Mickey, a champ at the ordinary. She envied the manageable size of Mickey's arena, the improved odds for achievement when it was only cakes and thought with a nostalgic twinge of having girlfriends, dreaming over coffee in each other's sunny kitchens, going shopping together, fixing each other's hair; thought about it and ran on.

When they finally did stop for the night she was so intent on her typescript that she lost track of everything else. Later she gathered she had gone blind and deaf. She remembered seizing Lance's typewriter the minute they stopped and Kath opened the trunk, after which she must have made an end run for what passed for a desk in the motel room, setting herself up before Mickey came puffing in with the luggage. She had it this time, Georgie was sure. Who wouldn't love her seriocomic treatment of the girls who weren't girls any more, their diverging lives and the questions raised on the trip to the funeral? She was not ready to address the fact that it was Ralph Schwartz's funeral.

She emerged around half-past supper at some unnamed North Carolina watering hole where the asphalt shimmered in the evening heat and the sky above the parking lot was aflame with the afterglow of neon or the blush of belching factory furnaces or maybe it was the trace of a distant forest fire. Semis crashed past in stinging bursts of exhaust while beside the central swimming pool three brassy local beauties cavorted under the lights. Yes, she'd had to file her story by wire: two copies, charge to her home phone. At least it was done. She was beginning to feel improved.

Mickey sprang from the shadows by the ice machine. "There you are."

"Oh, hi Mick."

"After all this time. You took *hours*."

"Sorry. How was dinner?"

"Dinner? What dinner? I haven't had any dinner."

"Why not?"

"I've been waiting for you."

"I told you not to wait. I told you to go ahead and eat."

"All by myself? Where was I supposed to go?" Mickey's smooth hair had accordioned into tight, angry-looking kinks; her face was red and her expression clearly wounded; underneath the modest Ship'N Shore blouse her breasts were heaving. "I've been waiting forever."

"You were supposed to eat with Lance and Kath."

"I don't go where I'm not wanted."

"In the *restaurant?*"

"Oh no, not in the restaurant," Mickey said. She was trying to sound careless, but her tone betrayed her. "They had room service."

"Well, for Pete's sake, you could have gone to the restaurant."

"Not all by myself. What would people think of me?"

Georgie said, patiently, "They would *not* think you were trying to pick them up. Everybody would see you were a lady." Mickey was glaring. "Oh, right, a lady doesn't go out after dark alone. OK, you could have waited in the room."

"Not after what you said to me."

"Oh lord, did I tell you to fuck off? Oh Mickey, I'm sorry." She saw that Mickey's mouth was trembling. "I really am sorry, OK? When I'm working I don't always know what I'm saying, especially if somebody tries to talk to me. Oh look, I tell you what"—Georgie knew she had to act quickly—"let's go into town, wherever that is, and I'll treat you to dinner at whatever is the best restaurant."

After a search they ended up in an ersatz French place where Mickey brightened after they began with quiche and split a carafe of wine. Georgie gratefully ordered another because for the first time today she could forget about her assignment and relax. She could feel her knots unraveling. Mickey was flushed and smiling like a girl, and everything might have been all right if Georgie hadn't been buzzed and careless when she went to the salad bar, where, she guessed later, she must have smiled too warmly at what she supposed must have been a flattering and she believed inoffensive remark from one of the locals. What did she say back? She couldn't remember. She was not sure of the sequence that followed, what words she exchanged with the local dudes, but it ended with Mickey lurching up without dessert, brandishing her MasterCard. She dragged Georgie out of the restaurant without so much as an after-dinner mint.

"Why are we running? What's the—"

"Hurry," Mickey rasped. "Get in and start the car."

Which she did, discovering only in transit that they were being pursued by the locals from the restaurant, who were belching drunk. They looked much less bucolic in the jacked-up Buick with the bloated rear tires, which rumbled alongside them at the first light with the passengers hanging out the windows to holler and thump Ag's fenders with good-natured roars. Grinning, the beefy Romeo in front opened a face like a Smithfield ham and bellowed, "Sweetbreads!"

Mickey clutched her sleeve. "What does he mean?"

"Don't ask."

"Oh lord," Mickey said, "this is awful."

"No it isn't." Georgie rounded a corner, fast. "It's just dumb."

"Remember *Sanctuary*," Mickey gasped. "Remember the end of *Easy Rider*."

"Shut up and let me drive," said Georgie, driving like a dog with a can tied to its tail. It took a series of passes through the highway interchange to lose them, which she did with an atavistic yip. Once she was shut of them her heart lifted as it always did at petty victories, but for Mickey's sake she drove past their exit and doubled back once more, arriving at the motel flushed with success. "Well, we did it. Right?"

Mickey's face was a tragic mask. "How could you," she said in a voice trembling with reproach.

"How could I what?"

"I saw you in the restaurant. You led them on."

"Mickey, they were only hicks out for a giggle."

"We could have been killed, or worse."

"Oh Mickey, oh good lord." When she looked at her friend she saw Mickey was not pleased by their escape or even relieved by it; instead she was fuming and miserable, upset and shaken and, Georgie saw, just about to cry. "Oh Mickey I'm sorry, please don't cry."

"Leave me alone."

Inside, reinforced by the gold-chased vinyl wallpaper and the comforting Formica and the sanitized toilet seats of civilization as they knew it, Georgie tried to apologize, but Mickey locked herself into the bathroom with her laden overnight case.

Temporarily relieved of duty, Georgie called home, talking to the kids and then hanging on the line with Bill in lovelorn silence; when it got too expensive she said love and he said love; she was almost feeling strong enough to hang up when he added, "By the way, I had a call from Serena, she's rounding up Ralph's letters."

"Ralph's what?"

"His letters. Some guy at Harvard is getting out an edition. I said all we had was postcards . . . Hey, are you all right?"

"I'm fine."

"You don't sound too good."

"It's this Flinc crap," she said, and signed off quickly because the hound of hell was running at her heels tonight; she could hear his jaws snapping and it was only a matter of time before she felt his teeth. The only safe place for her was bed. She might have made her escape into sleep if Mickey hadn't emerged from the bathroom still fully dressed and *in extremis*.

"We could have been killed."

"Hardly."

"All right then, I could have died."

"I've already said I was sorry." Too tired even for a shower, Georgie shucked her clothes and slipped into pajamas while Mickey looked the other way. When she turned back Mickey was still standing there with her hair tightly curled and her oxfords neatly tied and tears streaming down her face. "Oh, Mickey, I *said* I was sorry."

Abruptly, Mickey got to the point. "I wish I had died."

"Don't be ridiculous."

To Georgie's great discomfort, Mickey elaborated. "Nobody would care if I did."

"Of course we would, we would all care terribly." She went on as best she could, attempting to escape under cover of a diversion. "You're just tired, you'll feel better when you get some sleep."

But Mickey persisted. "You wouldn't care. Kath wouldn't care and Lance certainly wouldn't care."

Georgie knew it was a losing battle, but she said, "Mickey, we would *all* feel terrible."

"Nobody would notice." To her astonishment, Mickey went on. "Not even Howard."

Howard the paragon, Howard the St. Francis of Assisi of all husbands, Georgie thought, saying with some conviction, "Howard would care most of all."

Mickey may have said, *that's what you think,* but Georgie was too tired herself to be sure. She had a hard enough time imagining that marriage as it was—Howard the aggressive businessman and shy, virginal Mickey, who was so squeamish about sex that Georgie had been surprised that she was getting married at all. Why, Mickey, she'd said, that's wonderful, at which her old friend had blushed and quoted that terrible thing from St. Paul, "It's better to marry than burn." At the time Georgie had not known whether to be depressed because that's the way she thought about sex, or tickled to know that she thought about it at all.

"I just wish," Mickey said, and did not say what she just wished.

There was still the chance she could bundle Mickey into bed and get there herself unscathed. She said, in a tone she used with the kids, "Where did you leave your jammies? We've got to get some sleep."

"I can't sleep," said Mickey, who would not be distracted or diverted from her misery. In spite of Georgie's best efforts she was dragging them both inexorably closer to her point. "You know that poem we had in English?"

"'Each man's death diminishes me.'"

"How did you know?"

"It doesn't matter, Mick," Georgie said wearily.

"Well anyway, that's just how I feel."

"Well you shouldn't," said Georgie, wishing she hadn't understood so quickly. It was easier to deal with Mickey when she could pigeonhole her as just another frustrated housewife, but in her own way Mickey was troublesome and prickly, like a little blowfish; funny as she was in some circumstances, Mickey had spikes. Now she had made them kindred and Georgie was going to have to hear her out.

Apparently aware that she had Georgie now, Mickey made her opening statement. "It's just too terrible."

So they were going to have to go through with it. Beyond exhaustion, Georgie steeled herself. "All right, what's so terrible?"

"Everything," said Mickey, whose mouth was trembling. "Just look around you. Those awful men, we brought it on ourselves, and now, look at Kath, our friend Kath Hartley, that we used to sit up and talk all night with, and that dirty young man . . ."

"He's only a kid."

"I know what he is. Well it makes me feel dirty, lying down next to their adultery," Mickey was crying. "I thought this trip was going to be so wonderful . . ."

Georgie knew better than to reach for her Pearlcorder as her second installment came tumbling out. She began carefully, "What did you think was going to happen?"

"I thought we were all going to have fun together. It was going to be even better than it used to be," Mickey said miserably. "We were all going to be happy and it was going to be so nice, just like it was at Mount Maria, except now I would be the one with the lovely home and the . . ." her voice broke, ". . . beautiful life. I was going to be just as good as you and Kath."

"But you are!"

"No, Kath is beautiful and you—you are a success."

Georgie shot her an agonized look. "That's relative."

"Well, I was going to fix it with this trip. I thought we were going to, you know, talk and laugh and have a lot of fun and we would be wonderful and I would finally have something to tell Howard about. I thought I would . . ." she sputtered and exploded, "I thought I would stop being boring!"

Georgie strangled, "You're not boring, Mick."

"Then why are you swallowing that yawn?"

"Mickey, it's been a long day. You're a lovely sweet wonderful person and everybody likes you." Mickey was shaking her head. "They do." When Mickey was herself she was serene and disapproving, a walking icon: holier-than-thou, but at the moment, contorted by self-doubt, she was funny and endearing, which made Georgie work hard trying to buck her up, to make her stop crying and feel better, which she did, finishing with a guilty start because as she accomplished this, she was already searching for the words to order and frame what was going on. With a twinge of guilt she insisted, "In fact, you're really very interesting."

Mickey wept quietly.

"You're a wonderful wife," Georgie said loyally, "and a super cook and a really wonderful mother."

Mickey sniffled. "Do you really think so?"

"Of course."

"I wish I thought so," Mickey said. "God knows I used to think so. I used to think I was so much better than you were, staying home and lighting up my hearth, so I stayed home and did that, and now none of it works. I used to think I could, you know, *do* it, but something happened, and I . . . I lost my nerve, and now my cakes always fall and the house is filling up with dirt. Last week I found a ring around the inside of my toilet tank and the kids keep bringing home gross words from school and Howard . . . Howard and I have run out of things to say to each other. And now here we are, and there is Kath . . ."

"Kath!"

"It's all part of the same thing," Mickey said, without explaining. "You let one thing slip and everything follows. If you want to know the truth, I'm scared to death."

"Everybody's scared, Mickey."

"But I'm scared of everything, I'm scared of boring Howard and the kids getting in trouble and I'm scared about my cakes . . ."

Georgie thought she saw her opening and darted for it. "Oh hell, I have trouble with my cakes."

"Well that's all right for you," Mickey said in a mixture of envy and resentment, "It isn't your whole life!"

"Oh, Mickey!"

"And now Kath is . . . now I'm so ashamed," she said in a tiny voice, "I'm ashamed of not being good at anything and I was ashamed for Ag and now I'm ashamed of Kath, and I've always envied you and Kath, which I'm ashamed of . . ."

It may have been exhaustion or the teeth of the hound of hell closing on her Achilles tendon or it may have been that the last ten minutes of this scene had been played against muffled cries of delight from the next bedroom, thumping as of heels kicked in abandon, or it may have been her own guilt or Mickey's blind and naked envy that spurred Georgie to murmur, "Come on, everybody has something they're ashamed of, I've done lots of things you don't even know about . . ." Next door Kath cried out and the hound drove her straight into the abyss, so that although she knew she had admitted *something* to Mickey she could not be absolutely certain later whether she had said this last out loud, foolishly letting out her secret just to make Mickey feel better, or whether she'd done this only in her heart: ". . . some of them with Ralph."

"Ralph!" Did Mickey actually hear and did she say it, or was she so choked by emotion that all she could manage was a guttural cry? "What?"

"Nothing." *Did she hear me? Oh my God.*

"What did you . . ."

"Ah. Ah . . ." *In extremis,* desperate George did the only thing she could think of to create a diversion, clutching her throat with a strangled "aaargh!" after which she staggered backward and crashed, poleaxed, on the nearest bed, landing hard in a hastily contrived faint.

It was much later, after she had permitted the distracted Mickey to revive her and force aspirin down her and tuck her in, after Mickey had extorted reassurances that she was not in fact dying, and was all right, and had also gone to bed; it was after Mickey had finally quit sniffling and slid, snorting, into slumber, that Georgie decided it was safe to creep into the bathroom, which she had needed to do for more than an hour. God help her, she made notes. Coming back into the velvety darkness of the bedroom, she saw a slash of light where the heavy draw-drapes failed to meet the Thermopane. She heard splashing outside and slipped between the curtains and the cold glass so she could look into the courtyard, where the lights in the little swimming pool made it glitter like a Cryst-o-Mint Life Saver. In the water two figures swam in formation, curving and playing like porpoises: Lance, who had escaped Kath's bed somehow, and one of the brassy blondes of early evening, who slipped into his embrace in a dazzling display of precision swimming, circling in the brilliant pool of light.

12

"WHAT!"

"Oh, Mrs. Kendall, is that you?"

If this was morning she had gone blind. The room was blacker than the inside of an executioner's hood. She had fallen on the telephone like a Marine on a grenade, terrified it would wake Mickey and they would have to talk some more.

"Robin Lawton."

"What time is it?"

She could see him, her gaunt erstwhile employer, hunched over the phone in the exquisitely faded jeans. Never mind the time; the moneyed lived different lives. He and Anthea would have just come in from the Palladium, or coffee at some 24-hour deli where they went to put the dust cover on the night. "Mr. Lawton?"

"I thought we ought to talk."

Still half-asleep, Georgie would not know whether she had remembered much of this conversation, or imagined it. "Did you get my column?"

"It's too early."

Georgie muttered into the darkness. "When *is* this?"

"I just wanted to take this opportunity to let you know that whatever happens, I'm behind you." He lowered his voice to a confidential mutter. "No matter what Anthea does or says."

"I wired you ten pages." Georgie was blinking hard, trying to wake up. "Did it get there? I wired it . . ." she made a deductive leap; if this was happening, it must be morning. "I wired it last night."

"This *is* last night."

"Then why are you . . ."

"I just wanted you to know I'm on your side. When push comes to shove, remember, I'm the bottom line."

It was still so dark in here that she could not for the life of her figure out the hour. "I see," said Georgie, who did not see.

"So in the crunch, which will be upon us shortly, just keep it in mind." There was a series of clicks on the line. "Anthea, is that you?"

They were cut off.

Pay no attention to that man behind the mirror.

In the morning she could not be sure how much of this was only a dream. If she'd read Robin correctly he was letting her know that he was the money and therefore the power behind the magazine, but he had been so cryptic and she'd been so drugged by sleep that could not be sure whether he'd actually said this and if he had, whether she'd remembered this right. She would give the Lawtons an hour to read her piece and have their phone conference with Peter Flinc, and then she'd call Washington. She might be able to read the truth of the Lawtons' arrangement in Anthea's comments, or in Robin's tone.

Mickey was still sleeping and so she went out into the pink early morning and sat by the swimming pool. Grimly slouched in a wet plastic deck chair, she noted the distinct quality of each piece of debris floating on the surface and the unpleasant white bits suspended in layers down to the bottom, where they merged in an impenetrable murk. The Cryst-o-Mint magic of the night was gone. The pool had lost its iridescence, like a dragonfly in death.

She was anxious to finish this with the Lawtons because she was all rough edges now because of Ralph's death and all the collisions of souls it had created, and even in the best of circumstances, she was bad at suspense. She hated not knowing, which was why she had abused her body and alienated her roommates, crashing to have this over with. Trying to please these people she didn't even like, she had snapped at poor Mickey and made her cry. Distracted by her own self-imposed deadlines, she had ignored the business of Kath and Lance, and Mickey's rising level of, what was it, guilt by association, or was it diminishment. If she had been more careful of all their feelings she wouldn't have brought on the after-dinner car chase that had finished off poor Mickey and once it was over she wouldn't have expected Mickey to rejoice because she had won. She could not have prevented Kath from bringing Lance or from making audible love in the room next to theirs but she could have found some way to keep Mickey's mind off it and so forestalled their partial moment of truth. At least, she thought, she'd talk to the Lawtons in an hour and make them settle this. Either she'd have the job or else she wouldn't have the job.

At least she'd know.

Naturally nothing was this simple. The Lawtons were so smooth they must have rehearsed. There was nothing in Robin's tone to indicate he and Georgie had talked in the middle of the night or in Anthea's to suggest she had listened in. They appreciated her quick work but it was too soon to tell anything; they needed to straighten a few things out and they would telephone her at Fulcrum Saturday morning, without fail. By then maybe she would have lined up her Forrest Fulcrum interview. *(Oh lord, did I promise them a Forrest Fulcrum interview?)* Meanwhile, Anthea said as an afterthought, would she try to find a direction for the columns, like, longterm compass points?

This meant she either had the job or else she didn't have the job. She knew better than to ask. In a way it was a relief. She had been granted temporary amnesty from orgies of composition and cryptic phone calls and entreaties to Federal Express. She could get back to her life, things like whether it was sunny out and how Kath was and if Mickey was or wasn't speaking to her today, indeed, whether Mickey had picked up or registered her foolish half-disclosure about Ralph.

If Mickey had, her face didn't offer a clue. When Georgie came away from the telephone Mickey was standing by the car with a little heap of their things, waiting for Lance to wedge

Kath's bag in among Ag's heaped belongings and throw his pack on top. Guilty and remorseful, Georgie studied her friend for signs of permanent damage, but the disassembled Mickey of the night before had vanished, to be replaced by the sunny and serene personage Mickey liked to project. Whether in celebration of surviving the night or as a concession to their entry into the southland, Mickey had decided to relax her personal dress code. She was letting the people see her in the Mount Maria sweatshirt with the pleated skirt, along with what looked like her old gym sneakers, scrubbed to extinction and touched up with white shoe polish that only ran over on the rubber here and there.

Her thin smile put Georgie on the offensive. It was too warm out for the sweatshirt, so clearly it was a statement. Georgie said, "Going native, eh?"

Mickey pushed up her sleeves with a flourish. "When in Rome, it's *suave qui peut.*" Without missing a beat she turned to Lance, saying, warmly, "Oh Lance, these things are heavier than they look. If you could just ... That's it, wonderful, many thanks. By the way George, Kath is waiting for you in the restaurant, she says we're not moving until you eat." To Georgie's astonishment, she bent over the luggage with her head tilted like a flirtatious girl.

Next to the pool the brassy blondes slathered each other with suntan oil and stretched out. As Lance closed the trunk and came around in front of the car they sat up with matched waves and fluting yoo-hoos, which he chose to ignore.

Kath was waiting at a corner table littered with crumpled paper cups and ruined cigarettes. She seemed not larger than life, exactly, but somehow denser, as if the same hand that had drawn the rest of the world had chosen to outline her in dayglo; she wasn't even moving but she seemed to smoulder. Banked fires? Georgie wondered. Whatever fueled her at the moment was as steady as it was intense. Georgie sat down. "I didn't know you smoked."

"I don't." She stared into the coal of her Virginia Slim. "You'd better eat. You look green."

"I didn't get much sleep."

"Lance and I didn't . . ."

Georgie said, carefully, "No."

"You've had a spike up your ass ever since we started. I thought maybe me having a—"

Georgie protested too fast. "Certainly not. Don't worry. Of course not. If you want to know the truth, it's about this job I'm trying to get."

"Everybody has to have something," Kath said. "Don't you think? You have this career on top of your family, and I . . . Did I tell you I'm going back to school?"

"That's wonderful."

Her voice changed. "Not soon enough."

Because their conversations were always worth more than face value, Georgie assumed the subtext. "Kath are you all right?"

"No. Yes. I'm fine. Never better. Did I tell you I'm going to get back to my poetry?"

How long had it been now? Almost twenty years. Georgie had this fear that talent was too much like physical conditioning for this kind of easy reentry. Kath was like the college athlete who quits training after Commencement; she was already too old to take up the game where she had left off. "Gee." She couldn't keep her voice steady. "That's great."

"It is, isn't it? I'm starting my *life* now. About time, don't you think?" Kath's eyes were like little whirlpools, green and set in shadows; in another minute the irises would begin to spin.

"Please be careful."

"We're in love."

"*You* are." Georgie could not bear to ask: is Lance? Instead she began gently. "Sometimes people aren't as wonderful as you think."

Kath whirled in a swift, appalling display of teeth. "He has to be!"

"Oh, Kath," Georgie said sorrowfully, "You've mashed your cup."

"Lance is everything right now. We're everything. This is my life." Abashed by the force with which she had smashed the cup down, she dropped her voice to a confessional-booth husk. "It's all I have left to be."

"That isn't true."

"Then what the hell am I?"

"You could be that poet, you're already one hell of a designer, you could get decorating jobs just by showing your house. You're strong and tough and good-looking." Kath had snapped forward with her mouth open, voracious. She trembled as if stirred by unseen winds and it was clear that whatever Georgie said next was going to be of tremendous significance to her. Georgie took a deep breath and ran out of things to say. "You're going to write again, so you really are a poet," she finished weakly, "and a child of God."

"*Manqué.*" Kath shook her head. "What I am is, getting old."

"Well *I'm* not!" They were of an age.

Kath went on in a flat, matter-of-fact tone. "So I'm either this, with Lance, or else I'm nothing. Let me lay it out for you. When I got divorced I had a choice. Was I going to be another Catholic leftover, or was I going to have a life? I happen to like screwing."

"So do I."

"Well, you still love the man you're married to. I just couldn't see me spinning out the next forty years going on shrine tours and doing the fox trot at the Catholic Singles' Club, and waiting for Barry to die so it would be OK for me to get married again. As far as I know Barry and I are still married in the eyes of God, so what was I supposed to do?"

Georgie tried to take her hands but Kath drew them back. "Please don't get hurt."

"I won't. Not me. I'm a big girl now and I'm the one that hurts people, not the other way around. I snagged at least one person's husband and I've told a lot of lies. I'm a dangerous woman, which is pretty big stuff. Lance's father almost flew in from Rangoon to reason with me; he had to lie to his father to get him not to come and now he says I have to be careful because his mother has threatened my life. One girl he promised to marry spent three weeks crying on my doorstep, every time I went out I would fall over her, all that misery, all because of me." Kath drew herself up and ran her fingers through the punk cut. She looked tough and daring and energized, surprisingly young.

"But you're going back to school. You're going to write."

"Sooner or later. In case." Kath tossed her head. "Right now I'm doing this."

"I just wish it wasn't Lance."

"Because he's too young?"

"Because I don't trust him," Georgie said flatout.

"Well neither do I, but he's mine." Kath's eyes glinted. "He's mine and we're in love and when we're in bed together we do everything you've ever heard of, that Mickey hasn't heard of, and a lot of other things even you couldn't imagine, with your good man and your good sex, and sometimes his friends come in and we do even different things. Am I shocking you?"

Georgie could not tell how much of this was true. She was distracted by a pair of red arcs on Kath's wrist. "Not yet."

Kath lifted her head in a kind of pride. "Do you know what his father calls me, and can you guess what I call him? Do you know what his friends say about me? Can you imagine what the nuns would say? What did I used to be before I turned into this, what was I anyway? Just another nice Mount Maria girl, a boring good sheep like a million other good sheep, do you think God really notices what good sheep do? If He did He would never let certain things happen, you know? Now I'm a standout." She couldn't seem to light her cigarette but she was radiant.

"Your wrist!"

"It's nothing."

"Did Lance bite you?"

"No," Kath said with an apologetic grimace. "It was me."

"Are you all right?"

"I'm fabulous, I told you. Look, I'm living in sin. Way in, and I don't care who knows. Ag, what's happening to Ag is kind of an accident, you know? You're standing on the curb and you get caught in the fallout from a wreck, but me . . . This is on purpose. I looked for this. I picked it out." Her voice dropped.

"Maybe you ought to stay away from me, George. Maybe you should get out before you catch it off me. Quick! You'd better go!"

It crossed her mind that Kath might be mad. "Don't play games."

"I mean it."

"So do I."

Kath considered for a moment. "Sorry to dump all this on you."

"Please take care."

"Mickey would never understand, but you . . . Well, unlike the rest of us you went out and amounted to something. You're *somebody*. I knew you'd . . ." She overrode Georgie's self-deprecating mumble. "I figured you'd understand. So I'm going to get into some writers' colony somewhere and try to put everything into a verse cycle, Paolo and Francesca, probably, they go to hell in concentric circles and they never get to touch, right on target, don't you think? I don't know, maybe I'm into too many things and I'll never *be* any of them, but in the meantime I get to be this fallen woman, dangerous. It may be the biggest thing I ever do."

"That isn't true."

"I'm going to make the people know I was here. So what I'm doing is, what I think I'm doing is, I'm making some kind of statement. You know?"

"I think so."

"Do you think Ag is thinking some of the same things?"

Oh, Georgie thought, relieved. Maybe it's only an intellectual position after all. "I don't know what Ag thinks."

"Remember the thing from Genet, where God was supposed to be, there was only this black hole? Well maybe I think the black hole is blacker than God is God. Does that make sense?"

So there was that hard core of absolutism; all Catholics, all four roommates possessed it to some degree but in ways that sometimes conflicted and often collided with the ordinary, or the expected, of which ways this one was Kath's. In a universe in which there was even one absolute, certain things became possible: definite blacks and whites, yesses and nos, extreme acts that were absolute in intention and swift in execution, people running out on limbs to shout into the whirlwind; was it gallantry or folly? She did not know. It might be a crazy way to behave, Georgie thought, but it was not such a bad thing to believe absolutely. It admitted certain possibilities. She grimaced. "Maybe it does."

"So that's what I'm doing, which I hope you can see . . ."

She did not add what Georgie took to be the rest: *And I hope God sees.* What Georgie did see was that at Kath's back there seemed to be large shapes moving, massing in shadows whose nature she could not divine; here in the flat morning sunlight of the ordinary motel restaurant there was something that made her want to cry aloud: Watch out! which she knew better than to do. She covered her friend's hands with both of hers, saying, "I love you, Kath."

Then Lance came in and Kath whipped in his direction like a divining rod. As Georgie watched, the haunted woman became a laughing girl, assured, sexy, all the things she wanted to be. She got up to join Lance, leaving Georgie to sit alone in the rubble of their breakfast table while she let him put both hands on her neat bottom and hurry her toward their room for one last bash before the four of them got into the car.

13

LEVELED BY FATIGUE and the rubber-stamp squalor of the next night's motel room, Georgie suffered five minutes of Mickey's muffled phone call to Bronxville before she fled into sleep. She could not have said whether it was the impoverished, monosyllabic quality of the dialog that troubled her, or Mickey's apologetic tone. "Hi kids, it's Mommy, hi, hi-ii . . . oh Howard, it's you . . . Yes, Howard. No. Because I . . . Sorry. No, fine. OK. I just. We. Uh-huh. Yes." Hunched over the receiver with her back to the room, she talked to her husband in the same tones of stifled embarrassment Mickey the sophomore used to reserve for discussions of sex. (It. The husband—uh. Blush, whuffle. That. When the man puts. You know.)

Boy, when I get old I'm not going to be like that, Georgie thought flurrily, slipping fast.

Later, in the territory between sleep and waking, she thought she heard Mickey, apologetic and uncertain, whispering into the darkness, not so much for Georgie's sake as for her own: "I never was too good on the telephone."

So that she had to rouse herself just before crashing to pull Mickey back to familiar ground. She murmured, reassuringly, "But it doesn't matter to Howard."

"No," Mickey said, moving back to one of her old vantage points. "He knows I love him." After a three-beat pause she consolidated her position, saying, "You didn't call Bill."

Beyond exhaustion, Georgie rolled over and burrowed. "I guess I didn't."

"But I guess he doesn't mind." The rest was implied: with a working wife there are a lot of things he'd had to learn not to mind. Once she had said to Kath, who duly reported it: Do you know that when she works at home she hires somebody and *shuts herself away from her own children?* In seconds Mickey's tone slid from apology to smugness. "Howard would never put up with it." The rest sat between them: the angel-on-the-hearth speech, which she no longer needed to make because by this time they both had it by heart. Mickey had always managed to make Georgie feel guilty for being a careerist. "You know, I'm a very lucky woman."

Georgie said automatically, "And Howard is a very lucky man. Good night, OK? Right, Mickey?"

When she woke somebody was scratching at the door. It could have been any time except morning. Mickey was a swaddled hump in the other bed; in spite of the little volley of taps and scratching, she slept like a stone. The sounds were subtle but urgent; at first Georgie thought it was somebody trying to get in. When she was fully awake she understood it was, rather, somebody trying to get her to come out. She slipped on the chain latch and opened the door a crack. It was Kath. "What's the matter?"

"It's Lance."

"Is he hurt?" Georgie wrapped herself in Mickey's raincoat.

"He isn't anywhere."

"How do you know?"

Kath was wild. "Because I looked."

"The restaurant."

"It's closed."

"He could be in the office, watching TV."

"But he isn't."

"The bar."

Kath's hair was electric; her eyes were dazzling in her pale face. "Don't you think I checked?"

"Maybe he went to town."

Kath's violet eyes were lined in green; she was in full makeup and naked under a red T-shirt that swept the cement. She looked wonderful. "The car's still here."

"A walk?"

"He isn't the type."

Although she knew better, Georgie said, experimentally, "The pool."

Kath shot her a look that let her know she knew. "Not this time."

"What do you want me to do?"

"I don't know. Maybe I just wanted somebody else to know."

"Oh, Kath, please don't worry, he's not worth it."

"I'm not worrying and he is worth it. I'm in love with him." Her voice faded. "I'm sorry I bothered you."

"Wherever he is, I'm sure he's all right."

"So am I." She grimaced. "I'm sorry I got you up for nothing. I guess I was just tired of being alone with it."

"What if I came over? We could watch TV."

"That's the last thing I need."

"We could pig out. Better yet, we could tie one on."

"You know you're not the type. Neither am I. But thanks."

Her smile was so taut that Georgie was reluctant to let her go. "Let me do something."

"You already have. Thanks." Kath opened Georgie's door and pushed her back inside. "Really, thanks. Now go to bed before we wake up Mickey, and whatever else you do, don't worry. I know how to take care of myself." At a look from Georgie she said, "I *do*."

Georgie did the first, but the second became impossible. Within minutes there were sounds outside the room next door: laughter, muffled conversation, giggling. Then through the wall she heard somebody blundering into the room, more laughter mingled with talk, the sound of two people hitting the bed at the same time so that it skidded across the carpet and bumped the wall. This kept Georgie awake and vigilant because she could not be certain both voices belonged to people she knew. She didn't know whether that was Lance with Kath or somebody else, whether she was having fun with some unknown partner or might rather be in danger. She strained at the darkness, alert to any warning sounds: a change in the tone or timbre of the voices, sounds of hilarity sliding into distress or merriment skidding into alarm, anything that might let her know her friend was in trouble, in which case she would have to be ready to spring up and go for help.

She slept badly if at all. She was relieved when it began to get light. She got up and dressed as soon as it was decent and escaped to the restaurant. In spite of the ravages of the night she felt surprisingly bright, almost fresh. Sitting in a corner booth, she was seized by an attack of notes. She flipped open the spiral notebook and began transcribing entire sentences that had arrived whole, mysteriously given—about Mickey, about Kath, about assumptions and what happened to them when people were wrenched out of context, about three Catholic girls in midlife, make that four Catholic girls. Then the restaurant door opened and Lance slouched in, redolent of the night before. She flipped the notebook shut and put it out of harm's way. She hailed him because, whether or not it ended badly, it seemed important to her to confront this kid whom Kath had put so much hope into and who, as nearly as Georgie could make out, had already betrayed her. Absolutes came in a wide range of shapes and sizes, from grave to minuscule; she could not be sure which this was, but she loved Kath and she was going to confront him. "Over here," she said, louder.

As soon as he spotted her his aspect changed. He tucked in his shirttail and with quick fingers raked his hair into ingenuous-looking tufts. His grin reminded her of Matty Kendall. "Hi, Georgie, are those waffles? Are they any good?"

She looked at her plate. "Waffles? Did I order these?"

"They look good."

"Do you want these?"

"Oh, no thanks. I don't do waffles."

"We need to talk."

"No problem." He slid into the seat opposite with a careless grace that argued total innocence. His gray eyes were so wide and clear that it was hard to picture him debauching in any circumstance. Without even waiting for her to ask, he cleared up the immediate matter. "Funny thing happened to me, in the middle of last night? I was all wired, you know, from spending all day jammed up in the car, so I went out running? I was following this, like, path? behind the restaurant, and the next thing I knew I was lost. It took me hours to find my way back here. It was amazing."

"You went running in the dark?"

"There was plenty of moon." He studied her for a moment and then said, carefully, "You know there is a lot going on here. I was all right, I was feeling crowded, you three are a carful, OK? I already told you I went out running because I was wired, I ran about four miles before I even noticed I was lost, and by the time I found my way back . . ." he shrugged expressively.

It seemed better not to mention Kath. She said, without explanation, "You'd better be careful."

"Just because I run around doesn't mean I don't love your friend," he said anyway.

"You'd better."

He said, in a flash, "What difference does it make?"

"If you don't understand, there's no way I can tell you."

"Who put you in charge?"

"Who told you it didn't matter?"

"What gives you the right to say what does or doesn't?"

He was so swift that she drew back to a safe distance so she could study him. Pretending to be absorbed in her waffle, cutting a wedge that she knew she would not eat, she considered him. Nothing he said or did was true. Everything was. Which was it? She did not know. Would he please hold still and if he wouldn't hold still, would he just tell her? She knew better. If she could make him out she would know how to deal with him. All she could say was, "If you step out on Kath, if you so much as think about it—"

He hit the table with the heel of his hand as if he could chop off the end of her sentence: the injured lover. "Stop that."

She said, inadvertantly, "I'm sorry."

"Probably you don't know what it's like to be beaten up every morning before breakfast."

"What?" Except for the eyes his face had gone dark, like the sky on a bad day; she became silent and waited for the rest, which came so quickly that it must have been from the heart— or else from memory.

"Or to have to steal food from the neighbors. Your friend is very, very good to me, and I . . ." He sat there testing Georgie's silence. By this time the restaurant was shot with morning sunlight and some of it seemed to slant into his irises and ricochet. "I am good to her. This is a good thing for both of us."

She tried to keep the edge off her voice. "No kidding."

"Really." The candid gray eyes fixed hers. "My mother ran out. I never even knew her."

"I thought your mother . . ." What had Kath said? Had threatened to murder her for corrupting her darling boy, and so far from home, which as she remembered it was in some foreign embassy; Kath had painted an angry, possessive family.

"Gone."

"And your father . . ." What was the story? Rangoon, she thought, and was angry with herself because she could not remember well enough to nail him with a quick question.

His face darkened. "Don't ask. Wherever he is, I hope he's satisfied." He made what seemed to be a major effort to pull himself back from despair, saying, more or less bravely, "Kath is the only one who gives one damn about me."

"And she's helping you through school . . ."

"Yeah, well." He did not meet her eyes. "I'm, ah, taking some time off."

"She said you were a student of Barry's."

"Barry?" His tone was ingenuous. "I don't know any Barry."

"Look, I don't know quite how to say this, but Kath is my friend, and I care a lot about her."

He was swift. "What makes you think I don't?"

"I mean, if you . . ."

He leaned forward with a look that fell somewhere between injured and angry. "What makes you think you know what I'm going to do? What makes you think you know anything about me?"

She did not know whether to be angry or embarrassed, because she had been caught prying. She cleared her throat. "Maybe we should order you some toast or something, I mean if you were lost for half the night . . ."

"Running," he reminded her.

She said, in spite of her best efforts, "I just wish I could be sure."

"Shut up." He hit the edge of the table with force so sudden that it knocked the skin off his knuckles. Without knowing quite how, they had arrived at a place she didn't recognize. "When you have been through one half of what I've been through, then you can come back and judge me." He was fingering a scar on his wrist; it could have been the mark of a childhood accident or left by a paternal beating; there was no way for her to know any better than Kath did whether this guy was on the level. He was watching her carefully and now he said, "My mother left me this locket, to remember her? Except for your friend, it's the only thing I have."

"Your mother?"

"I told you."

"Ran away."

"I already told you. Like zip."

"She deserted your family."

"Left us flat."

"In Rangoon."

"Rangoon?" He looked bewildered.

"You know. What Kath told me."

"What did Kath tell you?"

Exasperated, she snapped, "Will you stop sliding around?"

"Will you stop trying to nail me?"

"Logic One," she said automatically.

He grinned. "Smokescreen Two."

Looking at him like this, as if through Kath's eyes, she began to understand that it might not even matter to her friend whether he was what he pretended. He was vital and swift and he said he loved her. He was bright enough, and smooth; he might in fact be from that diplomatic background Kath believed in. Besides, he made Kath happy. Going, going ... He was handsome and graceful, slouching as he did now in the corner of the booth with a careless ease. The accent could have been genuine. Had he learned his manner at embassy parties in exotic spots or was he only a gifted mimic? Had he inherited the signet ring or did he get it from some unwitting admirer? Going ... There was no doubt he was magnetic, he had come along at the right time for her friend, who was clearly on the verge of *something* without being precisely sure what, or why she was poised there. Georgie made one last effort. "So the locket is the only thing you have left except for Kath."

"Exactly."

"And you really do love her."

"Didn't I just tell you?" The look he gave her would have melted granite. "You don't know what it's been like for me."

Gone. She was astounded to hear herself offer: "What do you want me to do?"

"Let me be what I want to," he said with dizzying speed. Bullseye. On impulse he fished into his pocket and came up with a small object which he did not let her see plainly but flashed, perhaps in a fit of generosity: apparent proof of everything he had been saying, although if she lived for another hundred years she would never know whether it was, in fact, his mother's silver locket or only a piece of chrome from the parking lot. "I can make your friend very happy, if you let me."

"I . . ."

"Hi folks." Kath slid into the booth next to Georgie, bumping her to one side with her hip. Her voice was jagged but otherwise she seemed glossy and rested, bearing no trace of the uses of the night. "Lance, babe, could you get me some coffee and aspirin from the counter?"

"For you, anything."

When he left the table she leaned toward Georgie with her head at a conspiratorial angle, talking without moving her lips. "I want to push hard today, so we can make it to Fulcrum tonight."

It occurred to Georgie that this might give her time to find the letters. Still she had to say, "Ag told me Saturday at the earliest."

Kath's words came unevenly. "I don't care what Ag told you."

"If it's that important . . ."

Lance was on his way back with coffee and some milk for himself. Georgie was so confused by the scene she had just played with him, by the long view of Lance now, young and handsome and she guessed it was ingenuous-looking, ambling dreamily through a stripe of sunlight, balancing the saucers, that she was startled by Kath's urgent whisper.

Tears stood in her friend's eyes as she finished, "These nights on the road are just too damn much for me."

Which was how they happened to approach Snowy Egret, Florida, and the Fulcrum Foundation on Friday afternoon, a full day earlier than Ag expected them. It was a little like rolling toward the Rockies over hundreds of miles of barren plains; the triangular Fulcrum tower was visible from miles away. It appeared first as a slight irregularity in the shimmering skyline; blinking, Georgie took it for a rogue cloud, or the result of a trick of light. Then it took shape, popping out of the flat Florida sand with phallic self-importance, and her heart lifted with irrational excitement; they could have been coming into the land of Oz, where nothing was real and everything was an adventure.

What had happened to Ag and Ralph here? Georgie slouched in the back, sighing. Another question. So far this trip had raised more questions than it had answered. In the long drive made longer by the fact that they could see their destination now without getting any closer, Georgie mulled this.

Ag had come with Ralph to Florida where anything could happen, with certain expectations. She would begin a new life; she could be a new person. When Ag phoned to say goodbye Georgie had actually believed she was going to turn her life around; she writhed now with remembered envy. Was it Ralph she'd envied Ag, the physical Ralph who, to her embarrassment, she still strongly remembered, or was it the fact that Ag was making a break with a man so different that he could do this with no guilt and few worries? But when she talked to Ag on the phone she understood that even with her life turned over and set on its head, Ag herself was no different. She was the same Ag, as Kath was still Kath with or without a dozen Lances, would be in spite of her best efforts.

Georgie found herself measuring this consistency to which she and her three college roommates seemed to be damned or destined against the strangely equivocal qualities of Lance, or Ralph, now that she thought of it. Lance was driving now with his elbow on the windowsill and the other hand in Kath's lap.

He could be everything Kath said he was or whatever Georgie was afraid of: a cynical paid lover or a climber, one of those clever boys who screwed their way to success, stepping on a few heads in the process; he could even be an escaped ax-murderer. Ralph had been, in his own way, as equivocal as Lance; flat-footed, four-square Georgie had always been as drawn by this as she had been put off by it. Reckless, feverish Ralph had rolled toward her the next morning and talked about their passion in the larger context of protest. It was good to give each other pleasure, he said, because love made them brave, which they had to be, to overthrow the establishment. When the old order went everybody would be happy, he told her, and besotted Georgie was ready to believe everything he said. For a while there with Ralph, she had imagined—as Ag must have imagined—guilt would fly out the window, along with responsibility.

For Ralph even after he got married, these moments were no more than that—quick passions without guilt, without consequence, wonderful while they were going on and quickly forgotten, perhaps even by the patient Serena, who must have needed to forget so she could keep on forgiving him. But *in extremis* as she was after he died, Ag had called it adultery. Georgie's heart had twisted even as she understood.

So there it was, or there they were. In spite of everything that had happened to them and everything they did to change their circumstances; in the face of fire and flood and apocalyptic happenings, she and Ag and Kath and Mickey seemed always to be the same people. She did not know whether it was who they were that made them this way, or how they had been brought up, or whether it was something about the way they looked at things that set them apart and kept them stewing, weighing everything on some eternal scale.

Was this way of being a good thing or a bad thing? Georgie was either trapped by it or she was reinforced by it. Like her three friends, she was open to extremes: good or bad, happy or miserable, guilty or not guilty; if nothing else, she thought, there was one thing about it: no matter what you did or what happened to you, you always knew who, if not what or where, you were. At least she *thought* you did. In this respect, she thought, it was not such a bad thing. It was somehow steadying to know that no matter what she and her friends did or what befell them in this bizarre setting they would each be absolutely consistent.

But they were on the ring road around the little town of Snowy Egret now, heading for the exit marked with the Fulcrum triangle.

"Well," Kath said in a shaky voice, "here we are."

Mickey sounded uncertain. "Here we are."

"Not yet," Georgie said, "it's at least four miles to the gate."

"Lance, will you step on it?"

"I don't know." Mickey covered her mouth.

"Know what?"

"If we ought to be here," Mickey said stubbornly. "I think we should get a place in town."

"That's silly."

"She told us not to come until tomorrow. I don't like going where I'm not expected."

"She's dying to see us." Kath hurried them with her voice. "Besides, Lance and I have people to see here."

"Maybe Mickey's right."

"Georgie!"

"Ag's been through a lot. She may not be ready for us."

"Of course she will," Kath said. "We're her best friends."

Mickey said, "I don't like it." They were passing a golf course complete with carts covered by triangular umbrellas and propelled by what Georgie supposed were America's movers and shakers in their playclothes. Something about the spectacle drove Mickey to tuck in her blouse and feel her hair and try to put herself together. "What if Ag's taking this time to make her peace with God and we barge in on her?"

"What do you mean, peace with God?" Kath said angrily.

"After what she did."

"Good lord, we're talking about a grand passion!"

"It's still a sin."

"Mickey!"

Georgie tried to head off the fight. "But it's over."

Mickey sighed. "And he's dead."

"At the very peak," Kath said feverishly. "That's the whole thing. To die while somebody loves you."

"She didn't die, he did." Mickey said. "And what she did was wrong."

Kath wheeled on her. "Who died and left you God?"

Mickey snapped, "You leave God out of this."

"Hey, you guys . . ."

Mickey said, "You, of all people."

"You. You're so fucking pious. You don't know anything about God."

"I am not pious and please don't use that word, I'm not used to it."

"You are so too fucking pious and I'll fucking use any fucking word I fucking want to."

"I'm not pious," Mickey wailed, "I'm only trying . . ." She reached for the rest, but it escaped her.

"Well, cut it out!"

"I'm only trying . . ." She broke off. "I'm only trying . . ."

Thinking to put her out of her misery, Georgie supplied, "Trying to be good?"

Without shame Mickey said, "That's it."

Kath flamed, "Well so am I!"

"Enough," Georgie said, but Kath grumbled and Mickey fussed. Desperate to end it, she went on in a fit of invention, "Look, I think I see Robert Redford at the eighteenth hole."

Kath: "No shit!"

Mickey: "Oh, please."

Once they had quit craning she managed to get them focused on where they were going instead of their differences, and as they passed the last of the tennis courts and the shuffleboard courts and entered the outer ring of the spiral drive, even Mickey forgot her anger. The place was gorgeously manicured, with Bermuda grass tended like a good haircut and ornamented here and there by carefully trimmed flowering bushes. It was impressive and the tower itself was impressive, triangular and simple, with terraces recessed so that at first glance its face seemed smooth and monumental.

As they turned into the second ring, heading for the center, they drove into the shadow of the building, which seemed to be too much for Mickey. "Poor Ag," she said, when what she meant was: *Poor Mickey.* "What do you think is going to happen to her?"

Kath said staunchly, "It's a good thing we're here. She never could take care of herself. It took three of us."

Georgie herself was uneasy. Trying to look out of both sides of the car at once, she said, "I hope we can help her." Ag wasn't playing tennis and she wasn't with the group next to the pool; in this sleek company their gawky friend would stick out like a broken thumb. Georgie thought with a little twinge in the belly that in this elite citadel the four of them really were intruders; she tried to step back from the other three, to set herself apart, thinking: *when I get that column.* Could an absolutist make it in the big world? Good question.

"Poor Ag," Kath said unexpectedly. "No job and now no Ralph. How is she going to make it?"

This made Georgie even more uneasy. "Maybe she can get her old job back."

Mickey began a little threnody. "Poor Ag, cut off from her home and family. What if Brendan won't forgive her?"

"Fuck Brendan."

"Kath!" Mickey was shocked. "He's her husband."

Kath snorted. "Not any more."

"In the eyes of God."

Kath showed all her teeth. "Death before dishonor."

"That's all you know."

"She can start a new life."

Where was Ag? Still no sign of her. Georgie took a deep breath. "New lives are hard to come by."

Kath was right on top of her. "They're a hell of a lot better than old ones."

"We only get one life." Mickey seemed stricken—whether by Ag's plight or Kath's determination or only their flossy surroundings, Georgie could not say. Her plump friend was fuming in the seat beside her, anxious and threatened, casting about for a way to make herself feel better, and as Georgie watched she finally hit on it, saying, tremulously, "It's a good thing Ag has us."

"That's no big deal," Georgie said in rising discomfort. If she could just spot Ag she would feel better. As they circled the building for the last time she could find no sign that their friend was even here today.

Ag was not among the sleek bodies taking drinks on the patio, which was the last place where there were people gathered; she would be easy to spot, pale and out of place among the suntans. So would all the rest of them, she thought, wondering why she had ever imagined she might be welcome here. It was a little like the entry into El Dorado: welcome to Olympus, pal. Not you, Mrs. Kendall.

At that precise moment the Datsun's muffler fell out, dragging with a roar that made at least four of the sunning celebrities stare angrily. So much for fitting in.

They had spun into the inner ring, which would fetch them up under the porte cochere. The shadow of the building was overwhelming. Something kept Georgie from looking up. "She said Ralph fell from the twentieth floor."

"Or jumped."

"Whatever. I wonder where she is."

"I don't know," Kath said. "Do you see her, Lance?"

"I don't know what she looks like."

Georgie said, "Very sad."

"Ma'am?"

"It's sad." Why was she so shaky?

Kath's voice was uneven. "It really is kind of terrible."

Mickey said, uncertainly, "It's just awful."

"You want me to park here?"

Kath was scowling at the sounds coming from underneath Ag's rusty old car. She looked ready to ditch it. "Anywhere."

Mickey said, "I hope she's glad to see us."

Georgie could hear her own breath rattling because she had taken it in sharply without even knowing it. She let it out all at once. "I hope somebody is."

14

THERE WAS NOBODY inside to greet Ag's supporters or tell them how to find her.

The cavernous lobby was empty except for detritus left by the great and the near-great: briefcases with significant initials, clipboards, manila folders, all apparently abandoned at the end of a long day at the Fulcrum conference tables. The movers and shakers were playing in the sun or, depleted by hours of heavy thought, they were in their rooms napping or getting drunk. The Fulcrum Foundation was neck-and-neck with Aspen in popularity with the international intelligentsia, with a reputation for fostering Great Thoughts in the privacy of plush surroundings. It was a first-class place, a kind of luxurious observation deck where the people at the top of the world could hang out without being interrupted or approached or even goggled at by the rest of the earth's passengers.

Deserted as it was, the place spoke of eminent visitors. In front of the main desk a display board with movable letters carried the day's menu of speakers on everything from female-bonding to bondage and discipline to nuclear responsibility. The wall above the mailboxes bulged with inept caricatures of Fulcrum faces, whom the legends identified as, among others, President and Mrs. Marcos of the Philippines and Dustin and Abbie Hoffman and the McQueens, Steve and Butterfly, to say nothing of several unfortunate Secretaries of the Interior. At the far end of the lobby, clustered around one enormous painting, were oil portraits of more eminent visitors, who seemed to include Gerald Ford and Richard Nixon as well as either Kirk Douglas or Burt Lancaster, depending; the portraitist seemed to be good at everything but faces. These were strategically placed to enhance the main event, an outsized likeness by Norman Rockwell of the founder, the august Forrest Fulcrum, who at this distance looked twice the size of J.P. Morgan and might have come from the same period. He was enthroned in a carved and gilded chair with arms that ended in lions' heads, with his fingers arranged on the manes as if he alone kept the beasts from lunging at the beholder. A three-piece pinstriped suit contained his outsized and imperious person, with the vest lashed together by more gold chains with important-looking keys than Georgie had ever seen on one human being. She recognized the Phi Beta Kappa key and something that looked Masonic and the Fulcrum triangle, but the rest were ornate and coruscated and their origins eluded her. It was both strange and logical that all this eminence should have been assembled by this powerful but strangely old-fashioned-looking figure.

Their spoor was everywhere. One chair had been plaqued in honor of Jean-Paul Sartre, who must have distinguished some long-ago conference, and the intricately patterned Persian runner that bisected the tiled floor had been donated by the late Shah of Iran, probably before the troubles. In glass-topped library cases were enshrined first-class relics of some all-time favorites: Art Buchwald's glasses and a tie once worn by Walter Cronkite, a camera that Yousuf Karsh had abandoned, a book cited in a footnote by Buckminster Fuller and a polo mallet that had been broken by the future King of England in a pickup match at Fulcrum, if the handlettered placard with the illuminated capitals was accurate. Georgie studied these objects in a confusion of emotions. She was rather more excited than intimidated by treading where they trod, which came as a surprise to her. She could not help but imagine her own notebook neatly labeled and enshrined to impress future visitors; at the same time she felt out of place here because her arrival had nothing to do with her professional standing. She was just one more Mount Maria girl here with three others to help a friend in trouble, and it was going to be hard to prove to the people at Fulcrum that she was anything more. One of the *IN* people, she had forgotten which, had perked up when she mentioned that she was coming here and she may have rashly offered to rip the lid off, but where was the lid, and how could she get a purchase on it?

At her elbow Mickey was rumbling.

"What's the matter with you?"

"I told you we should wait."

Kath's voice spiked. "I've lost track of Lance."

"He's right here."

"Not any more."

"I don't go where I'm not wanted."

"Mickey, for Pete's sake!"

"I just turned around and he was gone," Kath said. "How could he meet people so quickly?"

"But I just saw him." Georgie was arrested by an apparition in tennis whites, a sinewy Nordic blonde striding toward them. She had swimming-pool eyes and a body tanned to the color of a Moroccan camel saddle. Everything about her made the three women fall into a flurry of patting and tucking, trying to rearrange their clothes and hair and prepare faces to meet this sleek woman who so clearly belonged.

"Is that your—ah—*car* out front?"

Georgie was not going to deny anybody thrice. "Well, sort of. I'm Georgia Kendall, of the . . ."

The vision looked down her nose. ". . . other Boston newspaper."

"I'm afraid my reputation doesn't travel."

"Even so, Mr. Fulcrum keeps track of arrivals. Can I help you?" She meant: What are you doing here?

Georgie blurted, "We're here for the funeral."

"Oh, right. More of Ralph's camp-followers." Her manner slid from imperious to matey. "Welcome to the club."

"We're not . . ."

Either she had something in her eye or she was winking. "You can't fool me."

". . . his girlfriends," Georgie said anyway.

"Relax, kids. Serena knows everything. Great thinkers have great appetites."

Georgie's heart lurched. "We hardly even know him."

"I don't know him at all," Mickey grumbled.

"Everybody knows Ralph," she said.

"It's not true," Mickey protested. "I personally never even met him."

Kath began, "Have you seen . . ."

But the blonde was looking at Georgie, who was afraid she might be blushing. "Come on, we're all friends here."

This went right by Mickey and Kath, who was fixed on her own problems. "I'm looking for a young man, he came here with us?"

"This place is loaded with his exes." The steely blue eyes frisked Georgie for secrets. "So to speak, that is."

"He's about five eleven, and handsome?"

"He's nothing to me," Georgie was saying.

"Come on, you're among friends. I'm also in charge of arrangements here. You can call me Danuta."

Still Georgie persisted; for whatever reasons, she had to separate herself from the rest of Ralph's women. "We hardly knew Ralph. We're here for Ag Fitzgerald."

"Oh." Danuta cooled fast. "That one. That's why you're on the arrivals list."

"Yes. Agnes Mary Fitzgerald." Georgie let her tone slide to glacial. "She's expecting us."

"Not today she's not expecting you," Danuta said without even consulting the signout book. "She's off to Bok Tower on a journey of introspection."

"She's *what?*"

("Lance! Where the hell have you been?"

"By the pool. I met some really neat people."

"Well, the least you could do is put your shirt on."

"One is a casting director."

"Movies!"

"Well, commercials, really."

"But that's so shallow—Lance! Where . . ."

"Later.")

"Just one moment and I'll see when she's expected." Danuta made a production of flipping through the signout book. "She went with Father Frank and Sister Mary Murphy, you know, the one who almost got elected to the senate."

Mickey grred, "Nuns ought to stay out of politics."

Georgie knuckled her. "Mickey!"

"Quit that! It's true, and another thing. Who is this Father Frank anyway?"

Kath said, *sotto voce,* "For Ag's sake, I hope he's cute."

"Is that all you ever think about?"

"Will you two shut up for a minute?"

"I thought everybody knew, Father Frank is the fern poet and a noted advocate of disarmament. They are gone overnight, it says so right here in the book, there is a lovely park surrounding where some people like to stop for meditation." Danuta was looking at Mickey with curiosity; the two women might have come from different planets. "Perhaps they will be back tomorrow morning."

"Tomorrow morning!" Mickey considered this slowly; after all her wheels had ground for a few seconds she brightened. "Oh, they must be off on a retreat somewhere. Maybe he's hearing her confession."

"I beg your pardon?"

Georgie could see Mickey was about to address this matter at some length. She silenced Mickey with a look. "It's something Catholics do."

Danuta was closing the signout book: Q.E.D. "So you see, this is something of an inconvenience."

Georgie did not apologize. Next to her, Mickey stirred uncomfortably; Kath was already drifting.

Danuta said, firmly, "Perhaps tomorrow." She was tapping her fingernails on the edge of the book, apparently waiting for them to back out, scraping.

"We've come a long way," Georgie said. "If you'll show us to our rooms . . ."

"Rooms?" The swimming-pool eyes were empty. "Your rooms will not be ready until tomorrow."

"I told you we should wait."

"Shut up, Mickey."

In another decade, Mickey would have pulled on her white shortie gloves and adjusted her bandeau with the veil before departing without a murmur. As it was she was already making her manners. "Oh, we'd better come back when it's more convenient."

Georgie said, "Wait."

"I have to find Lance."

"Georgie, please, let's go."

"I said, wait."

"So if that's all I can do for you people . . ."

"I said, wait a minute." It was Danuta's tone that bothered her, Georgie decided. The arrangements chairman or tennis coach or masseuse or whatever she was had finished making hand-washing gestures over them and was already checking items off the dinner menu as if she had completely disposed of them. No, she did not like Danuta. She was also at the end of her tether. "I'm only going to do this once," she said in a new voice. She leaned both elbows on the counter. "So wait just a minute and listen."

Mickey tugged anxiously. "Please don't make a scene."

"It's OK, George, I see Lance out by the car."

"You know I hate scenes."

"Let's split while we're ahead."

She said, with force, "We're not going anywhere."

Later when they were all in Ag's room, exuding travel dust and still breathing shallowly, Georgie was surprised by how smoothly she had accomplished this. Instead of being out on the streets she had a key to Ag's room and a locker in the bathhouse and a pool pass and dining privileges; what's more some invisible functionary had moved all her luggage into Ag's room and put a cellophane-wrapped fruit basket on the table. She and her friends had keys to the adjoining double room, from which Danuta had evicted a minor philosopher to accommodate Kath and Mickey. Lance had a place in staff quarters and not only was the Datsun being repaired, they had a Fulcrum parking sticker. What had she said to accomplish this? As far as she could recall, she had maintained a low and reasonable tone throughout, but she had achieved all this somehow and now Kath was looking at her with new respect and Mickey seemed a little frightened. Where Mickey came from, women did not show anger, or threaten violence. In Mickey's world, women did not push past the official greeter and seize the telephone. What had she said? The magic words were, "St. Petersburg *Times*? Get me Andy Barnes. There's trouble at the Fulcrum Foundation." In seconds, Danuta's hand was on hers, Danuta was entreating. What had she said then, that brought Danuta to heel? "This is only the first call I'm going to make. I also have friends at NBC and the Associated Press." Danuta personally had showed them to their rooms.

"I can't believe you did that," Kath said from the door to the balcony. "Do you suppose this is where Ralph did it?"

Georgie said, modestly, "I didn't do anything."

"Much." Mickey was still quivering. "I'm not used to terrible scenes. I'm not used to hearing that kind of language."

"Oh, did I have a tantrum?"

"I can just imagine what they'd say at Mount Maria."

"When you're used to doing business, you have to do business," Georgie said grimly. "I didn't get in to see Mama Rose Kennedy by being ladylike."

"Lord." Kath slid open the glass door. "I think there's still blood in the courtyard."

"You threatened her with those specially bronzed sandals. I think they used to belong to Albert Einstein, or was it Albert Schweitzer."

Kath mused. "Not a bad way to go. It's quick and it's certain."

"Don't even fool," Georgie said in a swift aside to her friend, who seemed drawn to the prospect.

"I was never so embarrassed."

"Well, I'm sorry, Mickey."

"I think I see Lance down there by the fountain. Hey, Lance . . ."

"Kath, would you not hang over?"
"I'm just trying to get him to look up."
Georgie seized her shirttail. "You know heights make me dizzy."

Alone in Ag's room later, while she was supposed to be dressing for dinner, Georgie was gripped by another attack of notes, this one brought on by a growing sense of disparity, or difference. Until this week most of the parts of her life had somehow jigsawed with most of the other parts but now she was having a hard time fitting together some of the pieces. In the car, approaching this place, she had been as uneasy as the others; she shared a past and, she thought, the present with her roommates, but now she saw that in spite of the common memory, they were very different people. It was not that she was any better than they were, or anything more, but it was clear that like it or not, she was different. Confronted by Danuta, Mickey had dissolved; she had been brought up in a genteel tradition of, what was it? What became a lady. Poor Mickey, handicapped by white shortie gloves of the soul. But what accounted for Kath? Without being certain she thought it had to do with having to have a place to stand before you could make wide gestures. Chic, handsome Kath had been willing to back out with an apology, while Georgie had to come too far to give up easily. What made her meaner than the others? She was ready to pillage and lay waste if she had to, level entire villages—anything to secure their position. Did this have something to do with bad temper, or was it identity? What made the other two avoid confrontation while she turned into Godzilla?

Only when she heard Mickey knocking and calling did she realize she'd been so gripped by the disparity that she hadn't even tried to locate Ralph's letters. Too late now: they were expected at dinner. A lifetime of time-motion study had left her expert at systems, the natural result of having to be two or three people at once. This meant among other things that Georgie was a quick-change artist. She called "Wait a minute," and managed to shuck her old clothes for a bright dress and do everything except hairspray and eyeliner in the three minutes before the fastidious Mickey grew impatient and resumed knocking.

"Oh, Mickey, your lavalier. How lovely."

"Isn't that color kind of extreme?"

"Relax, this is Florida."

"But the *two* of you . . ." Mickey wiped her palms on her navy silk.

"What?"

"Wait till you see Kath."

Kath was magnificent. She was twanging like a tuning fork in shades of red, and something about this made Georgie want to grab her arm just to ground her before her head flared like a Fourth of July sparkler and she fizzled to extinction. In the years with Barry her own intelligence had kept her from settling, because it was Kath's misfortune to *want* without being able to figure out what it was she wanted to have, or be, or how to go after it. She'd had brief flirtations with too many things to be able to fix on any; now as nearly as Georgie could make out she was trying to move in on evil—that absolutism again; maybe she thought she could stick with this elusive or was it illusory absolute long enough to snare or achieve it. This was both so sad and so alarming that Georgie wished she knew how to warn Kath or take care of her. Because she loved her friend, she couldn't do either. She tried to think of something to say that they could both hang on to, but the elevator doors were opening; her good friend spotted the object of her attentions on the far side of the lobby, Lance hastily disengaging himself from a furtive conversation behind a pillar, and before Georgie could think of the words, much less frame them, Kath had bolted.

Georgie said, after her, "Take care," but her voice broke and in any case, Kath was moving too fast to hear her.

From a distance came sounds of combat: the forces of Fulcrum engaged in the cocktail hour. Next to her, Mickey was already fretting. "What are we going to do?"

"What do you mean?" Georgie was preparing to join the fray.

"All those people."

"Go to the party."
"But we don't know anybody."
"Give me a minute." She girded herself and moved out.

Mickey trotted at her elbow, flushed and miserable. "We don't even know if we're invited."

"Of course we're invited. Stop being a jerk."
"Promise you won't leave me."
"Relax, they're only people."

The cocktail crowd was a revelation. With one or two exceptions the great and the near-great and the merely trendy were out of shape and badly costumed; they were either pallid and ectomorphic or florid and overblown, which led Georgie to understand that the Barbies and Kens in playclothes by the pool and on the golf course must be either staff or locals imported to give the place a little glamor. This did not necessarily build her confidence as, funny-looking or not, the group looked more or less unassailable: a tangle of intersecting rings of backs. Everybody was locked in conversation with everybody else and they were all like the prisoners who have memorized the page numbers in the joke book, using code words instead of numbers to stand for entire recitals which everybody but Georgie seemed to know by heart. *Semioticism* was one popular favorite; she picked up *internecine interface* after a moment's study, along with *nuclear irresponsibility,* but it was harder to get a handle on *mutually assured reconstruction.* It was either something the semiotics guys did after they deconstructed a perfectly innocent poem or else it was what followed the mad bombers' Mutually Assured Destruction.

She found herself shuffling her credentials; it was going to take more than a bright smile and an orange dress to win her acceptance in this company, even though the dress was a favorite and she knew what she looked like in it from behind. She envied Kath, who had come here with Lance; together they formed a private corporation; apparently in love, they were unassailable. Behind her, Mickey seemed to be twice as plump as usual, clingy and already fuming with an attack of the shys, perhaps exacerbated by the fact that everybody here was at least a little bit famous for something. Georgie could cling to her friend from the old days and pretend to be engrossed, but she already knew they looked like two country mice marooned on a traffic island in the middle of big-time white water. She could die here or she could jump in and sink or swim. Mickey was tugging and hissing the way she used to at the college mixers of their girlhood, and because she could not bear to be identified with the innocence and uncertainty of her own past, Georgie took a breath and launched herself, only faintly annoyed that Mickey was actually physically hanging on to her. Fixing Danuta with a determined glare of greeting, Georgie bore down on her.

"Danuta, how nice of you to include us."

"It was nothing." Danuta briefly considered flight but duty prevailed and she prepared to deliver her opening day address, which she would follow with one duty introduction, after which she would be shut of them. "Welcome on behalf of Forrest Fulcrum and the Foundation. As you can see this is the dining room; except for dessert, service is buffet. I hope you'll enjoy your stay. We all like to make up our tables during the cocktail hour. Dinner is billed to your room number, but it is a cash bar. Enjoy yourself."

Unless she worked fast, Danuta would escape, leaving her and Mickey high, as the saying went, and dry. "Once we know a few people—"

"People," Danuta said grudgingly.

"Some people."

"Oh yes, people."

"These people," Georgie said.

"People, yes." Danuta was regarding her as if trying to decide whether the bomb squad had truly disarmed her; she might be still ticking and ready to go off. She made a quick policy decision and snaffled a likely-looking dinner partner as if to buy Georgie off; she hooked a bearded, balding troll, nailing him in midflight and pulling them into their isolated little knot. "Perhaps you'll enjoy Dr. Felix Fessenden, the leading Egyptologist."

"How do you do, I'm Georgia Kendall."

Danuta arched a brow. "She's with the other Boston newspaper."

Dr. Felix Fessenden's face was a white blank. Light refracted from thick glasses rippled over it.

Georgie was determined to make a go of this. "I'm a columnist?"

Danuta said, "She's not very well known south of . . ."

"Don't say it."

"And you . . . ?"

Georgie's question was followed by an intense silence.

Mickey stood mulishly because she never spoke until she was introduced. She had learned this from Mrs. Belmont Greenough, who used to give lessons in couth to the girls at the convent school she went to before she arrived at Mount Maria.

Dr. Fessenden's expression was hard to make out because the eyeglasses preceded him by almost an inch; they looked like the business ends of twin microscopes. Georgie tilted her head to peer in the end of one. "Hello?"

Mickey was no help.

Neither was Danuta.

Georgie peered into the ends of the glasses to see whether the good doctor was really in there. The silence was thick enough to stick to the wall. She tried the only question that occurred. "Pyramid architecture?"

Behind the glasses the doctor's eyelashes waved like undersea creatures in a hugely magnified blink.

"Mummies, perhaps," Georgie said through gritted teeth. "Danuta!"

"Dr. Fessenden's *specialité* is early hieroglyphics." Danuta pronounced the conversation dead and moved on. "I have to go and talk to Stillman Sedley."

"Who?"

"You mean you don't know?"

"Sorry." Georgie blushed.

"Stillman Sedley is the legendary ornithologist."

Danuta escaped, leaving her to cope with the stony Felix Fessenden.

"Hieroglyphics," Georgie said thoughtfully, waiting for her only contact at this entire cocktail party to say anything. When he did not, she tried something else. "Oh Mickey, isn't that interesting?"

Paralyzed, Mickey was still waiting to be introduced.

"And what are you doing here at the Foundation?" Georgie said, louder.

The sea creatures behind the heavy glasses fluttered wetly. The doctor made a grudging answer. "Hieroglyphics."

"Oh," Georgie purred, quite by accident, "you mean duck duck fish cat chicken snake river."

"Georgia, oh good grief."

Dr. Felix Fessenden did not burst out laughing. "Not precisely."

To Mickey's horror she went on, not without malice. "You mean it's more like fish moon obelisk moon moon ibis?"

"Sorry. I have to go talk to Stillman Sedley." He took off like a fly leaving a corpse.

"Stop it, everybody's looking."

"Sphinx sphinx pyramid," said Georgie, who in fact would be grateful to see that somebody *was* looking.

"Now you've ruined everything." Mickey's tone brought back all the agonies of those college mixers when the two of them spent hours on the sidelines glued like Chang and Eng, twinned by unpopularity.

She would not have it. "Or, triangle, circle, wavy lines, if you happen to be a purist."

Mickey hissed, "What are you *doing?*"

"I'm trying to have a good time at this party," Georgie barked. She would have reason to regret losing her temper, but right now she was ready to fly. "Be back. Someday I have to see."

"Wait for me."

"Can't."

"Wait!"

With a cavalier twirl of the fingers, she cribbed her exit line from Lance. "Later."

"What am I going to do?" Mickey threw up her hands like a drowning mother of two.

"Mickey honey, it's sink or swim here." With a lingering twinge of remorse, Georgie darted through a trough that had opened in the waves of the cocktail crowd and abandoned Mickey, navy silk and lavalier notwithstanding.

After which she fared better. She had a brief conversation with one of the kid interns, which gave her the confidence to mingle, at which point she discovered that nobody here really knew anybody all that well, because Fulcrum was filled with short-timers. Mickey had retreated to the shadow of an enormous urn, near enough to Kath and Lance to be able to follow them to the buffet when they got tired of staring into each other's eyes and went for provisions. Why should she feel guilty about Mickey when they had both been thrown out of the same boat? The difference was, she was managing. This was a delicate matter. In places like Fulcrum you were what you did; she had a place to launch herself from which Mickey did not. She supposed she ought to be one of those generous feminists who would double back to pick up a floundering sister, but if Mickey was floundering, whose fault was that? Mickey herself had said, in another context, "When in Rome, it's *sauve qui peut.*" Amen, Mickey.

Later she would remember with some discomfort the frailty of the apostle Peter on the night his leader was arrested, his three denials, but at the time the sequence of events was so logical as to be inexorable. First the woman next to her, a leading epidemiologist, pointed to Kath. "Who is that gorgeous woman you came in with?"

"Kath Hartley. She's my friend."

The woman Supreme Court judge struck. "What does she do?"

"She's ah . . . She's a kind of a poet."

"Have we heard of her?"

"Probably not."

"What about the fat one?"

"She isn't fat, she's . . ."

"Not another poet."

"Wife and mother," Georgie said hastily. She was embarrassed for both of them. Anxious to fish it out, she said, "I'm a columnist, in Boston?"

"Oh look, there's Dr. Martin Abend," the judge said, departing.

Maybe if she took the offensive. "Do I want to meet that woman in the pink army jacket?"

"I don't think so," the doctor said indifferently. "She isn't anybody. Excuse me, I have to talk to Stillman Sedley."

"Oh." Who was she, to compete for attention with somebody that important? It was a little like being the new kid. She could either stand here with her mouth open and her hands hanging out like the gloves on Minnie Mouse or she could act. She had pitched a tantrum at the front desk today because she had come too far to back out scraping, and she was determined to make her way tonight. She was going to have to work fast because Mickey had spotted her standing unattended and launched herself, flailing in her direction.

"George . . ."

"Excuse me," Georgie said fast, and to her eternal shame, washed her hands of Mickey, perhaps forever, saying, "I have to go and talk to Stillman Sedley."

Mickey's despairing wail would echo for the rest of her life. "Oh, Georgie!"

15

MAKING THE PLUNGE into the deep end, Georgie startled three major thinkers with her energy. "Hi, I'm Georgia Kendall, from *IN* magazine?"

She thought she heard Danuta: "But you never told us you were from an important new magazine."

"It's going to be a major publication, and they're looking for work by people like you." She could have been wearing white gloves and black patent leather tap shoes; in another era she would have been wearing a boater and spinning a cane; as it was she was all teeth, grinning. "It's like a, ah, *People,* but crossed with *The New Republic,* with maybe a touch of *The Paris Review?* Not bad company, a chance for the major thinkers to reach a wider audience?" Inspired, she was not even aware she had made this part up. "I'm here to do a story on the Fulcrum Foundation?"

Danuta pushed into the center of the circle she had gathered. "A story?"

Georgie said, carelessly, "Probably a cover."

The minute she said this, it became true. Within seconds, everything was different. She was different. People parted like the Red Sea, free drinks came, followed by Amazing Free Offers: guided tours, exclusive interviews; luminaries jockeyed for position at her elbow. At dinner she captained a corner table far removed from the Fulcrum Siberia, or was it the

Galapagos, where Kath and Mickey were seated. The conversation was dizzying; Georgie didn't know whether it was champagne or the ozone but everybody seemed brilliant. Great ideas whizzed back and forth like shuttlecocks as the Fulcrum elite played to her, floating plans to change or save the world and, until coffee and after-dinner mints, at least, convincing her that they had the means to do it. She was flanked by a humanistic physicist and a political scientist, who were joined by a neurosurgeon, a philosopher and a minor poet, all of whom gave her their home addresses with promises to look her up in Boston so they could, how did they put it? pursue the ongoing dialogue. Later she would not be able to remember a word. At the moment she had the idea that for the first time in her life she was close to the center. Her favorite phrase from any novel was, "You see, there are thirteen of us, and together we rule the world." She didn't know whether it was the *Blanc de Noir* (compliments of Danuta) or the ether or her own foolishness, but as a student waiter touched a match to the Baked Alaska and set it before her, flaming, she thought giddily that for the first time in her life she fully understood this.

Maybe she could be one of them.

Flattered and excited, taken up and twirled around by the same people who had left her adrift and flailing at the cocktail party without throwing her a rope or even a backward glance, she discovered something new. It was given to her whole, like an unexpected present: that in these circles it was not necessarily what you did but how you went about it that made the difference. If you came on like a tiger, you could be one. For the first time, everything seemed possible, even easy. This piece about Fulcrum was going to be brilliant. Peter Flinc would forget about exposing her poor friends and go for this. They would use it for the cover and make her name. It would secure the job at *IN*, all right—for openers. Once she had the luxury of choice she might prefer to take a position with Fulcrum; they would fly her back to Florida first-class as soon as they saw the piece. Naturally they would let her do her job from home. Maybe she was a little drunk.

She had lost sight of Kath and Mickey and, for the moment, her private reason for coming here, and was surprised by a complete vision of her friends standing on a deserted wharf while she waved goodbye from the decks of a glittering ocean liner as it carried her away to a new land. *I love them but I am not like them.* It was a shameful thought. This made her feel guilty.

It was also true. She was not. This both saddened her and sent her high as a kite; she was so electrified that when she finally said goodnight to her new friends and valued colleagues and let herself into Ag's room, she went to the telephone with the idea that she was going to take her life into her own hands instead of waiting around for Peter Flinc to get back to her. *IN* Magazine. Nothing but a pack of . . . Didn't they need her more than she needed them? Wasn't she a hot property? It was her turn to grasp the bull by the horns and swing it around her head and fling it wherever she bloody well wanted.

"Oh, it's you." He was not thrilled. "I'll get back after I've read it."

"Listen, I have something big for you. You said you wanted the inside stuff on Fulcrum. I have an interview with the founder tomorrow morning at nine." *You see, there are thirteen of us, and together we rule the world . . .*

He sounded distracted. "I can't talk right now. Something has come up."

She sagged. "It's the first interview he's given in forty years."

If she expected him to be pleased, tough rocks. Silence jelled.

When she could no longer stand it she said, ". . . are you still there?"

At the end of another long silence he let five words explode. "There's trouble about the column."

. . . and I'm not one of them. "What do you mean, trouble?"

"Just trouble."

Is that your dress? "What kind of trouble."

He exhaled the words: *Pah.* "Somebody else wants it."

"Like who?"

"Nobody you know," he said hastily. "It's tied up with the . . .

Never mind, OK? I just thought—forewarned is forearmed, so it's good you called. I also thought you might want to make the part about the fat friend a little stronger."

It was like being snagged in the homestretch. "I thought you said you hadn't read it."

"Well, you know."

She didn't. "Not really."

"We're not humming the same tune yet."

"I gave it everything I've got."

"Listen, if you want this job, you're going to have to give it everything you've got. We're not only talking about a cover piece. They've upped the ante on the column."

"Upped the ante?"

He rumbled modestly, "We're paying three thousand a month for the column."

Three thousand. It was like hearing the starting gun. "Tell me what you want and I'll do it."

"So listen, I'm pulling for you, but it's going to take a lot more work, OK?" He sounded hearty and false, the coach of a losing team. "Just rework that lead for me. Want you in shape for them."

"For who?"

"Just get it on the wire tonight, we're meeting in the morning."

She groaned. "Tonight. And we can settle this?"

"Call you tomorrow by noon at the latest."

Her mouth was watering uncontrollably. Her problem was, she had always been bad at suspense. Uncertainty had left her strung out, edgy and vulnerable in the way that people who have undergone emotional traumas are susceptible to illness. She could imagine her antibodies throwing in the sponge and keeling over, but she also knew she was not going to be physically sick. Worse things were waiting in the wings. She told herself she would do anything to get this over with, one way or the other. What she meant was, she would do anything to get them to tell her she had the job. She began again.

It was only after she had finished dictating the new version that she realized she was alone with nothing to do except wait for morning. Worse yet she was alone in Ag's room, where Ralph had ... it was creepy. The party was over for tonight and the intelligentsia had all retired; the Foundation was silent except for the occasional hum of the elevator floor and her own increasingly noisy breathing. She didn't know when Ag would be back or where Kath was and she didn't know what had happened to Lance. She knew where Mickey was, all right. When she cracked the door to the adjoining room she saw a swaddled lump in the bed with the covers pulled up and the head covered with one of two pillows, Mickey shutting out the world, which had always spun a little too fast for her.

It crossed her mind that Mickey might be in a sulk and faking, so she murmured, "Mickey?" Even when Georgie called louder she twitched but did not stir. With a little sigh of regret, Georgie closed the door on her.

She was afraid of being alone. To her surprise she was pacing uncontrollably, looking because she could not keep from looking for the letters. She opened drawers gingerly: Ag's dresser, sad Ag things lying in scented heaps; she was embarrassed and shut them quickly. She discovered to her chagrin that the other dresser had been emptied of Ralph's things. There was nothing left in it, not even shelf paper. This was also true of Ralph's end of the closet. If he had kept her letters here they'd been packed off with the rest of his things. She had to find and destroy them before some library scooped them up and some academic published them. She could not for the life of her imagine where Ag would have sent them. To some dim basement storeroom? Back to Serena? To his sons?

In a way she was relieved. The last thing she needed was to be discovered sitting on the bed with the incriminating evidence in her lap. In her current weakened condition it was altogether possible that she would fall on Ag's neck in a welcoming, apologetic hug and accidentally confess everything. Without them, she could go on pretending it had never happened. She wished to hell it never had. It was going to be hard enough to face Ag, whose privacy she was invading.

In absence, Ag reproached her for intruding. On the dresser Ag's Hummel figurines squinted at Georgie, cute kids in porcelain lifted straight from her desk at college, cherished over the years and set down in these unlikely surroundings in precisely the same order. Was Ag trying to cling to her old life even as she fled it or had she set them out after Ralph died in an attempt to climb back into the safety of her girlhood? In the closet Ag's assembled costumes gave conflicting messages. Here were old Ag clothes, her no-color pants suits and jumpers from her days as a wife and juvenile probation officer that would forever hold her shape in spite of frequent cleanings, drab Ag uniforms elbowing unworn and unlikely-looking Hawaiian prints and white linens, a resort wardrobe that had lost the courage of its convictions. The closet gave off a faint smell of Ag, and the neatly paired loafers and espadrilles made Georgie want to weep for her.

She deserved better, Georgie thought; Ag was one of eight children and never in her life had anything that she didn't have to share, nothing that was hers alone, not even Ralph, as it turned out. What would she do if she found out even her renegade lover was a hand-me-down? It was bad enough for Ag to have to relinquish the urn that contained Ralph to his legal widow. She did not need to know that she was not the only Mount Maria girl to be stormed off her feet by the passionate Ralph Schwartz. She was not even the first—just the one who was going to be permanently damaged. After her moment of temporary insanity with Ralph in the early Seventies, Georgie had put herself back together so smoothly that only she could detect the seams. Not Ag. Her bridges were burned and her life irretrievably altered. Ag had given up everything for her new love, only to have her life totaled, along with her lover; damn Ralph, he had always been careless. If nothing else Ag should have exclusive custody of her tragedy, Georgie thought in a certain delicacy. Was this the real reason she had to keep her secret? She wasn't sure. She only knew she had to keep it.

Spooked, she found herself at the door to the hall, only two steps ahead of a case of the screaming shakes. She had to get out of here. Maybe she needed a cigarette after all these years. Maybe she needed to smoke a carton. If she died of lung cancer, it would be no better than she deserved.

If nothing else it gave her a reason to go down to the lobby.

There were no cigarettes anywhere. The lobby was empty. Outside, the swimming pool glowed green, drawing her. Unlike the motel pool this one was clean, with reflected light casting ripples of light on the Fulcrum tower. She circled the glamorous empty pool, regarding the tiled triangles in the bottom, the design clear even at the deep end. She wondered if she would ever get a chance to swim in it. Probably not. She thought: *I am tired of hustling,* and with a sigh turned and headed back. As she crossed the deep-piled lawn she was aware of something going on in front of one of the elegant ground-floor suites that overlooked the pool. There was a swift shifting of shadows indicating movement on the balcony, a stir as of a couple disentangling, somebody slipping over the rail and crossing the lawn at an angle. It was Lance, who seemed not to see her; in the light from the pool she saw he was holding something that glinted like a piece of jewelry, and knew without having to think it through that by morning Kath would be wearing it. He was about to brush right past her when she stopped him:

"Lance!"

In a flash he turned and gave her a rough push; quick on her feet, she pushed back without even thinking. Did she hear him laughing as he caught his balance? The next thing she knew he had grabbed her and pulled her toward him like a randy eighth-grader. Unless she dodged fast and pulled loose he was going to kiss her in an assumed complicity that would compromise her forever. His very carelessness infuriated her. She brought her forearms up and out and down in a swift, hard gesture and as he yipped and let go she stepped back quickly, breathing hard.

"Who the hell *are* you . . ."

"It's me, Lance. Don't you know me?"

". . . and what do you think you're doing?"

"Who, me? I'm not doing anything."

"What's that in your hand?"

He shoved the object in his pocket. "Nothing."

"And who the hell do you think you are?" She pushed him hard.

"I told you, it's me. Now cut it out." He grabbed her wrists a little too hard but his voice seemed to say they were still friends; it was husky, wheedling. "Come on, you know me."

"No I don't!" She was shaking with anger. "I don't know you at all. I don't even know what you have in your pocket. Is that all you are? Is all you are a petty thief?"

"Think what you want."

"What were you doing on that balcony?"

He was clever. "What did it look like?"

"I don't know, that's why I'm asking."

"I was either going in or coming out."

"Well, which was it?"

"That's the trouble with you people," he said, "you always have to know."

"What's the matter with that?"

"In or out, right or wrong, black or white," The tone was meant to be light and mocking, but it had a spiteful edge. "It's always got to be here or there with you people, you'd think life was some kind of equation that you could solve it and get it over with." In spite of himself, he sounded angry. "What is it with you people anyway?"

"If you don't know, I certainly can't tell you."

"Well, lay back a little. Give me a break," he said angrily. "Why can't you just go with the flow?"

She barked: "Because that would be quitting. When Kath hears—"

He gave her wrists a painful wrench and then let go, saying in a low voice: "Nothing you say is going to surprise her."

Then he turned, and without even bothering to see whether she was watching, sauntered back to the balcony. He was making it clear that he didn't care whether she saw, or whether she told Kath; he was going to go on doing whatever he had been doing. Tomorrow he would smile and present himself, the lovable, brand-new kid whose face was not marked by guilt or fatigue, who bore no traces of the night before. Was he forever innocent because nothing he did had any meaning? Was he one of a new elite that never had to think about consequences? Maybe there really was a separate moral continuum in which there were no rights and wrongs, no blacks and whites, there was only being, and maybe people like Lance really did live there, no problem. What had he been doing there in the dark, and with whom, and what was he playing at?

She was not surprised to find Kath waiting for her in Ag's room. Her makeup was gone; her hair was a mess and she was drawn and shaking, huddled in the chair with her arms ringing her knees and her bare feet drawn up on the plastic upholstery. She greeted Georgie with a shaky grin. "Sorry to bother you. Mick's asleep and I just couldn't go in there."

"Lord, I'm glad to see you." Georgie saw no need to dissemble. "It's about Lance, right?"

"He's out with somebody. Or something."

"I saw him."

"You saw him?"

"Down by the swimming pool. He was . . ." Georgie swallowed it.

"It's OK, you don't have to spare me. He met this talent agent, a woman, she wanted us to do a trio and I just . . . Blame it on my convent upbringing."

So much for Kath's wilder claims to scarlet womanhood. Georgie said drily, "I told you it would come in handy."

"I personally could do without it. Signposts on everything. Wow, good. Watch it, this is *bad*. Didn't you ever want to be some kind of heathen so you wouldn't have to think about these things?

"Right. We could go live in a nice gray area, where we could be safe." It was an old conversation without much possibility for development because they weren't, and they could not. "Look, can I send down and get us a drink? We could get plotzed and wait for Ag."

But Kath had quit smiling. "Oh George, we just got here and I'm already losing him."

"You would be mad if I said good riddance."

"I can't . . . Ah." Kath's breath shuddered. "Right now I can't do without him."

"But he's a—"

"I don't care, I have to have him."

Loyal Georgie spoke without thinking. "Then you'd better go after him." Horrified at what she had just suggested, she said, "No. Wait. That's probably a terrible mistake. I want you to be happy, Kath. Maybe you should have a showdown."

But Kath had seized on it, brightening. "Do you really think I could get him back?"

Kath was wild, driven; because she loved her, Georgie would say anything to buck her up. "You can do anything you want."

Kath's eyes blazed. "I don't know why this is so important."

"I don't either, but since it is, you'd better use Ag's Chanel."

Tears had pulled Kath's eyelashes into starry spikes. Her eyes were so bright Georgie had to look away. "Oh God, I look a mess."

"You look wonderful." The red dress was a little forlorn, but with the right accessories, they could probably fix it up. Georgie rummaged in her overnight case.

"I know it's dumb, but if I can't do this . . ." Kath's voice was squeezed by compressed emotion. "If I can't do this . . ."

"Shh. Shh. Where's your purse? You need lipstick. Wait, you can take mine."

Kath was fixed on some inner self, struggling with an agency Georgie could not see. Finally she pulled out the right words, saying, with passion, "If I can't do this I can't do anything."

Georgie still thought Lance was a bad ticket, but Kath was so unhappy that she said, "Sit down and let me fix your hair."

Kath bowed her head. How many times had they sat this way in the old days, Georgie working magic with Kath's curls so they could knock the socks off the bright college kids waiting for them in the Mount Maria parlor, promising, magnetic new guys? Together, they had made quite a team; getting ready for those evenings they had fixed each other's hair; they used to wear each other's clothes. She was not doing this for Lance, she thought. She was doing it for Kath. Submitting to the comb now, Kath was not so much returning to that shared past as trying to gain confidence from it, which Georgie understood as she finished with the hair and fished in the closet for something she remembered seeing among Ag's things.

"Here. Ag's cashmere stole. You can wear my silver chain." Kath looked as fresh as if she had just gotten out of the shower. She was brilliant. "Am I all right?"

"You're wonderful." She had a visionary look that would have been more appropriate to one of the Round Table setting off on a quest. What if she got down there and she couldn't find Lance? That would not be so bad. What if she got down there and found him with somebody else, and what if he laughed at her, or sent her away? Georgie already knew that was a possibility; deciding to go after him, Kath knew this. What if . . . Georgie could not imagine the other alternatives, nor would it make much difference if she could. Nothing was going to stop Kath. Conscience spurred her to add, "You know this is dumb."

"Yes I know this is dumb." The glow from Kath's eyes illumined her face; she could have been lighted from within. She seemed larger than life; she was trembling, with a passion that Georgie could see was not necessarily sexual, which might have been a first indication that there was something else going on here, or something more. All her life Kath had wanted to be something out of the ordinary, vivid, somebody special; all her life she had *wanted,* without being able to say precisely what. Looking at her now, Georgie realized that the thing her friend was rushing out to meet might not be what she thought. Kath was poised now, tremulous. "Wish me luck?"

"Love," Georgie said instead, as the door closed on her.

Even though it was close to three A.M. there was somebody coming in: Ag Fitzgerald, who flipped on the light without even noticing that she was not alone. She bent over the lock with the fatigued grace of a woman pushed beyond the limit, perhaps ready to quit being cheery and brave. It was time to quit keeping a stiff upper lip for the sake of her comforters; she probably wanted nothing more than to do what she had been waiting to do since she got up that morning: to let down and cry here in the privacy of her room. Ag's fair Irish skin was so thin that all the blue veins were showing just beneath the surface; every line in her body drooped. Georgie felt guilty for seeing. Ag had the right to expect privacy. She cleared her throat.

Ag jumped and whirled. "What are you . . ."

"Here early. I'm so sorry." Ag was looking at her in such resentment that Georgie stumbled over her words. "Pretend I didn't get here too soon. Pretend I'm asleep. We can talk in the morning."

"It's OK." Backing into a straight chair, Ag tilted her head at a strangely artificial angle; she could have been miming attentiveness. "If you want me to stay up and talk to you, I'll stay up and talk to you."

"Are you all right?"

Ag shook her head but she said, "I'm fine."

"Let's go to bed, OK? We don't have to do this."

"No. I want to. Really." Ag's skin was transparent, stretched by exhaustion. "If you want to talk to me, go ahead and talk to me. I'm, ah, I'm trying to do a lot of hard things. It's one of the forms this thing is taking."

"I said I was sorry. The desk put me in here."

"It's OK. Really. It isn't you. I just mean, doing things I don't happen to feel like . . ." She finished as if she had explained everything. "It's what I need right now."

"Are you sure you're all right?"

"Couldn't be better. Working it out. This is part of it."

"Part of what?"

"It." Ag reached into the cathechism of their childhood and brought up the next thing whole, as if it did not so much explain as justify. "Temporal punishment."

"Ag!"

She seemed desperate to explain. "You know. Partial reparation. Right now it's the only thing that makes any sense."

"You're trying to—atone?"

Ag nodded.

"This awful thing happened to you and you think you have to make up for it? Ag, it doesn't make any sense."

"Wrong," Ag said. "It makes the only sense. It's going to take me the rest of my life to make up for this."

"Don't do this to yourself."

Weary as she was, Ag drew herself up, taking Georgie's hands in a kind of dignity that she found painfully touching. "I don't have any choice. Oh George, Brendan is taking the children."

"He wouldn't. He can't!"

"Right now it would serve me right."

"Losing the only thing you have?"

Ag managed a strange smile. "It's the worst thing I can think of. So probably it's right."

"That's crazy. All you did was fall in love with the wrong person."

"I took him away from his wife."

"You were only trying to be happy."

"Well, that was wrong. And that's not the worst thing about me." Ag grimaced. "Really bad."

Georgie was angry now, "Is that what that stupid priest told you? That you're bad?"

"What priest?"

"That Father Frank you signed out with. The one you took to Bok Tower. Did he lay some kind of trip on you?"

"Oh him. The fern poet. No, Father Frank isn't like that at all. He said God loved me and I had to love myself because I was one of His creations, you know. That stuff. Well, I don't think God even likes me, after what I did."

"You think you know better than this priest?"

"He's also a poet. Soft at the center," Ag said. "I'm OK, you're OK. That kind of stuff. I'm afraid Father Frank is just another Father Feelgood."

"If he says God wants you to be happy, he's right."

Ag's jaw seemed to get longer; all the muscles twitched in disapproval. "You've quit believing in last things?"

"I think life is longer than you think it is."

"Even God gets sick of handing out last chances." Ag spoke wearily, in a tone Georgie recognized. It came out of the same grim fixation that had sent her out running at dawn all one whole terrible winter at college, trying to make up for failing chem by conquering track; she had run hard, right into the pneumonia and a collapsed lung that forcibly removed her from competition. At the time Georgie had the idea that Ag was grateful to have that burden lifted; she had blossomed, aced chemistry. If she'd learned anything from that, she had forgotten it. She said morosely, "I've had my fun. Now it's time to pay."

"I don't understand."

"You know as well I do. We're talking about sin and punishment."

"I thought being sorry was supposed to be enough." Georgie studied Ag's face, which did not soften. She tried again. "Being sorry and then just going on."

"How could you understand?" Ag said in a light, dry voice. "You don't have anything to make up for because you aren't the one."

It was like being punched in the gut. Georgie swallowed.

"Look, Ag, you have to forgive yourself, everybody else has."

Ag's eyes squeezed tight, in spite of which the tears seeped. "I can't."

"Shh. Don't do this to yourself, you didn't do anything so terrible. You just fell in love with the wrong person. Is that such an awful thing? You just got caught trying to be happy."

"You don't know everything. What I—"

"That doesn't matter. It's over. You're sorry. That should be enough."

"Well, it isn't enough." Ag pulled away from Georgie, so rigid that she might have been turned into wood; her cheekbones could have been carved by an Indian making a primitive statue of an angel for a Spanish mission anywhere between here and Peru. It was if everything about her was fixed, her future precast. Now she laid it out. "I'm going to make up for what I did. I'm going to make up for it if it takes the rest of my life." She went on with a brave little smile. "And if God wants Brendan to take the children, then I guess Brendan is going to get the children."

"Ag, listen," Georgie began, trying to frame some mitigating thing, anything to soften Ag's penitential compulsion. "Maybe God doesn't want . . ."

Then Ag turned on her with her eyes glittering with anger

and to Georgie's chagrin she flashed, "What makes you think you know what God wants?"

"I don't know what God wants, I . . ." Georgie faltered.

"I'll tell you what God wants," Ag said. "Everything."

When Georgie was able to go on it was in a voice so fragile that it frightened her. "I can't talk about this any more, Ag. I've got to go to the bathroom now. So goodnight, and I'll see you in the morning, OK?"

Everything. Maybe Ag was right. An absolute God demanded absolute responses. Saints thought this way, and certain visionaries. Everybody who mattered was to some degree and in some way an extremist. Long after Georgie retreated to bed, mulling this, she could hear Ag's wooden beads rattling; not against her teeth, as of old, but in a steady progression through her fingers. Even in the dark Georgie knew her old friend was kneeling with her back straight, without even resting her elbows on the bed, finishing a rosary.

16

IN THE MORNING it was as if none of this had happened. When Georgie finished dressing and came out of the bathroom Ag was composed in a chair by the window in an outrageous embroidered peach nightie conceived on a trousseau scale that was completely at odds with Ag's rawboned and strangely unused-looking body. She had combed her thick, wiry red hair and touched her pale cheeks with powder and she was serenely studying a scrapbook Georgie recognized as Ralph's. With her head angled and her orange hair falling just that way, with the morning light on her bony, freckled shoulders, she was less the grim penitent than the fervent Agnes Mary of their girlhood, the dreamer whose romantic expectations had always outstripped her.

She was like a girl with her highschool yearbook, flushed and almost pretty. "This is Ralph's. It's like having him here. Well, sort of."

Georgie could feel her molars colliding. "I see."

"I love finding out what he was like."

The scrapbook dated from the Cambodia protest; Georgie herself had picked out the oversized red leatherette number with the black tassels, which still bulged with the memorabilia of Ralph's peace campaign. What had they thought they were doing, back then in the loft in the Sixties which, paradoxically, or was it characteristically, spun themselves out in the Seventies? They had brought leaflets and clippings and blurred snapshots and hastily lettered placards for Ralph to label and enshrine in the book, a makeshift time capsule for the unknown future. They had added missives from the White House, a button ripped from a police uniform, crumpled pamphlets, pasting them in like sober acolytes assembling relics of a dying civilization. Hundreds of years from now archaeologists could find this object in the postatomic rubble and know that somebody, at least, had fought to prevent the ruin of this planet. They had added verse by Daniel Berrigan and copies of Ralph's letters to the Joint Chiefs and even cloth armbands stenciled with clenched fists, one red, one black; the tag-ends of cotton still dangled from the scrapbook.

They were all so young they had imagined such gestures were for the ages, Georgie thought: *poor kids*. Yes she was one of them. They had believed they could do something final and magnificent and never have to look back. There was a sweet gravity to their extravagance, the solemnity of last times. It was, she supposed, the last time she had ever done anything with that kind of certitude. She had done all this before she was old enough to understand that life was not anything you could resolve or mark indelibly; instead of ending dramatically or artistically, it went on and on and on. Seeing the armbands dangling from the scrapbook now, Georgie quickened, which startled her. She hadn't been with Bill since Saturday. She remembered with a gulp that with Bill gone for six months, she had turned to Ralph, who found her ravenous, and to her enduring embarrassment, without reservations. She had probably wanted Ralph more than he did her. In spite of everything she'd told herself about that moment since, about susceptibility and coercion, about lack of free will or foreknowledge, or even about the significance of political gestures, she had in fact only been weak and foolish. And Ralph? What had Ralph been? Whatever it was, he was dead.

Unless she was very careful she was going to start crying right here in front of Ag. Why wasn't anything ever really over? If you were expected to do or judge things absolutely, she thought, then it would be absolutely fair for certain things eventually to be absolutely over, but after all these years here was Ralph's scrapbook, which came complete with that full physical memory of Ralph.

"What's the matter?"

"What?"

Ag said, "You look funny."

"I was just thinking about Ralph."

Her old friend's raw smile bared her teeth. "You don't know anything about Ralph."

"No, I don't," she lied, for Ag's sake, as she had lied all these years for Bill's.

Ag said, unexpectedly, "You know the shot heard round the world?"

"You don't need to tell me."

"No," Ag brightened. "No kidding."

"You don't need to tell me anything."

"No, really. That was the whole thing. The first shot fired. Ever. It was Ralph."

"You mean . . ." Georgie thought: *she couldn't possibly mean what I think.*

But she did. "There was nothing with Brendan. Nothing," Ag said.

"Really?"

Ag nodded, abashed.

In a hushed voice, Georgie said, "Oh wow." This came as a shock. It was like discovering that Ag had been blind or deaf from birth: you wouldn't know it to look at me, but . . .

"It's OK." Ag's blush made Georgie blush. "We made up for it."

"Ag, no wonder!" She had known Ag was starved for love; before, during and after her marriage to Brendan she had been hungry for romance—which turned out not to be all; poor Ag had so many reasons for running away with Ralph that Georgie felt the world owed her an apology instead of the other way around, while she, Georgie, had been given so much that it made her anxious, in spite of which she had betrayed Bill with Ralph. The contrast only made it worse. Ag had *reasons*. What was her excuse?

"And more." Ag was pink as a girl home from her first prom. "I'm just so sorry." *Bill I am so sorry.*

Ag said, brokenly, "So I just don't know how I am going to live without him, is all. Having him here. His hands."

Georgie knew about Ralph's hands. "Don't!" This came out on such a sharp note that she had to dissemble. "You're only making it harder."

"It's one way of keeping him alive. Let me tell you." Ag was puzzled. "Don't you want to know?"

"I don't think so."

"Let me just tell you how he made me feel," Ag said anyway. "For once I felt beautiful, he made me feel proud of myself for once. He would hand me into cars like Elizabeth Taylor or the Kohinoor diamond, it was like being put down in velvet when he . . . every time."

Raising her hands, Georgie wasn't sure what she was trying to forestall. "You don't have to tell me if you don't want to."

"Yes I do," Ag said, and began. "What else do I have left to do? Imagine, me and Ralph Schwartz, who used to get written up in *Time*. I bet you were surprised when I called and told you we were running away."

Surprised was only one of the things Georgie had been. "I was so scared you would get hurt."

"Oh, hurt," Ag said absently. "Hurt is nothing when you have what we had. You probably didn't even know I knew Ralph."

"Not really," Georgie said with an unnerving flash of jealousy.

"Well I didn't, until just this spring. I met him at a, you know, Rutgers faculty party? It was at one of those horrible houses where they have figured carpets to hide the food stains, and they still have the bookshelves propped up with bricks," said Ag, whose house was more or less upholstered in middle-class velvets and brocades. "This guy was in the psych department and he was trying to get tenure, which meant he had invited everybody he thought could help his case plus his friends plus me and Brendan, the place was jammed."

"Where did you meet him?"

"Ralph?"

"No, this guy from Rutgers."

"Oh, I was helping him with his research project: bonding among probation officers, you know the kind of things professors do when they're trying to get in touch with the world." For the moment, Ag had given herself to time travel; she was escaping her troubles in the recent past. "I answered a lot of his questions and let him meet some of the kids I see. I even took a Rorschach test for him. I guess he figured he owed me one, so he invited me to this party at his place. I had to drag Brendan. I told him there would be lots of new women. I laid it on thick."

"I never liked Brendan," Georgie said reflexively.

"Well, Brendan never liked you," Ag said, completing the old exchange. "So anyway, this guy from Rutgers was nice enough, but I guess he had been in graduate school so long he'd forgotten what grownups did. I mean, it was really tacky, they had Pepperidge Farm Goldfish and this ghastly vodka punch, everybody there was drunk." She blushed again. "I suppose I was drunk."

Georgie was quick to assure her. "That must have been it."

"No, that wasn't it. It was love at first sight."

"I see."

"Brendan tried to leave as soon as we got in the door," Ag said. "He was fit to be tied."

"Brendan!"

"Oh, he was fine as soon as he got drunk. I lost him after the first drink. Woman dance instructor. Leotard with a skirt over, dirty neck, you know the rest. So I wormed my way along to the kitchen, where everybody was hanging over the punch table talking about I think it was Kierkegaard, and I ran into this guy ... This guy! He didn't look like much, except he looked familiar? I only saw him that one time, at your first apartment?"

Georgie quailed. "While Bill was away ..."

"He was helping you finish an article."

"Right!"

"So I either recognized him from then or from that picture in *Time*, but there I was and there he was, this philosopher you used to know that went on to get big and famous with that crazy book, to think I met him at your house . . ."

"I guess you did." Georgie said unevenly. It was right before or right after her mistake with Ralph, probably immediately before, which would be why she'd found it necessary to say that about the article; she remembered being surprised that she needed a story to tell the virginal Ag. She'd kept explaining he was a professional friend, harped on it because there was already something in the air: intimations of immorality, she thought, and winced.

"Same guy, but he didn't used to be so *thin*. Or *sad*."

"Ineffable sadness. It was part of his pitch."

"What?"

"Nothing." There was no point in telling Ag she knew Ralph's old number too well. As it turned out she did not know this number. "So you asked, didn't you know him from somewhere."

"And he said, right, didn't he know me?"

"Imagine." Georgie forebore asking whether he had mentioned her. "So you got to talking."

"And he said this extraordinary thing."

"I suppose he told you his wife didn't understand him."

Ag was shaking her head. "No, he said he didn't understand her. No. I take it back. He said . . ." She blushed. "I can't tell you what he said, oh George, he has the most beautiful hair. I mean, had."

"I'm sorry."

"He was just standing there, twirling his hair on his finger, telling me this, and I couldn't stop watching the hair and I couldn't stop thinking about his fingers, and oh gosh, George I was feeling these things I never felt . . ."

Georgie said, thoughtfully, "That's the saddest part."

"It wasn't so bad, I didn't know." Ag was red to the roots of her red hair. "So I'm standing there with this strange famous philosopher that I hardly know and he's telling me . . . I can't tell you what, it's too . . . and I'm just watching the fingers and the hair, and the hair and the fingers and feeling this . . . and all of a sudden he says this . . ." She blurted, "What he said was, how am I going to put this. He had, you know, certain things had quit working for him. No. That isn't it. I mean, that isn't all. He said there was a place people got to, but there was this big zero in his life and he'd forgotten how to get there, or he couldn't, at least that's what I thought he was saying, you know philosophers, they're so *abstract,* but I got the idea that the love of a good woman could save him, can I help it if I thought I was the one? This is all in this smoky, crowded kitchen with everybody hanging over that rotten punch, I had on my blue jersey dress that matches my eyes . . ." She stopped for a moment, looking beyond Georgie. "I don't remember what came in between exactly, all I remember was R—" she gulped air "—Ralph saying no power on earth could help him now, and I just knew I could, I could not stop watching the hair and the fingers, the fingers in the hair, and then good Lord I said, oh my God, Georgie, do you know what I said? I said that's what you think, and then . . . oh wow, do you know what I did?"

"Ag, maybe you'd better not . . ."

But she was launched. "I up and grabbed him, I grabbed Ralph Schwartz, this leading intellectual and I dragged him around the corner into this kind of ell that was under the stairs? It's March out, I mean early spring, but it's one of those crazy warm nights and so we start something under the stairs that we can't in any way finish, not in this coatroom with people ready to barge in looking for their galoshes, but I am wild and he is wild, we have to finish it, and I am feeling, never mind what I am feeling, but Ralph is feeling . . . never mind what he is feeling all he says to me is I don't know who you are or what you're doing here but you're my saving grace, baby, my saving . . ." Her voice broke. "Saving! Look what I did to him!"

"Ag, don't torture yourself, you were—"

"I ruined him."

"Unless it was the other way around."

Ag did not even hear. "Oh Georgie, what he did was, we grabbed coats and went outside and I . . ." She gasped and, with a tremendous effort, managed to finish. "He took me into the garden. We both went." She was blushing violently by this time, and she put her hands to her midsection, gripped.

"Into this psych professor's garden," Georgie said helpfully.

"No no," Ag said impatiently. "You know what I mean. He took me somewhere I had never been. Don't you get it, I was there! In spades. In spades hearts and clubs, if you want to know the truth. It was like walking out of a dictionary into Cinerama, you had all the words and now finally you knew what they meant. Ralph said he couldn't live without me and I believed him, which is how . . ." She tried and failed to make her voice light. "Which is how we ended up down here. Which is how Ralph ended up . . ."

"Shh, shh."

There was a moment of silence while Ag pulled herself together and then smiled at Georgie through her tears. "So that was our story, more or less . . . It was amazing, oh hell, if it hadn't shaken down the way it did we would still be living in sin, OK, why beat around the bush, we would probably be in here right now in the bed, you would just have to leave, so it wasn't his mind I fell for, it was . . . me, Mary Agnes Flaherty Fitzgerald, can you imagine?"

"Shh. Yes. Of course I can."

Ag's eyes were wide with astonishment. "Imagine, convent girl me, turning into a sex pistol."

Convent girl. This was the second time one of her friends had used this, as combined context and self-accusation, or jumping-off place, or something more. It was complicated but she did not have the leisure to consider it. "I always said you had hidden fires."

"He said I made him feel just like a teenager, and I . . ." Ag burst out, "I loved it. I loved it all. I loved every minute of it. Does that make me a terrible person?"

Georgie was close to tears. "No," she said. "That doesn't make you terrible at all."

"I wish I didn't feel so damn *guilty,*" Ag said.

"Shh. Shh. We're just not used to these things," Georgie thought with a wrench of their different circumstances; *oh Bill!* As Ag talked on it got mixed up in her head—Ag's details, hers,

Ralph's words, some of them familiar, the way Ralph touched. Poor Ag could not be blamed, she thought, Ag with the prophetic wallflower droop and the inevitable bad marriage to that rat, while Georgie had walked away from *Bill,* for God's sake, whom she loved beyond expressing it, did this because she wanted him and he was not around; she had loved and been loved and betrayed her lover anyway. She wanted to end the flood of memory, to erase Ralph, but Ag was numbering details as if the simple accumulation would call Ralph up and recreate him here in the room today. "It's going to be easier if you try to forget."

"Are you kidding? This is *Ralph.*"

"I, ah." Georgie was squinting with concentration. She wanted to do this as gently as possible, not to hurt Ag but to help her, disassembling Ralph. If they could just do this together, maybe they could both put him away. She said, carefully, "You know there were other women."

"But I was the last!"

Georgie tried to move slowly. "The thing is, he, ah . . . He might not be as wonderful as you think."

"You." Ag raked her with furious Irish eyes. "What makes you so smart?"

Georgie faltered. Did Ag know? Had she guessed? "I was only trying to help."

"Well, cut it out!" Ag was studying her. "What makes you think you know anything about me and Ralph?" She probed. "What makes you think you know anything about Ralph?"

"Nothing!" Had Ralph told Ag anything? Had she found the letters? Georgie did not know. Watching Ag's face for signs, she went on carefully, "I just don't want you to feel guilty about something that isn't your fault."

"Not guilty? Me?" Apparently Ag did not know anything, except what Ralph had so cruelly pointed out right before he dropped: she was a Catholic girl, who would perforce take everything too hard. "Who, me? Who do you think killed him, Forrest Fulcrum?"

"Nobody killed him, he did it to himself."

"Oh come on, Georgie, how do you think he got out on that ledge?" Ag went on miserably. "We were so happy, and then I . . . When we ran away I told myself we were going to get married sooner or later, find grounds for annulment somehow, something that would make it possible, but I knew better. The end never justifies the means, isn't that what we learned in logic class? What I was trying to do—I was trying to make something beautiful out of what I did, when what I did was wrong."

"Don't be so sure it was all your doing."

"At the party? Of course it was. I grabbed him and he fell."

"Ralph doesn't fall," Georgie said without hearing what she was saying until it was out. "Other people do."

Fortunately Ag was too intent on her own version to hear. "Fell for me. Fell out the window, too. The whole thing was my fault. If I hadn't gone after him at the party Ralph would still be safe in New Brunswick. Imagine, me, that couldn't get a man to look at me in college, Ag Fitzgerald, *nouveau* home-wrecker, I got away with the great Ralph Schwartz. The trouble was, after we got here and unpacked, after we drank the champagne they left in our room and finished up the fruit basket, after I figured out what I was doing, I started crying. I just started crying and I couldn't stop." The scrapbook began to slide from her knees. Georgie caught it and put it back. "Is it terribly *Catholic* to want to make wrong things right?"

"Oh God Ag, I don't know."

"I knew running away with Ralph was wrong. I was just so dumb I kept thinking it didn't have to be, I could find some way to make it all right. We started having these . . . *discussions,* how, did we have grounds for annulment. I had this crazy idea we could erase Serena *and* Brendan, so we could get married in the church, Ralph doesn't even *believe* in the church, but there I was . . . I don't even know who I thought was going to annul us, so you can easily see how I brought it on. Him planning to jump, or not to jump. Poor Ralph, I guess I made him desperate. One minute we were just talking and the next . . . the next, he was out there on the rail, hanging by a thread. I think he would have jumped even if the damned thing hadn't snapped."

"What thing?"

"Do you believe it was the belt loop to his robe? He had his bathrobe cord looped around the pillar to the balcony, so he could lean out a little, and not fall?

"Ralph always did have a flair." In his early days as an instructor he had set fire to his coat in class just to make a point.

"There he was hanging by this bathrobe cord, Serena must have used thread when she fixed the belt loop, instead of button twist? I think he was going to make a speech after he had everyone's attention, maybe he thought they would spread a net or the cops would come or George McGovern would beg him to come in but while he had them all looking, he was going to make this speech . . ." Her voice broke. ". . . before he jumped."

"If he jumped. Oh hell, maybe he accidentally committed suicide."

Ag said, morosely, "Maybe he wanted to."

In a reckless desire to be helpful, Georgie dropped her guard. "Ralph was much too self-indulgent to jump." She rushed on headlong, still dissembling. "I mean, he looked like the kind of person who would do anything to keep from getting hurt."

Ag did not pick up on this, but she did brighten a little. "I guess the man did love a show. Anyway, he got out there and the people in the courtyard noticed him, Jesse Jackson was down there, if it hadn't snapped he might have talked him down; Joe Namath was there and I think I told you, Henry Kissinger, everybody who was anybody was down there and when they finally saw him, they all started running around. I was in here crying and begging him to get down off the rail but I was scared to try and grab him because I didn't want him to lose his balance and fall. The fire trucks came and the cops were in the hall, he was probably just about to begin his speech when he . . . just . . . went. If I hadn't gotten on his back about getting married, he wouldn't be dead. I wish I'd had my fling and sent him home, before . . ." She tilted her head in awkward grace. "I would have my memories and he would have his family."

"Not necessarily."

"Serena always forgives."

"That's one of the problems."

Ag's breath shuddered as she tried to keep from crying. "Now he's gone forever and it's all my fault."

"No it isn't," said Georgie; Ralph had probably been turned on by the novelty—this virginal lover in these casual times.

"Who else is there?"

"Ralph had a way of using people."

"That's what you think. I did it. Me."

"Ralph did it." Georgie grabbed her hands impulsively. "It could have happened to anyone."

"No it couldn't." Ag drew herself up in a lightning change. "Ralph said it was never like this with anybody else. Anybody. So he's mine forever now, in memory? And I may be bad, but since he's gone, I can't do anything worse. In a way, it's kind of a relief."

"Ag!"

"It's true. I was going crazy, trying to get the guts to do the right thing and give him up, and when I couldn't do that I kept trying to move it around this way and that way so that what we were doing would turn out to be OK, it was just too much for me, but now, now I can spend the rest of my life remembering."

"But what about your job? What about your kids?"

"I told you I don't *deserve* to have my kids," Ag said grimly, making it clear that in spite of the soft clothes, her brief pleasures in the world of recent memory, she had not moved away from the preoccupations of the night. Stop being ridiculous. "I thought I explained."

"Explained what?"

"Just how bad I really am. I didn't get carried away. I knew what I was doing and I knew it was wrong and I did it anyway. I loved it. I wish we were still . . . Which is what's so terrible. Which is why there's no hope for me. There's not going to be any forgiveness, either."

Ag's expression tore her in two. "That isn't true."

But Ag persisted. "How can I hope for absolution, after I—?"

"I thought Father Frank already—"

"Oh him," Ag said miserably, "That wasn't anything."

"Nothing! Absolution? That's the whole *thing* . . ."

Ag went on so bleakly that Georgie wanted to beg her to stop.

"You think a *poet* can absolve me?"

"He's a priest."

"Would God forgive me? Would Serena? Would you?"

"Of course I would!" Undone, Georgie threw her arms around her friend. "Oh God, Ag, of course I do." Because she did not want to break down in front of Ag, because she would do anything to keep Ag from having to break down again after so much grieving, she hugged her hard and fled to the bathroom, where she flushed the toilet three times and splashed cold water on her face.

When she came out everything had changed. Ag sat there with her head bent in the morning light, musing over the scrapbook as if none of this had taken place, not her confession, no tears, and because she did not know what else to do Georgie started all over at the beginning, saying, "By the way, where'd you find the scrapbook?"

"Oh, this? Out of the carton with the other stuff."

Her heart skidded. "What other stuff?"

Ag was not going to let her pursue this. She went on. "His things are all I have."

Georgie said weakly, "What about your things, that we brought down for you?"

"Oh, my things," Ag said absently. "What about them?"

"Your things from home. You said you needed them. Your things from college. Your white blazer," she said as brightly as she could.

"That old thing!"

"To face Serena in. You said it would make you brave."

To Georgie's surprise Ag covered a yawn. For the first time it occurred to her that of course the doctors would have given Ag something to help her get through this, she would have taken a couple this morning and they must have just started working. Maybe she'd just taken another with her tea. She seemed to be slipping, but into what? "I don't need any help with Serena. I'm not afraid of her." She touched the scrapbook. "I have all I need right here."

Surprised by her own urgency, Georgie was visited by an unbidden flash of Ag committing suttee, or doing something worse. "Promise you won't hurt yourself."

Ag blinked. "Hurt myself? Why should I hurt myself?"
"Last night. Those things you said. What you said just now."
"Me? What did I say?"
"About the guilt. Reparation. You know."
"Who, me? I don't know what you're talking about."
"Oh, Ag! You know what you said."

"Not really," Ag said, and fixed her with a pale blue stare that did not waver until Georgie let go her hand and picked up her pocketbook, because Ag was making it clear she wanted her to go. Georgie would love to have some of whatever it was she was taking, that had rendered her so sublimely calm. Her eyes were wide and empty as two ponds. "You must be crazy. I didn't say anything."

"I guess I'd better go."
"See you later." Ag's face was empty too. "Bye."

Rattled, Georgie closed the door on her. If this could happen to Ag, what was going to happen to the rest of them? She was mulling this on her way to the elevators when Mickey sprang out of the door to the next room so swiftly that she must have been lying in wait. She hurried after Georgie in her raincoat with the flowered nightie sticking out from underneath, trying to catch Georgie by the arm and hissing, "Wait!" She should have known Mickey was starving because she never did anything by herself. She'd rather die of hunger than venture down to the dining room alone. She was begging Georgie to come back inside and wait for her to dress. Georgie was in no state to sit on her thumbs while Mickey tried to decide which of several costumes would be the right one and whether pearls were going to be appropriate in this climate at this hour; she could not bear to watch Mickey spend her usual half-hour, going back again and again to the mirror for that last look that would just make her feel worse. Freeing herself after a brief tussle, Georgie apparently said the unforgiveable, because Mickey let go so suddenly that she staggered off-balance, retreating with magical speed. She disappeared, leaving behind only a raincoat button and the vestigial aura of Oil of Olay, which floated in the empty corridor like a sweet reproach. When she tried to think about this later, after it became important, Georgie had the idea that she hadn't even used words to plant the weed she would reap later; it was the fact of rejection that would sear and rankle until it became necessary for Mickey to get even; desperate, Georgie had pushed her away with an inarticulate, apologetic murmur: "Wump!"

17

ALL RIGHT, after she shed Mickey she doubled back and stood on her head in the mop closet, looking for the carton where Ag had found the scrapbook. No letters here, she thought, feeling diminished by the search. If Fulcrum liked her, maybe she could get into the basement storage room.

Going down in the elevator, she reassembled herself. She had half an hour to prepare for the Forrest Fulcrum interview. She would have Danuta bring the Fulcrum handbook and brochures and the official biography to her table in the dining room so she could do her homework while she ate. She should have done all this last night but it had come up fast when she was tied up with the column, which she was learning to hate, and the compulsion to succeed with Fulcrum, or at Fulcrum, she was not sure which. What did you say to a living legend? Hi, you don't know me, but . . . She had to win this one. She needed the kind of, she guessed it was standing, that would lift her out of her private preoccupations and end her vulnerability; if this worked out she would have, once for all, outrun that old folly with Ralph. She needed a triumph to offer Bill, in partial recompense. When they finally spoke she would offer it as explanation: why she had not been feeling, what, collected enough, or was it secure enough to call. *Sorry. I was tied up.*

If this worked out she might have something to give to her friends—assertiveness-training for Mickey, perhaps, or a week at the Golden Door; support for Ag, whether emotional or financial she did not yet know; and for Kath—what could she do for Kath?

She had to do something. Alarmed, she saw she was going to have to do it soon.

Kath was transfixed in the dining room, with Georgie's silver chain knotted at the neck of the red dress and the cashmere stole thrown over the chair. She had her head lifted at an angle that exaggerated the beauty of her throat; her eyes were fixed on something Georgie could not see. At a distance, she looked magnificent; unassailable. Spooked by the uncertainty of the night, she needed to ground herself; to see her reflection in Kath's eyes and know that whatever cataclysms fell between, she was still Georgie and Kath was still only Kath. *Good old Kath,* she thought, with a signal lack of accuracy, but hurried toward the table anyway.

At closer range, Kath did not look so good. How many more times was Georgie going to come down to some sun-shot dining room to find her friend sizzling like a cat with its tail in a light socket, with her face white and her black hair crackling, electrified? All her constructive plans for this half-hour sprouted wings and flew away.

"Are you all right?"

Preoccupied, Kath lifted her head after a long moment, apparently surprised in the middle of some private exploration; Georgie was not reflected anywhere. Her eyes gave back nothing Georgie recognized. Instead, somebody new flickered just beneath the surface—a Kath she had never seen but suspected had always been there, waiting to be realized. ". . . . Kath?"

"What? Oh, George. Hello, George."

"I said, are you all right?"

"Who me? I'm fine." Kath gave her a pale smile. "Everything is fine."

It was clear everything was not fine. She must have been nuts last night, sending Kath out for a confrontation with Lance. They had been like high school girls, giggling over her costume.

Had they imagined she would get him back? "Did you find him?"

"Oh, that. He was just where you said he would be."

Georgie said, hopefully, "So you had it out."

"Are you kidding? I. We. Let's say I convinced him to leave the lady. We went swimming. It was wonderful."

"If it was so wonderful, why do you look like a singed cat?"

Kath grimaced. "Oh well. You know. It wasn't, but then we went swimming and then it was. You know Lance."

"And you're not feeling strong enough to get rid of him," said Georgie, who was feeling none too strong herself.

Kath shook her head. "Not yet."

"But he's ruining you."

"No, it was—"

"He is. I can see it in your eyes."

Kath looked at her strangely. "What can you see?"

Georgie fell back. "I don't know."

"Right," Kath said. "You don't. You couldn't."

"What?"

"Know." She could have been fixed on the same bleak inner landscape Ag saw because she quoted Ag, verbatim. "I guess it's part of it."

"Kath?"

What was the matter? What did she think she was doing now? Whatever it was, it had transfixed her and it preoccupied her now. The thing about Kath was, even when she was chasing false leads—the aborted careers—she never did anything halfway. If Georgie could not make out what was going on, this was her fault, not Kath's. Her friend sat for a long time with her unsteady hands resting on the table while Georgie waited uncomfortably, discarding a dozen different things to say.

When Kath spoke again it was without preliminaries. "Yeah, something's the matter with me."

"I would like to murder Lance."

"No." The skin around Kath's eyes was blacker than usual, whether bruised from exhaustion or spoiled makeup Georgie did not know. At close range Georgie saw Kath's legs were covered with scratches and the beautiful red dress was stained along one sleeve and muddy around the hem. "Not Lance. Not really. It isn't really Lance."

"You don't look so good."

"That's the amazing part," Kath said. "I'm fine. Lance couldn't have been sweeter, we had a wonderful time. The two of us were dancing, right before the sun came up?"

"I thought you were . . ."

For a moment she was a college kid again, quoting with a raffish grin: "We were dancing, like they say in Ernest Hemingway, you know. Afterwards, after which we fell asleep in the grass and then . . ." Her hands shot out as if some huge child had pulled a hidden string.

"He took off again."

She shook her head. "He was still asleep, I woke up and rolled over and looked at him. He was beautiful. Then. Ah. Something happened."

"You weren't *attacked* . . ."

Her eyes were turbulent pools. "Much worse."

"Are you taking something?"

"Don't I wish."

"What do you want me to do?"

"Sit still and let me see if I can tell you this." In the silence Georgie reached for Kath's abandoned breakfast and began crunching abstractedly on her cold English muffin, which she finished, both halves, after which she moved on through the bacon while Kath sorted through all the words she knew, trying to find a way to explain. She was staring into her hands as if she ought to be able to find her next lines written in them, but when they yielded nothing she looked up and tried to begin. "Remember Marguerite Lattanza?"

"The weird girl from Bolivia."

"That's the one. Left in our freshman year."

"Creepy. Something about visions in the chapel."

"The nuns all said it was a nervous breakdown, but who knew? Well. Ah." Kath's hands jerked again. "Well. Ah. This is kind of like that." She blushed.

"Oh my God."

"Do you think I'm crazy?"

Georgie said, too quickly, "Of course not."

"I don't want you to think I'm having visions. Lord knows I'm hardly the type." Kath punched her arm. "Right?"

"You're hardly the type.—Are you?"

But Kath was fixed on it: what she saw that Georgie could not. "The trouble is, there was *something.*"

"What do you mean, something?"

"If I knew what I meant I would know what I meant, you know?" Kath said urgently, "What happened was, one minute I was lying in the grass with Lance, and the next thing I knew, no I don't know how I got there; the next thing I knew I was on the roof."

"The roof!"

"Don't panic, it's not what you think. At least I don't think it is. I was on the roof and there was just this kind of *buzzing* everywhere. That's all."

"That's all?"

"At least I think that's all. So, it's like . . . I'm probably just going crazy and you had probably better just forget it, OK?"

"I can't!"

"So I'm going up to get changed and I'll see you later, OK?"

"Wait." Georgie yanked her back. "Sit still and look at me. If it was somebody . . ."

Kath corrected her. "Some*thing.*"

"If it was something . . ."

"I think it was just this buzzing," Kath said.

"What do you mean, you think?"

"Well, there kind of was this something else."

"Else!"

"Something more, really. For a minute it was, I don't know. Blacker."

"What was?"

"Something. Blacker than anything else around."

"This black thing took you up there?" Was she crazy? Was that all? It would be a simple explanation and in its own way a relief.

"No, no," Kath said impatiently, "I'm not crazy, you know? I was there and for a minute it was there. Then it wasn't, that's all."

"So you saw something." Georgie wanted to pin it down, wanted her to name it, whatever it was, so it would not seem so huge.

"Not really."

"But you heard it."

"Sort of."

"What. Ah. What do you think it was?"

"Never mind, it's not important," Kath said hurriedly. "Your guess is as good as mine, you know? Look, thanks for listening. I have to get back upstairs and make sure Mickey didn't croak when she woke up and found out I didn't come home last night."

Georgie was judging Kath; how was she, really? She had to say something—anything she could think of to keep her here a little longer. "At least tell me what you think it was."

"Well, it sure as hell wasn't any stupid Catholic vision." Kath pried Georgie's fingers off. Perhaps to prevent any more questions she added, lightly, "The way things are going for me these days, you never know who's going to show up, but you know damn well who isn't."

"You mean the Virgin."

"I mean any of those folks. The good guys. You know. Look, if it turns out that I have the Lattanza problem in any dimension, will you see to it that Barry springs for a decent private hatch instead of stashing me in some state loony bin?"

"You're not crazy."

Kath whirled. "How do you know when I don't even know? I know Barry is going to try to stick me someplace good and cheap to serve me right. The man is losing patience. Especially after what happened before."

Georgie heard the words like stones dropping in a well. Splash. Splash. Splash. "What. Happened. Before?"

Kath said, matter-of-factly, "Nothing serious. Just this inexplicable thing. In the middle of our last fight. That happened. I was out of myself. That's all. I only had it once before, when Daddy died? The afternoon he died I was at the beach, I got this feeling, something huge moving, who knows what; it overtook me and I fell, like a goddam tree. I was out of it—how long? By the time I got back to myself it was getting dark and the tide was coming in. When I got home the cops were there with the news. With Barry it got black, or I got black, the middle of a storm—who knows? When I came out of it this time I had written this extraordinary poem—plus Barry had eight stitches. Said I'd tried to do something with a broken glass."

"To him?"

"Or me. He never said." She shrugged. "But if I have to go to the hatch, just see to it I go first class."

She stood for a moment, preparing to depart: the incomplete Kath of their girlhood moving toward some kind of completion; Kath Hartley, who had spent her adult life in an unfinished state, was clearly working out her own destiny with the strangest tools anybody had ever been handed; she was pale and driven, tense and concentrated because with or without a plan, with Lance's betrayal as means or as impediment, she was going to finish something now. Georgie found it necessary to say, loud enough for everybody in the dining room to hear her and make note of it, "You may be nuts, Kath, but I don't think you're crazy."

Kath turned in the doorway. "Remember Marguerite Lattanza," she said, and laughed.

In their freshman year at Mount Maria this Marguerite Lattanza, the homesick Bolivian, had claimed the Virgin came to her in the college chapel in the night. She only told her roommate, but by the end of January everybody knew. Who were they to say this never happened? If you believe in the supernatural, why not its manifestations? At one time or another every one of them had sneaked into the chapel to look at the spot. In February the Virgin came again and this time she called Marguerite by name, or so they heard. They managed to keep this from the sisters in the tough teaching order that ran the college until early March, when Marguerite, who had quit taking baths, told her theology teacher the Virgin wanted her sent home to Bolivia to await further instructions, at which point the sisters called in a doctor who called a psychiatrist. The faculty would have been delighted to write this off as a nervous breakdown but the girls gave Marguerite the benefit of the doubt. Saints were not usually your most attractive people; they were seldom your most sane. What sane person could walk the narrow line to sainthood without going nuts or falling off? Who could concentrate on the magnitude all the time, and not crack? Magnificent obsession, they said among themselves. Breakdown, the college president said and packed Marguerite off to Bolivia with a sigh of relief. Thinking about this now, with the tempered faculties of adulthood, Georgie knew it would be easier for both her and Kath to write off Kath's *something* as hysteria, or exhaustion, because nervous disorders were their own explanation. What's more they could be cured, while genuine visions usually came unwanted because they brought nothing but hardship and grief. *Vide* certain mystics in in the middle ages; *vide* Joan of Arc. Who in her right mind would not duck if she saw one coming? Oh no. Not me. No thanks. If you acknowledged supernatural nudgings, then at some point you had to respond to them. She wanted to dismiss the whole thing but there was the nagging possibility that there had indeed been something, maybe even the bad guys, Kath's black hole opening.

It was hard to know. When they were little, things either *were* or else they weren't. You always knew. Now, Georgie realized, she hardly ever knew. Adulthood had sharpened her critical faculties along with her defense mechanisms, which included the inability or unwillingness to judge anything absolutely, and specifically because she was Georgie, the particular inability to judge anything with a straight face. *Is that your dress?* She and stylish, funny, unlikely Kath would rather laugh over this one than try to take it apart and find out where it came from. It was both their failing and their protection.

"Sorry to disturb you, Mrs. Kendall, but while you've been sitting here gathering wool Mr. Fulcrum has been in the Verbarium, tapping his foot."

"The what?"

"Library to you." Danuta said. "You've kept him waiting long enough."

18

IT WAS STRANGE out today. How strange was it going to be? This morning's encounter with Kath hinted at prevailing atmospheric conditions beyond her control. Now that Georgie was alone in Forrest Fulcrum's office, her suspicions were confirmed. It was going to be weird all day.

The first thing was that Danuta's officious bustling was pointless. Forrest Fulcrum was by no means waiting. For a moment after Danuta rushed her in and slammed the door on her, Georgie imagined he was going to make his entrance through a hidden panel; then she thought maybe she would find him in a closet or waiting behind the portieres. He wasn't even here. His chair was here, all right, high-backed and carbuncular, as in the portrait, with mahogany lions ready to lunge. It was twirling behind the heavily carved mahogany desk. Had Danuta given it a bash on her way out—or had the founder just left it? She touched the velvet seat. Was it still warm? She could not be sure. Needing to impose some kind of control over her circumstances, she took out her notebook and itemized. The decor was a strange mixture of global and personal; on one wall a lighted map detailed Fulcrum holdings on three continents. As she watched new lights winked on, marking further financial triumphs. Today's issues of international newspapers sat on the conference table and stock quotations, details on troop movements, perhaps even statistics on the latest coup winked on his dozen computer terminals. The old man had autographed photos of himself with everybody from Albert Einstein to Alfred Eisenstadt, with F. Scott and Ella Fitzgerald, Reneé Richards and Ralph Richardson, John and Amy Irving and Irving Penn. His shelves were crammed with presentation copies of books by leading thinkers, who in some cases inked thanks to Fulcrum for fueling the train of thought. The hard hat the crusty founder had worn into the steel mill at thirteen was enshrined next to a yellowed satin woman's garter; Georgie half-expected to find Rosebud stashed, with rusty runners and her emblem peeling. He had a silver blotter holder and a gold inkwell. On his desk was an empty folder bearing her name.

This so unnerved her that she backed off hastily and sat down with her notebook, trying to decide what to ask the great man when he finally did show up. Too much time passed. At a sound she jumped to her feet and whirled to face the door. This had been such a long time coming that she was trembling, and all her carefully developed questions slipped her mind at once.

"Mr. Fulcrum, this is an—"

"Don't mind me."

"Mickey! What are you doing here?"

"Mrs. . . . Danuta let me in. Danuta told me where to find you."

"She *told* you?"

Mickey sat down with an embarrassed little grin. "I said it was an emergency."

"But I'm in the middle of an interview."

Mickey's eyes reflected the empty office. "So I see."

It was too hard to explain. She gave up on trying to remember what she had been thinking. "Well, is it?"

"What?"

"An emergency."

"Well, sort of." Mickey's eyes were pink and the tip of her nose was pink. Although they were alone she lowered her voice to a husky, conspiratorial whisper. "Kath's bed hasn't been slept in and when I knock Ag just tells me to go away, and I thought at least you . . ." She rasped like an obscene phone caller, or a kid in a confessional, "Georgia, I don't know what to do."

"About what?"

"I'm tired of being all alone here."

"And that's your emergency." Wearily, Georgie bent to her notebook.

"Of course if I'm intruding, I'll just go."

"Oh no," Georgie said with her head down, "you're not intruding. I'm not really busy."

Mickey said, "You're busy and Kath's in love and Ag is grieving, everybody has something except me. Which is why I had to find you."

"I see."

"I thought maybe you would come in while I had breakfast?"

"Mickey, I'd really love to, but . . ."

"You have to work."

Georgie kept her head down. "I'm sorry."

"No you're not. But maybe you won't mind if I just sit here?"

Georgie sighed and did not answer.

"You don't have to go to breakfast, if you've already been," Mickey said, composing herself on one of the uncomfortable chairs Fulcrum's designer had chosen to keep his visitors on their toes. For morning wear she had selected a serviceable navy linen with white piping and a complementary red scarf, navy espadrilles and white shortie gloves, which she held in one rosy fist. In spite of her apparent uneasiness, the color scheme gave her a rakish, nautical air. "As long as I can sit here."

Mickey had tilted her head at a winning angle that was at odds with her surroundings. It was a little like entertaining a Martian here in Forrest Fulcrum's office; Mickey and her manners had been beamed down whole from another world. When Georgie realized her old friend was sitting there with her head tipped and her mouth fixed in a genteel smile, pink around the eyes but waiting politely, she sighed again, knowing Mickey would not take the hint. *Oh lord,* she thought, and did not have the heart to kick her out. "OK."

"You don't even have to talk to me. I just want company," Mickey lilted, in a stab at being charming. She went on in a musical tone, "Imagine the four of us together, after all these years, imagine the four of us together in this glamorous place."

What if he found Mickey here? It would make her look like an amateur, when she had to come on like a pro. "It isn't so glamorous."

". . . With all these famous people . . ."

"They aren't even very famous."

". . . four Mount Maria girls."

Georgie sighed. "We haven't been girls for a long time."

"You know what I mean."

"Maybe you ought to go to the dining room and get something on your stomach. You sound a little faint."

Mickey said eagerly, "Would you come?" She deflated. "No, I didn't think so. I'll just sit here if you don't mind . . ."

"Mmm." Why not? She thought; she had nothing to show so far—not much to lose. She could start by asking Fulcrum about the mines.

"—You don't mind, do you? Go ahead, go on writing, I'll be quiet," Mickey said.

"Mmmm . . ." After she warmed him up on his childhood, she could . . .

"Really."

"Sure." Copying a quote from the Fulcrum brochure, Georgie became aware it was possible to do two things at once.

"I won't make any noise. So this is his office," Mickey said in a prefatory way. When Georgie kept writing she went on in a light voice; she could have been singing to herself. "It's all right, I can entertain myself. I'm used to having to do things all by myself, Lord knows I do at home. It was the hardest thing about graduating. I always had plenty of people around at Mount Maria. It was like the peaceable kingdom, you know, everybody coming from the same place, all wanting the same things. When we talked we were always on common ground, nobody argued and nobody laughed at you. At Mount Maria I was never lonely or out of place, but ever since . . ." Mickey's breath rippled.

Georgie murmured, "I know."

"It was kind of like being on a ship with appointed places for appointed things at appointed times, meals, going out, going to chapel, coming in, going to . . . going to bed," Mickey burbled giddily. "Remember, it was so *orderly,* your own neat bunk bed and your own shelves and your own little desk that you could lock things into and you could come back months later and they would still be there, a place for everything, that's what I loved, and everything in its place, and plenty of people to do things with, you never had to be alone, that was the whole thing about being at school . . . people to sit with at breakfast lunch and Christmas, people on the hall at night, and after Lights Out somebody at the desk on the landing, just to take care, you even had people to go to town with at night, so you didn't have to worry about, you know, being attacked. It was the only time in my whole life I felt like a part of something. I would lie there in my bed at night and think this was the way the world was, it was the only time I ever felt completely safe."

Perhaps with her head bent over her notebook Georgie had become the perfect listener, invisible but present, enabling the speaker to go on. As her mind strayed and she began making zigzags with her pencil instead of writing, Mickey went on. By this time she was fixed on her litany of memory, numbering the rituals of their girlhood in a little threnody of nostalgia that tugged her listener because different as they were, Georgie had at some time felt some of the same things. It was getting harder to keep her mind on her interview. She would rather die than let Mickey know she knew exactly what she meant and so instead she sat with her thoughts scattered and her head down while Mickey went on remembering.

"I was never happier in my entire life."

"That's awful."

But Mickey did not hear. By this time she was disgorging every nice thing the sisters had ever said to her, numbering them as if this would keep them true. This left Georgie fixed on her own thoughts, which Mickey had invaded and cluttered with memory. It had indeed been precisely like being in a ship; awake in the reaches of the night, spreadeagled in the top bunk, Georgie had been strongly aware of the silent building with its wings and porches extending to surround her, of the sprawl of the sleeping structure and her place in it. Even now she could see the yellow night light in the corridors, the gleaming expanses of waxed linoleum that led to empty marble stairs, the light burning in the silent chapel at the far end of the hall; she comprehended identical rooms on identical floors below, all harboring people on their way to becoming women, who in spite of Mickey's imagination of a single purpose, dreamed diverse and conflicting dreams. Mount Maria at night in the early Sixties had indeed been quiet and well-kept and safe—as safe, she thought, as the past.

It wasn't the place that they had loved so much, she thought. It was what it stood for: the kind of certitude that at the time had filled her with joy for what she was, a Catholic girl among hundreds of others like her. In those days, she thought, it all seemed all of a piece, which as much as anything explained why she used to wish everybody she cared about could share what she had, be what she was. It had been a long time since she had wanted to convert anybody. It was no longer a party it was easy to invite people to. What was she supposed to tell them about the conflicts between those who looked back and those who were trying to move forward? How could she explain why being *this* was important to her in spite of the church's interior struggles, division over so many things, from politics to what was moral obligation and what was meddling in private morality. How could she invite anybody to this in the face of her own discomfort with so many hierarchical public gestures? How could people who were trying so hard to do everything right do things that seemed so wrong? She couldn't explain it. At the moment, she didn't even understand it.

Mickey's passion startled her. "I wish I could go back."

It was hard for Mick, she thought, turned out into a puzzling world, moved from hushed stability to a state of flux with no choice but to sink or swim, which was, of course, the whole point. There were times when she missed the black-and-white simplicity, but she would not go back. "You couldn't live there even if you wanted to."

Mickey said, in a small voice, "I was so happy."

"That was before, Mickey," she said firmly. "This is during."

"There was a flurry in the doorway: Danuta, disturbed and trying to look ominous. "I hate to say this, Mrs. Kendall, but something has come up. Something most unfortunate."

(Alarmed, Georgie whispered, "Mickey, you have to leave now."
"Where can I go?"
"I don't care."
"*Georgie!*")
"There's been some trouble," Danuta continued darkly.
"What kind of trouble?" Georgie was too loud. ("Would you *leave?*"
"Couldn't I just stay here?"
"No."
"I won't make any noise. I won't embarrass you."
"Would you just *go?*")
"About your credentials: Mr. Fulcrum is still checking you out."
"I see." The empty folder, Georgie thought. What has he got on me? (Mickey was frantic. "Please?"
Georgie had bigger problems now and so unwittingly fed the weed of resentment with the fuel of rejection, pushing her old roommate out the door, hissing, "Will you just go away and let me *do* this?") "You mean I'm not going to see Mr. Fulcrum?"
"Not yet. Not until this is settled."
"Until what is settled?"
"Never mind. I will take care of you. Meanwhile . . ." Expanding her chest like a runner at the starting line, Danuta hit the mark. "He says I am to show you around the Foundation."
"But I've already seen the—"
"Top to bottom." Danuta got ready. "It will take hours."
Georgie's voice trailed off. ". . . Foundation."
"You have no choice." Danuta got set. Went, without even looking to see whether Georgie followed.
It crossed her mind as Danuta benched her at the exercise class that she should be hearing from Peter Flinc and his cohorts soon. What if they called Ag's room while she was watching these philosophers in sweatsuits leap and grovel in an attempt to better their bodies? ("*Mens sana in corpore sano,*" Danuta said brightly). What if she was slogging through the sauna ("Excuse me, Mr. Sevareid") or marooned out here inspecting the cabanas? ("All right, Lance, who is she?" "Go

away, we're talking business.") Would they bother to bring a cordless phone to poolside, where she feared Danuta would swim laps while she watched, and would they put her through, or would they make her wait until Danuta finished demonstrating the flip turn with Teutonic precision, or would they shove her in, clothes and all, and make her perfect her turn before they let her have the phone? (*"Mens sana* . . ." "I know, Danuta, I know.")

Yes she was on sufferance here, trapped in the Institute's version of *May I,* investigative reporter sidetracked on standard outsiders' tour. If she, what, passed the tour with a B-plus or better for conduct, she might get to talk to the Great Man and she might not. Right now she was neutralized, shooting along a diversionary channel that might just spill her out on the street. The route was set; even Danuta's recital was canned. By contrast, the Fulcrum fellows were frenetic: energetic scholars and thinkers seeking truth in the universal gym, at computer terminals, at triangular conference tables, life's would-be A students convinced they could dissect—she guessed it was *being,* because Forrest Fulcrum ordered it, everybody but George productive, busy and, above all, engaged, frantic to do—what?

Troubled as she was, stuck with Danuta while her circumstances rattled out of control, she thought: *interesting. People will go to any lengths to make their lives make sense.*

This so unsettled her that she cried, "What do they think they are *doing?"*

Danuta tapped the brochure, saying smoothly. "Pascal's wager. It's in here."

"Pascal's wager!"

"Mr. Fulcrum thinks there might be a God."

"I see. And all this?"

Inexorable, Danuta moved on. "In case."

She did not know whether it was her own exhaustion or the tiresome quality of all the scholarly babble that left her feeling jagged and critical, but it seemed to her that Forrest Fulcrum's money was being wasted here, as his hired thinkers chased truth like greyhounds going after a mechanical rabbit, tearing around and around the same old track. *Between the intention and the act . . . Hers too,* Georgie thought with a shudder . . . *falls the shadow.* Right. She didn't know whether it was anxiety that made her dyspeptic, or disparity, or only the unbidden shade of Marguerite Lattanza, which Kath had raised this morning when she blundered into the curtain between what they knew and what they could not know, and left it rippling. The shade of the unfortunate girl who said she had visions was present, hanging somewhere just out of sight like an old bathrobe, an unwanted reminder that at any level it was always more convenient to discount the unaccountable. Maybe she was depressed, Georgie thought, or too tied up with Kath. Or only exhausted. Whatever the cause, she was burning out.

The Fulcrum story. Was there one? Did she want to write the story, and if so, what for? What made her think she could?

As it turned out, the choice was removed from her. The great man was waiting in his office in a chilly atmosphere of disapproval. It was clear there would be no interview. Forrest Fulcrum looked like his portrait but not like it: the face of Dorian Grey, she thought; through some mistake it showed the marks of everything he had done instead of the youthful portrait, which was the thing that was supposed to age. He looked old and used-up. His soul was fluttering very near the surface, waiting to be released.

The folder bearing her name had notes in it, which he tapped angrily as she
 came into the presence and he looked up. "Your erstwhile employers," he snapped.

"How-do-you-do-Mr.-Fulcrum-I . . ."

"They say they never heard of you."

She faltered. "You must have gotten a wrong number."

"There is no time in my life for wrong numbers."

"Then you got the wrong person," she said, reaching hard.

"There is no time in my life for the wrong people," he said. "Peter Arnold Flinc, Brown University, 1969. Formerly of Gannett Publications. *IN* Magazine, a pilot stepchild of Magnum Publications, bankrolled by Robin and Anthea Lawton of

Washington, D.C., although that is becoming increasingly problematical as the financial picture changes. Mrs. Kendall, they never heard of you."

"I work for them."

"All you work for is that second-rate newspaper," he said angrily. "Which I happen to control. One word from me and you're fired. If you want to keep your job get out of here."

"Listen. There's been a mistake." She tried to pretend he hadn't already swiveled, turning his back to her. "*IN* Magazine really sent me here."

"Stop wasting my time. If I see you again you're fired."

"One phone call would clear this up."

"Don't waste your time." Why was he so angry? "Nobody lies to Forrest Fulcrum and survives."

Why was she so desperate? "Just let me make this call."

His heavily jeweled knuckles hit the desk, closing the seance. He was frigid, angry. "Get out or you're finished. Everywhere."

Danuta removed her before he could erupt, dragging the unwilling Georgie across the lobby and around the corner to the bank of elevators. "His heart. It is not safe. You understand you cannot stay."

At the elevators Georgie dug in her heels. "Wait. I can't go yet."

"I'll send somebody for your bags. You are finished here."

"It isn't cleared up yet. Please. You can't just cancel me."

"It's already done." Danuta's manner would have done credit to a storm trooper. "Your car will be out front in half an hour."

"I don't have a car."

"A car. You understand. Anything to take you away. Mr. Fulcrum is very powerful."

"I can't leave yet." *Not until I find the letters.*

"He can fix it so you never work again."

"I know, but I can't leave. It's a matter of honor," Georgie said, because this was true, and on a hunch she added craftily, "and love. I have to be here for the funeral."

"Funeral? Oh." Danuta tried to pretend she hadn't caught the hint. "You mean the Commemorative Moment. We don't have funerals here." She consulted her clipboard. "You aren't even on the C list. You will not be missed."

"No. Please. You don't understand." Because she had to buy time, Georgie either did or didn't lie, writhing out of Danuta's grasp to yank at her viscera. "Ralph and I were in love."

"Aaaaah." Bullseye. Stricken, Danuta went pink. She had hit the Achilles heel, or was it the heart? The change was magical. As Georgie watched she was transformed from storm trooper to Rhine maiden impaled on the arrow of sentiment. "My dear. I knew it all the time. I saw your eyes. We have this in common, you know."

It came to Georgie that if Ralph had had Danuta it wasn't before, in some remote and misty past, it was just now, after his arrival with Ag and before the scene on the ledge. He always was a rat. She murmured conspiratorially. ". . . So you do see how important it is."

"For just this reason," Danuta said softly. "Just this once. I will arrange for you to stay. But on one condition." So, it seemed they would collude. Her voice dropped. "Mr. Fulcrum must not see you. You will lose your job. I will lose my job. He is furious."

"It's such a shame. One phone call would clear this up."

"Don't count on it." Danuta took her shoulders, saying, hoarsely, "Mr. Fulcrum seldom forgets, and he does not forgive."

Bundled into the elevator, Georgie let the doors close and pushed the HOLD button, sealing them just long enough to convince Danuta she was really gone. Then she slipped out to the phone booth like an anxious wraith. She needed explanations, apologies. She had never been kicked out of anything in her life and she had to set this right. She emptied her pockets and settled in for a long siege. Unfortunately, by the time she finally got through to the offices of *IN* Peter Flinc was away from his desk, or said he was. Nobody was willing to speak for him or take a message, perhaps because nobody knew whether he was at his exercise club or in some smart Manhattan boite doing business over a four-Martini five-course carbohydrate-laden lunch, whether he was in the Magnum front offices, receiving accolades or whether, instead, he was opening his wrists in the last stall in the least populated men's room in the Magnum building, the natural result of some as yet unannounced defeat. In Washington, the Lawtons' maid said in broken English that the Lawtons were out of the city. Only after Georgie explained patiently that her suicide would be on the maid's soul forever did she admit that they were in fact stashed in bed in their Pan Am sleep masks after a late night and nothing Georgie could do or say was going to convince her to wake them up. All Georgie could do was head back to Ag's room to lie low and wait them out, powerless until she finally got through. This alone was enough to fell her but the persistent background racket that distressed and distracted her the whole time she was on the telephone had finally separated and identified itself (honkahonka) as her worst social nightmare come true and heading her way. Oh good grief. "Horace!"

"Georgia, Georgia Kendall. I've been looking everywhere." Beaming Horace Metcalf came trotting across the Spanish tiles in his gleaming white suit. "Georgia," he said, loud enough to rouse Forrest Fulcrum and bring down his wrath on her. "At last."

"Shh, Horace. What are you *doing* here?"

"Invited," Horace said with a triumphant grin. "Seminar on midwestern history—my specialty. I'm responding to a paper."

"Oh Horace," she groaned. "How nice."

"Bill's idea. Thought I might run into more people to interview for my piece."

"Your piece?" She honestly had forgotten.

He looked at her as if over nonexistent glasses. "American Catholic thought. Besides, he wanted me to look in on you."

"Bill!" she said, betrayed. What would she have done after several days of Horace at close range? Even Bill had his limits; even for the Mother Teresa of their household, Good Works palled. He had sloughed off Horace like the last card in a game of Old Maid.

"I was worried about you," he said on a rising note, in spite of her frantic efforts to make him shush. "Bill is worried too. He hasn't heard from you for days." His voice continued to rise. "You haven't called since Wednesday . . ."

"Please, shhh!"

". . . and today is Saturday."

She realized with a little shock of guilt that this was true. She had not forgotten, exactly, there had been plenty of opportunities. She just. Kept. Putting it off. After a long moment in which she considered and Horace watched her carefully, she said, with signal accuracy, "I've been tied up. You can tell him I'm fine."

"Well you don't look fine. Why are we whispering?" Horace whispered, but louder, "I thought you would be glad to see me. Aren't you glad to see me?" He was touchingly glad to see her, a note from home with the silvery hair and the freshly cleaned white suit. His enthusiasm made her squirm.

"Let's just say this is not the best time. So goodbye, OK? I'll see you later, OK? OK, Horace, OK? Maybe tomorrow, when it's saner out." She resisted the urge to push him with both hands.

"Not so fast. I have other business here." Horace forgot all about whispering. "Remember, I was invited. *Plus,* I'm something of an ornithologist."

"An ornithologist?"

"Amateur, but on a major scale. Ornithologist, Georgia, *ornithologist.*" He said, unexpectedly, "Oh Georgia, why are you so hard on me?"

"I'm sorry, Horace, I . . ." Touched, she had a sudden shot of INTERIOR: HORACE—DAY. Poor old man, he was spent after his long trip, feeling unwanted—not so different from what she felt. Across the lobby a door was opening—if she wasn't careful Forrest Fulcrum would apprehend her and the game would be over, but she had to make amends. "I didn't mean to hurt your feelings."

"You think I don't notice, but I can see you cringe."

Oh lord. It was true. "You're imagining things. Look, I . . ." The office door was wide open now; in the few seconds left, her wave of sympathy was followed by a spasm of inspiration. "Ornithology. I have just the person for you to talk to. The legendary Stillman Sedley."

She could see his heart leap up. "Stillman Sedley?"

"The very same."

"Is he here? Is he really here?"

"Really. I just saw him in the dining room," she said, right before she sprang into the elevator and made her escape. "You can use my name." Sped by the angels, she finished, "If you hurry you can go birding with him at Bok Tower."

In the relative safety of the hall outside Ag's room, she leaned heavily against the wall in a paroxysm of relief. She had made it this far. At the moment she needed sanctuary; she wanted nothing more than to be among old friends, where she was safe. If she could only make her key quit rattling and fit into the lock she would be home free.

When she wrestled the door open all three roommates looked up at her like raccoons surprised in a midnight raid on somebody's garbage. There were papers all over the bed—her handwriting, she realized, her typescripts, every draft of the column she had written so far. Her notes, she realized, shaken by guilt.

"Well there you are," Mickey said. "Mrs. Holyboly, Georgie the irreproachable."

She fought back waves of nausea. "What's the matter?"

"Are these not your notes?" Mickey was so pink it was frightening.

"What are you doing?"

"You've been writing about us," Ag said. She had turned white underneath her pallor and her large frame seemed rocked by conflicting emotions.

"All of us," said Kath, whose eyes were ringed in black. "Probably you should have told us, George."

"It wasn't anything I could explain."

"You've been telling our secrets, making us look like fools." Mickey was furious. "What did you think you were doing, anyway?"

"Trying to tell the truth, I guess."

"Writing about our personal business for God knows who."

How could she explain it to them? She was the only writer here. "I was trying to make something *more* of it, Mickey." This was true.

Mickey was shouting. "Well it wasn't yours to use!"

This was also true. She dropped her head. "I'm sorry."

"You should be."

"Let me try to explain." She put her hands to her face and pulled them down as if trying to drag her features into an expression they could all live with. She said for the second time that day, "This is not a good time." When nobody said anything she went on, "You know I love you all."

"Bullshit."

"Mickey!"

Mickey turned to Kath. "Well, it is."

"I never wanted to hurt anybody."

"Well it's too late for that now."

"Especially not you." She had never seen Mickey like this. Was Georgie aware that she had planted this weed herself? Had she known at the time that she was planting it? Whether or not she knew where it had come from, the weed of resentment was in full flower. Distraught, she understood first of all that right now Mickey was hurt and angry because of something she had found in one of the many drafts of the column she had wadded and thrown into the wastebasket, and she tried to reassure her. "I would never knowingly hurt you."

"Sure. Oh sure." Mickey quoted from memory. "'. . . bounding along like Piglet, always a little overweight and always behind . . .' Do you want me to go on?"

"I didn't even send that. I threw that away. Oh, please." She reached out, trying to take Mickey's hands. "I changed your names!"

"Well, big deal."

"I was trying to protect you," she said brokenly, still reaching for her friend.

But Mickey lowered her head and backed away, eluding her. "Listen to her, Mrs. beloved smartass bigtime writer," she said with astonishing bitterness, and before the others could do anything more than murmur in distress she went on thickly, "And don't you dare stand up for her, not after what she's done to us. Not after what she's also done that I know that you don't know about."

Georgie was too upset to see what was coming. "If I have hurt you, I'm so sorry."

"Oh shut up." Mickey turned to the others, going on in a

conversational tone. "You don't know what I know about Mrs. Georgia Kendall. Superwife, supermom, superwriter. Thinks she's so smart."

"I don't, I promise. I'm not."

"Thinks she's so much better than we are."

"Oh, Mickey, I don't." Her voice broke. "I'm not." There was so much truth to this charge that Georgie swallowed a sob, too disturbed and distracted to be able to see what was coming—where Mickey was leading them. "Really," she finished weakly, but Mickey was already overriding her.

All the stored-up slights of the past few days, real and imagined, propelled Mickey's words, so that they popped into the room with surprising force. "Well I can tell you a thing or two."

Kath touched her arm. "Take it easy, that's enough."

"If you knew what I know you wouldn't think it was enough. You wouldn't tell me to take it easy, either. If you want to know the truth, nothing is enough. Not in this case."

"Easy, Mickey. Easy."

"Not after what she did."

"I'm just so sorry," Georgie said.

"You want to know what I know? Do you?" Mickey spun out of Kath's grasp and moved center stage. Flushed with outrage, pinker than Georgie had ever seen her and intent on something Georgie still could not see, she confronted them. She seemed to swell until she filled the room. "Do you want to know what she is really doing here?"

Kath said, "She came for Ag."

Ag said, "I asked her to come."

"That's only part of it."

"I asked you all to come."

"You know, there's more."

Ag smiled thinly. "She came for the funeral."

Mickey snapped, "You're damn right she came for the funeral."

Georgie groaned. "Oh God."

"And that's the least of it," Mickey said. She turned to Georgie, saying, in almost conversational tones, "You thought I was asleep when you made your big confession, but I wasn't. You thought I didn't hear. I kept quiet because I thought we were friends. I would have kept it to the grave if *you* . . . All right," she barked, riveting the others. "She came down here because she used to be in love with Ralph."

Staggered, Ag turned to her. "With Ralph!"

"Oh please," Georgie mumbled. Oh God, what had she said to Mickey that night in the motel? *Everybody has done things they were ashamed of.* She had hoped against hope that she'd mumbled the rest, so Mickey hadn't heard, but she had. *Some of them with Ralph.* "Oh please never mind."

But Mickey was launched. "She came all the way down here to mourn your boyfriend, Agnes Mary, Serena Schwartz's husband? Agnes Mary, are you listening? Your wonderful friend Georgie had an affair with him."

For a minute, nobody said anything.

Then Ag groaned. "Oh lord. Georgie, you didn't!"

Kath covered her face.

Mickey stood there breathing heavily.

They were waiting for Georgie to say: *It's true.*

Georgie said, "But that was a hundred years ago."

Georgie said, "It's been *over* for a hundred years."

Georgie said, "I didn't come to mourn him at all, Ag. I came for you."

Then, because she had done everything but confess she said, "But there is this other thing, I have to find these letters?" When nobody spoke she went on impulsively. "Listen, I wrote Ralph all these letters that I'm ashamed of and I've got to get them back because if I don't . . ." She could not bear to look into their faces; she had run as fast as she could all these years, she had prayed and dissembled, but she understood that she hadn't fooled anybody, she hadn't fooled them at all. "Ok, you might as well know, I never told Bill."

After which she dropped her hands and stood with her head bent, completely at the mercy of them all—all three of them.

Ag said, in a hushed voice, "All this time."

Georgie was too overwhelmed to respond.

Ag's voice was filled with wonder. "All this time."

She was looking at Georgie with a complex and changing expression of what might be recognition, and Kath uncovered her face gradually and shuddered as if, from the head down, all her parts were clicking in a subtle realignment, while Mickey breathed hard and looked from one to the other expectantly. It was Kath who spoke at last, out of a silence that had stretched from the fearsome to the intolerable.

Kath said, slowly, "Well, there's only one thing to do."

"What? What are you going to do," Mickey challenged her.

"Take care of it."

"Where do you want to start? Shall we tell Serena first, or do you want to get in touch with Bill?"

Kath's voice was light but definite. "If you say one word to anybody, Michele, I am going to murder you."

"What are you going to do, let her get away with it?"

"Shut up, Mickey."

"You're going to let her get away with it after everything?" Mickey was breathing hard. "Kathleen? Agnes Mary?"

Completely disassembled, Ag faltered while Mickey waited and Georgie held her breath. "I don't know what we're going to do. Kath?"

"Come on, Kathleen, what are you going to do about it?" Unnaturally flushed and gasping with compressed excitement, Mickey faced them all. "What are we going to do?"

After a moment Kath looked up and began to smile. When she spoke it was quintessential Kath, in all her reckless gallantry. "Find the letters, of course. We have to get rid of them before Serena comes."

19

"I DON'T KNOW what got into me," Mickey whispered tearfully from her corner of the darkened bedroom. Ag and Kath were off somewhere on unspecified errands while Georgie crouched on the telephone like a bird of prey and Mickey lay across the bed as if flung by the hand of an angry goddess. Instead of letting Georgie telephone in peace she kept wheezing apologies congested by the fact that she had her feet dangling off one side of the bed and her head hanging off the other so that all the blood rushed to her face. Fixed on the sequence of telephonic clicks that would connect her to Peter Flinc if only she could concentrate, Georgie was distracted by another sally from Mickey, that one-woman pageant of repentance. "How can I ever make it up to you," Mickey said, as Georgie's call to Peter Flinc clicked off into oblivion.

Georgie said, drily, "You'd better sit up, all the blood is running to your head."

"I don't care." Mickey pulled her hair a little so it, too, would dangle.

"You're going to get apoplexy."

"It would serve me right."

"You're getting all red in the face. Operator, would you try that number again?"

"I don't care."

"Get up, you're making yourself sick. Operator . . ."

"I'm never getting up," Mickey muttered.

The Fulcrum operator cut in. It sounded suspiciously like Danuta. "Please hang up. We will ring when we have your party on the line."

"I don't deserve to get up," Mickey said, upside down. Her face had turned an alarming color. She cut her eyes to see how Georgie was taking this.

"You're no good to anybody lying there." Georgie resisted picking up to ask the desk how her call was progressing. "Why don't you pull yourself together and go help them find the letters?"

Mickey brightened. "Would you let me?"

"Why not?"

"After what I did to you?"

"We're still friends."

"After what I said?"

"Oh, that. I think we'd better forget it."

"I'm never going to forget it."

"It was my fault for saying anything."

"Probably it was the trouble with Howard . . ."

Where was her call? "Operator."

"Did you hear me?"

"Howard," Georgie said automatically.

"That made me do it," Mickey explained.

Georgie was fixed on the newest sequence of telephonic clicks. "Mickey, if you'd just . . ." disappear.

Mickey said ruefully, "There you go again."

"I'm sorry," Georgie said, because Mickey was right. She put down the receiver. "What trouble with Howard?"

"That's the trouble, I don't know. He hasn't said or done anything, he doesn't hit me and he isn't stepping out, he isn't doing anything. I just—" Mickey put her head into her hands. "I'm having a lot of trouble with marriage," she said in a choked voice. "Whatever it's supposed to be with us, it isn't there."

"You're upset."

"I don't think that's it," Mickey said. "It's like my *raison d'être* just *isn't* any more. I mean, as long as I had Howard, and the kids, it wouldn't matter what you wrote about me. It wouldn't matter what you did, or what Kath did."

"What we did?"

"I mean as long as I had my house in order it didn't matter what you did in yours, or what happened in the world outside. Don't you get it? I was all right as long as I had control of my own place. I could still look in the mirror and say, OK, Michele, you're no world-beater, but you're doing OK here, in your home, but now my household is falling apart. I don't know about Howard, and the kids are growing up. I'm supposed to feel fulfilled and all I feel is bad."

"Well, what did you think you were going to get out of it?" Georgie asked as gently as she could. She was afraid to ask if Mickey and Howard were in love.

To her absolute astonishment Mickey wailed, "I just never thought I would be so bored!" After a pause she collected herself and went on. "The thing is, until we came on this trip I could still kid myself that everything in my world was OK, I really thought I was doing all right for a Mount Maria girl of my age and station, but now . . ." Mickey reached for evidence, producing the best she could come up with. "You people still have *waists.*"

"Oh, Mickey." Georgie wondered why it was she who felt guilty when it was Mickey who had hurt her, not the other way around. She said, loyally, "You look fine to me."

Mickey went on in a low voice. "You know that isn't what I mean. It's everything. I was feeling OK about myself and then I got in the car with you and all your notes and Kath and Kath's—all right, Kath's lover, and I just didn't think I could *do* that, and then I realized there were a whole bunch of things I couldn't do—support myself if I had to, in case Howard . . ."

"Howard would never."

"I can't even decide what is the right thing to *wear.* I'm afraid to go anywhere alone, and everything you and Kath said and did just brought it home." Her voice dropped. "There isn't very much to me."

"You know that isn't true."

"Get me away from the house and I'm nobody. *Nobody.*

That's what came to me riding along in the car, and I rode along thinking, Georgie neglects her kids and Kath is living in sin but at least they amount to something, while I—"

"What do you mean I neglect my kids?"

"Going to the office. You know. Oh don't take it personally, that's the way it is. I used to think you were crazy, locking yourself away from your kids to work, but at least you're *somebody*, and I'm not."

"You're a terrific person, you're . . ."

But Mickey was in no mood to be cheered. "Don't bother, don't even try. I know what I am." Overcome, Mickey regrouped, squeezing out the rest. "Then there was that terrible cocktail party and you didn't want to get stuck with me, but it was really breakfast."

"What was really breakfast?"

"Why I told."

At which point Georgie came to a full stop. "You told everybody and did everything because of breakfast?"

"We were supposed to be friends, and you wouldn't even wait for me to go down."

"Oh Mickey, I'm sorry."

"And then I *got* down alone, which was a fairly big deal for me and you were so tied up with this interview that you wouldn't give me the time of day, and then . . ."

"I'm really sorry."

"No," Mickey said with tears bulging. "I am."

"Forget it."

"How can you forgive me?"

"Mickey, it's already done. I forgave you as soon as it happened. Besides . . ." Georgie was jerked to a full stop by the discovery. After she recovered her breath she said, astonished, "It was bound to come out sooner or later anyway."

"Not if I hadn't shot off my mouth."

Georgie looked into her empty hands. "Even if you hadn't."

Mickey said bravely, "You'd better get the phone."

"We're still talking."

"It's OK. I'm fine." With a little wave, Mickey ducked into the adjoining room.

Peter Flinc's breath filled the receiver. "You called?"

"I need your help."

"If it's about the column . . ." Her voice spiked. "You've settled it?"

"About the column, ah, we're going to meet on that. It may need work."

"Not now," she snapped. "There's trouble here. I need you to make a phone call for me."

"Listen," he said in a breathy voice like an obscene phone caller, "we see TV possibilities, but we need more on the affair."

She parried from habit. "There wasn't any affair."

"Trust me," he said. "You have to open up." Was it a product of her fevered state or did she think she heard him mumble, "What are you wearing right now?"

"Listen. Some fool in your office told Mr. Fulcrum you'd never heard of me." She was shouting, as if that would make him understand. "I need you to tell them I'm OK."

Mickey poked her head in. "Are you all right?"

"No problem," he said.

"Listen, what about the . . ."

"Operator," Danuta trilled.

". . . column," Georgie finished anyway. Flinc was gone. "No. Not you, Danuta. No, I was not disconnected, please go away."

She was breathing shallowly and trying to remember whether she had offended Mickey this time when the phone rang again.

"Danuta, I told you . . ." She recognized the sound at the other end. "Oh, Horace, I have to keep the line open."

"I've been looking everywhere for you."

"I'm waiting for a call."

"I couldn't find Stillman Sedley, either."

"Keep looking, I know he's around."

"You might as well know, I've been worried . . ."

"I'm fine. I'm waiting for a call."

". . . Bill is worried too. You know he wants you to call him. Why won't you call him like I told you to?"

"Because I can't!" Astonished, she slammed down the

receiver and covered her face. She sat like this for several seconds, shivering like a flu victim because Horace had stampeded her into the truth. Until now she had imagined she was just too busy and Bill would understand, she had to get straight with Mr. Fulcrum, she had to find out about the column, she had to find the letters, anything; she had too many reasons, which meant there was really only one.

She couldn't talk to Bill until she had figured out precisely what was going to be the next thing she would have to say to him.

Mickey popped in with her hair combed and her face returned to its normal expression, faintly hopeful if confused. "Well, here I am. I thought maybe I could help you with your calls."

"You?"

For the moment Mickey looked sweetly competent. "I know how hard it is to get calls put through."

A lifelong high-jumper, Georgie recognized her first thought: *only I can do this right.* Her first instinct was to refuse, but she also realized she was perilously close to saying the same kind of thing that had offended Mickey in the first place and so she reconsidered, something she seldom did because she had conducted her life so far on the premise that first thoughts were usually better than second thoughts. Right now her friend the housewife was in considerably better shape than she was, looking perky and helpful in her fresh Ship'n Shore blouse and navy wraparound skirt with her face freshly powdered and composed in an expression of unwavering good will. Mickey had confessed to Georgie and repented and now she was ready and anxious to redeem herself through as many corporal acts of mercy as she could manage in one day, which meant that like it or not, Georgie had better suffer her good offices. "That would be very nice. I've been trying to get through to these people in Washington, the Lawtons? If you could get Danuta to put you through to the long distance operator . . . and you might find out whether Mr. Fulcrum has heard from Mr. Flinc."

"Fink." Mickey was scribbling on a pad.

"Close enough. I need my typewriter."
"You need a nap."
"Are you crazy?"
"You look like you've been in a wreck. I'll work on your calls in Ag's room. After you lie down." When Georgie had accomplished this under her stern eyes, Mickey turned off the bedside lamp and gave the pillow a little pat.
"Leave it on. I'm not going to sleep."
Mickey gave her a push. "Lie down." She lingered in the doorway like Mrs. Cottontail, shaking her finger and laying down the law. "Now are you going to keep popping up like a dummy or are you going to lie there and let me start these calls?"

She kept crashing and bursting into flames and starting up. In a dive, she would be jerked back from the welcoming surface of sleep by an arm or a leg jerking out of control, or an overpowering sweat, which would be fine if she happened to be old enough for hot flashes, which she wasn't. It was anxiety that left her drenched and jangling, near-panic that scooped her out of sleep with a complete line of dialog spoken by somebody, perhaps herself, in her fragmented dream: *a death wish is what they call chutzpah when it doesn't work out.*

Ag came in. "Mickey thinks they'll talk to you at six."
"What time is it?"
"Around five."
"I've been in here all this time?"
"Looks like it."
"And Mickey has been trying all this time?"
"When she wasn't looking for the letters," Ag said. "She says they aren't anywhere in my room, as far as she can tell. Kath cleaned out his carrel in the Verbarium and she didn't find anything, and I checked out his things that he left downstairs with the valuables, and they aren't in the office safe."
"You're being too nice."
"Don't be a jerk," Ag went on brusquely. "I also checked the pockets in his suitcases."
"I'm really sorry about this."

"Why should you be sorry?"

"Putting you through this, on top of everything. It's bad enough you've lost somebody you love . . ."

"Reparation." Ag tossed it off.

"Stop that."

Ag looked at Georgie with clear eyes. "If these things don't add up to reparation, what sense do they make?"

"You shouldn't have to carry what I did."

Ag just shrugged. "Has Kath called?"

Georgie persisted. "You shouldn't have to know about me and Ralph."

"I can't find her anywhere."

"Ag, I am so sorry."

"I haven't seen her since three."

"Ag, listen!"

"I brought you a club sandwich." If Ag knew what was coming she chose to dodge it. She switched on lights and patted pillows, moving around the room like a nurse.

Georgie went on anyway. "I'm so sorry about what I did with Ralph."

"I also brought you a Coke."

"And all this crap about the letters. You shouldn't have to worry about the letters on top of everything else."

All Ag said to this was, "Shut up and eat."

Georgie sat up. "I don't know how to thank you."

"Eat."

"Really."

"Really eat." After a long silence in which Georgie listened to herself chewing, Ag spoke again, but very slowly. "So you really were with Ralph."

Georgie hastened to add the qualifying fact. "It was a long time ago." This was true.

"It's OK, I didn't even know him then," Ag said dreamily.

Oh Ag! Georgie knew better than to try and hug her. She wanted to give Ag everything she had, but the best she could come up with turned out to be, "He never loved me. I don't know if he even liked me very much." Upon saying which she understood this was also true.

"It's all right. Really. I'm OK," Ag said, with her mouth stretching in a beginning grin, "Don't torture yourself."
The rest came. "I didn't love him either."
The breadth of Ag's smile startled her. "Don't you think I know that? You probably already know, I really did."
"Oh Ag, he wasn't worth it. I was trying to tell you but I didn't know how. He really isn't worth all this suffering."
"You're absolutely right. I never met anybody softer at the center, and the center of Ralph was always Ralph. I know it, I knew it at the time, but I had to go with him anyway, you know? And while he was with me he made me feel like the most important person in the world. Everybody needs that at least once. The thing about Ralph was, I was doing something for him that no other woman could. It's like you're the last two people in the world and he needs you and only you can save him, if that makes any sense."
From the vantage point of her own unburied past, Georgie said, regretfully, "I'm afraid it does."
"And in a funny way it was going to be worth it even though it was never worth it, you know?"
"Worth it?"
"I have something to look back on, now that I'm going to be old and alone."
It was time to be firm. "You're not old and you're not going to be alone."
"I'm never going back to Brendan and I've lost my kids." Ag looked into her big hands and then looked up. "Scarlet woman like me."
"Stop that."
"It's true."
"You're never going back to Brendan, but you are going to get back your kids."
Ag shook her head, resuscitating the old misery and setting it in the room between them.
"You're so special you can't be forgiven?"
"After what I did . . ."
"What you did was no big deal, so you can cut it out." To her surprise, now that she had been found out, Georgie was

armed for this next task. With her hands, she reduced Ag's guilt with a gesture, compressing it to a manageable size. "After what you did, indeed."

Ag wavered. "You couldn't possibly understand."

So Georgie almost had her. "After what I did?"

"That wasn't so . . ."

Georgie leaned heavily on this shared guilt, saying, firmly, "Yes it was. But it didn't ruin my life and . . ." As she spoke she became aware that this was not necessarily true; because it was something not yet altogether settled, she had to take a deep breath and collect herself before she could go on. "I'm not going to let it ruin my life. And you—you can't let one mistake ruin your life."

"But it was a big mistake."

"Any mistake is big. Everybody makes them. Take it from me. What you have to do is wash your face and go on."

She had Ag at last. Her face changed. "I . . . Yes. All right."

"Whether or not you think you deserve to have the kids, you owe it to the kids. If you love them you have to put up a fight."

"I love them. That's why I wasn't going to put up a fight."

Georgie had saved her best shot for last. "Do you really want them to stay with a guy who used to beat you up?"

Ag whirled guiltily. "How did you know?"

What was it: the guilt of the victim? "Never mind how I know, I just know. I'm ready to testify. I'll get Bill to testify." She was thinking: If he's still speaking to me.

"You really think I have a chance?"

"If you don't try they'll think you don't love them," Georgie said on inspiration.

Startled, Ag blinked. "I love them more than anything."

"Then you're going to have to fight. You're not going to get them back unless you fight."

"Hey wait a minute," Ag said, with a grin of discovery. "I am going to fight!"

"I'm so glad."

As Ag went on, it became true. "And I'm going to go back to my job and find us a place, and when they find me crying and they want to know why, I'm going to explain that it's a hell of a lot better to have loved and lost than to waste your life on . . . Oh, George!"

"You really are going to be all right, aren't you?"

"Yes. I mean, I think so. Now shut up and drink your Coke."

"God, Ag, you are wonderful."

Ag was still grinning at her through tears of relief. "Are you ready to swear to that in court?"

"You bet I am."

She felt in the pocket of her resort slacks. "Listen, I have something for you."

"What?"

"I did find one. In the bastard's shaving kit," Ag said with that same crazy grin that had turned her mouth into a long wavy line. "I think you'd better have it."

When she held it out Georgie's first instinct was to recoil: proof positive. Had she really wanted this? "What shall I . . ."

"Flush it down the toilet if you want."

There was a commotion in the next room. Dear lord, she thought she heard a honk.

"There's somebody here to see you," Mickey said.

Georgie said urgently, "Don't let him in."

"Looking all over for you."

"I told you not to let him in!"

"Worried to death." It was too late. Horace was already hanging over her, brandishing massed gladiola. "My goodness, you look terrible."

"Oh, Horace, good grief."

"I'm sorry you aren't feeling well."

She looked to Ag or Mickey for rescue but they had tactfully withdrawn. She was going to have to cope with Horace after all. "There's nothing the matter with me, I'm positively fine," she said with a grimace of pain.

"You're not yourself," he said, proferring the glads.

"Probably not." She sighed. "So if you would just go away . . ."

"I'm not myself, either. Haven't been for years." Horace did not go away, he only stood there by the bed with his flowers drooping for so long that Georgie began to be afraid that he had died standing up. When he spoke it was in a new, flat voice. "You know, I haven't always been this way."

"What?"

"You know, an old horror. No, don't argue, I know it's true. It's what happens when you let important things go by. I should have defied mother and gone birding in Kathmandu with Stillman Sedley when he asked me, but it was going to be hard breaking the news that I was beginning a new career in spite of her, so I put it off. I kept putting it off until one day I looked in the mirror and it was too late."

His cloudy blue eyes were watering, whether with regret or good intentions she could not say. "It wasn't your fault."

"I'm afraid it was. We get what we want most of the time. Or what we ask for." In the half-light of the bedroom he looked like a wistful boy. "Don't let it happen to you."

"Horace!" What did he know?

Nothing, apparently. "I just thought if you weren't calling Bill because you two had a fight . . ."

"You came all the way up here just for that?"

His old face was a paper mask of good will.

"Well thank you for worrying, we haven't, really, but you're very kind. And thank you for being so thoughtful, you've made me feel much better, and now . . ." In her own confusion of regret and responsibility she had the sense that perhaps she and all the others were in this not so much to win as to look after and to be looked after. With this in mind she pulled herself to her feet with a manufactured smile and said, "Come and meet my friends."

"If you're under the weather, don't get up."

"Nonsense. They're in here."

"I did it," Mickey said triumphantly, as Georgie led Horace into Ag's room. "It took hours, I had to resort to threats, but I have the Lawtons on the line."

"Oh Mickey, that's great."

"Ag is holding for you," Mickey said, cutting her eyes at Horace, who was hard on Georgie's heels. "Oh, who's this?"

Horace bridled. "I don't believe we've been introduced."

The light bulb went on in Georgie's thought balloon: IDEA.

Overwhelmed by discovery, Georgie looked from Mickey to Horace, Horace to Mickey, trying to cover a beginning grin. With an automatic grace, they had slipped into the steps of a familiar dance. She loved it: different as they were, Mickey and Horace both exuded the same whiff of sadness at having outlived their function, and they were both adrift; it seemed clear that her genteel college roommate and her gentleman nemesis were made for each other, at least for now. "Oh, haven't you met?"

"No, we haven't." Mickey was demure. For all their awkwardness in this tough world they were expert at the social formula; Mickey owned all the costumes and Horace knew all the lines. Because they had both been gently reared, they could subsist on manners while all about them were losing theirs.

"Georgia, if you would be so kind . . ."

"My pleasure," Georgie said. They were, further, in some unmeasurable continuum, two likes. In white shortie gloves and white suit they could take care of each other here, even as they created the illusion that they were charming and delightful and did not need taking care of at all. With the sense of doing at least one thing right, Georgie said, "Mickey, I'd like you to meet my old friend Horace Metcalf, from West Newton. Horace published a landmark history of the American midwest, but he's really an excellent amateur ornithologist." She wheeled like a lighthouse, completing the social transaction with a frantic grace. "Horace, this is my roommate from college, Michele Hoover. Mickey, Horace is interviewing for a new project, on American Catholic thought? I think he could use your help."

"Me?" Mickey blushed becomingly.

Like most social formulae, this one had worked like a charm. Brilliant George added, "That is, if you wouldn't mind."

"I'd be delighted."

With a courtly little gesture Horace repeated, to Mickey this time, "I have a number of questions to ask. If you would be so kind . . ."

"Of course I would." Pink with pleasure, Mickey barely resisted dropping a curtsey. "Just let me go and get my things."

"You're lovely to do this," Georgie said.

"Wait till I tell Howard," Mickey said.

"You can tell him all about Mount Maria." Wanting to do something for Horace, wanting to do something for both of them, she added, "And if you'll see that he meets Stillman Sedley . . . Now be good and have fun," she finished, and she saw them out the door, feeling at least partially redeemed.

20

THE LAWTONS were on the phone up to a point; when Georgie took the receiver from Ag it turned out Mickey had reached the Lawtons' maid, who was either listening to some terrible ethnic station or performing her variation on Muzak, humming to fill the interminable wait until the Lawtons came to the telephone. While Georgie hung on the receiver, Ag talked to her.

"We have a problem," Ag said from the window.

Without having to ask, Georgie said, "You mean Kath."

"She's been crazy ever since Lance left."

"Lance left?"

"For good, I think. I think he's run out on her. The last time we talked she couldn't find him anywhere. She said all his stuff was gone. Something about this woman from last night. Casting director, she said, at least I think she did. She was not exactly in control."

"She was bad this morning," Georgie said.

"Bad?"

"I don't know. She's had this—psychic experience or something."

"Crazy?"

Georgie could not answer this. "That's the trouble, I don't know."

Ag looked worried. "Well she's crazy now."

"When I get off the phone maybe we can talk her down."

"Not a chance. She's gone."

"Kath is gone?"

"Even as we speak." From the window Ag said, "She just bombed out of here in my car. I hope she knows where she's going."

Georgie went as far as the cord would let her but could not reach the window because she was tied to the phone. "Maybe we should go after her—"

"Too late," Ag said from her vantage point. "She just hit the outer drive. She's headed for the main road."

But Robin Lawton spoke unexpectedly, and without missing a beat Georgie dropped into another world.

"Mr. Lawton?"

"It's me. Robin."

"At last. Look, I need your help."

"Never mind that," he said urgently. "Before Anthea gets to the extension there's something I have to let you know."

"I need you to make a call for me."

"Listen. There's been some trouble . . ."

Another voice knifed between them. "Mrs. Kendall." Anthea did not sound warm. "You called?"

"There's trouble here. I need you to verify me, with Forrest Fulcrum. He needs to know I work for *IN*."

"I think that's still in question," Anthea said. "I'm afraid I'm not completely satisfied with what we have. Robin, are you satisfied?" She did not wait for him to answer. "And Robin isn't completely satisfied."

"You want me to write about that—thing I mentioned," Georgie said, cutting her eyes at Ag, who colored and ducked out of the room. It crossed her mind that soon everybody was going to know anyway.

"You've got it," Anthea said. "Once more around the block, but from the heart this time. Confessions."

"Revelations," Robin said.

"I thought you liked my work."

"We do like your work, but you've got to open up to us."

"I don't know if I can do that," Georgie said.

"I thought you were as interested as we were in the column," Anthea snapped.

But Georgie had to complete her thought. "I don't know if I *want* to do it, then."

Anthea pressed. "I thought you wanted us to call Mr. Fulcrum for you."

"I want a little time to think!"

"I see." Anthea's voice was cold.

Robin said confidentially, "You can't afford to take too long."

"I'll take as long as I have to," Georgie said in exasperation, but too late. They had both hung up. Or Anthea had. Sitting more or less stunned but still attached to the receiver, she heard the phone click back to life.

"Listen," Robin said unexpectedly. "There's something I think you ought to know."

"No more!"

"Something has come up. Everything has changed," Robin said unevenly. "The kind of thing that shakes a person's confidence," he went on in a strange new tone. "I have been disinherited. This morning. I just found out."

"What does that have to do with anything?"

"Do you have your own money?"

"Only what I earn."

"Oh well," he said in the condescending tone she would forever afterward associate with the unconscious arrogance that comes with old money. "Then you couldn't possibly understand. Just take it from me, a word form the wise. I like your work but you're going to have to dance to Anthea's tune."

Before she could consider this or ask for a question period, he had clicked into oblivion.

In a better or a more just world she might have called the desk to discover that if nothing else, her name had been cleared here at the Foundation. If Peter Flinc hadn't called maybe Anthea had, or at the very least, Robin, in a partial attempt to make up for his defection, or defeat. Unnerved but hopeful, Georgie gave it twenty minutes, during which she showered and changed before she went back to the telephone, which she had learned to hate. When the desk picked up she said "Hello, Danuta," but instead of returning the greeting the voice identified itself only as room service, making it clear that even if it was Danuta, whose voice she was sure she'd recognized, she had written Georgie off. Clearly her days were numbered here, the trick was going to be hanging on until after the funeral. No, the desk said, there had been no calls from Mr. Flinc or Mrs. Lawton nor even Mr. Lawton. Nobody had bothered to call anybody on her behalf. There were no messages for Mr. Fulcrum from anybody who mattered to her and there were no messages from Mr. Fulcrum for her, either, he had washed his hands of her, the only message was from a Mr. Metcalf, whom she had taken the liberty of sending up, but that was before, wait, was that a call coming in?

"Babe, it's Peter."

"Where have you been?"

"What do you mean, I've been right here."

"You promised you would talk to Mr. Fulcrum."

"I got busy."

"I got desperate."

"Don't stay mad."

"How about I get the desk to patch you through?"

"No problem, but not now. You and I have got to talk." There was a rustling, as of a heavy body shifting; she could see him in the Papa Bear warmup jacket, slouching in his chair with his furry feet on the desk. He mumbled intimately, "Babe, are you sitting down?"

"Wait a minute. About this call you promised you would make."

"I told you, that is neither here nor there."

"It's important. If you don't clear this up Mr. Fulcrum is going to get me fired."

"So is this important," he said. "Don't you want to know why I'm calling?" His voice was so furry and warm that she expected him to ask, Do you want to know what I have on?

"If you say so."

"I want us to stay friends."

"But you want me to expose myself a little more." She was surprised by her anger. "Well listen. You have been diddling me for days and I've had enough: more this, show us that, I am not a striptease artist and I'm not about to start."

"Hold it, babe, that's not what I called to tell you."

But she was rolling, propelled by an enormous feeling of release. "If that's what it takes to get the job then I don't want the job..."

"No problem. Listen."

"... There are certain things I'm never going to do."

"Oh well," he said carelessly. "No harm done. Turns out Anthea's going to be our columnist."

"*Anthea!* Surely you jest."

"Would that I did. I warned you we were in a..."

"State of flux. And you've been leading me on."

"Sorry about that. It's a question of where the money's coming from."

"All this time you've been jerking me around."

"I had hopes," he said. "I really did."

"You've been lying to me all this time."

"Not really. It's Anthea. She's where the money's coming from."

"All this time, and I've been busting my ass, alienating my old roommates..."

"No hard feelings, OK, babe?"

"I don't think I have any feelings."

"Good, I knew we could be friends. So thanks for everything, I guess this is goodbye."

She said, "Same to you, fella," but he had already hung up so she guessed he didn't hear.

OK, she told herself when the roaring in her head had diminished to the point where she could hear the thudding of her heart, *It's not the end of the world.* After all it was she who had just pulled the chain on this arrangement, at least she thought it was. It was not the end of the world but for the moment it might as well be; she felt just as bereft.

What had getting this job meant to her, really? She knew she had in part conceived of it as an outside event that would somehow solve the immediate problem of this portion of her life, but this was only part of it. There was the matter of Trigger Matson, bright, prescient Trigger Matson, talented, raunchy little Trigger, that obnoxious Harvard sophomore punk. For nearly half a lifetime she had been running ahead of Trigger, trying to drown out the sound of his voice. Whether wittingly or unwittingly, that rangy kid who hardly knew her either dropped the starting flag or wrote her epitaph in three words some time in the late Sixties. They were all shoehorned into some nasty literary party in Cambridge with as many leading lights as the hostess could kindle to meet Yevegny Yevtushenko, who was rumored to be in the country but, as she remembered it, never showed up. Good thing—there would not have been enough room for him because the place was already filled to whistling with windy egos, and hissing like an overloaded steam pipe about to blow up. The fallout from Robert Lowell alone overflowed one entire room, as sycophants lapped up every line and pressed him with samples of their own verse, delivered *viva voce* in direct competition with John Berryman across the room. The door to the next room was rendered impassable by lion hunters trying to impress fragile, angry Jimmy Baldwin, every one of them secretly afraid he was going to light the fire next time, while in a corner a distinguished Baptist divine who had been a Freedom Rider got down on his hands and knees to let somebody they both thought was Gunter Grass write what might or might not be his true phone number, using his back as a desk. Georgie had been around long enough to know what the suppliant wanted: ". . . his new book is the most exciting event to burst on the literary scene since the invention of fried dough."—*Famous Author: (signed in his absence)*, a succulent blurb to help sell his one and only book. What did the others want, she wondered, all smarming and smiling and lying in an attempt to be noticed; what did she want?

At the moment she had thought all she wanted was to have a nice time at the party, which was difficult because she didn't know anybody in the place except Bill, whom she was putting through architecture school and who was miserable in this company and agitating to leave, and this fresh little asshole student who did a little dope. She was only a beginning reporter with an aborted book proposal wadded in her drawer at work, the first in what was to become a festering heap, but she could feel the hunger licking as she tried to slip past the clot of people around Baldwin and get a drink. This was where she encountered Trigger, whom she misapprehended as a friendly face. She was preparing to say hello with a dawning smile of relief when this kid looked straight into her to something inside and said, not altogether kindly, "Poor little George." He never even said hello. She was too astounded to say Fuck you, Trigger, too taken aback to say anything. *I'll show him,* she thought at the time: could not stop thinking now. Just once in her life she wanted to be secure enough to stop scrambling instead of forever scurrying after the parade, calling, Wait everybody. Wait up. Yes she wanted to be a star, not for the adulation or even the money but quite simply to shore herself up against her own ruin—what she had done to Bill, becoming the kind of person that might make of her, and she heard herself praying: *If I couldn't be good at that, please God, let me be good at this.* Was this, then, what drove her along? She had spent her life yearning for something she might not ever have, trying to be something she might never be. What was it anyway? She thought now that she might have spent her life tugging against the fact that she was not perfectible. She might never win. Still she had to try, running ahead of the possibility that no matter how hard she struggled she would never get it right.

Trigger, who had thought he was a poet, died in 1970 of a heroin overdose; Lowell was dead, Berryman was dead, half the people at the party were probably dead and she still hadn't shown Trigger, or anybody else. *I don't care, Trigger,* she thought, which was a lie. *I may not be any closer but I'm still here.* This was true; she had no choice.

Now after years of professional struggle and personal denial, in which she pretended it had never happened, she was spilled out the other end. Worse yet, fluttering on the dresser like a ticket to oblivion was her letter to Ralph, which she examined with physical symptoms so severe that a biofeedback trainer would have raced her to the emergency room. It wasn't much of a note. But it was everything.

RALPH. AGAIN. SOON. I LOVE YOU. G.

She had to burn it. Sobbing and fumbling, she extracted a book of complimentary matches from the desk and twisted the paper into a little spill and fed it into the flame. *It would kill Bill,* she told herself, watching the tiny spiral of smoke it made, but she knew this was not true. It was not Bill's feelings that had kept her from telling him what she had done, any more than it was success she had been running after all these years.

She had been running to keep from having to tell Bill. Indeed she had come down here to preserve the lie. As long as she did she could pretend that she was not the kind of person who . . . At the brink of discovery, she pulled back.

But she had blown it. She had lost the job and blown her cover with her friends, letting her pathetic secret out, and here she was more or less empty-handed, except for the ashes of the incriminating note. What had she thought she was doing all these years? She did not know. She had thought if she ignored her affair with Ralph maybe it would go away, suppressing it not because what she had done to Bill was unforgiveable, or even as bad as she thought it was, but for another reason: It was a demonstration not of weakness but of something more complex—the prevalence of failure in spite of the will to succeed; the natural persistence of evil, even in the presence of an active will to be good. *Between the intention and the act falls the shadow.* Had she wasted her life chasing after the wrong thing? How was she supposed to know precisely what was right? If she could love Bill and sleep with Ralph, if she was trying to make Bill happy and had only lied to him, then she was human, frail, fallible in ways that made it clear that there were larger powers at work. If people who were trying to do good could do things that turned out to be absolutely bad, it must be one more indication that there was indeed something behind the veil between the world and the supernatural. For her, at least, the existence of the bad agent, whatever it was, proved the existence of the good.

It took her a long time to collect herself so she could go back in the other room and face Ag.

"I checked the rest of his books and the stuff he left in the Fulcrum safe," Ag said, "You should have seen Danuta's face when I cleaned out his locker in the gym!"

"The letters were in his locker?"

"No." Ag shook her head. "Peanut butter sandwiches. Dozens of them. You look awful. Wash your face and we'll go out to dinner."

"But Kath took the car."
"Ralph hired a Rolls."
"A Rolls!"
Ag's smile brought him back: "He was a big kid about cars."

Ag had the car idling at the loading dock. She rushed Georgie down the backstairs, avoiding the Fulcrum dinner crowd because without having to be told, Ag had figured out that Georgie was *persona non grata* at the Fulcrum Foundation. Riding in the rented Rolls was a little like being shut in with Ralph. The car smelled of him. The backseat was littered with books and unused roller skates, a tennis racket in mint condition; a complete run of *Heavy Metal* competed for space with dirty athletic socks that curled like armadillos on the sandy floor. No papers, Georgie noted after a brief search; no more letters; no letters anywhere. It was a little like rifling a corpse. On the front seat Ralph had kept a Dictaphone to preserve every precious thought, and—pure Ralph—he'd put mother-of-pearl Tables of the Law on the dashboard and festooned the rearview mirror with a rubber hula girl and a pair of fuzzy dice. A flocked plaster dachshund with eyes that lighted up bobbed its head in the back.

More or less enclosed in Ralph's aura, they were both relieved when they reached the restaurant and got out. They drank too many spritzers under the illusion that they weren't drinking much—all that soda, after all—and they ordered desserts they didn't really want. Too queasy to cope with the ice cream-topped brownie she had ordered, Georgie spooned off the fudge syrup and ate it pensively; while all about her were losing theirs, this at least was sweet. Then as the last nice old couple batted their way through the fishermen's nets to the exit and the flame in their hurricane lamp guttered, Ag stirred her melted sundae with her finger, licked it and began to speak.

"I used to think I had all the answers. Did you?"

"Yeah." Georgie gnawed the inside of her mouth.

"They all said the way of God was hard, but who was paying attention? I thought all you had to do was do it right for long enough and you would reach this magic point one day where it was given. It would all be done, and you could quit doing it."

"They never said that."
"It's what I believed."
"Me too."
"It's never over. Are you going to drink that drink?"
"I don't think so." Georgie pushed it toward her. "Maybe it's finally over when you're dead."

Ag drained it and began crunching ice. Her kind, plain face was altered by what she had been through, and when she spoke again it was slowly, while Georgie leaned forward because it was getting hard to concentrate. They might have been two convalescents, discussing the nature of their recent illnesses in the dining room of some mountain-top recovery lodge. "It isn't fair," Ag said. "Every time you jump, you think you've done it this time. Then you turn around and somebody has raised the stick."

Georgie was dizzy with drink, or was it discovery. "I think maybe somebody wants us to jump a little higher."

"Right," Ag said.

"I guess that's what it's all about." It was. It was about being booted, belted, kicked and goosed into eternity, an unending effort that made individual successes—and failures—irrelevant because nothing was ever really finished here. She said, "Nothing is ever enough." She wanted time to think about this, but Ag was off on another track.

"If the people in the church can't even agree on it, how are we supposed to know?"

Between the intention and the act . . . "Know what to do?"

"What God wants."

Georgie shrugged. "It's getting harder to figure out."

Ag let out all her breath: Q.E.D. "So it turns out Ralph was right," she said, sounding vindicated.

"About what?"

"About Catholic girls."

"Catholic girls what?" She already knew; she had spent her life on it, was doing it now.

"Taking things so hard."

"Right." She was surprised by a flash of pride. She grinned. "We really do take things too hard."

21

RETURNING TO FULCRUM, she was not feeling reconciled so much as *suspended,* her shoulders high and her breath taken in, waiting to be expelled. She had the idea there was something significant waiting to happen—exposure, she supposed, Fulcrum tripping over her in the lobby and ending her career, the Lawtons arriving to have her cast out, or worse, some confrontation she hadn't known enough to worry about. As they rolled out of Snowy Egret she understood this wasn't it. Instead, riding along the flat roads in the hired Rolls, Georgie scanned the sandy fields, the vistas where very little grew, in the uneasy realization that whatever happened, it would not be to her. She didn't know why it was so important, but she had to look for Kath. Partly, she supposed her distress was barometric; the air was completely still, the early evening sky a bizarre green, but that wasn't it. She was worried about Kath.

Ag said, "Where do you suppose she is?"

Georgie jumped. "How did you know?"

"You've been glued to that window ever since we left the restaurant."

"She was so wrecked this morning," Georgie said.

"She was pretty wrecked this afternoon." Ag slowed the Rolls so they could both look. "D'you think she's hurt herself?"

"Not on purpose," Georgie said, "but she could have bombed off the road somewhere, or hit something."

"You don't think she would, like, take pills."

"Not Kath. That's not her style."

"Lance," Ag said in disgust. "I never liked that kid."

"I don't even know if Kath did. But she fell into it anyway." Georgie considered this. "Went right over her head even though she knew what he was."

"When you're in love," Ag said, complete with implications, "that kind of thing doesn't even slow you down."

This was almost too much. Georgie shot her a look which Ag did not return; instead she kept her unsmiling Irish eyes on the road, leaving George to brood. "If anything's happened to her I'll kill him."

"You'll have to find him first. Listen, what are we going to do if she flips out?"

"She won't. Kath's OK." Georgie remembered the Kath of this morning, that strangeness about *the other times.* "At least I think she's OK."

Then Ag said, with alarming accuracy, "The trouble is, she never does anything halfway."

Fixed on the window, Georgie checked groves and culverts for the wrecked Datsun, half-expecting to find the car heeled over and their friend wandering distractedly. With a rising sense of urgency, she made Ag double back and circle Snowy Egret looking for the rusted Datsun in front of bars and motels and next to the lake. They didn't find it and they didn't find Kath or any sign of Kath.

By the time they got back to the Foundation parking lot there was a Florida thunderstorm lowering, a dark shape swelling in the sky like some enormous, gravid beast. Getting out of the car, Georgie automatically ducked her head as if to ward off a blow. Black clouds collided as they ran for the back door of Fulcrum in front of an advancing sheet of rain. Drops the size of robins' eggs slapped the asphalt and spattered into fragments on Georgie's head as she ducked inside. Lighting thwacked into a nearby Royal palm, splitting something inside her like a rock.

She screamed in pain. "My God!"

"What's the matter?"

"I know where Kath is." Compelled, she ran for the elevator

without even trying to explain where Kath was or how she knew, turning at the last minute to say, "Wait here."

"Hell no."

"You wait. Please." Setting her hands on Ag's shoulders, she quite simply *placed* her outside the door, saying as the doors closed, "I know where she is but I don't know what she's going to do."

With her heart thudding, she took the long ride as far as it went, thrust her shoulder against unmarked doors on the top floor until one yielded and she found the stairs leading up.

Yes, Kath was at the top of the tower. As Georgie came gasping out of the door at the head of the stairs she saw Kath near the edge even as she'd feared, a wraith in a red dress swaying with her arms outstretched and her body turned to meet the driving rain, her beautiful friend caught and held by some force Georgie could not identify. There was the crazed or driven Kath Hartley with her face upturned to the violent thunderstorm, hands extended to: what for the split second pulsed like absolute blackness within the dark rain, Kath galvanized by something Georgie could neither see nor hear.

Whirling with her mouth open as if in an exultant shout, she advanced into the sheet of rain with her arms spread and her mouth wide: wild, lovely, miserable Kath, so electrified that Georgie could not be sure whether she was listening to something or speaking or simply gulping wind and rain because she was getting ready to vault the barrier and jump.

Oh no, Georgie thought, or yelled, Oh no you don't!

But Kath was completely caught up in or with this— whatever it was! and neither paused nor turned to face terrified George.

"Kath, my God, what are you doing?"

Nor would she hesitate as Georgie began to shout.

Nor would Georgie stop to reason before she ran at her friend headlong, pelting across the heat-stressed surface like a tiger with its tail on fire and lunged for Kath's midsection and brought her down hard on the asphalt roof.

Kath either sang or shrieked, "My God, my God!"

"Kath, don't do it!"

"Aaaaaa . . ." Gobbling rain, Kath gasped and pulled away from Georgie's grasp, changing so rapidly that Georgie could not be certain of the stages, which might have been measured in three shots: out of herself, returning, *there,* so swift that no one could interpret them. She shook her wild, wet hair over her face and then combed it away with her fingers, smoothing the red skirts before she turned around, and when she faced Georgie she looked lovely and ravaged and utterly confused.

Georgie was crying. "Please don't do it!"

"Do what?" Kath blinked and shook her head. "Georgie, what are you doing on the roof?"

The rain had slacked all at once and now it was retreating gradually as if finished with them, but Georgie could not stop shaking or sobbing. "Oh just, oh please don't."

"What's the matter? What are you talking about?"

"You," she said into an increasing stillness. "The roof. Please don't go off the roof."

"What? Are you crazy?" Wet as she was, her red dress sodden and her hair streaming, Kath was gorgeous, and completely in control. "Who's going off the roof?"

"You. Just now," Georgie gasped; she could not get her breath.

"Me, just now? You are going nuts."

"But you looked so . . ."

"Oh, that," Kath said carelessly. She shrugged as if nothing unusual had happened. "It was just the buzz again."

"The buzz?"

"You remember, that I told you about, maybe it was yesterday."

"It was this morning," Georgie said miserably; had Kath lost all track of time?

"Whenever. Whatever. It's not important. I was up here, is all, and I just . . ." Matter-of-fact as she sounded, her eyes shone with the afterimage of something, what, inexpressible. "I would never, ever do anything like jump."

Abruptly the rain slacked. It was so gentle now that Georgie wondered if it was she who was over the edge, if Kath was fine and she had imagined this. "You looked . . ."

"Well, I wasn't." Kath pushed her dark hair back and let the dwindling rain wash her face, and then she looked at Georgie in such composure that she might have been speaking not out of a thunderstorm but in a greenhouse on a summer day.

"George, I heard something speak."

"It was me."

"Not you."

"Me, when I came out the door just now. I called your name."

"It wasn't you." As if Kath had willed it, the rain stopped. Now she looked at Georgie as if daring her to interrupt. "Listen. I think I know what it was."

Georgie said doggedly, "It was the wind."

"No."

"The ventilator. It makes . . ."

Kath's eyes were bright and strangely clear. "It wasn't the ventilator. I know all the sounds now, OK? I've been up here for hours."

Remembering Marguerite Lattanza, Georgie set her teeth. "But you don't know how you got here."

"In the elevator," Kath said. "I didn't want to come up here, it was the last thing I wanted, probably because I was scared, but, you know? I didn't have much choice. I went looking for Lance even though I knew I was never going to find him, just to put it off, but I probably knew I would end up here. No choice, you know? Not after last night. After what happened. That I told you about."

"The, um, ah . . ." Georgie said uncomfortably; she found this embarrassing. "Vision."

Kath said matter-of-factly, "The buzz. So I was probably, you know, hoping? But nothing happened until a minute ago, when it got all black."

Georgie rushed in. "That was the storm."

"Something else. After it started." Kath lifted her head. "Blacker than black. After which I heard this thing. Do you want to know what it said?"

"No!" Georgie softened. "I mean, no, please."

"Don't worry, you don't have to, it's all right. So probably

I'm crazy," Kath went on almost blithely, "but. Something. Did. Call. And sooner or later I'm going to find out what it was, if it takes the rest of my life." She slicked her hair again and grinned. "Now let's get out of here, George, I think this place is a dump."

Then Kath got up from the asphalt and shook her dripping crimson skirts and without looking back, started across the roof to the utility column and the stairway down, her bright image shimmering as the line storm moved ahead of her in a glistening sheet. Maybe she was the one who was going crazy here, Georgie thought, or they both were; she could not be sure even of this because she could not shake the sense that something huge had just quit moving somewhere just beneath the surface of the observed. Whatever this was, it was not going to let her see it; it had only stirred a little, to let her know it was there... So it was that Georgie found herself standing on the Fulcrum roof more or less wide open—mouth, eyes, arms, straining because in some complicated spiritual way she had become the receptacle, or instrument, although whether waiting to be filled or picked up and used she could not say. *What I am called upon to do,* she thought, willing but ignorant. *What am I called upon to do?*

"George! Hey, George!" When she turned Kath was standing in the door to the stairway like an impatient kid, holding the door open with one jaunty hip. Yawning, she waved. "Are you coming or what?"

On the way downstairs behind Kath, Georgie was too polite to say anything more than you're welcome when Kath thanked her for coming, and too confused to ask her any more questions, which left her to construct her own explanation for what had just taken place, trying to build a logical formula as they followed the orderly sequence of stairs and landings down to their floor. She was, after all, a writer. It was her business to make sense of things. Whether revenance or conversion or simple hallucination, she decided, Kath had indeed experienced *something* up there on the roof, and whether it was one of these things or all of them or none of the above, it was going to enable Kath to construct her survival narrative, her version of the stories people have to tell themselves so they can make it through.

Whether it had been a vision or an hallucination or sheer invention Georgie could not say. This was not important now. It had fulfilled its function, Georgie thought, surprised because, strange as it was, it seemed appropriate—right. Kath had been given the means to go on with the rest of her life.

As they came out of the stairway on their floor the elevator doors opened, disgorging Mickey and Horace Metcalf, who was giving Mickey's gloved hand a gentlemanly shake as prelude to an avuncular goodnight. Mickey complained, "I bet there isn't any Stillman Sedley."

Horace honked. "There is too a Stillman Sedley, he just wasn't here tonight."

22

I WONDER WHERE *they think Ralph is now,* Georgie thought at the funeral, which was not so much a funeral as a celebration of Ralph's contributions to the world of thought, according to the Engravatoned message on the program emblazoned with the crest of the Fulcrum Foundation. It was billed as a Commemorative Moment because, according to Danuta, Mr. Fulcrum did not like to think that anybody ever died. This struck Georgie as sublimely logical since it was clear that the old man was uncomfortably close to the moment.

The event was taking place in the triangular Fulcrum auditorium, which had been banked with flowers and arranged so that the distinguished speakers in academic regalia sat on-stage in folding chairs in a half-circle around the inurned vestiges of Ralph. Ralph himself took center stage under a pin spot with a bastard amber gel that made the urn glow with a golden sheen. His urn was silver, and could have been mistaken for a tennis trophy if it hadn't been for the figures of Truth and Beauty and Knowledge pursuing themselves in an eternal circle of copper chasing around the rim. Someone had thought to put a brazier next to it: first tongues of what was supposed to be an Eternal Flame. Now the great and the near-great and the venerable Forrest Fulcrum (on a dais behind Ralph with the light glinting silver in his thick white hair) and newsmen and camera people from all three networks and the Foundation cinematographer crowded the auditorium, waiting for the entrance hymn to end. Danuta had engaged the Boston Pops, and the music was glorious. Ag and the committee had agreed on the *Largo* from the *New World Symphony* to open because it sounded appropriately memorial without being churchy. Since even a hint of religion would offend at least half the people here, a nonspecific service had seemed well advised. *Where, then, do they think Ralph went? Where do I think he is?* All she knew for certain was that the vital part of Ralph was definitely not in that urn, nor was it in the collective memory of the people in this room. When she tried to visualize the rest she could not, and sitting there, she imagined all these other hundreds of people sitting there, each with a separate and differing vision, so many and so wildly unalike, from the literal picture of the lumpy rubble in the urn to (Horace, she bet, perhaps reborn Mickey) Ralph in the white robe complete with wings and halo and a harp.

Next to Georgie, Mickey stirred, perspiring but happy in her appropriate costume of navy silk with the white shortie gloves. Mickey loved ceremony. Now that Georgie thought about it, so did she. It gave an order to major events and endowed lesser ones with a certain dignity, creating the impression that what people did and what happened to them really did matter, at least for a while. On the other side of Mickey, Horace sat quietly in his white suit, with his jaw hanging ever so slightly and his hands folded in a prayerful attitude that seemed heartfelt. He was still a mess, but in his fumbling way he had helped Mickey through a hard time, and pushy and ungraceful as he was, he was kind. He had been truly good to Mickey when nobody else had time; last night she came in glowing with excitement because she had gotten to sit at Mr. Fulcrum's table, even though Mr. Fulcrum wasn't there, on top of which Horace had offered her a job as research assistant on his new project on American Catholic Thought. ("Horace says he needs an insider's views," Mickey said proudly. "I can work at the New York Public and we'll meet once a month.") Georgie looked at creaky, awkward Horace almost fondly, and in this unbidden affection felt linked to Bill. She was never going to be absolutely Mrs. Nice but it was clear she had to try. Or wanted to.

Three seats down, Serena sat, Ralph's widow flanked by her two handsome sons. Ag was gone. Now that she and Serena had met and talked, she had wept for what turned out to be the last time. Forgiven, she yielded custody of the funeral to Serena and hugged her friends. She was heading north, she said, to make her peace if not with Brendan, then with herself. She had to find a good lawyer to help her get shut of Brendan and keep custody of the kids: she was almost looking forward to the rest of her life.

Kath was not here either. Altered by the events of the night before, she had met them out front as they came back from Mass, Kath with face bright and eyes glistening, looking fresh as a newly washed slate. They were all different this morning: Mickey because of her adventures with Horace, Ag because she had survived Serena, and Kath because of—whatever had happened to Kath. So Ag was gone and Kath was gone and if Georgie was still here it had something to do with ceremony, the element of art in these public gatherings that people found necessary because it seemed important to mark beginnings and ends to things. She had to make her own termination; she was approaching closure, and she needed to make public acknowledgment of the fact that while life went on and on, certain things were indeed truly over.

She had to bury Ralph for good.

What had happened to her this morning so far? Sitting with her head bent, she tried to sort it out.

Mickey got them up at dawn so they could get to early Mass in Snowy Egret and still make it back in time for Ralph's send-off. She jostled Georgie with an apologetic grin because it was so early, but this was the only game in town. Feeling drained and gritty from lack of sleep, Georgie rolled out. This was a given; if Mickey hadn't checked schedules last night Georgie would have done it, or Ag, anybody but Kath, who had been, what, transfixed or transformed by whatever it was that had befallen her on the roof, a moment so grave that she slept as if smitten by a broadsword, or as if she'd been laid out by major surgery, reamed of what ailed her and left to mend. The rest got up without question, paddling down the deserted hallways and out to church. It was what they did every Sunday of their lives. It was not so much what they did as who they were.

Georgie drove through the early morning while Mickey yawned next to her and Ag dozed in back. It was so quiet that she could hear the gravel crunching as they cleared the turnaround, the whisk-whisk of the sprinklers.

Mickey was brighter today, perhaps because for the first time she had done something on her own. She carried herself with more assurance. If she wanted, she'd said last night, when they were all too wild and distracted to listen, she could take over the book when Horace got too old or sick to work; yes she was beginning to outstrip her opinion of herself. This did not prevent her making a half-turn to consider the Fulcrum tower, where everybody but them still slept, and then her own hands in the shortie gloves, still apprehensively curled. Mickey said pensively, "Do you ever get the idea the whole world is going in the opposite direction?"

Georgie didn't have to ask what she meant. "Yes."

The church Mickey had found was a mission chapel, planted at a crossroads down the road from the phosphate plant and bordered on three sides by pastures populated by blanched-looking longhorns which grazed listlessly on brown weeds. The people in the drab rural church were of a piece with the land: strangely leached of color. In clothes put on for Ralph's sendoff, Georgie, Ag and even Mickey were well-dressed by comparison. Looking like exotic birds snared among so many chickens, they knelt among knotty oldsters and sagging women and children who seemed to run to fat, everybody not so much dressed as decently covered in polyester weaves and double knits.

The priest was probably on the first of his round of three or more mission churches, which accounted for the hour. As they stood to sing the syrupy entrance hymn, Georgie wondered whether he minded as much as she did that the music was poor and the parishioners' voices thin and disspirited, and did he mind that, like her, many of them were half-asleep, present but not really here, thinking about any number of things not directly related to the Mass. It was a good thing she wasn't in this for the aesthetic experience, she thought, because except in abbeys and some college chapels and certain urban churches, the aesthetics were almost always terrible.

Why was she in this? What was she doing here when she could be safe with her head under two pillows in the Fulcrum air conditioning, sleeping off everything that had happened to her?

Pressed to explain, she would have named what was for her the only possible reason—the existence of a life beyond the visible and tangible. It was the only thing that made sense of this otherwise puzzling activity. Thinking about this, she tugged against it—the absolute; she had been tugging against the absolute when she fucked Ralph and again, more strongly, when she did not so much deny as hide it. She had imagined that she could confess Ralph and not tell Bill and so, accepting immediate consequences, efface the eternal marks and pretend it had never been. But it had been. It absolutely had taken place, and she understood what she was tugging against: the ethic, or truth or ultimately mystical belief that what you did in this life had consequences beyond the temporal. Whatever you did, for better or worse you were writing on eternity. Which explained why she was here. She was here, she thought, because she absolutely had to be.

It was a matter of definition, which was why Georgia Kendall and all the other ragtag worshipers came to this and every other temporally unsatisfying Mass being celebrated anywhere. She had gone nuts once, in the golden period when she wanted everybody to have what she had, trying to explain the Trinity to some guy from was it Princeton who really wanted to know or said he did; she struggled to explain until she arrived at ground zero, saying with some relief: It's a mystery. The whole thing is a mystery. This was the amazing part. It was. She and all these sleepy others were, OK, participating in a mystery. That this was necessary, no, essential to them, was a puzzle; and God, the puzzle was the answer: for her the need in spite or because of everything, to do or be *this* reaffirmed the mystery.

Instead of speaking from notes the priest began to read his sermon in a drone that for Georgie in her present state was better than white noise: perfect background for her reflections. Preoccupied, she mulled it, standing with the others for the Creed. Interestingly, now that they were speaking the old words, the little congregation that had not much bothered to sing the bad hymns sounded like twice as many people.

She had a hard time pulling herself to attention as they knelt for what used to be the *Sanctus*. The translation was not wonderful. With the old Latin, with bells and incense, would she have been more attentive? Maybe and maybe not. If there was an absolute God, Georgie thought, then why couldn't His people manage to do things better, and why could she not even manage to be absolutely attentive? Why did she and the others not spend their lives running around being absolutely good, in anticipation? She did not know. *Between the intention and the act . . .* but they didn't. *Falls the shadow.* Which was the misfortune and the wonder—that inescapable uncomfortable, preternaturally acute sense of responsibility to the mysterious; the trying, over and over, even when you knew ahead of time that you were going to fall short. Trying was the whole thing back then, at the beginning, and it was the whole thing now, in this dreary little church with its sleepy congregation, which of course explained why in spite of what she took to be the source and reason for what they were doing, what happened in church could be so true in spirit and sometimes so tacky in execution. *Trouble is, this part gets done by people.*

Lord, while she was blundering around in her head they had come to the Consecration.

Here I am. I can't even keep my mind on it but here I am.

Beaten as she was, with no accounting for the way this morning found her, Georgie was Godstruck and wild: in love with it. *Because here it is.*

Thus George, through the Last Blessing.

It was just as well they had to sit through the final hymn before Mickey would let them leave; it gave Georgie time to collect herself. There was a church bake sale under the pastor's carport and the three friends stood in the shade breakfasting on coffee and orange bread, standing apart from the local faithful as Georgie, at least, had stood apart from congregations in a dozen different places. They stood with their heads bent in the harsh Florida sunlight, smiling, blowing crumbs and mumbling.

"God," Ag said in the car going back to Fulcrum. She was in front now, trying to fix her hair in the rearview mirror. "I look terrible. This dress is hideous. How am I going to face Serena?"

In fact she looked quite nice in a lilac silk that hid the stern lines of her frame and made her hair look gold instead of orange. Georgie kept one hand on the wheel, patting Ag with the other. "I think you look wonderful."

"I feel like a scarlet woman."

"Well you're not, OK? You're just a nice person that got hurt."

"I guess you're right," Ag said, "but Lord, I wonder. Georgie, what are the kids going to think?"

"They're going to think you're back."

"I never meant to be gone so long," Ag said. "What are they going to say to me?"

"They're going to be very glad to see you."

Sitting in back now, Mickey said out of a morose silence, "Mine have stopped going."

In any other company this would not have made much sense, but Ag responded immediately. "Oh, Mick, I'm sorry."

"Oh, that's too bad," Georgie said. Looking at her own sons, she wanted to rip out her faith and hand it to them, whole, to spare them doubts, or questions; how could she, when nobody was spared? Could they see what she saw? She did not know. All she could do was want it for them. "It happens."

"I don't know what I did wrong," Mickey said, "I couldn't figure out what to say to them."

"It wasn't anything you did, Mick, OK?" This was what you said to Catholic Moms whose children presented their backs on Sundays when it was time to get up for Mass. "For all you know it's a passing thing."

Mickey sighed.

"Shh. Shh. Chances are, sooner or later they'll come back to it."

Ag was thoughtful. "That's the amazing thing, isn't it? One way or another, we all seem to come back to it."

"God," Mickey said, "I hope so." Then she went on in the way she had worked out for playing whatever hand fate dealt her: pure Mickey. "Oh, George, do you think I ought to do jewelry for this thing we're going to, or is it too early in the morning?"

"Your lavalier by all means," Georgie said, navigating the Fulcrum driveway. "And the gloves are lovely. Hey, there's Kath! Kath, hey!"

Kath stood by the pool, staring as if she had never before seen water. After a moment she turned and came toward them; she was in shorts, thus making clear without having to tell them that she was going to finesse the Ralph Schwartz memorial. Ag proferred a piece of leftover orange bread that Kath devoured without even tasting it, wiping away the crumbs with a careless hand and saying without having to explain, "OK, guys, shall we do this?"

Together, the four addressed the Fulcrum building which was awake now, teeming with people from guests to caterers to the entire Mormon Tabernacle Choir, which had been marshelled for the service.

As they came into the lobby Ag and Kath and Mickey formed up more or less in front of and around Georgie, a protective phalanx. She was here against orders and if Forrest Fulcrum spotted her, there would be trouble for her and Danuta both. He was crusty and used to getting his own way. Foiled, he could even be mad enough to send for the police. But she had to do this. Once they had her inside the thousand-seat auditorium for the service, she could slouch unseen behind all those rows of the pious. All she had to do was make it across the lobby. They had no way of knowing Serena had arrived, or that as they made this run, they would find her standing with her bags under the grand archway in front of the auditorium.

Preoccupied, discovering that she felt unaccountably joyful, Georgie had more or less forgotten Ralph's wife and his sons until now. She thought of them as distant figures in New Jersey, not here. Therefore she came unprepared through the main entrance, protected by her friends in a flying wedge, Ag first. So it was Ag who bumped into Serena—Ag also unprepared, vulnerable, ragged. Shaded by a potted palm, she was tucking the ends of her full, dark hair into a French roll. Flanking Serena were two tall boys whose handsome faces carried intimations of Ralph—not as he was, but unflawed Ralph idealized by a future. She was smiling.

Serena saw them. Putting her sons behind her with a murmur, she approached Agnes Mary with her hands outstretched. With a little cry, Ag ducked as if she wanted to run and hide from whatever might be Serena's accusations, or reproaches. Although she herself was feeling none too strong, Georgie steadied Ag. Serena was large and calm and handsome in plain white. Her face glowed with what Georgie took to be the enhanced light of relief that comes with knowing that in a lifetime of bad moments with a rat, the worst thing imaginable has already happened. For Serena, whose life with Ralph must have been a misery, there would be nowhere to go from this point but up. Grieving though she must be, she would never again have to worry about where Ralph was, or what worse thing he was doing.

"Don't run away," Serena said to Ag, who had covered her face. Tall as Ag was in the lilac silk, she seemed to think she could hide herself from Serena. "It wasn't your fault."

"I feel so . . ."

"Don't," Serena said matter-of-factly. "It wasn't the first time."

"That he died?"

"What he did. It was one of Ralph's oldest tricks."

Caught off-guard, Ag fell back a pace. "What?"

"He always attempted suicide when the going got too tough."

"Always!"

"Really." Serena shrugged. "It was one of his survival tactics."

Changed by this knowledge, Ag grimaced. "He told me you didn't understand him."

"That was another one of his tactics," Serena said. Dressed in white as she was, handsome and stoic, she could have been a nurse, or an elegiac survivor of a Greek tragedy. "He always tried it when things got too thick."

"Too thick!" If Ag had already begun to crumple under the burden of new information, this finished her. Gripping her arm, supporting Ag, Georgie considered this, considered everything.

"He knew if he just tried suicide, I would come and rescue him."

The word hung between them: *rescue.* Ag cried, "I knew it was my fault. Oh, Serena, this is so terrible."

"It was nobody's fault but Ralph's." Serena said. "He brought it on himself. I'm just sorry you got pulled in after him."

Ag put her hands to her face. After a moment she spread her fingers. "I am so sorry—"

"It wasn't you. It was his stupidity." Then Serena said, for all their sakes, "It was an accident."

Ag said in a low voice, "Are you going to be all right?"

"Me? I'll be fine. Now. If you want to know the truth, Ralph was a nightmare." Serena was almost offhand, like a mother describing a cherished hellion. "I stood by him because I loved him in spite of it, and besides . . ." Her rich voice suggested a lifetime of closeness. ". . . We promised each other something once. Now that he's . . . Well, now maybe I can have a life, so please don't worry."

"If there's anything . . ." Even though she was the one who needed it, Ag tried to make the offer.

"I'll be fine. That is, I'll be fine *now*," Serena said, adding, surprisingly, "I'm sorry he caused you any unhappiness."

"I'm sorry I was so dumb."

"Shh. Shh. It's over, and face it, it's a relief." Serena went on softly, reminiscent, "He was a restless spirit, Ralph."

Ag gave a little cry.

"Listen. It was never your fault. Whatever you do, don't go around thinking it was ever your fault. It was always Ralph. It was his way of *being.*"

Georgie was clinging to Ag's arm for support now. If back then she had known but not comprehended that she was one of many, now she truly knew it.

"Ralph was Ralph, which was why we both loved him, you

know?" Serena hugged the speechless Ag. "Thank you for making him happy."

Ag flushed; pink with relief, looking soft and almost pretty in the lilac silk, she stepped out of Serena's arms for a moment so she could take her hands. She could barely say, "Thank you."

In the brief lull that followed as Ag wept and Kath and Mickey fussed over her, Serena turned to Georgie, speaking in low tones. "I can see why Ralph liked you. It wasn't only the intelligence."

Georgie started. "How did you know?"

"We shared everything."

"Everything!"

"I suppose it's what kept us together, through everything."

"God. I am so sorry—"

"Look. I brought you a present." Serena slipped her hand into her shoulder bag and pulled out a manila envelope, thick with paper.

The letters. "Where . . ."

"He sent me the extra key to the rented Rolls."

"The Rolls," Georgie said. She and Ag had been riding around in it only yesterday. How long had they spent searching? "The Rolls."

"This was in the trunk along with his pool cues and all his canceled checks. That's where Ralph always kept documents. No. Don't thank me. Don't apologize. Don't give it another thought. You're needed." She indicated Ag.

Georgie began, "And you . . ."

Serena inclined her head toward her two handsome sons, who had stepped forward to stand on either side of her. Together, the three of them formed a neat corporation: the family. "I am needed too. I have my boys." She finished simply, saying, "And now that everything is done and finished, I have Ralph. For good this time."

"God bless you," Georgie said, and blushed.

"You too." Serena pressed her hand and then went on into the auditorium, where the first mourners were already finding seats.

When she turned back to her friends, Georgie discovered

they had clumped in an altered formation: Ag with her head and shoulders back, resolute and valedictory.

Ag said, "George, I need you to do something?"

"Name it." Georgie looked at Ag: the wet, spiky eyelashes, the tremulous smile smeared across her pink Irish mug. She would have done anything for her.

"This." Ag's gesture took in the four of them, the lobby, swept wide to include the Fulcrum faithful filing into the auditorium. "I don't think I can do this right now."

"Right," Georgie said. "You shouldn't have to. Mickey and I will take care of it for you."

Ag said, shakily, "And Serena."

"And Serena. Serena will take care of it."

So they saw Ag to the elevators. The two who had children understood that Ag had been away from hers long enough, that she had to get them back before she could begin to mend. They were all going to testify at the custody hearing. Surprisingly, it was Kath who would provide written proof that Brendan was a philanderer. So Ag would use the long drive north to regroup: mourn, plan, do whatever thinking she had to so she would be ready for the struggle. Embracing her in a flurry of farewells, they sent her up to finish packing.

Then as the doors closed on Ag, Kath, who had been standing with them but was not really among them, tugged Georgie's hand. "You know I'm not going to do this funeral."

"It's OK." Georgie looked at her irises, which seemed to be whirling. "Are you?"

"I'm fine. Terrific. I think I'm wonderful."

Georgie took her hands. "Kath, what's happened to you?"

"I don't know. It's amazing."

"What was it last night," Georgie said raggedly. "What did you see? What was that?"

"I don't know," Kath said, with her voice lifting like a flight of birds, "but whatever it is, I've got to find it." She was crazy with it, gorgeous; she could have been the Maid of Orleans going out to do battle, although the enemy she prepared to meet might change its face a dozen times before noon. "Look, sorry about the funeral and all, but I need to go out and think."

"I love you Kath."
"Me too, Georgie."

Feeling strangely bereft, Georgie saw her out the main entrance, watched her set out across the blasted landscape, disappearing into the blaze of Florida sunlight.

With the departures completed, Georgie and Mickey went to the auditorium to pay their respects to what remained of Ralph. Horace snagged their elbows at the door, where he had been lurking. Georgie broke free and dodged toward the back row, where she would be safe from Forrest Fulcrum, but she was apprehended by an usher, who must have been told to look out for her. A second fresh-faced college intern took Mickey by the left elbow since Horace refused to let go of her right. Struggling, Georgie wondered if they were going to be thrown out. She was being inexorably drawn into the front row because, she understood as Ralph's smiling widow greeted them, Serena wanted them to sit with her. Georgie wanted nothing more than to cut and run for hiding, but if Serena was brave enough to take the front row after everything that had happened, with half the congregation knowing how Ralph had betrayed her, the least Georgie could do was support her.

The music ended abruptly, and on the platform the first speaker, a deconstructionist philosopher of a certain age, began an interminable reminiscence about a colloquium he had once attended with Ralph. He went on at length even though Stillman Sedley was waiting to speak and Leontyne Price was preparing to sing, after which John Cage, according to the program, was going to perform a piece composed in Ralph's honor. He was sitting stage-right with what looked like a garbage can filled with Ralph's old lecture notes, an electric fan and a portable shredder. Still the speaker babbled while Georgie did her best impression of an intent listener, disassembled and distracted as she was, and fixed as she was on her own turmoil and confusion. "Naked we come into this world," said the speaker, overriding instructions to keep it secular, perhaps because it proved an academic point Georgie had not bothered to catch, "and naked we go out."

Except, Georgie thought, feeling disproportionately exalted, *for what we have become.* It was this, of course, that had kept alive the knowledge that she was not yet straight with Bill, and this that had propelled and driven her through the defeat at *IN* and would keep her going in spite of it—the sense of endeavor, or incompleteness, the knowledge that at the end, whenever that was, whatever it was, she had to have something to show. Another proof of the existence ... It did not, she thought, make much real difference whether she came to the accounting a success or a failure—only that she kept on hurling herself at the wall in the hope that eventually she might make it up and over. Whether or not she ever figured out precisely what was wanted of her, she did know that it *was* wanted: something expected, the passion of trying to exceed herself. *Bill!* Caught in a fever of introspection, she noted briefly that the eulogist's mind had wandered and then she lost the thread altogether. She sat with her head bent as the others' heads were bent, one sheep among several hundred others here in the auditorium, docile Georgie blending in, suffused with emotion and mellowed by ceremony, looking up at the urn that represented Ralph, bathed in golden light, at . . .

At the eyes of Forrest Fulcrum, who was looking right at her. She blanched as their eyes clashed. Right, she had defied him. Right, it was dumb. For a second she was not certain he recognized her; if she shrank she might blend in. But this was not right. She had not come all this distance to dissemble; she was tired of trying to pretend to be somebody else to please people, and so she sat a little straighter, fixing him with her eyes until she was certain that he did indeed recognize her.

He glowered. *You.*

Yes it's me. Georgia Mahan Kendall, and I'm not afraid of you.

For the moment, she was not afraid of anybody.

She held his eyes just long enough to let him know that she would stay now in spite of his wrath if she wanted to. She would stay precisely as long as she liked. Therefore when she stood, it was clear to her—to him, she hoped—that she was saying goodbye to all this by choice. Then in an unhurried way she turned and began to make her way down the aisle, patting

Mickey's knee and touching her mouth to hand a silent kiss to Serena as she left. She had buried Ralph for good this time; she had made a mental adjustment that would send her back into her work on her own terms, not anybody else's. There was only one thing left to do.

Feeling a hundred pounds lighter, Georgie escaped. Grinning, she caught a cab and sped away from Fulcrum without a thought for the great and the near-great who were still inside, warmed by the glow of the Eternal Flame and cheered by the Mormon Tabernacle Choir, which as she left began to sing the *Ode to Joy*. She was heading for the local airport, where she would take the next plane home. If the old man wanted to have her fired, let him try. She could sell the Fulcrum story to bigger fish. The real story. But first, she had to get straight with Bill.

She didn't even have to write her speech, she knew it by heart:

I came home early because I have to tell you something. I love you, Bill, and there's something you have to know.